Sarah Canary

Sarah Canary

Karen Joy Fowler

HENRY HOLT AND COMPANY

NEW YORK

Copyright © 1991 by Karen Joy Fowler
All rights reserved, including the right to reproduce
this book or portions thereof in any form.
Published by Henry Holt and Company, Inc.,
115 West 18th Street, New York, New York 10011.
Published in Canada by Fitzhenry & Whiteside Limited,
195 Allstate Parkway, Markham, Ontario L3R 4T8.

Fowler, Karen Joy.
    Sarah Canary : a novel / by Karen Joy Fowler. — 1st ed.
    p. cm.
    I. Title.
PS3556.0844S26 1991
813'.54 dc20   91-9746
    ISBN 0-8050-1753-4 (acid-free paper)   CIP

Henry Holt books are available at special discounts
for bulk purchases for sales promotions, premiums,
fund-raising, or educational use. Special editions
or book excerpts can also be created to specification.
For details contact: Special Sales Director,
Henry Holt and Company, Inc.
115 West 18th Street, New York, New York 10011

First Edition—1991

BOOK DESIGN BY CLAIRE NAYLON VACCARO
Printed in the United States of America
Recognizing the importance of preserving
the written word, Henry Holt and Company, Inc.,
by policy, prints all of its first editions
on acid-free paper. ∞

1 3 5 7 9 10 8 6 4 2

For Hugh

You only comprehend things which you perceive. And as you persist in regarding your ideas of time and space as *absolute*, although they are only *relative*, and thence form a judgment on truths which are quite beyond your sphere, and which are imperceptible to your terrestrial organism and faculties, I should not do a true service, my friend, in giving you fuller details of my ultra-terrestrial observations . . .

CAMILLE FLAMMARION
LUMEN, 1873

Sarah Canary

i

The years after the American Civil War were characterized by excess, ornamented by cults and corruptions. Calamity Jane rode her horse through Indian country, standing on her head, her tangled hair loose along the horse's sides. Chang and Eng, P. T. Barnum's Siamese twins, hunted boar, fathered children, and drank like the gentlemen they were. The Fox sisters held seances and secretly cracked their toe knuckles to dissemble communication from the beyond. T. P. James, a psychic/mechanic in Vermont, channeled Charles Dickens, allowing him to complete his final book, *The Mystery of Edwin Drood*, posthumously. Big Jim Kinelly plotted the kidnap of Abraham Lincoln's body. Brigham Young married and Victoria Woodhull told everyone who was sleeping with whom. Football and lawn tennis had their first incarnations.

In 1871, strange events took place in the skies over the central and northern United States. Eyewitness accounts allude to spectacular meteor showers, ghostly lights, and, on the ground, a number of fires whose origins were unknown and whose behavior was, in some ways, disquietingly unfirelike.

In 1872, the residents of the asylum for the insane in Steilacoom, Washington, were thrown out of their beds by earthquakes resulting from volcanic activity in the Cascade Mountains. The event was so profound it cured three of the patients instantly. These cures were responsible for a brief and faddish detour in the care of the mentally ill known as shake treatments.

Across an ocean, in China, the Manchus prepared for the Year of the Rooster and the end of the female Regency. The power of the Dowager Empress shrank. The influence of the palace eunuchs grew. Neither had much energy to spare for the Celestials dispersed abroad.

In 1873, in the fir forests below Tacoma, Washington, a white woman with short black hair and a torn black dress stumbled into a Chinese railway workers' camp.

CHAPTER ONE

THE YEAR
OF THE ROOSTER

To this World she returned.
But with a tinge of that—
A compound manner,
As a Sod
Espoused a Violet,
That chiefer to the Skies
Than to Himself, allied,
Dwelt hesitating, half of Dust
And half of Day, the Bride.

EMILY DICKINSON,
1864

The railway workers were traveling from Seattle to Tenino on foot
and had stopped, midday, to rest. They hadn't really made a camp,
just a circle of baskets and blankets around a circle of damp dirt that
Chin Ah Kin had cleared with his hands prior to building a fire.
Chin was briefly alone, although in the distance to his left he could
hear the companionable sounds of two men urinating.

It was midwinter, the tail end of the Year of the Monkey and

3

just before noon. There was no snow, but the ground was wet with the morning's frost and the trees dripped. Underfoot, the fir needles were soggy and refused to snap when stepped upon, which might explain why Chin Ah Kin did not hear the woman approach. It was a mystery. She was just there suddenly, talking to someone, maybe to him, maybe to herself. Her speech had no meaning he could discern. Chin, whose mother had worked as a servant for German missionaries and later for a British family in the ceded area of Canton and briefly for a family of Mohammedans, had been surrounded by foreign languages all his life. People speaking a foreign tongue often appear more logical and intelligent than those who can be actually understood. It is inconceivable that extraordinary sounds should signify something trivial or mundane. But this woman's speech felt lunatic, and it was cold enough to give Chin the momentary illusion that her words had form instead of meaning, were corporeal. He could see them, hovering about her open mouth.

In spite of the cold, the woman wore only a dress with crushed pannier and insubstantial leggings. This, too, was a mystery. Chin Ah Kin had been told that the Puyallup Indians could sleep in the woods at night without blankets or shelter, but he had never heard this ability attributed to a white woman. Initially, he mistook her for a ghost.

He had been hoping for a ghost. Ghost women often appeared to men of his age, luring them away, entrapping them in seductions that might last for centuries. Such men returned to bewildering and alien landscapes. The trees would be the same, though larger; there the apple tree that grew in the corner of the yard, there the almond that once shaded the doorway. Trees are as close to immortality as the rest of us ever come. But the house would be gone, the people transformed; granddaughters into old women, daughters into the grass on their graves. Popular wisdom held that these men were lucky to have escaped at all, but Chin had his own opinions about this. Chin was a philosopher, his uncle said. Philosophers and running water always sought the easy way out. No more mining. No more working on the railroad. No need to send explanations or apologies to your parents back in China. But I was *enchanted*, he could always

4

say later. Who was going to argue with this? Who would still be alive?

The ghost lover was so beautiful, she broke your heart just to look at her. She wore the faint perfume of your sweetest memories, a perfume that would be different to every man, depending on his province, the foods he liked, what his mother had used to wash her hair. The ghost lover dressed in clothes that were no longer fashionable. She seldom appeared in broad daylight, preferring shadows, and seldom faced you directly. There was something strange about her eyes, a light-swallowing flatness that always seemed to be an illusion no matter how closely you looked at her. Chin looked more closely at his apparition. She was the ugliest woman he could imagine. He revised his opinion. His second guess was that she was a prostitute.

To the best of his knowledge, he had never seen a white prostitute before. It was always possible that he had and not known it, of course, since the white men called prostitutes *seamstresses* and they called seamstresses *seamstresses*, too, and occasionally, like the famous Betsy Ross, revered them. It could get tricky. He recalled briefly the prostitute he had seen last year in eastern Washington. He and his uncle had been sluicing on the Columbia when a big-footed woman from Canton was taken through the mining camps. She wore the checkered scarf, so there was no mistaking her, and also a rope, one end tied around her waist, the other in the hands of the turtle man. While the man talked, the woman's head had drifted about her neck; her eyes rolled up in their sockets. She was ecstatic or she was very ill. She had a set of scars, little bird tracks, down the side of one cheek. Chin had wondered what would make such scars. "Very cheap," the turtle man assured them and then, to make her more alluring, "She has just been with your father."

The woman in the forest gestured for Chin to come closer. Chin asked himself what could be gained by any intercourse with a white woman who had hair above her lip and also a nose that was long even by white standards. He looked away from her and into the trees, where his uncle was returning to camp holding two small birds that appeared to be domesticated doves. It was not at all clear that the woman had been gesturing to *him*, anyway.

5

"There is a small white woman with a large nose here," his uncle pointed out. Of course, he said it in Cantonese in case she understood English; it would not be so rude. "She is very ugly." Chin's uncle dropped one of the doves onto his blanket roll and shook the other; its head bobbed impotently on its neck. He took his knife from his boot and spread the bird on a tree stump fortuitously suited to this purpose. It was not a large stump, maybe two hands across, but it had many rings, each one fitting inside the next like a puzzle. People were like this too, Chin thought. A constant accumulation— each year, a little more experience, each year, another layer of wisdom. Old age was a state much to be envied.

Chin's uncle severed the bird's feet in a single motion. "So very sad. So tragic, really. The life of an ugly woman. If she does not leave soon, she will bring us all kinds of trouble. You must make her go away."

"She is looking for opium," Chin suggested, opium being the obvious antidote to the woman's state of overexcitement and the only thing he could imagine that would bring a white woman into a camp of Chinese men. He had smoked opium himself on several occasions and drunk it once. At no time had it left him in anything like this agitated condition. Poor ugly woman. He was overcome with sorrow at the situation. He moved to the other side of a tree, out of sight, and shouted at the crazy lady to go home. Her voice rose in response, an unpleasant, exultant clacking. It was possible she did not know that he was talking to her.

"You must be forceful," his uncle said. He had an unusually mobile face and one mole to the left side of his nose, which quivered distractingly when he spoke. He himself held forceful opinions, which he hinted had brought him powerful friends as well as potent enemies. He lived life inside the fist, belonging, or so he claimed, to the secret Society for the Broadening of Human Life and the Chinese Empire Reform Association as well. He hated the Dowager Empress, Tz'u-hsi, with a particularly forceful passion. "Overthrow the Ch'ing and restore the Ming," he might say, instead of "Good day," or "The Manchu Dowager contains twelve stinkpots that are inexplicable," but only if there were no strangers present.

6

He disapproved of Chin, whose philosophy of life was more flexible. Chin didn't care anymore who was Emperor in China. Chin could read American newspapers and would say anything anybody wanted to hear, even when no strangers were listening. It was a shocking attitude.

"You must make a place for yourself in the world," Chin's uncle told him. "And not always shrink to fit the place that is made for you. You must make the big-nosed woman go away. I am cooking." He picked up one of the dove's severed feet and curled its toes around the index finger of his left hand, sliding it up and down like a coin on a string. "This is not a good time for opium-eating white women to be found inside our camp."

When would have been a good time? The gold was gone and the first feverish speculations in transcontinental railroads had ended in disaster for the investors. The economy was depressed and so were the white men. The American Congress had just announced its intention, given the alternatives, to depend in the future on *Nordic fiber*. Nordic fiber had settled the Midwest. Nordic fiber could win the West as well. The Chinese, according to this thinking, while well suited to railway work, were not otherwise needed. They had no families and were absolutely indifferent to human suffering; wore their hair in long pigtails, which they prized above all other possessions; and relished a dish called chopsooey, whose main ingredients were rats and snakes. They had been massacred in Los Angeles's Nigger Alley and in Martinez, and they were picked off one at a time, like fleas, in Union Square in San Francisco and, like fleas, they just kept coming. Chin understood quite well, his uncle did, too, though he didn't always admit it, that it was best to be invisible and, when that could not be achieved, then quiet, at least. All the alternatives in this current dilemma were noisy ones.

Chin came out from behind his tree. The woman stood before him, spine straight as a hanged man's, face transfigured, tongue fluttering in a strange, noisy speech of clicks and bangs. "Go away," Chin told her. "Go home." He said it in English. He said it in German. *"Gehen Sie nach Hause!"* He said it with his hands and facial expression. She fixed her eyes upon him. Were the pupils curiously flat? Or was that just a drugged dilation? She answered him with a steady and joyful stream of nonsense. Chin gave up.

"You are not being forceful enough," his uncle said. The mole on his cheek quivered.

Chin tried to change the subject. "Why doves?" he asked. "Was there no rat?" It was a joke. His uncle did not laugh. His uncle began to remove the dove's feathers with one hand, a repetitive up-and-down motion at which he was very accomplished. He was ignoring Chin. A snow of feathers fell at his feet.

"When I first saw her," Chin said, "I thought she might be the ghost lover." This was even funnier than the rat joke. His uncle did not pause in his plucking. Chin said something serious. "Sometimes," he said, "the immortals send someone in disguise to test us. Where did this woman come from? I have never seen this woman before."

If she were an immortal, merely feeding her would not be sufficient. She would have to be given the very best parts of the bird—the soft meat of the breast, the dark meat of the heart. His uncle resisted this explanation. In Tacoma, maybe, he said to Chin, they had seen everybody. But in Seattle there were some three thousand people and Chin had seen almost none of them. Was it so hard to believe a crazy woman could have traveled here from Seattle? Hadn't they just traveled here from Seattle themselves? Or Steilacoom? Wasn't there a hospital for crazy people in Steilacoom? "She is not immortal," his uncle said. "She is just lost. We cannot arrive in Tenino, ready for railway work, dragging a crazy white woman behind us. There would be questions. If you cannot convince her to leave on her own, then you will have to go to Steilacoom and ask someone to fetch her." The disadvantages to this plan did not even have to be stated.

"She will soon grow tired and go," Chin suggested. She will take her gifts of long life and many sons and excessive prosperity and give them to someone else.

They waited. Her words continued, frenzied, high-pitched gibberish delivered in a cat-gut voice. The other railway workers arrived

8

with water and wood for the fire. "There is an ugly, noisy, long-nosed white woman," they said. "Right there. By the tree." They seemed to think it was Chin's problem. Chin had seen her first. "Make her be quiet. Make her go away."

Chin's uncle reached inside his heavy right boot and scratched his ankle. "She has come for opium," he assured them. "And we have none. She will soon grow tired and leave."

"She is a crazy woman," Wong Woon said. "Crazy people never grow tired."

All the crazy people were supposed to live together at Fort Steilacoom, where the asylum had enough opium and opium tinctures for everyone. They were not supposed to wander the country alone, turning up in Tacoma or Squak or who knew where else. Neither were prostitutes. Neither were women of any other kind. Chin lowered his voice. "She is an immortal," he said. "The ugliest woman in the world has been created as a test for us." There was no response to this theory. Chin waited a long time for one. "Where did she come from?" he asked. "Seattle? Then she has been walking for days. With no food. With no blanket. Tacoma? Steilacoom? She would still have had to walk all night. And wouldn't she have frozen, dressed as she is dressed?" Chin wished the woman in black would be quiet for a moment. Her constant noise obscured the complex point he was trying to make.

"Not if she kept walking," his uncle said, but the woman's voice had risen so Chin was able to pretend he hadn't heard.

"A woman appears out of nowhere. We should feed her. We should give her a blanket."

Wong Woon began to make the fire. He sat on the ground and stripped bark away from dead wood. He put the bark in one pile and the wood in another. "The person with two blankets can give her one," Wong said. He had to raise his voice suddenly on the word *one* so as to be heard over the woman. It was a disingenuous suggestion. The person with two blankets did not exist.

Wong Woon lit the pile of bark and Chin's nose filled suddenly with the sweet, smoky smell of transformation. He envied the bark, which had been, in the course of one lifetime, both forest and fire.

One endured; one destroyed. Chin said it aloud. "One is one," he said. "All is all." Could Wong Woon deny it?

Wong Woon looked at him with irritation. Wong Woon had purchased *Sam Yee's English Phrasebook* in Seattle and had been lead-ing them in a chorus of useful phrases as they walked: *I have been cheated of my wages. I have been attacked and robbed. Where is it permissible for me to eat?* They depended on Chin for the correct pronunciations. Apparently it brought no gratitude.

Chin's uncle spread a naked wing to its full extension and sev-ered it cleanly. "She cannot stay here. Even for one night. Even if we had a blanket. Even though she is ugly. Opium addicts are like cats. Once we have fed her, she will never go home." He raised his knife again.

Chin looked at the body on the stump. A bird with wings was a star in the sky. Wingless, a stone on the ground. Star. Stone. One was one. But a bird with one wing, Chin thought, would be some-thing beyond the inescapable unities. A bird with one wing would require an entirely different world to support it. *Chop.* The second severed wing closed like a fan on the tree stump.

Chin's uncle's knife thudded into the wood of the tree. When he lifted it, he had made a new line, which bisected the two inner rings. There were many of these lines. His uncle was speaking in straight lines. Chin was hearing in rings. Circles. Lines. People. Trees. Chin's mind completed this ring in the time it took his uncle to clear his throat and continue. "If she will not go home, someone will have to marry her eventually." *Chop.* Chin had no doubts as to who that would be. Though surely even the immortals would not demand this. "Or you can take her now to Steilacoom." *Chop.* "Maybe you will lose her on the trail. Regrettable, certainly, and not something you would want to have happen, but then you could rejoin us in time to get some sleep before morning. We will try for Fort Lewis."

A dusty column of sunlight slid between the trees. It came in at a slight angle, then righted itself, sheathing the woman. She looked up, struck silent, and Chin imagined her pupils constricting from circles to points. Chin knew men who could tell time by reading the pupils of a cat's eyes. He knew that the ghost lover might have the eyes of a cat, which told you she was doomed to appear in the form of a tiger for part of every day until some man learned her awful secret and loved her in spite of it. The spell would break; your lover's eyes, which had always been jade, were suddenly black. Then your own enchantment began.

Chin saw the woman's dark, round eyes close, allowing him to stare at her rudely. The lines at her mouth and her forehead—this was not a young woman—disappeared in the dazzling sunlight. She was haloed. She was so bright, it hurt. She was wonderfully, wonderfully silent. "I will eat first," Chin told his uncle. He had been chosen. Such things were not to be resisted and nothing would be gained by regretting them. What Buddha sends, he sends.

Chin's uncle had seasoned the dove with five spices purchased from Chin Gee Hee's Emporium in Seattle. There was rice and there were turnips. The spices made Chin's eyes run. He offered food to the woman in black. She put her head into the bowl to eat it, her hair falling forward. Chin gave her his chopsticks and ate with his fingers. The woman watched him, then put the chopsticks aside and ate with her fingers, too. She finished quickly, wiping her nose on the back of her black sleeve. Mucus glistened on the fabric like a snail's slick. It was a rainbow of many colors. It killed what remained of Chin's appetite. He turned his head aside, emptied his own nose onto the fir needles, then went to get his blanket roll.

He added a cooking pot, put on his coat. He wiped his Double Happiness porcelain bowl clean and set it inside the pot with the wok brush and his abacus. He checked his left boot for his knife. The boots were for mining, big and waterproof, purchased from a white man's store in Seattle. Chin had almost bought pants as well— stiff, metallic pants made by Levi Strauss. He had tried them on, but they chafed the insides of his thighs when he walked, binding his testicles in a particularly constricting way, and his uncle had warned him against them. Repeated wear, his uncle had said, would affect his ability to father children. The Society for the Broadening of Human Life, according to his uncle, was working toward the day when every white demon on the West Coast would be wearing

Strauss's insidious pants. Generation by generation, they would tighten the fit. It should be no harder to accomplish than foot-binding.

Chin's uncle was a farsighted man. "Ask the doctors," his uncle said, "in Steilacoom if they have powdered tiger's teeth. Buy red pepper if you can."

Chin returned to the woman for his chopsticks. She followed his gaze to them with some uncertainty, then picked them up and held them tightly. At last she offered Chin one back. She put the other into her own pocket. Chin looked at his single chopstick with the character for good fortune etched into it. What good is one chopstick? What good is one wing? What good is one man?

The woman did not want to accompany Chin. He had to take hold of her sleeve. She smelled soggy. He pulled her toward him. She nearly fell before consenting to move her feet, but she retained that transported look on her face. There were dark, indented circles under her eyes like moon shadows. Chin continued to pull. She did not look down and stumbled frequently. Occasionally she laughed. Nothing could have been more disconcerting.

The noises of the camp faded behind them, irritatingly common-place noises, the noises of people who have no problems of their own and no reason to honor anyone else's. Chin chose a path along the creek, keeping as close to the water as he could. Even as he picked his way, even though patches of bare earth were rare and brambles flourished at his feet and ankles, even though the walking was not thoughtless walking, there was an inertia involved. Once started, it was easier to continue than to stop. The woman must have felt it, too. Soon Chin was able to drop her sleeve and move farther ahead of her. The way was much easier single file. He could hear her trailing him; her breathing was congested but not labored. She hummed from time to time. She spoke occasionally, single, un-connected syllables full of joy. Syllables like *wark* and *shoop*. Her inflections rose or fell much like the intonations of Cantonese.

The creek sucked itself over rocks. The trees sawed in the wind. Waterweeds rubbed together, singing with friction like insects. Chin was a small ant, picking his way over the melodic body of the world.

Her syllables began to connect again into whole nonsensical sentences, at first quietly and then gratingly. Her voice rose and followed after Chin. His queue bounced in the small of his back with each step. He thought about opium. He thought about the great silences of opium and the mysteries of the great silences opening like peeled fruit so that you could swallow them, segment by segment, until the mysteries and the silences were all inside you. He must never take opium again; he had recognized this the very first time he tried it. Chin craved tranquillity and clarity too much. Opium was a danger to a man like him. If only he had some opium now. Panta opium. Dangerously fine.

"Seattle," he said to her once. "Did you come from Seattle?" Her shoes were big and black and buttoned, heeled and caked with mud. She was limping a little; clearly she had already walked a long way. He slowed his own pace, in annoyance, in pity. They should have stayed in camp overnight and begun this journey in the morning. She should have washed her feet and wrapped them in rags dipped in water and just a little pulverized horny toad skin. They would never, never make Steilacoom before dark; she was already limping and he would spend a cold night with the indifferent, almost immortal trees and a woman who was, at best, very ugly and, at worst, some sort of demon spirit.

She smiled at him and her nose hooked toward her mouth. She hummed her answer. Her skin—he noticed this suddenly—was poreless and polished. It shone like Four Flowers porcelain. It was beautiful. He was a little bit frightened. Why was he seeing this? Why hadn't he seen it before? Why was he seeing it now? Chin faced forward and walked again.

Perhaps three hours later they arrived at a lake. Chin paused beside it hesitantly. He had expected to follow the creek all the way into Steilacoom. He didn't know the area well, saw no path, had only a vague sense that the Sound lay ahead of them. There should be no lake. He had come too far. They would need to cross the creek now and head directly west. Chin hated to leave the creek behind. He could lose his bearings so easily in the woods.

The woman shouldered past him and slid down the lake bank.

The trees on the bank grew at a slant. Chin saw a stain on the back of her black skirt that might have been blood; he didn't want to think about the implications of this. The stain did not look recent. She found a large, flat stone exactly one step into the water and dropped to her knees on it; her skirt collapsed around her like a shriveling flower. The stain vanished into a fold. Leaning forward, the woman thrust her face into the water where the creek joined the lake. The water parted around her mouth. The tips of her short hair floated and she drank with her tongue like a dog. When she sat up, her face was white where the icy creek had touched it. The excess water drained off her teeth.

She began to remove her shoes. Chin did not want to see her feet. "No," he told her hastily, sliding down into the creek after her. "We can't stop. We don't have time to stop." There was no room for him on the rock beside her. He stood in the creek itself where it was shallow and only washed over the toes of his boots. Leaning down, he forced her foot, halfway out of her shoe, back inside. He tried to fasten the buttons. An instrument was required; he knew this; he had seen such instruments, although he had certainly never used one. He had, in fact, never put a shoe on anyone's foot but his own before. Even with the sort of shoe he was accustomed to, he would have been awkward. All his movements had to be done backward, like braiding your hair in a mirror. She kicked at him once, playfully, and then did not resist. Chin was able to fasten the top two buttons. The rest defeated him. He disguised this by knocking the shoe lightly against the stone to loosen some of the dirt. Her expression was alarmingly coquettish. He dropped her foot. "We want to be in Steilacoom before it gets dark. A few miles still to go. Please," he said. "Please. You come now."

She came liquidly to her feet and stood on the rock with her hands out, forcing him to lift her over the water. Her dress was damp beneath her arms where his hands touched her. He wiped his palms on his pants.

Looking down at them, from the mud wall of the creek, were two Indian children. Chin hardly saw them. They were there, black-haired and black-eyed and solemn, and then they were gone. Chin's legs buckled beneath him and he fell on his knees. Water slid inside his boots. His heart refused to return to his chest. Indians, it thumped. In-di-ans. The woman, who was looking at him and seeing nothing, lifted her voice in rapture.

Some years back the Indians along the Columbia River had murdered the first Chinese they saw simply because they did not recognize them as a viable natural category. They were not Indian. They were not white. They were like one-winged birds; they were wrong. They were dead. The Caucasians, according to the second Chief Steilacoom, had brought disease and war; they had killed Indians just to demonstrate the versatility of the bowie knife. They had injected a tartar emetic into their watermelons to teach the Indians not to steal, and very effectively, too. Still, the Caucasians clearly worked to a higher purpose. They had come to bring potatoes to the Indians. Much could be forgiven them. The second Chief Steilacoom weighed more than two hundred pounds. What had the Chinese brought? Nothing they were willing to share.

There had been another ugly incident when the Indians back in the eastern part of the state had driven a camp of Chinese miners over a cliff, herding them up the slope and into the air. They were stars against the sky; they were stones against the earth. Chin wanted to see no more Indians. He wanted this badly. His pants were wet up to the knees. They would not dry by nightfall; they would never dry in this weather; they would make a cold night that much colder. The crazy woman had no blanket and might die of exposure if she was not inside after the sun went down. Who, exactly, would the immortals hold responsible for that?

Chin took hold of the woman's wrist, but she resisted. She was looking out over the lake at some apparition of her own. Chin saw it, too. There was a dark shadow under the water, the size and shape of a woman. He held his breath. A spray of water appeared for a moment, just at the waterline, and was instantly followed by a black snout. Water rolled away and the entire head slid into the air, hairless, with a long nose and whiskers. He let his breath out. A seal stared at them. Its body twisted beneath the motionless face so that the seal now floated on its back, fanning the water into patterned waves with its flippers. Chin leaned down, scooping some of the lake water into his hand to taste it. There was no salt. He separated his fingers and let it drip through. The woman called to the seal. Her voice was happy, urgent. The seal stared at her impassively and then sank away. The ground at their feet trembled slightly. The waters of the lake rocked against the bank in waves.

There was no time for safe, easy routes. Put your faith in your fate. See how it comes to you. Walk toward it. Walk away. See how it comes.

They headed for the Sound and the landscape changed; the trees grew thinner and there were fewer of them. Suddenly it was hard to see. Not only had the sun vanished, but as they got closer to the ocean, there were patches of fog. One moment Chin would be there with the trees and the woman in black, the next he would be walking by himself in the clouds. He could have taken some comfort in his own blindness—if he couldn't see, at least he also couldn't be seen—but the woman continued her keening. Her speech was vowel-laden, one running into the next running into the next, like the noise at a hog-slaughtering. The continual din obscured other noises so Chin was deaf as well as blind, but instead of cloaking them like the fog, the woman's words exposed them. Chin could not be tranquil and accept his fate with this annoying vocal accompaniment. The thought of Indians panicked him; he could not control it. The noise was driving him mad. He felt the trees leaning in to listen to it. "Be quiet," Chin begged her. "Please be quiet," but she wasn't.

Chin stepped inside a drifting patch of fog and stopped. The world was shapeless and moved. The woman in black did not stop. See your fate come. See how it stumbles into you from behind, how it pushes you forward. Chin felt the woman's teeth jar against his shoulder. Her mouth was loose, her jaw was slack. Her vowels continued. He turned around and hit her with his open hand. "Be quiet," he said and hit her again, across the mouth, slapping it closed. He was surprised and he was sorry to be hitting her; it was just the noise he couldn't stand anymore. It was profoundly possible that she was just a crazy old woman, after all. That he was a fool to be taking her through the forest when railway work awaited every Chinese man in Tenino. That he would pay a fool's price.

Chin forced his hand shut and held it with the other hand against his chest. "I'm sorry," he said to the woman. "So sorry." She had moved away from him so he couldn't see her in the fog and she was quiet now, but he thought he could still hear her, a fruity kind of breathing that suggested tears. The dress rustled slightly as though she might be shaking.

"Sorry," Chin said again. "Forgive me." He felt a wave of self-pity. "I am so far from home," he told her. "You can't know what that is like." She couldn't know how hard his life was, how it tried him. In none of the languages he spoke was there a word as vivid as his loneliness, and she wouldn't even understand the pale approximations he could offer. He stepped in her direction, but she wasn't there. He didn't hear her at all now, put out his hands and groped through handfuls of cloud and found nothing. Whirling around, he felt through the fog in the other direction. His hand hit stone, a large, flat slab, sticking up from the ground with letters carved into it. The fog dispersed so that he could read the words:

Chas M. McDaniel
Born in Iowa, 1834
and died at the
HANDS OF VIOLENCE
Jan. 22, 1870
aged 36 years.

The fog was back. Chin felt something unseen brush against his hand. It was sticky and ghostlike. He jerked away, stumbled. Something or someone caught at his foot and threw him against the stone. Chin bit through his cheek as he hit. Blood drained into his throat. Putting his arms around the marker, he slid slowly down it to earth and on the way he passed through the gate into unconsciousness.

CHAPTER
TWO

A FULL MOON
IN STEILACOOM

Not a Tomorrow to know its Name
Nor a Past to Stare —
Ditches for Realms and a Trip to Jail
For a Souvenir —

EMILY DICKINSON,
1872

"Groggeries. Unspeakable revels. Drunken dancing. Dancing without partners." The voice was female and Caucasian. Chin lifted his head painfully and let it drop again. The blow resonated through his skull. He located his hands, sprouting limply from the ends of his arms, and pressed them into his temples to keep his head from splitting into several pieces. He was on a stone floor. There was a small window with bars. He could see the moon through it, a great white plate on the outside. He smelled urine. Closing his eyes, he searched for unconsciousness again. The woman's voice prevented him from finding it. "We know what goes on here, Jeb Chambers. Don't think that we don't. The noise you and your friends make. We heard Dash Away Boys last Saturday night. We heard the Fireman's Dance. We heard the Portland Fancy. Satan's own music. Real inconvenient for you to have actual occupants in the jail, isn't it? Unless they're your own good friends."

On the floor directly opposite Chin's face stood a heavy pair of boots with creases across the toes. Chin followed them upward with his eyes. An Indian sat on a folding cot against the opposite wall. He watched the moon out the window and he didn't move.

There was the webby sound of someone clearing his throat and then spitting. "You just behave yourself, Jeb," the woman said. "You're in the presence of ladies."

Chin sat up slowly. His head pulsed. A patch of moonlight lay on the ground between him and the Indian, patterned with the shadows of bars. Outside the cell door, a white man perched on a chair tipped on the back two legs. He rocked slightly, smiling at Chin. "If this was San Francisco," he said, "we'd be cutting your hair already." He opened his first and second fingers and then shut them like a scissors.

Two women dressed in black stood behind him. Neither was Chin's woman; these were cleaner and larger. Their cheeks were flushed with resolution. "Tom. Tom Mays," the older of the women said. She was looking at the Indian. "Trust the Lord. The Lord is your shepherd."

The Indian gave no response. He sat and watched the moon.

"Repent, Tom. Rejoice. You're going somewhere beautiful."

"You go," the Indian said.

The woman swung her head to look at Chin. "I'm Mrs. Taylor," she told him. "I run a Sunday school for the Chinese here in Steilacoom. Are you a Christian?"

"I don't think you want this one," Jeb said. "Attacked a white woman. Lured her out into the graveyard right behind the hospital and then beat her when she resisted. Nasty business. Greene had to take her right into the asylum. Driven mad by the experience. Any decent woman would be."

Chin's forehead was suddenly slick with sweat. "I found her in the woods," Chin said. "I was trying to help her. She was already mad. She was lost. I thought she came from the asylum. I was taking her back."

Jeb shook his head. " 'Course I believe you," he said. "But you see how it looks. It don't look good."

Chin tasted the dove with the five spices again. It happened so quickly he couldn't even try to stop it. His dinner lay in the patch of moonlight. His queue fell over his shoulder and into the mess. His head spun. He stretched out on the floor again.

"Now, that's nasty," said Jeb. "Someone's going to have to clean that up. A nasty thing for ladies to have seen." Chin heard the front legs of the chair slam down on stone as Jeb got heavily to his feet. His footsteps came toward the cell. "Mewling and puking. Shakespeare said it, but that don't make it art when it happens. Mrs. Taylor, Mrs. Godfrey, I'm going to have to ask you to leave now. We've got some cleaning to do, and I can't open the cell door with two such decorative women on the outside. Old Tom here, he might want one last look at the earthly pleasures he's leaving behind. And the Chinaman has already ruined one white woman."

The two women conferred in whispers. Chin heard the sibilants in the intervals when his head was not pounding. He had a desperate inspiration. "The Lord is my shepherd, Mrs. Taylor," he said. He kept his eyes closed and did not raise his head for fear of throwing up again.

There was a brief silence. "We're going then, Jeb. Because it's late, not for any of your nonsense," Mrs. Taylor said stiffly. "But we will be back. Tom, you think about what I told you. I'll bring psalms in the morning. Comfort and cheer. The Lord will never desert you."

"The Lord will never desert me," said Chin. He heard the heels of the women's shoes as they left, a sharp sound that faded on the street outside. He heard the keys clank together and then the scraping of one key in the lock. The door opened. Chin looked up. Jeb had a mop and a bucket.

"You get up now, Chinaman," he said. "If you think I'm cleaning up your puke, you're crazier than you look."

"I'm dizzy," said Chin. "I don't know if I am able to stand."

"Makes my heart break," said Jeb. "Tom here has already killed one Chinaman and is going to glory for it tomorrow. Shall I ask Indian Tom to clean up your stink?"

Chin looked at the Indian, who looked at the moon. He was seated on the mattress with his back against the wall, yet his feet were flat on the floor. It occurred to Chin that this was probably a very big man. Chin stood up heavily. When Jeb handed him the mop, he leaned on it like a crutch, swaying slightly, forward and backward. Jeb set the bucket next to the vomit. "Do it proper," he said, "or you're the one who'll have to sleep in it."

Chin had never used a mop before. The strings went in a dozen different directions; the water splashed over his boots. "Nothing to stop Tom from killing another Chinaman, neither," said Jeb. "Can't hang him twice." A puddle of water replaced the mess on the floor. Chin was going to even it out, but Jeb took the mop. Chin stumbled slightly without it. "I'll just leave the two of you now. The Chinese lecher and the homicidal Indian. Last time Tom had a knife. This time, nothing but his bare hands. What can a man do with nothing but his bare hands?" He thrust the mop into the bucket, pumped it up and down to rinse it off. "Well, I'm off to my own sweet bed. Whatever happens, I won't hear of it till morning. You go to sleep now, too, John Chinaman. Perchance to dream. Or you stay up and watch the Indian all night long. That's what I'd do. If I was Chinese."

A cloud floated across the moon. The edges of the cloud remained dark, but its heart was round and luminous. The light in the cell diminished. Jeb threw Chin's blanket into the cell, just missing the water. He disappeared through the door. Chin heard Jeb cough and spit onto the ground outside. The Indian's face was all shadow. "I'm not going to kill you," Tom said. "I never set out to kill the other one. I just needed money. You people always have money."

"I have no money," said Chin. He reached inside his boot in the dark. He had no knife either.

"I don't need money now," said Tom. "That's one thing I won't miss. Always needing money." The cloud passed. Chin could see

21

him again. What he saw in Tom's face did not calm him. He watched Tom and tried to think of things to say.

"Do you believe in omens?" Chin asked. He was speaking very rapidly. "Tonight I stood on the shore of a lake and a seal appeared. In a *lake*. And the ground shook. I thought it meant something."

"Steilacoom Lake," said Tom. "There's an island in it that sinks and rises." He turned his face back to the window. His nose was large and hooked. "The ground has been trembling for weeks. Trees falling. I haven't seen a bird in forty days. They all left when the mountains began to smoke." His voice softened and smoothed. "The earth talks to us, but we don't speak its language. Why should it not mean something just because you don't understand?"

"The woman I was with," said Chin, "she was a goddess."

"Indians call that lake Whe-atchee. It means underhanded or deceitful. Because the shoreline changes like the ocean. Because sometimes there is an island and sometimes not. Why were you beating up a goddess in the graveyard?"

Chin seated himself again on the floor with his back to the wall. There was a wooden shutter outside the window and the cell would probably have been warmer if they closed it. Chin reached for his blanket instead. Only half the moon showed through the window now, the bar bisecting it. Lines and rings. Chin repressed the thought. He had seen the unities and he had awakened in jail. He dealt with Tom's question carefully, one piece at a time. "I didn't beat her up," he said. "She might be a goddess. I didn't know I was in the graveyard. There was a lot of fog. I couldn't see."

"They want you to kill me," said Tom.

This struck Chin as a particularly awkward turn in the conversation. He could think of no polite response. He spent a long time looking for one.

"Sportals," said Tom, "is a deceitful lake. It narrows in the direction of the sunrise. Sometimes a great hunter will swim the narrow part, chasing a herd of deer. Suddenly the water will turn out of its customary currents, round and around itself. The hunter will hear music and will see something never seen in this world—a beautiful striped horse. If you see the striped horse, you are destined for greatness."

"Have you seen the horse?" Chin asked.

"Have I become great?" Tom's voice was flat and unfriendly. "Does this look like greatness to you? In China, would this be greatness?"

"You said the lake was deceitful," Chin reminded him. "In Africa there are striped horses," he added. "Herds of them. Sometimes so many you can't see the ground beneath them. But I never met anyone from Africa who has become great."

"You've met many people from Africa," Tom said. Impossible to know if it was a question or a statement, if it expressed derision and disbelief or admiration and faith. Tom's voice was flat and unhelpful.

"Many," said Chin. "In the South." Tom had probably never heard of the Memphis Plan, an attempt by white plantation owners to replace their Negro slaves with cheap Chinese labor. Tom had probably never heard of Cornelius Koopmanschap, the notorious slaver from San Francisco who was hired to provide the Chinese. Tom had probably never heard of the *Ville de St. Louis*, the infamous ship on which Chin had been an unwilling passenger. Tom said nothing to invite these details. Chin returned from the personal to the philosophical. "Do you know what would really never be seen in this world? A one-winged bird. I mean, not a bird that has been damaged, but a bird that was supposed to have only one wing. Who wants me to kill you?" Chin asked. "Not that I would."

"Jeb Chambers. Hank Webber. The judge. The doctor. Maybe even those good Christian women, though you'd never hear it from them. That's why you're in jail. I heard Jeb talking about it when he carried you in. 'A live Chinaman in the graveyard,' he said. He said you were the answer to a prayer. And a damned peculiar answer. Nobody really thinks you beat that woman."

The sudden loosening in Chin's stomach was almost more than he could bear. Was there really a way out of this? Was the woman in black still protecting him in spite of what he'd done? No human, not even a crazy human, would be so forgiving. Only the immortals were capable of such charity. And Chin would be worthy of it. If he got out of this jail, if he was alive and free to go where he wanted, he would head straight for the hospital and make sure she was all right. This was a promise. His honor attached to it. In his relief he had allowed himself to forget some of the details of Tom's statement.

Tom cleared his throat, which helped Chin remember.

"Why do they want me to kill you?" Chin asked.

"They probably wouldn't mind if I killed you," Tom said. "I mean, it wouldn't solve the problem, but it wouldn't be a great loss either. There it goes, the moon." His voice flattened again. To Chin, who was used to the six tones of Cantonese, all English was expressionless. But he had never heard a voice as empty as the Indian's. "I'm not going to see it again," Tom added. "I suppose I should be grateful there was a full moon on my last night. Could have been moonless."

"You said you weren't going to kill me," Chin reminded him. Chin had not forgotten; it would be a shame if Tom had.

"I don't plan to," Tom said. "You show me how I gain by it."

"You don't," said Chin. "I don't see how it benefits you at all."

Tom closed his eyes. "Don't hurt me much either. And keeps you from killing me. I'll tell you what, Chinaman. I have only this one night left. Half a night now, and I want to see something never seen in this world. You show me something like that and I won't kill you. You Chinese are supposed to be so damned clever. You do that. You do that for me."

"I will," said Chin, thinking desperately and futilely. What did he have? His abacus? His wok brush? "But you have to trust me a little. I can't do it right now. I've got to have just a little time."

"I got just a little time," said Tom.

"I bet you didn't know that the Chinese came here before the Caucasians," Chin said divertingly. "Came, looked around, and went home again. Never tried to move in. Came as guests. Hui Shen, a Buddhist priest, returned to China from a land he called Fu-Sang. He said the people there drank deer milk, lived in wooden houses, owned oxen and cattle, had copper but not iron. This was thirteen hundred years ago."

"He didn't come here," said Tom. "My people would have remembered."

"He may have been farther south," Chin conceded.

Tom slid a heavy boot along the stone floor. It made a scraping noise. Was he getting up? Chin spoke rapidly again. "Where do you think they're going to end the railroad?" he asked. "You think Steilacoom has a chance? The terminus will be an important city. I bet Steilacoom is hoping for it."

"Steilacoom is a pile of dung on a pile of dung," said Tom. He slid his other boot forward.

"Good point," said Chin. "We think it will be Tacoma. We Chinese."

"You tell me," said Tom, "how it is that you Chinese make a dollar a day in a job where a white man makes a dollar seventy-five and you always got more money than anyone else."

"Frugal," said Chin. "It's a frugal culture."

"Your women, is it true they have little tiny feet they can hardly walk on? That you fix them when they're little children so that their feet never grow again? You like them that way?"

"Yes," said Chin. "Yes, I do. A woman's foot is a work of art. She creates it. It shows what she is. It's a manifestation of her inner character."

"It's sick," said Tom.

"I can see how you might think so. Is it true that you Indians take many wives?"

"Is it true that you Chinese do?"

"Lucky men. Prosperous men."

"Well, we don't," said Tom. "You're thinking of the Puyallups."

"Still, you must have known many beautiful women."

"I must have. It would be hard to die without that, wouldn't it, Chinaman?"

"Yes," said Chin. His throat constricted suddenly. How many beautiful women had he known? Lily-footed women. Women whose feet curled like petals. Or even big-foot, flat-footed women? Once while they were mining, his uncle had told him there were only two Chinese women in all of eastern Washington. Chin had never set eyes on either of them. He was a young man and all the beautiful women were an ocean away. Or in San Francisco. The Temple of United Justice smuggled beautiful, shameless women into San Francisco in bulk and sold them on Dupont Street.

Tom was standing up. He was probably a whole head taller than Chin. He shook his pants out, smoothed them down with his hands. Very big hands. "Did you ever hear of the beautiful Ah Toy?" Chin asked him. His voice came out rather high. He coughed to lower it, which made his head ache again. "When she lived in San Francisco the white miners stood in line and poured gold dust onto her scales just to look at her."

"No, I never heard of her," Tom said. "But right here in Steilacoom we have a woman named Soldier Sal. You wouldn't want to just look. You could die for her, if you felt like dying."

"I don't," said Chin.

Tom stepped to the window and wrapped his hand around one of the bars. Chin thought how cold it must be, the metal on his bare hand. But Tom didn't seem to mind. His shoulder-length, unbraided hair was a blacker shadow in the black room. "Are you ready?" Tom said.

Ready for what? "No," Chin answered.

"I don't have much time left. You don't have much time left. I'm ready to see what you promised to show me."

"You have to trust me," said Chin. "You will see it. I will show you. But I can't show it to you now."

"Can't be a dead Chinaman," said Tom. "I've already seen one of those."

"I wasn't planning for it to be."

"But you're lying to me," Tom told him. "You've got nothing to show me. You Chinese are no smarter than we are. And don't think that I'm so dumb. Just because I haven't killed you yet." Tom swung just perceptibly left to right and back, hanging on to the bar.

"I never thought that was dumb." Chin was sweating again. His head beat. He was a small man on the inside of a pounding drum.

"Listen." Tom's voice came alive suddenly. "Listen." He turned his face to Chin. His eyes and his mouth were open. "The birds are back. The birds have come back."

26

Chin heard an owl outside the window. "Who," it asked. "Who?"

"Me," said Tom. "Of course, me. My owl."

So Chin knew for the first time, knew with certainty, that he would not be dying that night after all. "Who?" the owl repeated. Not me, thought Chin. He wrapped himself in his blanket. "Tomorrow night," he said to Tom sleepily, "I will look at the moon for you. Every night I will do that."

"But don't say my name. Even though it's not my Indian name," Tom answered. "Don't ever say Tom after I'm dead." And then Chin let his head hurt until Tom's glistening face and the window and the cot began to move past him, chasing each other around and around the room. He had the discursive half-dreams of early sleep. The demonic dreams of full sleep. He was just about to begin the prophetic dreams of morning when he woke up.

Jeb Chambers was bending over him. "Chinaman," he said. "There's someone here who wants to talk to you. You come with me now."

Chin rose in some confusion. He wiped his eyes, and the back of his hand scraped against a lump on the side of his head. In one painful stab he remembered everything. He turned to look for Tom, who was seated again, the way he had been when Chin first saw him, back against the wall, feet on the floor. The green, pasty light of pre-sunrise illuminated the cell.

"Good morning," said Tom. His voice was even. His face was drawn and taut. "I hope you slept well."

"I'm surprised you slept at all," Jeb said. Perhaps there was admiration in his voice. "You Chinese don't care about dying, do you? You think you're just coming back, only as a cow or something."

Chin did not answer. He could not imagine where Jeb had gotten this information or why anyone would think the prospect of returning as a cow could resign one to one's own death, more than going to heaven would.

The cell door was unlocked and Jeb pushed it open. Chin followed him through and it swung shut heavily, metal hitting metal.

The shutting rang like a gong, revealing the ceremonial nature of Chin's temporary release. Jeb locked the door behind them.

A very clean man sat in Jeb's chair in the little anteroom and scraped the undersides of his fingernails with a tiny blade. His head was a globe on the globe of his body. His hair was thin and his skin was pale. "Thank you, Jeb," he said. "Well"—he directed these words to Chin—"you look like you had quite a night." A smile, and his teeth were all white except for one dead incisor on the left side. "I'm Hank Webber," he said. "And your name is?"

"Chin Ah Kin."

"Now, does that mean I call you Chin or Kin? I can never remember. Calling you kin would be a good joke, wouldn't it? Do I call you Kin?"

"Call me Chin," Chin told him.

"All right, Mr. Chin. I'm going to come right to the point. We want you to do something for us. And you'll get something in return. But before I get too specific, I want to remind you that your bargaining position is not good. We found you in the graveyard last night with a helpless, witless white woman. Now, I don't know what your intentions were. I just know an unsavory picture when I see one. There are places where they wouldn't even have bothered bringing you in to jail. I'm sure you know this is true. Do you know this is true?"

"I know this," said Chin.

"You're a hell of a lucky man even to be alive this morning."

"I am lucky."

"You're even luckier than you know. Because I'm prepared to let you walk right out of this jail today a free man. I have the authority to do that. And all I want is a favor from you first."

Chin stood silently. Hank Webber had a mole much like his uncle's, only Webber's was closer to his ear and had hair growing out of it. Chin imagined that he was dealing with a forceful man who had powerful friends, and Chin expected to do whatever was asked of him. But he didn't expect to be happy about it. Hank waited for Chin to ask what the favor was. Chin remained in that innocent, blissful state of not-knowing for as long as he could.

"All we want," Hank said (he was whispering now; Chin had to lean forward from the waist, bowing, to hear him), "is for you to put the rope around Tom Mays's neck. You should be pleased to do it. We're only hanging him because he killed a Chinaman."

Chin said nothing. He stood upright again, moving his face away from Hank Webber's mouth.

Jeb cleared his throat. "Cook over't the asylum," he added. He was whispering, too. "Popular man. Always smiling. Always had a piece of candy, a little story for the children. One of Tom's own, little Indian girl, turned Tom in, stood witness against him. She saw the whole thing. There's really no doubt about his guilt. Not that he ever denied it."

Chin said nothing.

Jeb lowered his voice even further. "The Indians aren't happy," he confessed. "We figure they can understand this better—you kill a Chinaman, a Chinaman kills you. Simple and fair. They don't see why *we* should care." He looked at Hank and shook his head. "Hell, why am I explaining? We don't want Indian trouble, Mr. Chin. You don't live here. You just do this one thing and then you go back where you came from. Or you stand trial yourself. Like Hank told you, your bargaining position, it ain't strong."

"I just put the rope around his neck?" Chin asked.

"And string him," said Jeb.

"You want me to kill him."

Hank Webber put the small blade away and withdrew a clean white handkerchief from his breast pocket. He blew his nose carefully, first one nostril and then the other. He folded the material over twice and wiped the corners of his mouth with it. He put the damp cloth back in his pocket. "The law is killing him," he said. "He's been tried and sentence has been passed. If you don't do it, someone else will. It's not as though you can save his life. We're giving you a chance to save your own."

"To be or not to be," Jeb said. "It's as simple as that."

Two years earlier a lynch mob, which included businessmen and bandits and men of the cloth and men from the ranchos and one member of the city council, had hanged every Chinese in Los An-

29

geles that they could find. They had hanged doctors and cooks and children. When they ran out of rope, they sent their own children running home to beg for clothesline from their mothers. They hanged the Chinese from the gutter spouts and the awnings of Goler's black-smith and wagon shop, from balconies, in twos and threes, until they had hanged eighteen and there was no more room. The *Oriental* had carried the story and Chin had read it in a ragged copy brought from San Francisco almost six months later. He had seen nothing about it in the American papers. "I will do this," Chin said miserably.

Jeb locked Chin back in the cell. Down the street he heard Mrs. Taylor and Mrs. Godfrey. They were coming toward the jail and they were singing, "God, I am your instrument."

"They want me to kill you," Chin told Tom. "They'll kill me if I don't."

"You want my permission," said Tom. "You'd like me to say it's all right." In the pale beginnings of daylight, his straight hair was greasy and unclean. Last night at the window in the moonlight, he had seemed to have a certain potency, a large heart. The moon had been full for him. The birds had returned to say good-bye. Chin had sensed a malevolent majesty. This morning he only appeared to be dirty.

Chin himself felt a movement on his scalp he supposed to be fleas. He reached into his hair in pursuit. "Just your understanding," he said to Tom. He had the tiny, husked body between his fingers, but as he pressed them together tighter, *because* he pressed them tighter, it slid away. "I want you to see that I did not choose this, but have been chosen. My fate is to cross paths with your fate. This is not a personal thing. I am not doing this because the man you killed was Chinese."

"I'll keep that in mind," said Tom.

The music reached a crescendo. One of the women had a beauti-ful voice, came down on each note from the note above it. The other could not sing at all. They threw open the door. "God is here," said Mrs. Taylor. "God is here this morning with you, Tom."

Jeb brought Tom water and soap and a cloth. Tom knelt beside the bucket to clean his hands and his face. He had very little facial hair, no more than Chin himself. And the hair on his head was as black as Chin's own. Around his face it was wet and locked together in clumps. "We're ready for you now, Tom," Jeb told him. "We're taking you out and you can talk to people if you like when we pass, but don't touch anyone. And no stopping."

"Yea, though I pass through the valley of the Shadow of Death, I shall fear no evil," said Mrs. Taylor.

"You come last, Mr. Chin. Stay to the back."

Tom rose and turned to look at Chin. Chin could not meet his eyes, bowed his head and watched Tom's boots. They moved out of the cell in small, slow steps. Everyone was mindful now of the immensity of the undertaking before them. The law was about to kill a man. A man could be killed by another man in anger, for fun; the occasion could be a small one. But this required ritual and attention to detail. This required a procession. They moved slowly and with care, each one trying to mesh with the others, to be a proper part of the larger whole. Chin was the last out the cell door, which rang again with ceremonial finality, then the jail door, and into the streets of Steilacoom. They did not walk far. Ahead of them was a large tree with a rope, already knotted and looped. There were people all around; the Indians stood together, thirty black heads, thirty unsmiling faces to the left of the tree. Through the empty frame of the noose, Chin could see Mount Rainier.

Tom stopped beneath the rope. "Now, boys, it's all understood that we have nothing to do with this," Hank Webber said loudly. "The Chinaman is doing it all."

The sun swam upward in the East, a great red concentration. "Look there," said Tom to Chin. He pointed into the open fields. "That's Scotch brush. The Sisters of Charity brought it here. They missed Scotland so much. Now look at the way it's spread. It'll own this land in another ten years." He closed his eyes for a moment. "But it's beautiful when it blooms. You should be here in the spring just to see it." Sunlight filtered through the tree branches. Tom stuck one hand into a patch of sun and turned it slowly. He spread

31

his fingers until all the shadows were gone. "You've been a lot of places, Chinaman," he said. "You've been a lot farther than I have. Is there anywhere more beautiful?"

Chin looked at the peak of Mount Rainier. The distant ice glittered and beckoned. If you let go for an instant, your soul would fly to it. If you could walk inside that combination of light and ice, its beauty would blind you. Powerfully beautiful. Dangerously beautiful.

"You lived in paradise," he told Tom.

It was important that a man live somewhere. People were not meant to blow over the grass as Chin did, footless and rootless, like ghosts. It was important that a man die at home. Nothing was more important than this.

"Hang him," Jeb told Chin. "Do it now."

"Embrace God," said Mrs. Taylor. "Do it now."

Chin lifted the heavy rope with two hands. It slid without catching over Tom's head, settled on his shoulders. "Maybe I'm going to show you what I promised you," Chin said to Tom. "Something never before seen in this world. Maybe you'll see it soon."

Tom said nothing, looked neither up nor down, not left or right. His eyes were open and empty, as if he had already gone on, gone ahead without Chin's help, was past seeing. His body was cooperative in a distracted, sleepy way. Chin pushed the knot into the hollow spot on Tom's neck where it seemed to fit. He helped Tom mount a chair, which rocked slightly on the natural unevenness of the dirt around the roots of the tree. Hank Webber pulled the slack from the rope and anchored it. He gestured that he was ready.

Chin removed the chair. He killed Tom as invisibly as he could, there with everyone watching. The law killed Tom, the natural law of gravity. Chin thought of the Chinese miners falling and then of the birds, which did not. He was sorry that Tom's body did not go as gracefully into death as his spirit, but kicked and flailed and smelled, his feet seeking the ground again and again, until it finally stopped.

"You're a free man," Hank Webber told Chin. "My word is good on this. But let me give you a little advice. Go now. I don't think you should stay around."

"I'm going," said Chin. He caught the bundle of his belongings that the sheriff threw at him. Everything was tied up in his blanket now, white-man style. He kept his eyes on the ground so that he could pretend no one was looking at him. He watched the toes of his heavy boots alternately striding into view, now the right, now the left. He took big steps. The ground before him was wet and still retained the impressions of earlier shoes. Behind him he left his own tracks. His heels dug into the mud, making a trail of holes, each one looking like a small, open, angry mouth. Chin knew this. But he would not turn around to see.

11

In 1873, Georg Cantor developed set theory, based on several practical suggestions for proofs made to him by God (the proofs have held); Joseph Sheridan Le Fanu, master of the ghost story, died from an overdose of laudanum taken to ward off his nightly dreams of being buried alive; Cornell's President White refused to allow Cornell to face Michigan on the football fields with the words, "I will not permit thirty men to travel four hundred miles to agitate a bag of wind." Is there a madman here? Which one is he?

Sanity is a delicate concept, lunacy only slightly less so. Over the last few centuries, more and more of those phenomena once believed to belong to God have been assigned to the authority of the psychoanalyst instead. Some of the saints can be diagnosed in retrospect as epileptics. St. Theresa was almost certainly an hysteric. St. Ida of Lorraine seems to have suffered from perceptional insanity. She only thought that her body was amplified to monstrous proportions in her desire to be acceptable to God; we doubt this swelling actually took place, in spite of the testimony of the astonished and crowded nun who shared her bed. The prognosis for such cases in our own age is excellent; saintliness can often be completely cured.

We owe these advances, at least in part, to experimental alienist physicians such as the doctor who worked at the Steilacoom Territorial Asylum in 1873. The same year Freud entered medical school in Vienna, Dr. James Carr was duplicating the experiments of William Hammond, cutting the heads off coupling frogs to isolate the physical location of instinct in the frog's body. Hammond claimed to have kept the headless male frog alive for up to ten days, and in all that time the male never released his purposeful grip on the female. The seat of instinct, Hammond concluded, was in the spine. Dr. Carr had great difficulty getting his frogs to couple at all, and then they lost all interest in sex when they lost their minds. They were, perhaps, less instinctual to begin with, more cerebral, more effete, these western species of frog. He had experimented with Red-legged Frogs, identifiable by their short hind legs and warty skins; Tailed Frogs, smoother, olive green, and named for their tail-like copulatory organ; and the smaller Cascades Frogs. He had switched to East Coast varieties now.

His patients were not expected to couple at all, were, in fact, segregated by sex, at least in their sleeping quarters, to prevent this very thing. Dr. Carr had little to say about their care. The asylum was run according to the contract system, and the authority of the physician was secondary to the authority of the contractor and his profits. Dr. Carr made the original diagnosis. He chose what medications were to be tried and in what dosages. Beyond that there was little he was permitted to do. His recommendations that particular patients be discharged were often opposed by the contractor, one Arnold Greene, who was paid ninety-one cents a day by the Territory for each patient and saw, therefore, in each cure the loss of revenue. When the doctor and contractor differed, the superintendents for the asylum invariably ignored the doctor. Research might have been a great comfort to Carr if he hadn't been faced with these intransigent frogs. It was so unjust.

MORNING AT
THE STEILACOOM ASYLUM

Assent — and you are sane
Demur — you're straightway dangerous —
And handled with a Chain —

EMILY DICKINSON,
1862

Despite his isolation, Dr. James Carr tried to keep up with current developments in his field. He had written several letters to colleagues detailing the astonishing earthquake cures at Steilacoom last year. There had been a flurry of gratifying interest, but no one could duplicate the results. The cure only seemed effective when it had the authority and scope of an Act of God. Nothing smaller worked. He had spent several weeks designing the Carr Quake Chamber, a tubular cell suspended from the ceiling by rope. He had drawn up plans, specified dimensions, sacrificed nothing in the way of patient comfort or the gyrational range of the device. It would never be built. Certainly not at Steilacoom, where even outmoded technologies such as the Autenrieth Mask, the Cox Swing, Reil's Fly-wheel, or Langermann's Cell were deemed beyond the austere budget of Contractor Greene. For a time, Carr had been quite interested in the fat-and-blood cure popularized by Dr. S. Weir Mitchell, a leading neurologist during the Civil War. The fat-and-blood cure emphasized overfeeding, massage, and complete rest. But someone had told Contractor Green that Leland Stanford found it cost-effective to supply the Chinese railway workers with opium, which acted as an appetite suppressant and reduced food costs. Most of the patients in Steilacoom were on some sort of medication anyway; many of them took opium derivatives. Contractor Greene cut their meals to two a day. He called this trimming the fat from the budget.

The regimen Dr. Carr now envisioned for Steilacoom rested, like a footstool, on three solid points. The first was hearty food—beef, in particular, as so many of the insane are lacking in iron. He described to Greene a fortifying dish that could be made by scraping the tender parts of a steak away from the tendinous connections so that the juice is retained and then salting it heavily. This diet would be contraindicated, of course, in those cases where patients suffered from the delusion that they were made to eat human flesh or the blood of their friends.

The second point was exercise. Steilacoom boasted its own roller-skating rink; all that was required now was the provision of a reasonable number of skates so the patients would not have to wait so long for a turn. Dr. Carr would have liked to see the insane on horseback, too, and participating in guided gymnastics, but he tried to deal in realities.

The final point was music, music and dance. The medicinal benefits of music, he told Contractor Greene, were hard to overstate. A piano or melodeon in the female ward would answer the purpose. Violins for the men. There was already an asylum band and Dr. Carr would have liked to see every inmate participate, the most incapacitated being asked only to play the triangle or the sticks.

The superintendents, led by Hank Webber, their most illustrious member, had promised Greene that when Dr. Carr's contract expired, he could replace him with a physician of his own choice.

"Get the patients out in the open air," Dr. Carr was always nagging the wardens. "The breath of God's free atmosphere, the open face of Mount Rainier, these things are a wonderful tonic," and they took this advice when wood needed to be cut or water drawn, and they did, out of respect, refrain from kicking the lunatics in the physician's presence. Even so, they resented him. Dr. Carr could feel this and he complained to the patients about it often.

One of the most sympathetic of the insane was the young man named B.J. Voisard, who now stood outside Dr. Carr's office, trying to figure out how to open the door with one hand and not drop the load of wood he was carrying with both hands. The problem proved insoluble. Fagots of wood clattered to the floor and B.J. had to dance to protect his feet. When the wood had settled, he swung open the door.

"I heard there's a new woman in the ward," he told the doctor, dropping to his knees to gather up the scattered kindling. "What's wrong with her?"

Dr. Carr was seated at his desk with his notebook open before him and the tip of his pen in his mouth. He had undone the cuff of his right shirt sleeve to allow the free flow of blood to his writing hand. "I've only had time for the most cursory examination," he answered. His eyes were a pale, filmy blue and he blinked them often. The lashes were white and almost invisible. "Might be an ecstatic. She makes those meaningless, ecstatic noises, so that's the direction in which I'm leaning now. I'm going to send for her again after breakfast. Then we'll see. Anyway, a new patient in January is not too surprising. Lots of people go mad in January. Not as many as in May, of course. Nor June. But January is your third most common month for madness."

When he had been admitted, late in October, B.J. had been delirious. He had no memory of this, but he had read the notes Dr. Carr had made at the time. Tongue coated, breath very offensive, bowels constipated. Intellectual monomania with depression, Dr. Carr had concluded. B.J. still spoke rapidly and often appeared to be uneasy, but his physical health was much improved—his digestion was better, his secretions more free—and he was often quite lucid now.

He glanced at the contents of Dr. Carr's desk. The glass office window defined a small neat square of sunlight about the size of a blotter. Inside it, the colors made vivid by illumination, were a slab of obsidian that the doctor used as a paperweight, a letter opener shaped like a golden feather, and his notebook, pressed open to a clean white page. On the edge of the desk, pushed out of the sun, there was an empty whiskey bottle. At the bottom of the bottle, two frogs sat and ignored each other.

"It's not mating season," B.J. told the doctor. "It's winter." He wondered where Dr. Carr could have even gotten the frogs. One of them had the pale palm of its hand pressed against the glass, four fingers spread wide. The curvature of the bottle magnified the hand so that it seemed all out of proportion to the frog's body. "Where did you get the frogs?" B.J. asked.

"Boston," said Dr. Carr. "I sent away for them. In the big hospitals in the East, where there's lots of money and the doctors earn big salaries, frogs mate like weasels. There's never any shortage of frogs." His voice had an abused edge to it. B.J. liked the doctor and wanted to make him feel better.

"Would you like to talk about it?" he offered.

"I ordered six. Four of them arrived dead. I'm just lucky a male and a female survived. Count your blessings, right, B.J.?"

B.J. dropped the wood by the fireplace and approached the desk, dusting his hands off on his pants. He had a splinter at the base of his left thumb. He picked at it until it came out, leaving one small drop of blood, which he licked away. "Can I see what you've got on the new woman?" he asked.

Dr. Carr flipped back two pages in his notebook. "Just the observations I made last night when she was admitted. I haven't gotten back to her yet today." He passed it over the desk to B.J. Dr. Carr's lines slanted upward and he had a rounded, feminine hand. His "e's" yawned from the page like "o's." B.J. underlined the words with his index finger as he read.

According to Dr. Carr, the woman in black who had appeared so suddenly in the graveyard the night before had the classic facial features of the criminally insane. He cited the work of Cesare Lombroso at some length and included a description of the new woman. Thick black hair, gray eyes, diastema of the teeth with exceptionally large canines, a repulsive, virile air, and big, sensual lips. This tallied closely with Lombroso's description of the accomplished or potential poisoner. Contractor Greene tended to employ reliable patients in the kitchen to save himself the wages of an additional Chinaman. Dr. Carr had made a further notation restricting the new inmate from this duty.

He had also written that the woman appeared to have menstruated recently. Dr. Carr had seen this immediately, had, in fact, been looking for it and said so forthrightly in his notes. This, more than any other factor in her appearance and demeanor, had made him tell Sheriff Jeb Chambers that the Chinaman who had been found with the woman could well be an innocent victim in the case, however much the layman might be tempted to draw the other obvious conclusion. If called into court, he would be forced to say so. He could cite authorities on this subject. Delasiauve, among others, had been quick to call attention to the abnormal mental condition into which many women are thrown at each menstrual period. Their desires are exaggerated or perverted; they may even be impelled to criminal acts. In his own practice, Carr noted parenthetically, he had once treated a young lady who, while menstruating, suffered from the delusion that a large Negro man was entering the house through the window and pointing a pistol at her. He had read of more extreme cases, such as Marce's account of a patient who furiously attacked with a knife anyone who offered her the most trifling

41

opposition during her menstrual period. He knew that the menstrual cycle, which represented the disappointment of the maternal instinct, could occasion a gross perversion in which the natural feminine desire to procreate became instead a desire to kill. There were already legal precedents for what he was saying; he had told Jeb so. Last night's entry ended with a list of them. Dr. Carr had gotten as far as the Lydia Palmer case, which had yet to go to trial.

B.J. handed the notebook back. "What's diastema?" he asked.

"Excessive spacing between the teeth," Dr. Carr told him. "There is so much room beside her upper canines that the lower ones occlude when the mouth is closed."

"Oh," said B.J., returning to the fireplace. He knelt on the hearth and turned back the edge of the rag rug so that it would stay clean while he swept up the ash from yesterday. "It's too cold in here for you to work," he said solicitously. "Maybe if it were warmer the frogs would think it was mating season. Let me get things going." He arranged the logs, hoping they were dry enough. He tore strips from an old newspaper and stuffed them into crevices so that the logs would light. "There's an article here about Belle Starr," he said. Much of the article was now on his hands. There were actual, decipherable letters across his palms. Raven-ha, they read. He stared at them for a moment before wiping them off on his thighs. Indian talk, he supposed. Lake Raven-ha. On the shores of Raven-ha. "Now she's flayed a man with her quirt just for being saucy. She's married another damn Indian half her age. And it set me thinking, you know, how masculine a lot of these women who like to ride so much are. Do you think it's possible they're just wishing they had what men have? I mean, is it too farfetched to think the horse could be a sort of substitute for . . . a male member?" B.J.'s voice fogged slightly on the last words. He coughed, looking over at the desk where Dr. Carr had stopped writing and was regarding him, his fingers slipping absently up and down his pen, which now rested its nib on the paper in his notebook.

"A horse is a lot bigger than a penis," Dr. Carr said. His voice was gentle. "Think about it, B.J. You know this." He put the pen down and withdrew his watch from his breast pocket. "Come here, B.J.," he said. "Look at this. Perceptional distortion is not an uncommon symptom for a man with your condition. I once had a female patient tell me my watch was as big as a carriage wheel. Could you hold this watch in your hand?"

"It's a perfectly normal-sized watch," B.J. lied. Really he had never seen a watch so huge. It was a pumpkin of silver and glass, and the doctor's hand trembled under its weight. "I know that horses are bigger than penises. I was abstracting. Maybe these horses are the closest thing to a penis these women can get."

"I don't want a penis as big as a horse. Do *you* want a penis as big as a horse? Is this why you think Belle Starr wants a penis as big as a horse?"

"She doesn't," said B.J. "She just wants a penis, and a horse is the closest she can come."

Dr. Carr put away his watch. "A pen is closer to a penis than a horse," he said. "The root word is even the same. A knife is a lot closer. Do you think Belle Starr has no access to a pen or a knife?"

B.J. sat back on his heels and stared into space for a few minutes. "I guess it was crazy," he concluded. "Now that I think about it more. You're right, of course. It's ludicrous." He shook his head cheerfully. "That's why you're on that side of the desk and I'm on this one."

"You're just overexcited." Dr. Carr's voice was soothing. "Your progress has been excellent. You mustn't expect the treatment to be a straight road. Bound to be some twists. Let me finish the fire here. I want you to go back to your room and lie down for a little. Will you do that, B.J.?"

"All right," said B.J. He stood and brushed off the bits of bark and dirt that clung to his clothes. There was a dark ink smear on Dr. Carr's notebook where the pen tip had run when he stopped writing. B.J. could see it clearly from where he stood. "You've spoiled your page," he said. "Sorry."

Dr. Carr looked down. "Well, I'll be," he said. His voice carried a message of surprise and pleasure. "It looks just like two frogs coupling, doesn't it? See, here's the male. . . . "

"It looks like a puddle," said B.J. "Like a rain puddle." He looked at the blot again. "Only smaller," he added and then shut the office door carefully behind him and moved through the dark hallways to the male part of the asylum.

He had to pass through the female section on his way—not directly through, of course, but through the corridor around it. Someone was howling inside. The introduction of a new patient always threw the ward into chaos. He stood at the door and listened for a moment. The howling was guttural; it was the woman from Germany. She was in love with him; B.J. knew this, much as his natural modesty coaxed him to demur. She watched him all the way through breakfast, trying to mesmerize him with her eyes. Snake eyes. Sometimes he could hardly eat. And *sometimes* she invited him to her room, where she claimed to have two dead fleas dressed as a bride and a groom, laid out in an old jewelry box. She had made their clothes herself, she said, and caught the fleas herself as well. Killing a flea without crushing its body was not an easy thing to do. She had finally starved them in a stoppered medicine bottle, a project which had taken a surprising number of months. And the tiny veil had taken hours to attach. Almost a year of work was represented. B.J. would have liked to see these fleas. If only it hadn't been wedding clothes. If she had dressed the fleas for the opera, perhaps. Or in ceremonial Indian dress.

The floorboards in the corridor tipped suddenly upward, forcing B.J. to walk uphill or wait until they tipped back. It was either part of his condition, landscape distortion, or it was another earthquake. Both were too common to alarm him. He waited for the floor to flatten.

A woman in black, a woman he had never seen before, curled out of the doorway, soundlessly, like smoke. Diastema of the teeth. Gray eyes. Large, sensual lips. She wore her hair cut short in the current fashion of the Duchess of Austria; B.J. had seen illustrations of her haircut in advertisements in the paper. Her dress was a complicated affair, though very unclean. He was surprised by her hair and her clothes, which suggested money. People with money didn't end up at Steilacoom. She stood directly in front of him. She probably thought he had been listening at the door.

"No, I wasn't," B.J. told her quickly. B.J. was often rather frightened of women, but this woman was so very small. Her mouth was slightly bruised, which showed that she had already been initiated by the wardens into life in the asylum. She had an air of fragility about her. B.J. felt protective. She had no business being in the corridor.

"You go back to your room," B.J. said to her, hastily, looking around to see if anyone was listening. "Or you're going to be hit again." He tried to remember which warden was helping with the women this morning. It was a popular duty. Was it Houston's day? He thought so. "Are you crazy? Go back," he said more strenuously. She smiled at him, but he would take no more responsibility. He didn't want another woman falling in love with him. Expecting things. Flowers. Gifts. Notes. Time. Women, all women, whatever their mental condition, had this unnatural need for attention. It wasn't enough just to be with them, even. You had to talk about them. You had to talk about nothing else. How you felt about them when you first met them. How the feeling was even stronger now. How you had never felt this way before in your whole life. He pushed past her. When he turned to look back, she was gone.

B.J. could not really go to his room and lie down. The doctor might actually not know this and B.J. would not have wanted to be the one who distressed him with the truth, but the penalty for not finishing assigned chores was one he had paid only once and was never going to pay again. He decided not to return to his room at all, but made his way to the kitchen to see if wood or water was needed for breakfast. A new Chinaman had just been hired. He wore a filthy padded coat and fiddled with his braid while William Ross, cook by trade and inmate by circumstance, instructed him in the preparation of graham mush and boxty.

"Staples here at the asylum," Ross was telling him. "Scarcely a day goes by when boxty isn't served in one form or another. You could say the asylum runs on boxty." He laughed. "A joke," he explained. "It goes right through the patients like grain through a goose." He waited for the Chinaman to express amusement, but there was no response. When Ross spoke again, his voice was less familiar. "B.J., here"—he gestured toward B.J. with the point of a large kitchen knife—"is an example of the fine, strapping health boxty can provide. If you ever need wood fetched or water, you can ask B.J. But remember, he's not to go out alone. None of them are. He needs to get the key and a warden. If he's not quick about it, then *you* get the warden yourself and tell him so."

Ross acted more like a warden than an inmate himself, and on special occasions, like the birthday of one of Greene's many daughters, Ross was called to the contractor's own home to cook. B.J. knew that Dr. Carr had recommended Ross's release weeks ago. Dr. Carr thought, and B.J. agreed with him, that Ross had never really been insane. B.J. was afraid of Ross.

He looked at the Chinaman to see if he was afraid of him as well. The last Chinaman had once thrown his cleaver at B.J. There was still a slice in the wall over the water bucket where the blade had lodged, the handle trembling in the wood like the shaft of an arrow. B.J. sometimes stroked the scar for reassurance when he set the bucket down. The bucket would soon be empty again. He would fill it and then it would be empty. The world seemed to conspire to erase his efforts, to erase him. There were times at night when B.J. tried to touch himself and could feel nothing but the blankets and the empty bed. He would reach for himself and miss, clutching air in both fists. There was no other terror like the one that came over him when he had ceased to exist. But there on the wall was something permanent. "B.J. was here," the gash said to him. November 23, 1872. B.J. dropped the water bucket and the water puddled on the kitchen floor and seeped between the floorboards and the Chinaman threw his cleaver into the wall by B.J.'s head. "B.J. was here."

The new Chinaman wore the same thick braid, the same dark, baggy pants, and the same oversized boots as the old one. He stood there looking blankly down at the pulpy mass in the pot. B.J. thought he seemed very tired. He had a large lump on his forehead from which rays of black and purple and green extended. It made B.J. wonder if he could be an inmate. They had inmates from France and Scotland and Holland and Germany. But no Indians and surely no Chinese. How would you know if a Chinaman was insane? All Chinamen were insane. He watched the Chinaman give the mush a tentative stir. It took both his arms to pass the spoon through.

Ross's knife caught the light at the edge of B.J.'s vision and he turned toward it. Suddenly it was the largest knife B.J. had ever seen. Sunlight spread on the flat blade whenever Ross's hand was still. When it moved, the blade of the knife sliced the sunlight into small, flashing pieces.

There was a code to the flashing light. The knife wanted many things. The knife wanted the winter turnips and the last of last year's potatoes and the side of beef hanging in the pantry. The knife wanted the Chinaman's braid. Lay it across the table and cut it off. Three blind mice. Three blind mice. The knife sang insinuatingly. B.J. shut his eyes so as not to listen. The knife whispered directly into his ear. Say nothing about the woman in black, it told B.J. You better not. B.J. pressed his lips tightly together so that he wouldn't. Ross went into the pantry and took his knife with him, leaving B.J. without guidance.

The Chinaman was looking at him. B.J. panicked. "There is a new woman in the ward today," he confessed all in a rush. The words flooded from him. "All in black. A tiny little woman. I saw her." He moved closer to the Chinaman, lowering his voice. "She was *outside* the ward."

"Is she all right?" the Chinaman asked. He was much easier to understand than the last Chinaman. He spoke more slowly and his words were less accented.

B.J. shook his head, wondering at this naïveté. "She's crazy," he pointed out.

"Don't tell anyone I asked," the Chinaman whispered. They heard Ross's footsteps returning and moved apart again. B.J. thought it best not to face Ross's knife after his betrayal. He turned and fled back into the asylum dining room for breakfast.

C H A P T E R
F O U R

DR. CARR'S THEORIES ON
ANIMAL MAGNETISM

Had we our senses
But perhaps 'tis well they're not at Home
So intimate with Madness
He's liable with them

EMILY DICKINSON,

1873

In a well-run asylum, the female and male wards would each have their own dining room. Contractor Greene was in the middle of building repairs; the Steilacoom facility originally had been a fort during that part of the Territory's history when the Indian threat was the greatest, and certain changes were required to make it function optimally as a sanctuary for the insane. He had been given a budget of three hundred dollars for the renovation and repair of existing buildings. When he submitted his bill for a little more than four thousand dollars to the Territorial legislature, they asked if daily association with lunatics had rendered the contractor stark mad. Work on the facility halted. The men and women of Steilacoom ate together in a single dining room. They sat on benches at four wide-planked tables. They had tin spoons and tin bowls. They bowed their heads and spoke the grace.

"Truly grateful," B.J. said, resting his forehead on his locked thumbs. "Amen."

There were twenty-three inmates in all at the asylum—sixteen men and seven women. They represented the following forms of insanity in the following proportions: Idiophrenic insanity, 6; Sympathetic insanity, 14; Toxic insanity, 1; Anaemic insanity, 1; Insanity resulting from arrested or impaired development of the brain, 1.

Ada, the woman from Germany, entered. She was late; she was dragging the new woman behind her. Ada pushed the new woman onto the bench first, then sat next to her, leaning sideways with her body until the other woman had moved farther down the bench and Ada was directly opposite B.J. She gave him a fluttery, conspiratorial look. Her gray hair was combed up from her forehead and away from her face. But when she turned to see that the new woman had a spoon and a bowl of mush, B.J. noticed Ada had forgotten to comb the back of her hair at all. It ruffled up from her neck like the feathers of an angry chicken.

"What's her name?" B.J. asked.

"Sarah," said Ada. "Sarah Canary, because she sings like an angel. She's been put in my room. I'm in charge of her. I'm to help her settle in." Ada made many of the sounds of her speech deep in her throat and spit often when she talked. B.J. had never been around many Germans and did not know if they all talked this way or if this was a symptom of Ada's illness or if this happened because Ada was missing one of her front teeth. He had discussed her case on several occasions with Dr. Carr.

"The woman from Germany is in love with me," he told Dr. Carr as a way of introducing the topic.

"Men and woman have profound physiological differences," Dr. Carr answered. "Some more obvious than others. The capacity of the skull is greater in the male and, what is really remarkable, is that this masculine advantage increases as the race becomes more civilized. Thus the skulls of the Negroes in Africa show less sexual differentiation than those of the Europeans." He blinked his eyes rapidly and leapt from his chair, unfastening the glass door of the bookcase and removing a large black book. He opened it roughly in the middle, flicked through a few pages with his thumbnail. "The average cranial capacity of the male German, for example," he said, his index finger floating over the text, "is 1538.76 cubic centimeters, but the German female capacity is only 1265.23. This is a difference of 273.53 cubic centimeters."

"She stares at me when we eat," B.J. said.

"The gray substance and white substance in the male brain are also heavier than in the female. It is not necessary to ascribe superiority to any of this, of course. Merely difference. Men are better at manly things. Women are better at being women. This current trend to provide them with similar educations is very wrong-headed." Dr. Carr shut his book with a sound like a clap.

"She's always trying to get me to come to her room."

"Well, that's not allowed," said Dr. Carr. "Surely male patients aren't allowed in the rooms of female patients. What are we running here, a hospital or a bordello?"

"A hospital," B.J. said. He'd been in both.

"Women feel the tyranny of their bodies so much more than men do. Love affairs are seldom a good sign." Dr. Carr shook his head. "One of the saddest cases I ever encountered was a woman, happily married, aged forty-six, in whom there were no discoverable hereditary influences toward insanity. Just at the time her catamenia were becoming irregular, she was seized with uncontrollable libidinous desires. Prior to this she had never exhibited any sexual proclivity, and intercourse rarely afforded her any pleasure at all. Now she could scarcely be taken out into public without making indecent propositions to the men she met. Sometimes in the presence of her *husband*. She remained in this condition for about two years, until her menses ceased altogether and she recovered her health."

"Is this the case with Ada?"

"Very likely. And very much to be pitied. Don't encourage her,

B.J., but don't despise her. Somewhere, trapped inside her body, is probably a very high-minded woman who would be ashamed if she knew how she was behaving."

Ada appeared quite satisfied with herself now. She was ignoring B.J. in favor of the new woman, making clucking, consoling sounds and feeding Sarah Canary from her own spoon as if she were a little child. "Here's a big bite," she said. Sarah Canary reached for the mush with her fingers, but Ada slapped her hand quickly with the bowl of her spoon and Sarah withdrew.

"Does she talk?" B.J. asked.

"Not yet. I'm teaching her. Here's another big bite," said Ada. "You eat nicely now." She looked over at B.J. with a dreamy smile. Her attention was elsewhere; her eyes no longer penetrated. "I'm going to make some clothes for Sarah Canary," she said. "Some lovely party dresses."

While Ada's face was averted, Sarah Canary slipped her fingers into the mush. She was licking them when Ada turned back to her. "No, no!" said Ada sharply. Her voice was extremely loud. "You eat nicely or you don't eat at all." She rose in a fury, picking up the bowl of mush and overturning it onto the table. The warden was there instantly. A silence fell over the entire room. It was Houston. B.J. had been right about today's assignments. The air thickened so that he could hardly breathe.

"Now, that's a mess," Houston said quietly. "And a mess is something I will not have."

"It's her mess," said Ada, pointing to Sarah Canary. "I didn't—"

Houston put his hands around Ada's neck and pulled her upright. "Some time in the wash house for you," he told her. The ideal hospital would have, as a matter of course, a cell for the punishment of recalcitrant lunatics. Fort Steilacoom had no shortage of cells; this was one of the aspects that recommended it for its current purposes. But females were always sent to the wash house in deference to the delicacy of their sex and to permit them to pass their sentence in some useful manner. The wash house was not a cell, but it was not dry and it was not heated. There were no windows. At Steilacoom everyone was used to making do.

Houston took hold of Ada's hair with one hand and struck her across the face with the other. "Papa," said Ada, pleadingly. "No, Papa." Houston fastened his hand about her throat again, shutting off the words. He began to pull her by the neck from the room. Ada's shift rode up her legs, which were limp, whether by design or out of fear B.J. could not tell. Her heels bounced off the floor with each of Houston's steps. Her face when B.J. last saw it was puffy and changing color.

B.J. felt suddenly that someone was looking at him and not at the more compelling scene Houston and Ada were making. He scanned the room to see who it was. Sarah Canary had her fingers in the mush on the tabletop. She put three of her fingers in her mouth and began to hum around them. These were the first sounds B.J. had heard her make. A cold spot on the back of his neck grew colder and he knew the person staring at it must be behind him. He turned around. The Chinaman stood in the doorway and his eyes were fixed intently on B.J. He made a small gesture. Come here, it said. And then he disappeared back into the kitchen.

B.J. got to his feet. The guttural sounds of Ada choking grew fainter and fainter. The corridor into the kitchen tipped upward. B.J. could climb it, but it made him pant. The Chinaman was alone, standing at the large basin, scraping the pots prior to washing them. "Did you need water?" B.J. asked. He looked to the bucket. It was still full. A moth floated on top, its wings extended. He hoped the Chinaman wasn't going to expect him to fetch a new bucket every time a bug drowned.

"Do things like that happen often?" the Chinaman asked. "Is this a bad place to be?"

It took B.J. a moment to understand that the Chinaman was talking about Ada and not the moth. And another moment to wonder how to respond. B.J. didn't like questions unless he knew what answer was wanted. He had no idea what the Chinaman hoped to hear. Perhaps the Chinaman wanted to hear about Louis Bergevain, an inmate who'd been beaten to death three months ago when he'd become too ill to do his chores. Houston had told B.J. people might come around asking questions. B.J. was not to even say the word

53

Bergevain. Not to Dr. Carr or to anyone else who asked. The people with questions, Houston told B.J., might be very cunning, but he would not accept this as an excuse if he was disobeyed.

He had not told B.J. the people with questions might be Chinese. This was *very* cunning, but B.J. would not be tricked. He said nothing at all.

He watched the Chinaman cross the kitchen to the black stove and pick up the mush pot. The mush had coated the inside with a grainy film. The Chinaman scraped at it with his spoon, but it adhered to the pot's sides. He scratched a tiny line clean with his fingernail. He stood staring into the pot.

"Soak it first," B.J. suggested. It was a generous offer since it would use a great deal of water and the bucket would have to be filled that much sooner.

"Perhaps that woman is just very difficult," the Chinaman suggested, setting the pot into the sink and ladling water into it. "Perhaps things like that happen only to her."

"Perhaps," said B.J. carefully. "And perhaps not."

"Which?" asked the Chinaman.

"One or the other," said B.J.

"Shouldn't a woman be in charge of the women?" the Chinaman asked.

"Yes," said B.J. "One is."

"Was she there at breakfast?"

"Yes."

The Chinaman stood staring at B.J. He was considerably shorter; B.J. could see every detail of the top of his head, his scalp where the hair divided, the way it flowed into the rope of the braid. There was a red spot on the bare skin between the hair that flowed to the right and that which flowed to the left. A flea bite, B.J. thought. Not that this was the season for fleas. "If I wanted a woman's help in the kitchen, could I request a particular woman? The way I can request you when I want water fetched?" The Chinaman was speaking very carefully, just the way B.J. himself was speaking. B.J. understood suddenly that he was not happy asking questions. B.J. was not happy answering them. He looked for a way to rectify the situation. He changed all his answers into questions.

"Fetching water is my job, isn't it?" B.J. said. "And not anybody else's, is it? You say what job you have and the warden sends the person who does it, doesn't he?" Now all the Chinaman had to do was answer. Instead he asked another question and looked unhappy about it.

"Are the new patients assigned jobs quickly?"

"Sometimes. Aren't they?" B.J. stressed his last two words. The Chinaman still had not caught on.

"Has the new woman been assigned a job?"

"Has Sarah Canary been assigned a job?" B.J. asked. His voice was getting louder. "Sarah Canary sings like an angel, doesn't she? But she doesn't talk. Does she? So I don't think she does jobs. Do you?"

The Chinaman waved his hands in a quick unhappy gesture to tell B.J. to be quiet or to go away, B.J. was not sure which. B.J. was sorry about this. He had only been trying to help. He returned to the dining room and his mush bowl. It was gone. Sarah Canary had two now. One was empty and clean as if she had licked it. The other was B.J.'s. He reached for it and she turned her eyes on him steadily. She made a low, threatening noise in her throat. It was a growl. B.J. dropped his hand and stared at her. "That's my breakfast," he said. "You had your breakfast." Sarah Canary growled again. Houston had returned and was pacing between the tables.

"Is there a problem here?" he asked at each. "Any problem here?" The man from France had no problems. The syphilitic farmer had no problems. The man who spoke only in rhymes had no problems. The woman who did things only in threes had no problems. Sarah Canary certainly had no problems. She smiled and hummed and licked her fingers. B.J. had no problems. And he had no breakfast.

He stared coldly at Sarah Canary. "Dr. Carr hasn't finished his diagnosis of the new woman," he told Houston. "I'm supposed to take her to him after breakfast."

"The hell you are," said Houston. "I'd like to see the day when inmates escort inmates around the asylum. When male inmates are asked to escort female inmates."

"Well, he wants to see her," said B.J. "And he wants to see me."

"The hell he does," said Houston. "Who the hell does he think is running this asylum? He'll see you when I say he can. He'll see you in hell." Houston cracked the knuckles of his left hand with his right. He reached under the overhang of his belly and began to undo his leather belt. B.J. put his own hands up to cover his face. They were interrupted by the female warden.

"On your feet, dear," she said to Sarah Canary. "The nice doctor wants to see you now." Sarah Canary did not respond. There was nothing to suggest that she had even heard. Houston gave B.J. one final look, fastened his belt back into place, and then turned to help. He gripped the collar of Sarah Canary's dress and slid her along the bench to the end. Still holding her collar, he lifted her and held her in midair for a moment. She seemed to shrink, pulling her arms and legs closer into her body.

"The nice doctor wants to see you now," Houston said, setting her down. "Let's not keep the nice doctor waiting. I'll take her," he told the female warden. "I'll take her more quickly than you could." He prodded Sarah Canary from the back. She stumbled slightly, then moved in the direction of the push. He prodded her again and she was unresisting. They disappeared through the dining-room door.

B.J. reached across the table for his bowl. Sarah Canary had not had a chance to finish; some of his breakfast remained. It was cold and congealed, but he ate it hastily. He left with the other patients, shuffling in a line through the yard for exercise time on the roller-skating rink. B.J. had fetched the water at sunup. It had been cold enough to see his breath. Now the yard was in full sunlight and the day was a beautiful one. Might rain later, but it really didn't look like it. This was two days now it hadn't rained. Both the wardens commented on it.

B.J. waited for his turn at the skates. He was quiet and unobtrusive. Ordinarily B.J. enjoyed skating. Most of the inmates did not. Most of the inmates strapped on the skates and then stood precariously on the rink without moving until the wardens came and gave them a push and they fell over. Some of them fell even without the push. Ada was a wonderful skater; she had done a lot of ice skating in Germany as a child. Ada's arms pumped about her body when she skated, not one at a time, the way most skaters moved, but both together as if they were wings. Ada was in the wash house and it was Sarah Canary's fault. B.J. was hungrier than usual and that was Sarah Canary's fault, too. He let several people ahead of him in line.

"Thank you, thank you, thank you," the blond woman with bloodshot eyes told him. She coughed three times. She did everything in threes. It was an S.O.S., but B.J. refused to admit he understood it. That was all he needed, another woman in love with him. He shook his head at her.

Eventually he had let everyone by and stood at the very back of the line himself. When no one was looking, B.J. slipped out. He followed a circuitous route to the doctor's study, creeping through the old barracks that had been converted for storage. He avoided the part of the asylum that once housed young subalterns and was the current quarters of the asylum attendants.

The doctor's study was in the old officers' quarters. B.J. listened at the door, which was solid wood and heavy. He could hear the sounds of humming inside. Making a fist, he tapped with the last knuckle of his hand. There might have been a response that didn't carry through the heavy door. Or he might not have knocked loudly enough to be heard over the humming. He opened the door and the humming stopped. "Excuse me," he said. "I don't mean to intrude. I just wondered if you were able to get that fire going." He could smell and he could hear the fire as he spoke. The wood snapped and gasped in the fireplace. Some of the wood was perhaps a bit too wet; the air was smoky, but the fire seemed a robust and reliable one.

"Oh, B.J.," said Dr. Carr. "Come in, come in. I need your help." B.J. turned to look at him. Sarah Canary sat in the patient-chair, a comfortable winged piece; her back was to B.J. and her head and the chair obscured much of the doctor. B.J. could just see his

57

face. He was flushed from exertion, perhaps, or emotion. Dr. Carr was one of those people who reddened easily. He stood close to his patient, holding one end of his watch chain a few inches before her. B.J. could not see the watch. Sarah Canary's dark, thick hair was in his way.

"I was just about to perform an experiment in animal magnetism," Dr. Carr said with some excitement. His pale eyelashes fluttered. "Something I'm ordinarily reluctant to do since it can get out of hand so easily. You've heard of Mesmer's group? The original public exhibition in Paris? No? There's quite a good account in Prichard. Not only were the infirm magnetized with mixed results, but a number of natural objects as well. Trees, for example. When the experiment was repeated in the garden of one Dr. Franklin, a susceptible boy who came into contact with a magnetized tree fell at once into a crisis. He lost all consciousness. The hypnotist tried to argue that additional trees had become spontaneously magnetic, which had concentrated the effect. Balderdash. If trees had this ability, it would be worth your life to take a walk outdoors. The susceptible would always be fainting dead away. It was a naked attempt to disguise his own culpability. Truly irresponsible behavior on the part of the hypnotist. And ultimately tragic. Most of those involved in the French experiments were from the upper classes. Axed during the Revolution. The people, that is. The hypnotists. The magnetized trees remain to this day. Is it too implausible to argue that some link between those trees and the madness that followed the Revolution might exist? Is it?"

This was the kind of question B.J. liked. "It isn't," he said firmly. He knew he was right.

"Caution, you know, has always been my guiding principle," Dr. Carr told him. "I'd rather err on the side of caution. But now, here we have a woman who doesn't speak. There appears to be some impediment to the woman speaking. Not a physical impediment. God knows she makes sounds. A mental impediment. I thought perhaps hypnosis could provide us with a way around it. And M. Petetin, in Lyons, reports such successes with cataleptic women. He has had eight cases in which the seat of sensation was transferred to the epigastrium. I was just reading his remarkable account of one of these cases. Young woman, completely deaf to sounds in the ordinary way, but, under hypnosis, able to hear M. Petetin's slightest whisper if he bent close to the epigastrium.''

"You thought Sarah Canary might be able to speak with her epigastrium?" B.J. asked.

"I was open—I *am* open," said Dr. Carr, "to anything. But then she swallowed the watch. Reached out quick as a cat. I had no idea what she was about. You know how fast an ecstatic can be." B.J. took a few more steps into the room and around Sarah Canary's chair. Now he could see that the other end of the watch chain was in Sarah Canary's mouth. Dr. Carr tugged gently on the chain. Sarah Canary allowed her face to be pulled forward but kept her mouth resolutely closed. Dr. Carr slackened off. He looked as if he was playing a big fish. "It's actually gone down into her throat. The woman has no gag reflex at all. And an unhealthy impulse to fill any available orifice. Women of a certain age are so prone to this. I suspected this the first time I saw her.''

"How old do you think she is?" B.J. asked him.

"The shady side of thirty. Maybe even the shady side of thirty-five. Premature wrinkling is a characteristic of the female criminal profile, of course. And there's very little gray in the hair. Let's say thirty-three. I'd rather err on the side of caution.''

"She ate my breakfast," B.J. told him. "Remorseless." He tapped Sarah Canary helpfully on the shoulder. Sarah Canary swung her head to look at him, jerking the other end of the chain out of Dr. Carr's hand.

"Oh, God," said Dr. Carr, diving after it. "Get it, B.J. Don't lose it! Don't let her swallow it!"

The watch chain was slipping away like a noodle into Sarah Canary's mouth. B.J. seized the end and held it tightly. It was much shorter than it had been. He pulled on the chain. Sarah Canary had it clamped between her teeth. There was no give. Dr. Carr retreated to his desk and rummaged through the center drawer. "Here," he

59

said, returning, holding out his hand. "Here's a nice peppermint for you, Sarah Canary. A trade. Give me the watch and you can have the peppermint."

Sarah Canary reached for the candy, but Dr. Carr closed his hand over it. "First the watch," he said sternly. Sarah Canary inclined her head questioningly. She looked sullen and stubborn. Dr. Carr opened his hand again and showed her the peppermint. She did not respond.

Dr. Carr grew tired of waiting. He transferred the peppermint to his left hand and gripped her jaw with his right. His thumb drove directly into the bruise at her mouth. Sarah Canary winced. "Give me the watch," Dr. Carr said loudly. He applied pressure on the jaw hinge. Slowly, painfully, Sarah Canary allowed her mouth to be pried open. As soon as a gap appeared between the upper and lower teeth, B.J. began to reel in the watch chain. The gap widened. The watch slipped into sight at the back of her throat, slid over her tongue, and dangled wetly in front of her face at the end of its chain. It was so large. He looked at Sarah Canary in awe.

He looked back at the watch, wiping it on his sleeve and examining it more closely. He held it to his ear. "It's still ticking, Dr. Carr," he said. "Can you believe it? An ordeal like that? And it's still ticking away. I wonder what else you could do to a watch like this? I wonder if you could put it in a box and drop it off a boat into a lake and leave it overnight. Would it still be ticking then? I wonder if you could hit it with a hammer."

Dr. Carr reached for the watch without responding. He put it into his pocket along with the peppermint. "I don't think this session can usefully continue," he said. "I think the basic trust necessary between patient and doctor has been somewhat violated." He sounded hurt. "Perhaps you'll return the patient to her room for me, B.J. I'll be prescribing phosphorus for her in the meantime. I really don't see what else I can do. I am not one of those doctors who thinks phosphorus is a cure-all, mind you. The dictum 'Without phosphorus, no thought' may be absolutely true, but it doesn't necessarily follow that phosphorus will always rectify abnormal mental processes. How easy the alienist's job would be if that were the case.

60

No, it is perfectly possible to crowd the stomach with phosphorus and see no improvement in the patient's condition whatsoever. But what else can I do at this juncture? You tell me, B.J. Suggest something. I'm open to suggestions.''

"What else can you do?" B.J. echoed. "You've done everything you can." He took Sarah Canary by the sleeve and tugged. She stood, shaking loose of his hand. She spoke to him, a happy stream of noise that must have been in some foreign code; B.J. didn't understand it at all. She smiled, first at him and then at Dr. Carr. Her noises continued, but her eyes began to wander. She was no longer directing her speech at either of them. She stepped around the desk, pressed a palm on the glass front of the bookcase, then tapped the glass with one arched finger. She was quiet for a moment, listening to the sound. Sunlight glanced off the panes at an angle now, making a mirror in front of the books. Sarah Canary pulled her hand back and bent into the sunlight. Her face appeared in the glass. She stooped to look at it, looked more closely, and the closer she came, the larger her reflected face grew. For a moment she stood still, merely staring. She pulled back and the face shrank. Then, quite suddenly, she leaned over and kissed the glass. The two mouths came together, but one was only an illusion and made no mark, while the other left behind an imprint, shaped vaguely like a butterfly, at just that place on the glass where the mouth that did exist tried to kiss the mouth that did not.

Houston found them together in the corridor. "What did I tell you," he cried, "about male and female lunatics escorting each other around the hospital? What did I tell you?"

He inserted himself between B.J. and Sarah Canary, drawing back his hand, knuckles out, to hit B.J. For a moment his hand wavered in the air by B.J.'s ear, a moment's pause so that B.J. could anticipate its sting, but Sarah Canary, standing behind Houston, saw the motionless hand, rose onto her toes, and bit it. B.J. sucked in his breath in a long, horrified gasp. There was blood on the corner of Sarah Canary's mouth. There was blood on Houston's hand, just where the little finger joined the palm. Houston's face went a terrible white, with bright red patches on his cheeks. He caressed the right hand with the left, wiggling the injured finger experimentally. His expression was one of disbelief. It seemed to B.J. that Houston grew larger.

Sarah Canary had begun to run the moment she released Houston's hand. She disappeared down the corridor back toward the doctor's office. She ran well; her skirt was torn and did not inhibit her and neither did her heeled shoes, but where was she going to go? B.J. watched Houston's back, receding from him in furious pursuit. The corridor twisted. He could hear their footsteps long after he could see either of them.

B.J. had not moved. He stood and tried to adjust to the fact that he had not been hit. How had this been avoided? Bringing his hands up to his face, he patted his cheeks and his nose and his eyes inconclusively. He couldn't be certain he felt anything. He began to suspect that he hadn't been hit because he had ceased to exist. There was only silence around him and an arrhythmical ticking in the distance. B.J.'s hands shook. In the kitchen, he told himself, was proof. There was a scar in the wall. He could go and see it. He could feel it. He forced his shaking legs through the courtyard. A platinum lizard scuttled out of the sun and disappeared beneath a thinly veined rock. The Chinaman stood in the doorway to the kitchen.

"You look like you've seen a ghost," he said.

I've *been* a ghost, B.J. thought. It was much worse. He tried to push past the Chinaman; he was still light-headed with terror. The Chinaman stopped him with an arm.

"Did you come to tell me something about the woman in black?" the Chinaman asked. "Have you seen her?"

"She's running," said B.J. "Please let me by."

"Running? What does that mean?"

"She was found in the corridor alone with a man," B.J. told him. His voice caught. "What is this, a hospital or a bordello?"

"What will be done to her?" the Chinaman asked.

"What did they do to Bergevain?" B.J. slid by the Chinaman at last and crossed the kitchen to the water bucket, his eyes on the mark in the wall. He reached his fingers to it. The gash itself was slick, though the wall around it was rough and splintery. He felt relief moving like heat through his body. His heartbeat began to slow. Warmth filled every extremity and testified to his completeness. He had fingers. They were warm. He had toes.

"Who are you talking about?" the Chinaman asked.

"Louis Bergevain." The Chinaman had so many questions, he had tricked B.J. into answering them. B.J. was beginning to not like him.

"Who are you talking about?" It was not the Chinaman asking. Ross, the cook, stood in the pantry doorway, chewing on a piece of raw turnip. "What are you saying, B.J.?" His voice flattened with menace. "We never had a Louis Bergevain here. Now, did we?" Ross turned to the Chinaman. "You have to forgive him. He's crazy. You can't listen to anything he says." He pivoted again, turnip dangling from his lips, looking at B.J., who could not look back. "You go to your room now, B.J. You're in the way here."

B.J. watched the ground as he left. He walked past the brown pants and the baggy black ones with the large boots. He thought there might be some message, some sign from the Chinaman, now that he had sacrificed himself to answer him, but there was nothing. He needed guidance. He needed to stay in those places where Houston was not for as long as he could. When he had last seen the warden, Houston had been heading in the direction of the old officers' quarters. B.J. went the other way, toward the wash house and the old Laundry Row, but he circled it, doubling back along his own route to confuse his tracks. It took him perhaps fifteen minutes to come back out by the kitchen, where he had started.

There by the door stood the Chinaman and the woman in black. The Chinaman had Houston's keys in one hand and the woman's sleeve in the other. There was a large bedroll tucked under one arm. His expression was one of absolute misery. B.J. was surprised at how easily he could read it. Usually he found Oriental faces hard to decipher. The misery deepened when the Chinaman noticed B.J. "Go back to your room," he said. "Everything here is fine. The woman is helping me in the kitchen."

"The woman is not allowed in the kitchen," said B.J. "Dr. Carr thinks she may be a poisoner."

"I will watch her. I will watch carefully," said the Chinaman. "You go back to your room now."

B.J. looked at the keys that dangled from the Chinaman's hand, winking in the sunlight at him. "You are escaping," said B.J. "You are kidnapping Sarah Canary."

"No," the Chinaman said. His voice was suddenly high. "Go back to your room or I will get the warden."

B.J. stood for a moment indecisively. The keys clicked together in the Chinaman's hand. B.J. looked into the Chinaman's face.

"Go!" said the Chinaman. He and Sarah Canary backed into the kitchen. B.J. followed. "No," the Chinaman said. The hand with the keys shook violently. He closed his palm over them to silence them, but it was too late. They had already spoken to B.J. The Chinaman opened the kitchen door into last year's vegetable garden. He stepped through and pulled Sarah Canary after him. B.J. followed.

"I am saving the woman as I promised. But I cannot be responsible for another lunatic." The Chinaman might have been speaking to B.J. or he might have been speaking to no one—to the air, perhaps, or to the keys. Nothing answered him. He began to run with the woman, through the empty furrows of the garden, and B.J. ran after them. They stopped at the main gate. "It is too much to ask," the Chinaman said. "You know it is too much." He began to speak a language B.J. did not understand. The words were low and then high like big and small bells. They rang with pleading. "Don't follow us," the Chinaman said to B.J. in despair. "They will only find us and bring us back. You will end up like Louis Bergefin."

"Louis Bergevain," said B.J. He took the keys from the Chinaman's unresisting fingers. He opened the gate and dropped the keys on the walkway. "We'd better run," said B.J. "Can you make her run?"

But Sarah Canary was already gone. She favored her right shoe slightly, like a dog that has picked up a thorn. Even so, B.J. had a hard time keeping up with her. Her black skirts fluttered ahead of him. She ran eastward, in and out of the shadows of trees, and away from the town of Steilacoom. B.J. was panting and had to stop often. Whenever he stopped he looked back, but no one was following, except the Chinaman in his awkward boots, his bedroll in his arms. The asylum gate remained open and empty behind them for as long as B.J. could see it.

In 1870, an excessively introverted six-year-old boy named Benjamin MacDonald disappeared from his family's farm near Winnipeg. He was found by his older brother two months later, emerging from a hole in the ground, filthy and thin, but unexpectedly alive. He had been fed and cared for by a female badger who followed him home, watched his tearful reunion with his parents somewhat protectively, and moved into his bedroom.

The experience left Benjamin with a sort of ambidexterity. He could function quite well on all fours as a badger, but he was a more successful human as well. Prior to this experience, his shyness had been so pronounced, his parents feared he was mentally retarded. Now he was companionable and outspoken.

In 1871, Champion Ira A. Paine and Captain A. H. Bogardus shot a match of one hundred birds each at the Long Island Pigeon-Shooting Club. Henry Bergh, president and founder of the SPCA, objected to the event. Why sacrifice a living creature to mere marksmanship? he asked. Were people aware that the birds were often tortured before they were released—stuck with pins or blinded with turpentine and cayenne pepper to make them whirl around and around before the gun? He was accused of sickly sentimentality. Roosevelt's *Citizen and Round Table* said Bergh was "the best intentioned and least practical man in the community. The idea of cruelty in field sports has long been exploded, and now it is admitted that no persons are more tender in protecting and preserving game that they pursue, and small birds that they do not, than sportsmen."

In 1872, an aquarium for the study and preservation of marine life was built in Brighton, opened to the public, and named the Crystal Palace. Octopuses were admired, dolphins adored. Southport was seized by a sudden rage for the baby alligators sold in the aquarium gift shop. The ladies in Brighton let them sleep on the parlor hearth like puppies, fed them table scraps, and it was absolutely unfashionable to be seen on the promenade without one.

The Victorians studied nature through the lens of morality. What is God's purpose for animals? they asked themselves. Are animals good? Are some animals good and some not? Geese, for example, but not tigers? Earwigs, who were argued to be tender mothers, and pigeons, who were monogamous and missed their mates, but not foxes or carnivorous plants? Why would God create animals that were not good?

Are animals happy? they wondered. In George Johnston's book, *Introduction to Conchology*, he says of oysters "in due season, love visits even these phlegmatic things, when icy bosoms feel the secret fire," but others in his field had doubts, the happiness of oysters being so hard to ascertain.

Despite such concern and controversy, the result for the animal seems to have been curiously invariable. Benjamin MacDonald's badger mother was shot and killed by a hunter in the MacDonalds' front yard. Champion Ira A. Paine won his match by eighty-eight pigeons to Bogardus's eighty-five. And the great advantage of baby alligators, as Frank Buckland pointed out, was that when they died, usually within a few weeks of purchase, the pet could be stuffed, gilt, and put on a hat for an ornament.

"I have just now killed a Large New Falcon, yes positively a new species of Hawk," Audubon exulted in a letter to Dr. Richard Harlan. ". . . I will skin it!!!"

In 1873, the word *ecology* (spelled oecology) appeared in print for the first time.

C H A P T E R
F I V E

THE STORY
OF SU TUNG-P'O

We like March
His Shoes are Purple —
He is new and high —
Makes he Mud for Dog and Peddler,
Makes he Forests dry.

EMILY DICKINSON,
1872

Nature was everywhere Chin looked. He was trapped with no knife in an oecology of Douglas fir and hemlock. A dead squirrel lay beside a boulder on the path, its tail stiffened in a final gesture of alarm. Its body had become a village for ants, who settled in thickly, building roads over its back, bridges and homes in its cavernous eyes. Chin stopped, staring for a moment until the ants blurred into black lines that tightened and loosened and tightened over the squirrel. "Honorable ant," said Chin. "Unselfish ant. You build a dream on a dream." The trees might have said this same thing to the railway workers. The stones might have said this same thing to the transient trees. Chin looked upward, following the line of a trunk past the small isolated mistakes of lower branches into the full opening of higher ones and beyond, into the sky. The sudden movement of his head made him dizzy and the sky went black. He stumbled over his next step.

He was a young man and his physical condition was very good. He had worked the rivers as a miner; he had driven steel. He could put in ten hard hours and he could do it on very little food. But in the past two days he had eaten almost nothing and thrown part of that up again; he had sustained a nasty head wound; he had killed a man and he had kidnapped a woman. He was tired. He told B.J. it was time to slow down. There were Indians before them and Indians behind. What did it matter how quickly they got to the nowhere they were going? Sarah Canary was so far ahead, he could no longer see her. B.J. responded with an ambiguous wave.

Chin shifted his bedroll from one side of his body to the other, wishing he had two of them. With two, weight could be distributed evenly across the shoulders. Especially if you had baskets and a pole. Your balance was better. And, also, if he had two, then three people would not have to share one blanket when night came.

"B.J.!" Chin called out again softly. "Wait for me. Wait there for me."

B.J. turned around, smiling. "It's sunny!" he shouted back to Chin. His voice rang and echoed in the stillness. *Anyone* could hear him. "I smell moss. I smell a stream. It's never going to rain again!" B.J. brushed his limp, colorless hair back from his forehead and stood still inside a patch of yellow light. Closing his eyes, he extended his arms out from his sides, palms up. He began to turn slowly like a top. The light made his face even paler; it shone like a small moon as it spun by Chin. This was the color of lunacy. Chin had seen this color before. The Chinese faded in this same way when they lost their minds. Probably even the Indians became this bleached, bloodless color. Maybe even the black demons, the Negroes.

He walked slowly up the path toward B.J. "I am hoping," he said, catching one of B.J.'s hands with a clap to stop him spinning, "that you have a suggestion as to where we can go now. Someplace where we can spend a night inside. I have the only blanket between us. I have the only coat."

"You can't be certain they're yours, all the same." B.J. was cheerful and matter-of-fact. "Just because you brought them. You learn that when you've been in a hospital as long as I have. Any time you start to think you own something, you should remember. Someone can always take it away from you." He hid his right hand behind his own back suddenly. "Then it's theirs," he said. He laughed. "Not that I would. Take your blanket, I mean. Though if it were my blanket, I'd share it. But Sarah Canary doesn't care. She's got no scruples. She's crazy." His voice dropped to a whisper as he looked from left to right for Sarah Canary, who was nowhere. "You probably shouldn't let Sarah Canary even see that you have a blanket," he suggested. "You don't tell her. I won't tell her."

"B.J.," said Chin tiredly. "Do you know someplace we can go tonight? Someplace we can be safe and inside?"

"No."

Chin stared at B.J., who smiled more broadly. His back teeth were stained with something greenish. Boxty, Chin supposed. Boiled boxty. If Chin had stayed on at the asylum, he would have tried steaming it. Or frying it quickly in very little oil. Cooking food in this manner intensified the color. Chin imagined rows of inmates sitting down to the brilliant green of stir-fried boxty. "Where did you come from before the hospital?" he asked.

"Squak." B.J. said the word without moving his lips. "Squak, Squak. We're going in the wrong direction. We couldn't get there tonight anyway."

"We couldn't get there tonight anyway," Chin agreed. He knew Squak. There were lots of Indians in Squak. Hop-pickers for the German farmers. Wrong season, of course. They were probably somewhere else now. They could be anywhere. A soft sound might have been the wind through a hundred leaves if it wasn't a hundred voices whispering behind them on the path.

He jumped slightly when B.J. spoke. "Sarah Canary is happy to be outside. She's talking to the birds." B.J. stood looking ahead of them, up the incline through the trees. Chin tried to follow his gaze. He couldn't find Sarah Canary's figure anywhere, just trees and trees and more trees. A sparrow dipped through the branches of one, circled Chin's head, and went north. It was an omen, but Chin wasn't sure if it boded good or ill. To see a sparrow walking was good luck. Chin had only seen them hop. To have a wild goose land in your courtyard was good luck. The year he left for Golden Mountain, their domesticated goose had joined the wild ones overhead and never come back. The geese were flying in formation that day; they wrote the character for man and took it east across the sky. It had made his mother cry with fear for him and for her own old age without him. Very bad luck. He thought of Tom's owl. Very bad luck.

"She's waiting for us," B.J. said. "Maybe she knows where she's going. Maybe she knows a place we can stay." He walked away and Chin followed, shifting the roll to his other, stronger shoulder again. It threw his weight to the side, making him stumble and hop. He was filled with self-pity. Poor little bird with one wing. Very bad luck, little bird.

B.J. continued to look up. Chin watched B.J.'s back and then his heels and then looked down at his own feet. When a journey has no destination, progress can only be measured by counting steps.

The path went down and then up and then down. The tree shadows shortened and shortened and disappeared. A stream appeared at their left, parallel to the path, masking the sounds of the two men walking with its own running commentary. The earth talks to us, but we don't speak its language, Tom had told Chin. Chin listened harder. Fallen tree here, the stream said. Rocks. More rocks.

B.J.'s voice was almost as incessant. Chin had not seen Sarah Canary since they left the asylum, but B.J., walking ahead, gave him regular reports on Sarah Canary's activities. "She's picking up leaves now," B.J. said. "She looks happy." Chin counted steps. The path ceased to be a path and became the ghost of a path. They stayed beside the stream. Chin stepped over a puddle. He stepped over a rock. He saw Sarah Canary's heel-print in the crushed leaves of a fern. "She's leaning against a tree and looking up at the sun," said

B.J. "She's hugging herself like she's cold." The fir needles beneath Chin's feet were bound together at the tops like miniature wok brushes. Chin walked in and out of the sunlight. He noticed that the pine smell was sharpest in the shadows. He noticed he could smell wet rocks in the stream.

"She has a stick in her mouth.

"She's throwing a stone at a tree.

"She's stopped to . . . urinate." B.J.'s tone was hushed. He turned back, facing Chin with his eyes closed. "Into the creek. Don't look." They waited a few moments and then began to walk again. The trail sloped downward and the trunks of the trees bent at identical angles, keeping the branches upright. Hemlock crowded out the fir, long cones abundant at the ends of the branches, the top shoots curving over in an arc of new green. Chin saw the scars of an old fire.

"She's caught a frog!" B.J. said. "She's getting smaller. Are we going down now?"

"Yes," said Chin.

"Oh, well, that explains it. I mean, she would then, wouldn't she? Get shorter."

"I don't see her at all," said Chin.

"She's just ahead. She's putting flowers in her hair. Phlox. Pink phlox."

"Where is she getting the flowers?" Chin asked. He saw no flowers. It was the wrong season for flowers. B.J. did not answer.

The absence of a path led to a narrow gap between two rounded stones. The stream turned sharply to the left. B.J. chose the passageway. His shoulders were almost too wide for him to walk through squarely, and Chin had to hold the bedroll in front of his body. It was slippery underfoot; between the stones and the trees, no sunlight penetrated, so the ground was perpetually damp. As Chin passed through, the stones around him shuddered. A ripple of earth lifted Chin slightly and then set him down. He heard a tree crack. "Did you feel that?" Chin asked B.J.

"Feel what?"

The passageway ended in the air. Chin stepped out beside B.J., who stood staring over the edge of the cliff. Chin's next step would take him out onto the treetops. A cold wind blew the loose hair from his queue back off his face. "Where did Sarah Canary go?" Chin asked.

B.J. shrugged. "I'm hungry." His hands and knees were shaking. "I think it's time for my medication. I feel kind of trembly."

"Where is Sarah Canary?" said Chin.

"Really. I feel sick."

"When did you last see her?" Chin sat on the heels of his heavy mining boots in the small square of ground they shared and opened the bedroll. He had taken some of the asylum bread; he removed it now from his blanket. B.J. sank beside him, holding his legs with his hands to try to keep them still. Chin watched him. You're an opium addict, Chin did not say. I see what kind of medication they had you on. "You're just tired. You probably haven't walked for a while." A second tree cracked behind them. "I don't think we should sit on this ledge." Chin gathered up his belongings. "Just go back through the passage. Then we'll eat. You'll feel better."

Once B.J. had mentioned food, Chin became ravenous. He broke the bread with his fingernails. It was hard and had retained its shape. He tore off a piece for B.J., puncturing the crust and wedging his thumbs inside. The second piece came away easier. Chin went to the stream and bent over it, drinking water from his cupped hands to help him swallow the bread. He drank until he began to worry about stomach cramps. Later he noticed how tasteless and odorless the bread was. He noticed how much chewing was required. He noticed how wide B.J. opened his mouth for each bite and how loudly he chewed. He remembered with a start that he had lost Sarah Canary. He should have called to her. How could they follow when the path was no longer a path? Why hadn't he called to her hours ago? The bread in Chin's stomach turned as hard as the bread in his hand.

Coward, he accused himself. He had not called because she had been so far ahead, he would have needed to shout, and he was afraid that someone else might hear. He had been prudent and now she was lost. Or he was. And everything she could have brought him was lost.

Such a small decision, not to call to her. It had come to Chin ready-made. He had not thought about it at all.

He folded his arms and told B.J. a story of despair. "In Penglai there is a statue of Su Tung-p'o. He was a poet in the Sung dynasty. One day, the eight Immortals appeared to him at the Marble Bridge disguised as eight blind beggars. He followed them to the pavilion of Shelters from the Wind and fed them food from his own hands. It was a great feast. There was duck and monkey brains and thousand-year eggs." Chin's tongue coated with saliva. He broke off another ragged piece of bread and offered it to B.J.

"Maybe they only looked like thousand-year eggs," B.J. suggested.

"Then one by one, the eight beggars leapt off the cliff above the sea. 'Leap out with us,' the last one said. Su Tung-p'o looked over the edge. He saw the eight beggars each on a lotus throne. There was a ninth throne, which was empty. But below the thrones was a three-hundred-foot drop into the sea."

"Jump," B.J. encouraged Su Tung-p'o. "Jump!"

Tears came to Chin's eyes. "Would you jump?" he asked. "Would you really jump?"

"No," said B.J. "It would be crazy. Wouldn't it? Unless it only looked like three hundred feet and was really a lot less. A *lot* less."

"I wouldn't jump," Chin admitted. He remembered how, when he'd removed the chair, Tom's boots had taken their last walk several feet above the ground. He thought again of the Chinese miners herded into the air by Indians. No illusion of thrones then. No leaps, no choice, just the unavoidable indifferent rocks of fate. Someday Chin would be pushed over that cliff. And who could say this was not what he deserved? How many mistakes could he expect Sarah Canary to forgive him? Assuming she really was an immortal, which Chin didn't, in fact, believe anymore. Not that he believed otherwise, exactly. He allowed himself to occupy the narrow ledge of belieflessness. The tears disappeared back into Chin's eyes without falling. "Su Tung-p'o didn't jump. He was prudent. He was afraid of losing everything. How many people are offered a lotus throne? He waited too long. The Immortals disappeared and he kept on waiting.

He thought they would come back and give him another chance. The statue is of him waiting. I have never actually seen it," Chin said. He redid the bedroll, saving the small stone of bread that was left, wrapping it up in the blanket.

"I heard a story like that once," B.J. said. "Only instead of a poet it was a princess, and instead of eight Immortals it was seven swans, and instead of having to jump off a cliff she had to be silent for twelve years, and instead of immortality it was love she wanted. Except for that, it was the same story."

"So she lost love?" Chin asked.

"Oh, no. She did what she was told. She was silent for twelve years. Women will do anything for love." B.J. shook his head, wiped bread crumbs from the corner of his mouth with the back of his hand. "Oh, I see what you're saying," he added. "That's another difference. I was forgetting. No, women will do anything for love. Women would jump." B.J. sat another moment, absently staring downward. His hands twitched; his mouth was open. "Oh, I see what you're saying." He looked at Chin. "You're wondering if Sarah Canary jumped. Well, she would. Women prefer love to immortality."

"No, I don't think she jumped." Chin stood, shouldering the bedroll. "We should go and look for her."

"They think love lasts forever. They think love *is* immortality. Women are crazy," said B.J.

B.J. walked behind Chin now and his movements were slow and vague. Chin, who felt a constant pressure to go faster, had to stop and wait for him on several occasions. Of course, if Sarah Canary had gone to the right at the passageway instead of the left along the stream as they had done, then going faster was only taking them farther away from her. There was no correct course here. There was only walking and not walking. Chin walked. Chin stopped and did not walk. Chin walked. "Have you ever heard of ghost lovers?" he said. He was still thinking about love and immortality.

"People who love ghosts?" B.J. asked.

"Ghosts who love people. Beautiful women who seduce you for a single night and when they leave, centuries have passed."

"I've heard that story," B.J. said. "Only it wasn't beautiful women, it was dwarves. And it wasn't centuries, but it was a very long time. And he wasn't seduced, he bowled. But except for that, it was the same story."

This information was like cold fingers in Chin's chest. Chilling. Clarifying. Predictable. Chin began to walk faster, trying to leave B.J. behind.

Everything in Golden Mountain was a fraud. Cross an ocean and find a cracked-mirror version of a world. Three dollars' wages becomes seventy cents when *costs* are deducted. Nice rooms and fine foods and play all day becomes the *Ville de St. Louis* and the Memphis Plan. Mountains of gold become mountains of stone, and you lay the dynamite no matter how many of you send your bones back to China afterward.

Seduction becomes bowling.

So why was he following a crazy, ugly white woman through an Indian-infested forest with angry asylum attendants following behind? Even if it were a test set by immortals, who could say, here in Golden Mountain, what his reward might be? Railroad work? Bowling?

He was glad she was gone. So he had struck her once. So much noise as she made was not safe. He had done it as much to protect her as to protect himself. And he had paid by staying in Steilacoom, where the Indians were so angry with him, long enough to release her from the asylum. Now he had put her back in the forest just as he had found her. No harm done. The immortals should be satisfied with that.

Chin turned quickly to the right because there was obviously no path in this direction. If he could only lose B.J., too, he could retrace his steps, not all the way to Steilacoom, of course, nor any place very close to Steilacoom, but back in the direction of his uncle and Tenino and the railroad.

A huge tree blocked Chin's way. He tilted his head to look up at it, stretching his neck so that his mouth fell open. It was a Douglas fir, the beautifully clear shaft clean of limbs for a hundred feet. It rose into the air above all the other trees and yet, sadly and obviously, was through growing. Chin could see the brittle, golden needles on the branches high above him. He was aware of the enormous weight of the dead tree.

He circled the trunk on the right. He could hide on the other side until B.J. was gone. If B.J. followed him this far, then he could circle the trunk again and again, keeping the tree between the two of them until B.J. decided he was mistaken as to Chin's whereabouts.

The tree coughed. Chin stopped walking. He examined the motionless tree. He put out a hand, touched the scabrous surface of the bark, and quickly pulled his hand back. He took seven careful steps around and finally came upon a white man, poking what appeared to be a pen into a horizontal crack in the tree's trunk. The man withdrew the pen and measured a distance along it with his fingers. He dropped to his knees and made a notation in an open ledger which lay on the ground. He looked up at Chin.

"Hello," he said. "Were you looking for me?"

"No," Chin answered. "I'm walking to Tenino."

"Not the most direct route," the man said. "Look at this." He sprang up again, indicating the crack in the tree with his pen. "Give a look. Here we have an old tree and its old wounds. How did this happen, do you suppose? A quake? A storm? A drying spell in the weather? Whatever made this crack is ancient history now, before you or I lay in our cradles, listening to our dear mothers singing. And yet? What else do you see? Take your time. Look carefully."

Chin looked at the man instead. He moved lightly on his feet, but he was really quite large, considerably taller than Chin, and built like a barrel with rounded shoulders and legs. His hair and eyes were dark, but his heavy beard was shot with streaks of red. He waved Chin closer with the hand that did not hold the pen. His accent, rather than being flat and English, sang up and down in his excitement. Chin recognized the intonations as Irish. There were many Irish working the railroads. In general, Chin had found it advisable to stay away from Irish people. The working people, they called themselves and only themselves, which seemed to carry the suggestion that the Chinese were not.

On the other side of the tree, Chin heard B.J. panting toward them. The large man gave no sign that he heard anything.

"Well, you see sawdust, don't you?" The man pointed with his pen. "And if you wait and watch—look here, you don't even wait long—here's your cause." The tip of the pen slid from one side of the crack to the other, where a large black ant was emerging with a small bit of fresh wood in its mouth. "A home is being built inside this old tree," the man said. "More than a home. A fortress." He rapped sharply on the wood four times; several ants rushed out, climbed up and down from the crack, and eventually went back inside. "Easily defensible," the man noted. "Canny, canny little creatures. 'The whole world has gone mad for bugs!' Audubon said that. He was complaining, of course. Couldn't understand that people might have had enough of him and his birds. My name's Burke, by the way. Naturalist. Wanderer. Wonderer. Claiming no allegiance to any particular genus or species. And where have you come from?"

"Steilacoom," said B.J. incautiously. He had rounded the trunk and stood with his arm out, leaning against the tree and trembling like a small flame in a soft wind. "Have you seen a woman? We were with a woman. We lost her."

"Ah, now, I've lost many women. You never get used to it. You never like them so much when they're around as you miss them when they're gone, though. There's a wide world out there. Larger than women. It has *mountains* in it."

Burke put his pen into his pocket, picked up the ledger, and closed its pages together. "You were closer to Tenino in Steilacoom than you are now. You'll need to go back," he said. "I know a woman who lives in Steilacoom. The gentle Miss Anna Blue. Teaches Sunday school. Wonderfully Christian. Beautiful woman. I love her." He directed his words to B.J. now; his back was to Chin. "Listen!" He raised a finger in the air. "The liquid notes of the water ousel. Owls hoot in B flat, cuckoos in D, but the water ousel sings with the voice of the stream. She builds her nest back of the waterfalls so the water is a lullaby to the little ones. Must be where they learn it. They sing it themselves when they grow up. Can you hear? Have you ever seen the little gray water ousel walking on the bottoms of the creeks? Sweet feathered fish with legs?" B.J. shook his head. His hand shook. His knees shook. His shoulders shook.

"Ah, well, that's a shame. It's a sight you'd remember. You'll never get back to Steilacoom tonight. It's a half-day's walk when you're fresh. Perhaps you'd better sleep with me. You and your Chinaman. My name is Burke. I have a cabin." He inclined his head. "About a quarter of a mile distant."

"B.J.," said B.J. It was the last thing he said. He closed his eyes and toppled over as if the ground had been pulled from underneath him. He fell into the arms of a small tree and twitched there.

Chin abandoned his plan of abandoning B.J. in favor of a cabin in which to spend the night. "His health is poor," Chin said.

"He looks like a man who needs a drink." Burke handed the ledger to Chin and plucked B.J. out of the tree, slinging him over one shoulder. "Follow me," said Burke, and he led Chin home. They met Sarah Canary on the way. Chin was unexpectedly relieved. He hadn't realized how tense her absence had made him. Of course, he wouldn't have just left her in the forest.

"I am so happy to see you," he said guiltily.

She responded to his greeting with silence. The limp stalk of a dead flower dangled over one of her ears.

CHAPTER
SIX

BURKE'S THEORIES
ON GOD AND DARWIN

I thought that nature was enough
Till Human nature came
But that the other did absorb
As Parallax a Flame —
EMILY DICKINSON,
1873

Burke's cabin was a single room obviously built in some haste. The floor was dirt. The walls were wood. Any gaps had been blocked with mud and occasionally with fists of crumpled paper. A rock-stick-and-mud fireplace filled one half of the room, and any number of shadowy items swam in and out of focus in the light of the flickering fire: birds' nests, feathers, blown eggs, rocks with the skeletal outlines of fish stamped into them, chains of dried leaves, corked bottles with severed paws inside, pinecones, and seedpods. Chin might have just stepped into a Chinese pharmacy. Even the smell was familiar, a mixture of spicy leaves and dead fish and formaldehyde. In one corner, a larger item showed mysterious curves through an old brown blanket.

A man was already seated in the cabin when they arrived, tending the fire. The flames flickered in his eyes and a large black mustache curled over his cheeks. He was clearly surprised and displeased to see them. "The gentleman warming the hearth for us is Harold," Burke said. "A business associate of mine. Harold, this is B.J." He deposited B.J. onto the floor next to the fireplace. B.J.'s eyes were open and he forced himself to sit up.

"A pleasure," said B.J. "Really." He coughed wretchedly. The fire sputtered and sighed in the fireplace.

"Now I'm going to get you a whiskey, B.J.," said Burke. "Miss Anna Blue doesn't approve of drink. It's sort of a sticking point between us. But even she would concede that something stiff is required at times. For medicinal purposes. We'll get the blood running through your veins again. We'll see the roses bloom in your cheeks before the night falls." The bottle rested softly on a stack of pelts. "There's a glass somewhere," said Burke. "Give us a moment." He removed a lizard skin and a seashell from a wooden crate, peered into the bottom, and then replaced them. "Isn't this always the way?" He picked up a sketch of several different curvatures of bird beak and looked underneath. "For weeks at a time I don't see another living soul. Then I have more company than chairs." Chin looked around the cabin. It contained no chairs at all. "I have more company than glasses. I can't make you all comfortable. I can't even complete the introductions. I don't know the name of your lovely companion."

"Her name is Sarah Canary," said B.J. "Because she sings like an angel."

"Lovely," Burke repeated. "Perhaps she'll sing for us later. When we've settled in a bit, we'll be in the mood for a song. Something light-hearted and romantic. Something about love." Holding the bottle upright above his head, he bowed to the corner where Sarah Canary sat huddled. "You can't know what a rare treat a woman's voice would be. Are you cold, madame?" He set the bottle down, then picked up Chin's bedroll, which he undid without asking, shaking out the blanket and hanging it gently over Sarah Canary's shoulders. "The poverty of the room becomes an embarrassment to me when a lady such as yourself graces it. If there is anything I can do to increase your comfort, you've only to ask."

He turned back to his skins and pods. "Ah!" he called out in triumph, brushing aside three long black feathers and revealing a small glass. He upended it, tapping on the bottom until three dead moths fell out. "I knew it was here somewhere." Uncapping the bottle, he poured a finger of whiskey into the glass. He took a long pull himself on the bottle's mouth, crossed his legs, and sank to the floor. He passed the glass to B.J. and the bottle to Harold. "Let's drink to the great naturalist Louis Agassiz. He gave us the ice ages. And I understand he's failing now. Drink to his health."

Outside, the sky darkened abruptly and a heavy rain began to blow against the western wall. An occasional drop fell down the chimney and boiled away instantly with a sound like a snake. Chin slid to the floor and sat on his heels, exhausted. No moon tonight, Tom, he thought. Not here. Maybe where you are.

Chin was lucky to be inside. He was a lucky man. "We still haven't heard your Chinaman's name," said Harold, and his tone reminded Chin that luck was, after all, only an illusion in a transient world.

B.J. sipped his whiskey and looked confused. "I guess I don't know his name. I'm sure I knew it once. I must have forgotten." No one else spoke. Burke drank.

Harold poked at the fire. "John?" he suggested. "Every Chinaman I've ever known answered to John."

"Chin," Chin said finally. "My name is Chin." The wind and the rain obliterated his answer. The three men sat and looked at him uncomprehendingly. "Chin!" he shouted. The wind dropped just before the word. He shouted it into a sudden silence.

"Chin," B.J. agreed in a tone that suggested there was really no need to shout. "Of course, Chin. A cook."

"They're on their way back to Steilacoom," said Burke.

"Possibly." Chin spoke quickly before B.J. could. "Our plans are not definite."

"You're an odd bunch to be wandering the woods with no definite plans," said Harold. He seemed to wait for an answer. The wind came up again, but with less force. The rain tapped on the wall outside.

"Do you think so?" said B.J. agreeably.

Sarah Canary crept forward on her knees. She seized the uneaten bread that had fallen out beside Chin's dishes on the floor, retreating quickly back into her corner. Holding the bread in one hand, she tore at it with her teeth. The dead flower slipped from her hair onto her lap. She made a sound deep in her throat.

Burke and Harold watched her curiously, passing the bottle of whiskey back and forth. The heat of the hike began to leave Chin's body and he wished for some of the liquor. Since coming to Golden Mountain, his uncle had acquired a taste for tiger whiskey, whiskey with the color and bite of a tiger. Chin also had grown to like the drink. How many weeks had it been since he'd had any? Seattle. Not since Seattle.

Burke's whiskey washed against the glass and glowed in the light. When the fire was directly behind the drink, a mirage of flames appeared inside the bottle. "Would you be offended if I offered you whiskey? You had a long walk today." Chin turned, but Burke was speaking to Sarah Canary.

There was no reason to keep Sarah Canary's condition a secret. And even if there had been a reason, there was no way to do so. Chin cleared his throat. "She doesn't talk."

"Yet she sings?" Burke looked thoughtful.

"I haven't heard her sing," said Chin.

"Sounds, but not words, perhaps?" Burke turned to B.J.

"That must be it." B.J.'s glass was empty. He held it out for more.

Burke took the glass and refilled it. He rose to his feet and offered it to Sarah Canary, who looked passively back at him. She hummed a little, through her nose. "It's all right," Burke said softly. He put the glass on the floor by her feet. "Go ahead, my darling."

Sarah Canary reached for the glass. She picked it up and sniffed. She took an experimental sip. Her lips twisted, disappearing and reappearing as her mouth worked. Then she spat the whiskey back into the glass. Burke retrieved it and returned it to B.J., who raised it to his lips, then caught himself and lowered it again.

"How long have you known her?"

"Since morning," said B.J.

"Two days," said Chin. "I found her in the woods two days ago."

"Interesting." Burke took another drink.

"Interesting," Harold agreed. "So you . . . adopted her." An unpleasant smile curved his mouth upward in opposition to the mustache.

Chin tensed. "I am trying to help her." He spoke quietly to avoid giving offense and kept his face still. He had made the mistake of becoming visible. As long as Burke and Harold had thought of him only as B.J.'s Chinaman, they had hardly thought of him at all. Now he had given them something to think about. The fire flickered behind Harold like an extra inch of flaming hair all around his head. Harold stared intently at Sarah Canary. Chin looked at Sarah Canary, too, and then at B.J. and then at Burke. He had no friends in this room. It was an important thing to remember.

Harold was helping to remind him. "I haven't known many Chinese," said Harold. "But I would have said that the race has a gift for self-interest." He shifted his position to make it clear that he was speaking to Burke and to B.J. and not to Chin. "I drank once with a man who supervised a Chinese crew on the railroads. He told me about an accident he'd seen. They were tunneling with dynamite and a charge didn't go. They sent a Chinaman in to relight it, but the charge had only been delayed. Took both his legs right off. So he lay there, screaming and covered with blood, and his legs were the whole distance of another man away from his body. But none of the other Chinese workers would help him. They kept carting out the baskets of rock like they didn't even see. They had to be ordered to tend to the victim. They had to be promised that any time they took would be compensated the same as if they were working, before they would do anything to relieve him. Damned inhuman, if you ask me."

Chin kept his eyes down and his mouth shut.

Harold was unaffected. "This Chinaman, of course, is different. He sees an abandoned white woman and he just wants to help her. It's very good of him."

Burke spoke. "Your English is remarkable, Chin."

Chin did not look up. "Thank you."

"Remarkable. How long have you been here?"

"Three years only," said Chin. He resisted the impulse to provide more details, to tell them he had learned English back in China and that he also spoke German. He tried instead to divert attention from himself with a deft change of subject. "You study nature, then," he said to Burke. "Have you ever heard of a kind of bird with only one wing? Do you think such a thing could be?"

"No," said Burke. "Nature being fond of symmetry. And partial to pairs. Two eyes, two arms. Two sexes."

"One head," said B.J. as if he were agreeing. "Five fingers."

A moment's silence followed and then Burke laughed abruptly. "You've put me in mind of the legless birds of paradise. Have you heard this tale? Stop me if you have." He paused only briefly before continuing. "Well, it's a bit of a joke on us, really. The first naturalists in South America sent back beautiful specimens they called the birds of paradise. Lovely birds with no legs. The scholars in London were beside themselves, contemplating the lives of the airy creatures, eating and mating and sleeping entirely on the wing. They wrote papers of praise. Later they learned the legs had simply been cut off to make the birds fit in the boxes for the mail. Oh, it was a great embarrassment all the way 'round." Burke laughed again and handed the bottle of whiskey to Chin. "Drink up," he suggested. "Drink to paradise and the legless birds who live there."

"Thank you," Chin said, inclining his head slightly. The bottle was wet on the outside of the neck where Chin grasped it and the dirt on his hands turned to mud. He took an especially long swallow, a tiny celebration of Burke's approval, though how he had won it, he wasn't sure. The whiskey was harsh; tears came to his eyes and his nose filled. He wiped his fingerprints off the bottle with his sleeve and handed it back to Burke, who passed it to Harold. Harold cleaned around the mouth with his cuff before he drank again.

"Chin, I want to show you something," Burke said. Swinging his legs around, he reached into a box behind him, sorting through several stoppered jars. "Are you familiar with this?" The jar he handed Chin contained a single small stone. "I bought this off a man in San Francisco who said he got it off a Chinese boatman in Hong Kong. I'd like to get another. Have you seen such things?"

"It's medicine," said Chin. "It's a dragon's tooth. A very good one. Liung tse. Very valuable."

"You Chinese use that name for any fossilized tooth. But this tooth is rather peculiar. You see how the internal slopes have filled the intervening valleys so that the surface is nearly flat? Leaving only a few fissures and those are particularly narrow. You would expect this kind of wear on a human tooth. Homo sapiens. But the tooth is far too large to be human. It comes from some animal that lives in China. Humanlike, but gigantic. What could it be?"

"An ape?" Chin suggested.

"Even that's not large enough. And it wouldn't explain the wear. Have you seen other teeth like this?"

"I've seen many dragon teeth," said Chin. "I've never looked that closely. I don't remember another one so large."

"Ah, well." Burke put the jar away behind him. He smiled at Sarah Canary, who was noisily finishing her bread. She smiled back. "Droop," she said. "Whulp. La."

"The world is full of mysteries," Burke observed. "And a very good thing, too. Harold, here, makes quite a little living from the world's mysteries. Don't you, Harold?"

"People have a natural sense of wonder," Harold said stiffly. "I try to provide them with a little oddity now and then. Takes them out of themselves and away from their own troubles."

"Don't apologize." Burke gestured extravagantly, knocking a book from the top of a crate. His voice was the loudest in the room, louder than the rain, which hit the wall with a sound like a thousand stones, louder than the wind, which rang like a celestial gong. Wherever Burke sat, Chin felt that the center of the room shifted to that spot. Harold's movements and speeches were miserly in comparison. B.J. was mouselike. Chin found himself admiring Burke's largeness and loudness. It seemed to him a kind of courage. "We all have to make a living," said Burke. "We all have to do things we can't be proud of." He tipped the bottle straight into the air and gulped. He handed the whiskey to Chin. His face had taken on a drunken redness, and Harold's eyes were glassy. Chin took another sip, smaller this time.

"What kind of little oddity?" asked B.J.

"Entertainment," said Harold.

"Carnival entertainment," said Burke.

"Have you ever seen a display of performing fleas?" B.J. asked. "A woman I knew had been to a carnival and she'd seen trained fleas who could draw water and turn a windmill and fire a cannon all with little silver wires fastened to their necks. She said there was a tiny carriage drawn by fleas and carrying fleas all dressed up inside. Have you ever seen an oddity like that?"

"No," said Harold. "I never have."

"I think it was in England," B.J. said.

Chin's scalp itched and he scratched at it. It itched even more.

Burke turned his head to gaze at Sarah Canary. "Here's a mystery for you. A beautiful mystery. A mysterious woman. You're familiar with the categories of Linnaeus?" Burke asked. *"Systema Naturae?"*

"No," said Chin.

"No, of course, you wouldn't be. If you were, it might have occurred to you that this is not an ordinary woman you've found."

"I never thought she was an ordinary woman," said Chin.

"And did you ever think that Sarah Canary might well be an example of Homo sapiens ferus?" Burke's eyes brightened in excitement. "A wild woman?" He drank recklessly. "Just last year a feral boy was captured near Mynepuri, India. His name is Dina Sanichar. He's been raised by wolves since infancy, like Romulus and Remus. Had to be trapped like a beast himself and dragged in ropes, snarling and spitting, back to civilization. Of course, we have to make a distinction between human children adopted by the animals and taught bestiality and the true Homo sapiens ferus. I'm looking at Sarah Canary's rather distinct facial characteristics—the prominent brow, in particular—and thinking she could be either one." He retrieved the bottle from Harold and passed it to Chin.

"The feral child," he continued, "has a natural aversion to intoxicants. Miss Anna Blue would make much of this if she only knew it. I offered drink to Sarah Canary and you noted her reaction. The feral child does not laugh. Have you ever heard Sarah Canary laugh?"

Chin considered the question. "Yes," he said. "I believe I have. Once or twice."

"Perhaps you mistook a guttural sort of vocalization for laughter. The feral child must be taught to walk upright. Have you ever seen her run on all fours?"

"No."

"Does she not recognize herself in a mirror?"

Chin paused. "Yes," said B.J., sounding excited. "I mean, no. She does not. Well, that settles it, doesn't it? And Dr. Carr thought she was a poisoner. Remember, Chin? How she couldn't go into the kitchen?"

"So she has been examined by a medical man?" Burke wiped a dribble of whiskey off his beard with his hand.

"He only had time for a cursory examination." B.J. finally finished his drink, setting the empty glass down and curling onto the floor beside it. He belched softly, laid his cheek over one of his bent arms and closed his eyes. "But he did the mirror test."

"What about the dress?" said Chin. "She was wearing the same dress when I found her."

Burke waved this away with one hand. "Obviously, you weren't the first to find her. She has escaped or wandered off from some previous attempt to civilize her. A special course of education is being designed for the Indian boy; naturally, you can't just throw a wolf child into an ordinary school with other children. The process of reclaiming these souls is a very delicate one, best left to an expert. I don't think a true wild man has ever been civilized. It would be a real challenge."

The wind shook the little cabin. Rain pounded on the walls

outside and blew into the chimney. Harold got up and added a handful of pinecones and another log to the fire.

"Do you notice that Sarah Canary has your blanket, Chin?" B.J. said sleepily. "What did I tell you?"

"You would start by teaching the names of common objects, of course," said Burke. "Especially those objects whose value would be readily understood by the primitive. Blanket. Fire. Water. In a simple setting. At first, the wild man should deal only with a few other humans and those should always be the same. Perhaps only two. One human to tend to physical needs—cleanliness, food. A second responsible for education. How are most children civilized? Why, within the family, of course. Create a family for the wild man. A mother. A father. Avoid the temptation to move too fast, to overwhelm the wild man with too many facts, too many philosophies. You wouldn't expect the wild man to appreciate opera immediately, for instance, even if that was one of your eventual goals. You wouldn't even take him to church right away. No, the best possible situation would be a sort of bridge between savagery and civilization. A remote cabin somewhere with a very few human companions. A life with elements of the familiar. And then the wild man could be taught to perform certain simple tasks. I'm not talking about tricks here. I mean, we're not talking about a dog."

"We're not talking about a flea," said B.J.

"It would take a great deal of time," said Burke. "A great deal of patience. But so much could be learned on both sides."

B.J. yawned widely. Chin heard his jaw crack. A pinecone burst apart in the fire, sending a shower of sparks upward. The sparks were small, brief stars, like those of a firecracker, smaller and briefer than the lives and affections of men. Yet somewhere beyond the clouds and the rain were the real stars. What did human sorrow matter to the real stars? And was it too implausible to suppose that something even larger existed, that some larger Chin sat and watched the real stars and thought that they were, after all, only a blink in time and tried to imagine something smaller still? Chin made a satisfying ring of this image in his mind, connecting the large and little stars, the large and little Chins. An afterimage of red lights danced above the fire for a moment more. Then the sparks existed only in memory.

"It would be holy work," said Burke. "I truly believe that. God created nature for man, and when we study it, whenever we can find the pattern to unravel part of it, what we are seeing then is the mind of God. I can't concede the objections to Darwin. The more pattern, the more perfection."

"What about women?" B.J. asked.

"In what way do you mean?"

"Are women part of the man God created nature for or are they part of the nature God created for man?"

There was no answer, just the wind and the rain, just the fire and the small sound of Sarah Canary's dress as she settled herself onto the floor for the night. Minutes passed. Sarah Canary pulled Chin's blanket over her. She took several deep breaths. Chin turned and looked at B.J. He had stopped trembling and his chest rose and fell in a steady rhythm. "He's gone to sleep," said Chin. "And so has Sarah Canary."

"It's a good question, though," said Burke. "It's one I hadn't thought of. Speaking scientifically, it makes sense to treat women simply as a less highly evolved form of man. Their brains are smaller. They're more delicate, evidence lower levels of metabolism and energy. This works out rather well for men, of course. We can do without them, but I don't think the reverse can be said. Is that answer enough?"

Harold reached for a crumpled blanket on the floor by one of the crates. Another crumpled blanket lay beneath it. He tossed the second to Burke. Wrapping it around himself, Burke stretched out between B.J. and Chin. Harold took a space closer to Sarah Canary. Chin lay down. He slept fitfully, waking whenever his position became uncomfortable. He woke because he was hungry. He woke because he was cold. The rain continued, but the wind had stopped. The fire was out. Burke snored like a beast beside him. B.J. sighed with every breath. Chin rubbed his arms and held himself. He went back to sleep. He woke again when B.J. screamed.

"Lord preserve us!" cried Burke. "What is going on?"

B.J. was standing in the dim light by the far wall, holding the corner of the brown blanket whose mysterious lumps and folds Chin had noticed when they first entered the cabin. Chin jumped to his feet and joined him. Underneath the blanket, underneath B.J.'s shaking hand, was the black, twisted, and open-eyed face of a dead child.

"What are you doing there?" said Harold sharply. "That thing there is none of your business."

"I was cold," said B.J. "I just wanted the blanket." He looked at Chin, his face white in the dark room. "I wasn't *taking* it. Nobody else was using it."

"Calm yourself," said Burke. He produced a second bottle of whiskey and picked up B.J.'s discarded glass. "Calm yourself. Have a drink." He poured again, stepping across the room to join them. He pulled on the blanket gently, but it was frozen inside B.J.'s fist. Setting the glass down, he unwrapped B.J.'s fingers and finished peeling the blanket back. A stale, medicinal odor filled Chin's nose. The little body, topped by the agonized human face, ended in a fish's tail. "What do you think of it?" said Burke. "It's an embalmed mermaid. She comes from the coast of Australia. Australia is a young continent, so its fauna is a bit strange." He picked up the glass of whiskey again. B.J.'s hand had not moved; it still clutched and shook in the air above the body. Burke put the glass inside B.J.'s fist and curled B.J.'s fingers around it. "Drink up," he said. When he released B.J.'s hand, the whiskey spilled from the glass.

"I can't," said B.J. "I can't hold it steady enough. Am I here, Chin?"

"Yes," said Chin.

"Are you sure?"

"Yes."

Burke guided the glass to B.J.'s mouth. He tipped it and the liquor ran down B.J.'s chin. "I can't swallow," said B.J.

Chin turned again to the little figure whose face expressed such anguish. She must have died in terror. So much terror that she had, in fact, become terror; her facial expression was more vivid to Chin than her strings of hair, her tiny, exposed breasts, or even her un-expected tail. He turned away, queasy, the whiskey shifting in his stomach. He remembered the promise he had made to Tom, to show him something never seen in the world before, and how Tom had imagined it would be something beautiful like striped horses. Would Tom have been satisfied with this? Would anyone want to go to his death too soon after seeing such a face?

Harold spoke softly. " 'Where the winds are all asleep,' " he said.

" 'Where the spent lights quiver and gleam,
Where the salt weed sways in the stream,
Where the sea beasts, ranged all round,
Feed in the ooze of their pasture ground;
. . . Where the great whales come sailing by,
Sail and sail, with unshut eye . . .'
"Poetry," he said. "Matthew Arnold."

"I'm sorry to have woken everyone." There was a quiet hysteria in B.J.'s voice, a quality Chin recognized, even in as short a time as he had spent in the Steilacoom asylum. It was a tone of voice by which any patient there could be identified. Yes, I'm crazy, it said, but I'm no trouble. Yes, I'm crazy, but look how quiet I am. "Let's just pretend it didn't happen. Let's all go back to sleep now. I liked the poem."

"I don't suppose you're familiar with a book called *Vestiges of the Natural History of Creation.* Of course, you wouldn't be." Burke stood, staring sadly down at the mermaid. "Curious volume. Authorship something of a mystery. But it attempts to explain the monstrous in nature. Uses the metaphor of the railroads—you'll be interested in this, Chin. The idea is that the embryos of all animals begin on the same main line but take a turning off at some point. Evolution hap-pens because an embryo stays longer on the main line. Monstrous births occur when the turning is taken too early. You get these mixes, like the duck-billed platypus, which is something halfway between a bird and a rat. And this mermaid."

"The mermaid is mine," said Harold. "Burke bought it from a ship's captain in San Francisco and I bought it from Burke and came here to collect it. I plan to exhibit it. It's none of your business."

93

B.J. returned to his spot on the floor and curled up on his side. "Did you want the blanket?" Burke said.

"Not anymore. Cover it up again."

Sarah Canary lay back down in her corner. Chin returned to his spot. He was awake a long time, thinking of Sarah Canary and the mermaid and of Tom. He was never aware of having fallen asleep, but he must have done so, because Burke woke him with a whisper toward morning. Burke had obviously spent the night with the whiskey bottle. His hair pointed in a variety of directions and his eyes expressed the same energetic confusion. The slurring of his speech made him spit on Chin while he talked. The quieter he tried to make his words, the more he spit.

"I'm giving her up," he said. On the "p" a drop of whiskey landed on Chin's left hand. It was filled with tiny yellow bubbles. Chin drew his hand across his sleeve. "My darling Sarah Canary." Burke shook his head. "My angel. I *have* to give you up. B.J. is right. If you were a man, it might be different. Then we might convince ourselves you had a profitable, productive life ahead. Work. Philosophy. Contemplation. But what can a woman expect? A woman of your age. A woman who can't even eat prettily." Chin wiped spittle off his cheek with one hand and pushed back the hair that had come loose at the sides of his face. He was surprised at his own sense of disappointment. He had not said to himself that perhaps Burke would take Sarah Canary and relieve him of responsibility. He had not said to himself that perhaps Sarah Canary would be safe with Burke. But clearly he had thought it, somewhere deep and unheard inside.

Chin sat up to work more at this conversation. His braid fell forward on his shoulder and he picked it up, held it in his hands, examined it while he tried to concentrate on what Burke was saying. Drunkenness had obliterated many of the hard edges of Burke's words, leaving only the open sounds, the singing. Chin was used to dealing in foreign languages. But liquor imposed a second translation. He had to decipher the drunkenness just to get to the foreign tongue.

"Strutes," said Burke impenetrably. "Struth. You can't teach, my pet. You can't be ornamental. There's little chance you'll marry. It's not a gallant thing to observe, but let's be honest. Unless you'll marry her, Chin. I'd do it myself, but I'm in love with another. Heart's pledged. Godswash." His voice gained intensity and then faded on the last indecipherable word. Chin's breath quickened nervously. Miscegenation was illegal in Oregon. Racial suicide, they called it. In Washington? He couldn't remember. He decided to pretend he had understood none of Burke's words, but even as he made the decision, he heard Burke go on. "No. No," Burke was saying. "Please, forget I asked. I promised myself I wouldn't ask."

Burke's eyes flowed with drunken tears. When Chin's uncle drank, he turned a bright red color all over his face. He became noisy and posturing, like a rooster. When Chin drank, he filled with a hollow kind of laughter, arising from nothing, aimed at nothing. If he emptied himself of it, nothing was what remained inside. Often he laughed so hard he was unable to speak. He had never seen anyone who became moist and abject like Burke.

"Let's have no lies between us." Burke sniffled loudly. "No dissembling. No cunning. No deceit. The truth is that no one has had much luck educating these children. I didn't tell you that, Chin. I *concealed* the fact. Now I lay it bare. With an adult, there's been even less success. I could work twenty years and only manage to teach her to dress and feed herself. Maybe one or two words you or I might understand but would have to be explained to anyone else. Maybe she'd be able to comb her own hair. I can't take the responsibility for condemning her to that kind of life. A life in the darkness of a few small rooms." Burke wiped at his eyes and nose.

"It would be a sin," he whispered. "I know that. I know that. And one more sin will be one more than I can rid myself of. The little mermaid—you mustn't tell a soul. I made her for Harold. The top half is monkey. I sort of shaved the fur from it. Added human hair and the breasts. The bottom is just salmon. I was proud of the work, at first. God forgive me. Time and care made her as seamless as one of God's own creatures, and I took a reckless pride in that. It seemed a good joke and a little money on the side. I didn't expect the face to turn out that way. Does it haunt you, that face? Tell me she won't haunt you. And then imagine how she haunts me, her father. I'm afraid to sleep sometimes.

"I shouldn't have done it. The study of nature is a kind of holy worship and I've created a perversion, a false idol, a sin against the mind of God. No. Tomorrow," said Burke, "you and I will take Sarah Canary as deep into the forests as we can and then lose her. We will find a lovely spot with a stream and a water ousel's nest and a host of wildflowers come spring. Anemones and the like. Let her return to the happy, natural life. Let her return to the fellowship of the deer and the wolf. Let her return to freedom and to the God she already knows."

"It's very cold," said Chin.

"Sarah Canary can handle that. Sarah Canary can curl into a hole until the weather turns warm. She can catch fish with her hands and find the early berries. She's as comfortable in the woods as any creature. Aren't you, my angel? Aren't you, my pet?" Burke directed his whisper over Chin to Sarah Canary's sleeping form. Sarah Canary had covered herself with Chin's blanket completely. No part of her face or her hair or her feet could be seen.

She was still that way at dawn. The rain was quiet and steady outside, but Harold had arisen early and appeared to be gone for good. The mermaid was no longer lying by the wall and neither was her blanket. Harold's own blanket was gone as well.

Chin stretched, rose, and began the fire for breakfast. Burke's eyes were gummy with sleep and regret and his face sagged. He stirred the porridge, looking with longing at Sarah Canary's still form. She was drawn into an impossibly tiny ball beneath the blanket. "Perhaps we shouldn't take her out in the rain," he said. "Although it would make it harder for her to follow us back. Wipe out the scent of our tracks and all."

Chin began to eat his own bowl of mush. It was tasteless, but it was hot. He felt hungry and hopeful. He was pleased that Harold was gone. He was pleased that Burke was wavering. Perhaps B.J.

would marry Sarah Canary, should such a thing be required. Perhaps he could leave both B.J. and Sarah Canary in Burke's care and consider his duties fulfilled. Perhaps he could still catch up with his uncle in Tenino.

"Wake up, Sarah Canary," said B.J. "Wake up and have breakfast." There was no response. B.J. ladled a bowl of porridge out and carried it into her corner. "Sarah Canary," he said. He leaned down, gently folding back the edge of Chin's blanket. The black face of the mermaid stared up at him. "Oh, God," B.J. cried, dropping the porridge, which overturned and spilled onto his shoe. "Dear God." He threw Chin's blanket back over the little creature and covered his own face with his hands. Outside the wind came up again. Chin heard its high voice and its low voice and all the unidentifiable voices in between. Women's voices, contrary and confused, but all of them somehow parts of one another.

iv

The magnificent Tom Thumb Wedding was P. T. Barnum's gift to a country whose sensibilities were being bludgeoned by civil war. It alleviated the scandal created when Tom allowed the cockney courtesan Cora Pearl to carry him off to her bedroom, balanced in one hand on a silver dish like a Christmas pudding.

America had lost her sons. They had killed one another. Or they had died of disease and neglect far from their homes. America didn't even get to keep her slaves. Surely, the survivors deserved a little oddity now and then to take them out of themselves.

Fortunately, there was no shortage of oddities. During one of Barnum's circus performances, a giantess was run over by a chariot and fatally crushed. Barnum shrugged. "Oh, there is another waiting for the place," he told his horrified companion, Major James Pond. "It is rather a benefit than a loss."

There was always another giantess, another bearded woman, another human skeleton, another slave, another soldier. They had names sometimes. The oddities often had first names: the Dog-Man Lionel; Nellie, the armless wonder; Maximo and Bartola, the Aztec Children.

Fiji Jim was really Ruto Semm, an ordinary Fiji Islander, lured with his wife to the United States by an unscrupulous manager who later abandoned them. Ruto spent the rest of his life trying to earn the money to return home and finally died of pneumonia in a top-floor tenement after saving a drowning swimmer off the coast of Rockaway Beach.

The Ugliest Woman in the World was Julia Pastrana, referred to by Frank Buckland as "the female nondescript." Darwin examined her and wrote: "This woman had a strong beard, a very hairy body, particularly on the forehead and the neck and, a phenomenon of particular interest, an irregular double row of teeth in the upper and lower jaw which gave her a prognathic appearance and a simian profile." Julia fell in love with her manager. He married and impregnated her, inviting much of Victorian society to attend the birth. The child was delivered, also abnormally hairy. Neither mother nor child survived. But Julia lived long enough to whisper her own epitaph. "I die happy," she said, "for I know that I have been loved for myself." Her grieving husband immediately sent for a taxidermist, had both bodies stuffed, and exhibited the pair all over Europe.

In 1704, Nicolas Sauvage made an engraving to commemorate Johannes Palfyn's dissection of a stillborn pair of Siamese twins, who were, of course, not called Siamese twins until Chang and Eng Bunker rose to international prominence. "God is Marvellous in All His Works" is Sauvage's title, so Howard Martin, the author of *Victorian Grotesque*, reminds us that the word *teratology*, used now to refer to the study of monstrosities, once meant tales of the marvelous, in an earlier age when monsters were marvels.

C H A P T E R
S E V E N

THE WILD WOMAN
PERFORMS IN SEABECK

The power to contain
Is always as the contents
But give a Giant room
And you will lodge a Giant
And not a smaller man

EMILY DICKINSON,

1873

In 1873, the residents of Seabeck, Washington, and the men in its outlying logging camps faced an unusual choice. The great magnetic doctress, Adelaide Dixon, was scheduled to speak in the schoolhouse at the very hour that, halfway across town, in the upstairs parlor of the Bay View Hotel, the Alaskan Wild Woman was being exhibited, fresh from her triumphal engagement in Port Gamble. One show only.

Adelaide had scandalized Philadelphia and Boston and St. Louis less with her belief that women and men should enjoy a variety of sexual partners than with the underlying suggestion that women should, in fact, be enjoying sex at all. Adelaide often said so explicitly. She even said that when women did not enjoy sex, men were to blame. But the Alaskan Wild Woman had been raised in the Yukon by wolves since infancy and, though she now wore clothes and slept in a bed with pillows, nothing would break her of her canine compulsion to howl at a full moon. Entertainment of this caliber rarely came to Seabeck. If only, the residents thought, there were some way to see them both.

The curtains were drawn and a lantern was lit. The audience consisted only of men, and most of them had been drinking. The maleness of the audience was no surprise. Fathers would not let their daughters attend such unwholesome entertainments. Husbands would not let their wives. The woman stood quietly at the front of the room, dressed all in black. Her hair was tidy but not arranged; her face was pale and somewhat tense. "I am very glad you came tonight. What you will see and what you will hear is not something you will soon forget. The woman before you is an enigma," the men were told.

"Women are enigmas to you. She . . .

". . . was raised by a she-wolf in a damp, flea-infested . . .

". . . bed where one partner is taking pleasure at the expense of the other, shameless as . . .

". . . a child who has suckled at the teat of the beast . . .

". . . and yet, of course, I need explain the effect of unconsummated intercourse to no woman who is . . .

". . . old enough to eat the raw meat for which she still retains . . .

". . . an unnatural appetite, you men would have her believe, knowing nothing about her, and denying her a common humanity with . . .

". . . the hunters who came upon her, hunched over the body of her 'mother,' absolutely and innocently unclothed . . .

". . . but she feels what you feel and needs what you need . . .

". . . and now you may come forward, gentlemen, and examine her for yourselves."

"A lady just lays there," a man in the front informed Adelaide hostilely. "It's part of being a lady. I don't see how it's my fault. I didn't make the rules."

"Is she just going to stand there?" someone complained to Harold. "Make her do something."

Men were always being told that women behaved like animals and never getting to see it. No wonder they were upset.

Harold was drinking heavily. The initial draw in each town was unaffected by the audience's dissatisfactions, but it meant that Harold could only schedule a single show in each location. The unhappiness of the audience followed him now, always a bit behind, but ineluctable as a shadow. As sure as the sun rolled daily from east to west, failure would catch up with him and, eventually, even precede him into town. Harold should have taken the mermaid instead. No one would blame him if she just laid there and did nothing. At least the men could look at her breasts. Even if they suspected the breasts were artificial, no one would be complaining. Breasts were breasts. You couldn't demand your money back, you couldn't claim you'd been cheated, if you'd gotten to see breasts.

He was drinking as much as he could afford to, but he had somehow lost the ability to wrap himself in an alcoholic fog so thick his memories wouldn't penetrate. Last night he had awakened all in a sweat, dreaming he was back in Andersonville, crawling those last fevered feet into the deadline like Jimmy had done. "Come on, Harold," Jimmy had said. "Just a few feet and your problems are over. Just those few feet between hell and paradise." The guards were free to shoot anyone who crossed into the deadline. They shot Jimmy, once in the leg, so that he collapsed, bent over his knees, his hands on his ears. The next bullet went through his right palm on its way into his head.

More than 40,000 men had died or were wounded at Gettysburg, and yet the odds of surviving the prisoner-of-war camp at Andersonville were smaller than the odds of surviving that battle. But Harold had done it. It made him special. It made him so special he could hardly get through the night. It made him an oddity.

It made him immortal so that death lusted after him, beckoned to him, pleaded with him, made the same promises alcohol had once made. Come on, Harold, said death. Then your problems are over. Stop the dreams, death promised. Or maybe the promise was to dream forever.

"So give her some raw meat," a fat man in the front suggested. "Show us how she eats like a dog." Harold rolled the end of his mustache between his thumb and index finger nervously. In fact, he had already tried raw meat at an early show in Snohomish. Harold booked the rooms and drew the posters, which made Sarah Canary look a great deal younger than she was, and arranged the transportation, which was sometimes horses and sometimes steamers and sometimes the train, and entertained the audiences and kept Sarah Canary as well as he could out of the earnings. Sarah Canary did nothing. Sarah Canary would not even eat raw meat.

"Raw meat has been removed from her diet as a part of the process of civilizing her." Harold bent his fingers around the neck of a silver flask of whiskey and drank.

"Make her talk. You said she howls. Make her howl."

Harold gave Sarah Canary a piece of bread. She took it in two hands and held it in front of her face. She looked more like a chipmunk than a wolf. She didn't eat it. "She's not hungry," Harold said.

"Notice the canines." Harold put a hand into Sarah Canary's mouth, pulling the lips back to expose her teeth. The men crowded around. She made a small, warning sound in her throat. "A growl," Harold pointed out. "She's growling like her wolf mother."

"She don't look so wild to me," the fat man said. He reached out and petted Sarah Canary's hair. Sarah Canary was stiff beneath his hand.

Harold drank. He held his flask under Sarah Canary's nose. "The Wild Woman will not touch intoxicants," he said. Sarah Canary did not touch the whiskey. Sarah Canary did nothing. "The Wild Woman does not recognize herself in a mirror." Harold turned the

silvered side of the flask to reflect Sarah Canary's face. On the con-
vex surface, she was all nose. Sarah Canary did nothing. "See?" said
Harold. Harold drank. A man with a red beard examined Sarah
Canary's hand. He pushed her sleeve up as far as it went and looked
at her wrist. When he let go, her arm fell limply back to her lap.
"Is anything else going to happen?" he asked.

"Her father," said Harold, stroking his mustache grimly, "was
a Russian sailor shipwrecked off the coast of Kodiak Island and
enslaved by the Aleuts." A chilly breeze came into the parlor
through the open door and made the lantern flicker. Sarah Canary's
shadow rippled on the wall behind her like water. "He fell in
love with a beautiful Indian maiden who shyly returned his affections, until"—Harold filled his mouth with whiskey, sieved it
through his teeth, and swallowed—"their love was discovered."
Sarah Canary's shadow flickered across the curtains. She shook her
hair and it flew about her face, settling back slightly out of place.
The men were quiet and Harold thought he felt them mentally
leaning forward. He lowered his voice. "The sailor was beaten to
death with stones." He paused to drink and let the pathos of the
sailor's fate penetrate. Killed by savages. And for love. He let them
think about it for a moment. "The maiden was sent into exile, but
her beauty immediately captured the heart of another Aleut, a war-
rior from a different tribe who did not know her shameful secret
and married her. All would have been well had the maiden not
been expecting the child of her Russian lover. The birth of the
baby would reveal her secret and lose her, she feared, the love of
her husband."

An unkempt man with a smell like ripening cheese put his fingers
on Sarah Canary's face. She made a noise, blowing through her lips
like a horse so that he pulled his hand back in surprise. The men
laughed. Harold struggled to control a momentary rage. He was
trying to build a mood. Sarah Canary was actively undercutting
him. She began a series of nonsensical noises, she panted, she moaned.
Harold put a hand on her shoulder, pinching her hard but invisibly.
Sarah Canary flinched and was quiet. He withdrew his hand. When

he resumed her story, his voice was louder. "Her time came and the little mother stole away to a cave she had discovered to deliver the child alone. But she was not alone. As she made her way to the back of the cave, she came suddenly upon a she-wolf. The little Indian maiden shrank back in terror. She prepared to flee, but just before she ran, the wolf whimpered suddenly, a sound of such agony, the maiden paused in spite of herself. The wolf, too, was giving birth, but in pain and in terror. The maiden's heart was touched. She returned, hesitantly, to sit with the other expectant mother, stroking and calming her and calling her *sister*. When the wolf cub was born dead, the Indian maiden sobbed as if it had been her own child." Sarah Canary made a series of clicking sounds. There was more laughter. She repeated the sounds. The laughter was louder. Harold's hands shook on the flask. He turned his back on Sarah Canary.

"But now her own child was coming. A girl. A misbegotten, hairy, ugly girl." The words came out of Harold's mouth before he knew he was going to say them. Usually the baby was beautiful, at least, Harold was careful to add, in the eyes of her mother. Usually the sobbing maiden entrusted the child to the care of the wolf and slipped back to her husband and happiness. Anger and frustration were telling the story now; Harold was merely drinking and getting out of their way.

"More wolves came to the cave. Whether they saw the dead cub and blamed the human for it or whether they were merely maddened by the blood of the childbirth is a question we will never be able to answer. In any case, they tore the Indian maiden apart with their pointed yellow teeth. Then they turned to her cub. The she-wolf shielded the baby from the pack with her body. She fought, taking and giving many injuries, until the blood-lust of the beasts was sated and they left her alone with the child."

Sarah Canary hummed. Sarah Canary trilled. Harold turned with his hand out, striking her with so much force, she was thrown sideways to her knees, where she remained, looking up at him with a face that was bestial in its lack of expression. "Or perhaps not," he said coldly. "Perhaps the woman we have here is the product of a different sort of union. Perhaps the sailor mated directly with the wolf." He was aware of the silence in the room again. Sarah Canary made no sound at all. The audience might have stopped breathing for all the noise they made. "The show is over," said Harold. He turned away from the woman on her knees. "Go home now."

CHAPTER EIGHT

HAROLD
RECITES TENNYSON

Further than Guess can gallop
Further than Riddle ride —
Oh for a Disc to the Distance
Between Ourselves and the Dead!
EMILY DICKINSON,
1864

It was strongly suggested to Harold that he join his audience in the saloon downstairs, where he could stand drinks for everyone out of the night's profits. It might make him more popular, he was told. He could use a little popularity, he was told. He was told this two or three times and everyone who told him was wearing a pistol.

Harold returned Sarah Canary to her room, checking the windows and locking the door from the outside. He went to his own room and picked up his own gun, stuffing it into the pocket of his jacket. He could feel the cold of the metal even through his layers of clothing. He walked down the flight of stairs, arriving about the same time that the men who had come to see Sarah Canary were joined by the men who had gone to see Adelaide. There was no fireplace; the room depended on liquor and bodies for heat. Harold smelled sweat and cigar smoke and spilled whiskey. His boots stuck to the floor and made sucking sounds as he walked.

Harold could see no way to buy drinks for one group and not for the other. He suspected that when the evening was over he would find the engagement in Seabeck had actually lost him money. His tentative plans had included touring the lumber camps with Sarah Canary. Now he thought it best to put more miles between Seabeck and the next show. He was thinking of heading down to Oregon. Or back to Steilacoom. When he was ready to admit that Sarah Canary was just not going to work out, then he could leave her, leave her somewhere safe, of course, and go back for the mermaid. Had the time come to do that?

"What do you have?" he asked Bill Blair, a half-breed Indian who owned the Bay View and tended the bar. Harold had met Blair earlier when he took adjoining rooms in the hotel for himself and the Alaskan Wild Woman.

"More liquor than you'll find anywhere else in the Washington Territory," Blair answered. "Just ask for it. Jersey Lightning, California port wine, grape brandy bitters. Whiskey, of course. Beer. Seabeck is seeing some fat times and I'm full-stocked for it. Sorry the show didn't go better." Blair had not attended the show. Obviously, the men who had preceded Harold into the saloon had already been complaining.

"Give everyone a drink," Harold said. "Give me whiskey."

A shadow passed in the doorway. Harold caught sight of a black dress and a white face. His heart beat twice, very fast, before he realized it wasn't Sarah Canary. The woman was going upstairs, not down.

"Miss Adelaide Dixon is on her way to her room," Blair observed. "Turning in early."

"And looking just like a lady." Someone behind Harold cleared the phlegm from his throat and spit. Harold turned. A man in kid gloves was seated among the mill workers, stroking a silk plug hat that he held over his lap. He had a white beard and a round face. "Which I assure you she is not. No more than I would be were I to put on a lady's dress." A tarnished copper spittoon sat right at his feet and yet he had managed to miss it. The spittle glistened on the floor by the toe of his new shoe. He raised his glass to Blair. "I'll have a Chinee Stinker," he said. "Made the way they used to make them in the old days when John Pennell, the mad squaw-master, ran Seattle."

He breathed on the crown of his hat, then made a series of small circles with his cuff, polishing. He turned to Harold. "Who is more the lady—the woman who provides it for money but talks about it free, or the woman who talks about it for money but provides it free? My name is Jim Allen, by the way. Clerk at the Washington Mill Lumber Company." Jim Allen removed his gloves. He was wearing a fat gold ring with a large opal on his little finger. "Thank you for the drink," he added. "Sit with us?"

His name made Harold think again of Jimmy. Harold sat down with his private flask of whiskey in one hand, the glass of whiskey he had just purchased from Bill Blair in the other. The liquor Harold had already drunk lit him up inside like a lantern, shedding light on everything around him, so the world was all edges and hollows and shadows.

This was the dangerous stage of drunkenness, when the separate faculties of reason and vision and memory began to bleed into one another so you couldn't be sure which was which. Harold saw each hair in Jim Allen's chin, each color in each hair. He saw the reflection of his own face, diminished by the prescription glass of Jim Allen's spectacles. He saw that he was really quite a little man, quite second-rate, and all the success in the world wouldn't change that. So what did failure matter? Drink. Just keep drinking. He saw how Jimmy's hand, with its ragged, bloody nails, had continued to clutch and open even after the bullet had gone right through it, like it was butter, and shattered his skull. Jimmy and he had survived the Battle of the Wilderness together when General Seymour's Black Brigade, an all-Negro unit that was supporting them, had fallen. They had survived the fire after the battle when some of the wounded had clung to trees, trying to climb away from the flames until trees and bodies were fused together forever in ashy formations like giant sand castles. They had survived the march to Andersonville. And then Jimmy had just crawled into the deadline as if all that surviving didn't matter at all. Harold held the whiskey flask so tightly his fingers began to cramp. "I'm Harold," he said.

There was a second man at the table. "Will Purdy," Jim Allen told him. "Postmaster here in Seabeck." He turned to Purdy. "Harold," he said.

Will Purdy was tall and thin, with dark brown hair and a curly beard. "Pleased to meet you." He held out his hand. It was damp.

"Have you ever heard of Pennell's Mad House, Harold?" Jim Allen asked.

"No."

"Ah. Well." Jim Allen sighed philosophically. "Lovely times. When you pay cash, of course, you don't have to ask if the lady is enjoying herself. Not that they didn't." The lens of his glasses magnified the wink he gave Harold. "At the Mad House"—Jim Allen's voice rose reverentially—"they cared about their customers. They attended to the body and the soul."

"The women were tattooed," Purdy explained to Harold.

"Tattooed? Well, I guess. One of Pennell's ladies had an entire Clipper ship, *The Flying Cloud*, emblazoned across her chest. That's not a sight you forget." Jim Allen thumped his glass on the table emphatically. The yellow Chinee Stinker rose in a wave toward the side. "And patriotic themes. A man who opens a thigh and finds the face of Nathan Hale there, with the noose already on his poor neck, well, that man knows the moment when the spiritual and the carnal meet in happy union."

"So what was Adelaide like, Jim?" a man at the next table asked. He was a smaller and a younger man, beardless, with a prominent red-veined nose. Harold recognized him. Third row. Fourth seat. Piercing finger-in-the-mouth whistle. "Did she heal you? Did you require a healing touch?"

"I wouldn't let a rude bouncer like Adelaide Dixon lay hands on me," said Purdy. "If I had a daughter like that, I'd drown her on the next steamer out of Hood Canal. We showed her, though, didn't we, Jim? About halfway through the 'lecture,' we got bored and Jim began to tell us about the new baseball field. After three years of carting sawdust from the mill to fill in the swamp next to the schoolhouse, Condon is finally ready to admit that his new field isn't big enough."

"Any hit to left field lands in the logs. Do you play baseball?" Jim asked Harold. Harold shook his head, both to answer the question and to express his sympathy over the situation in left field. "Automatic home run," Jim said.

"I can't abide these women's-rights women." Purdy spat, briefly and accurately. "Unmarried croakers, the lot of them."

Jim Allen set his empty glass on the table with a decisive click. "You've put your finger on it. *Unmarried.* Soured throughout by disappointed affection. Miss Adelaide Dixon's face tells the whole story. Some man has broken her heart and the rest of us must pay."

"If it were really rights these women wanted, they've only to ask," Purdy said. "A woman can coax a man into anything with a soft approach. What these women's-rights women really want is revenge."

"You buying the next round, too?" The fat man from the exhibition stood beside Harold's chair. Harold looked up. He squinted but could not quite bring the man into focus. Two flat faces overlapped so that their noses were only an inch apart. Two fat right hands fingered two pistols at about eye level. "Sure," said Harold. "Sure I am."

"It's usually understood that the fellow who treats has the floor," Jim Allen told Harold.

"Jim was treating until you arrived," said red-nosed Jack. "Apparently he's had a little windfall."

Jim Allen waved a hand modestly. "When a man comes into money, he shares it with his friends. You'd do the same."

Will Purdy raised his glass. "To the Washington Mill Lumber Company. To Company towns."

"Absolutely," said Jim Allen. They drank. Harold took one sip from his glass, one sip from his flask.

"But tell us about yourself, Harold," Purdy asked. "How do you find yourself in your current line of work?"

Harold coughed. "Just luck. I've always been a lucky sort. I won the woman in a card game up in the Yukon from the hunter who killed her wolf mother. Pair of black sevens. I played a bluff, and then it turned out I had the best hand anyway. Of course, she wasn't much like you see her now."

"I didn't see her," said Jim Allen.

"When she first came to me, she was absolutely wild. A beast, really. Well, it was all she knew. I worked months to civilize her."

"I heard she was very well-behaved."

Jim Allen's tone made Harold defensive. He took an angry drink, emptying the glass. Drops of whiskey clung to the hairs of his mustache. He licked them off. "What's so damned great about being human?" he asked. "What makes that such a damned prize?"

Harold felt suddenly claustrophobic, packed into the small saloon with so many other sweating bodies. His tolerance for human company had reached its limits. He stood up, clutching his flask, and put the last of his Seabeck earnings on the bar. "Drink it up," he said to Blair. "I'm going to bed."

He went to the kitchen first for some bread and milk to take upstairs to Sarah Canary. He would never starve anyone into good behavior. He would never do that. Hunger was like having something alive and separate from you inside you, a beast that grew in your belly. If you gave the beast nothing to eat, then it ate you instead. Harold knew what it was like to feel those particular teeth. Rations at Andersonville had been carefully calculated. The men at Andersonville had not been starved into submission. They had been starved to death. The architects of Andersonville were great believers in death by natural causes.

Liquor severed the connection between Harold's will and his body while he was on the stairs. He made it halfway, balancing the plate on his hand and concentrating on holding the glass upright. Then gravity took him down two steps. He was able to stay on his feet and to save most of Sarah Canary's milk. He leaned against the wall until he thought he was steady again. Up four more steps, down two. Up one. Down one. This was no good. Harold was forced to abandon the milk. Now he had one hand free for the stair rail. He pulled himself to the landing, spent several minutes inserting the key into the lock on Sarah Canary's door, and went inside. Somewhere he had lost the plate with the bread on it as well. He couldn't imagine where.

Sarah Canary sat on the window seat, looking out. To her right, half a moon was rising over the tops of the ghostly trees. To her left, the bay glittered with icy waves. She had let the fire go out and it was as cold as the saloon would have been without the men and the drink. Her knees were bent up to her chest and her arms were around them. She rocked slightly, back and forth. Harold thought he heard the sounds of a bird leaving the window. Even through the glass he heard it, the puffing of air under curved wings. A sound almost like breathing.

Sarah Canary ignored him. He pulled the flask of whiskey from his pocket and unscrewed the lid. "We're going to have to take the cheapest way back to Port Gamble," he said. "Do you know what that means? Indian dugout canoe. Over the canal. If the weather's as bad as it's been, we'll overturn and we'll drown. You'll drown. Even if you can swim, your skirts will fill with water and sink you. I won't drown. I've survived against odds worse than these before. Nothing's ever killed me yet."

He took a drink. For a moment he considered the possibility of tattooing Sarah Canary. Something big. Something brazen. He dropped the idea. Good money after bad.

Sarah Canary sat and rocked and stared out the window. The moonlight came in at an angle, silvering the few gray hairs she had. It was kind of pretty. Kind of like frost. Her dress and her face took on a yellow cast. A cloud passed over the moon so that Sarah Canary flickered into blackness and then out of it again. She made small, birdlike noises with her tongue and her oversized teeth.

"Damn you to hell anyway," said Harold quietly. Looking out the window, he tried to guess if it was going to rain tomorrow. There was a ring around the moon. It either meant that it was going to rain or that it wasn't. He couldn't remember which. But didn't it always rain out here on this godforsaken coast? Could you ever go wrong predicting rain? Harold's head was spinning and he could hear his own heartbeat, increasing incrementally in volume until it exploded in his ears, reminding him that, in spite of everything, he was still alive.

He fell onto the window seat next to Sarah Canary. Her shoe touched his thigh. She did not draw away. "It's very cold, isn't it?" Harold said to her. "Aren't you cold?" Her hair stood out from her head in a sort of nimbus. He moved closer, reached out to her knee and ran his hand down from it toward her foot. She twitched slightly, like a dog having a dream, but she looked out the window and not at him. She warbled. Harold closed his hand over her ankle, then began speaking softly:

" 'And by the moon the reaper weary,

Piling sheaves in uplands airy,

Listening, whispers, "T is the fairy

Lady of Shalott." ' '

"That's poetry." He returned his hand to her knee and this time he stroked upward along the thigh. "That's Tennyson. I could heat you up," Harold said. Her dress began to move up her leg under his hand. She kicked him suddenly, perhaps reflexively, catching him just above the elbow. It didn't really hurt, but the kick had enough power to push her away, to slide her further along the window seat. She still wouldn't look at him. His hand closed on her ankle and he pulled her back. "What do you think?" he said. "That I should do all the work, make the engagements, plan the shows, *do* the shows, and that I should sit afterwards, drinking with the men you've disappointed and buying them drinks, and I should get nothing back? That I should feed you and shelter you and lose my damned money on you and get nothing? Does that seem fair to you? Does that seem right?" He pulled her foot into his lap and tucked it between his two legs, pressing against it, rubbing himself to life with the sole of her shoe. He opened his legs to undo the buttons at her ankle. Sarah Canary kicked again. Her foot escaped from his hands and her heel dug into his crotch, filling him with blunt, pervasive, and utterly compelling pain. He couldn't see through it. He couldn't hear through it. He couldn't speak through it. He could only live through it.

When he recovered, Sarah Canary was standing away from him, beyond the splash of moonlight in the room. Her head was down and she was hugging herself, her arms crossed, her hands on her shoulders. Like a stone angel. Like the angel over someone's grave. She stared out past him from her lowered face in the shadows.

"Well, it doesn't seem fair to me," he whispered. His voice rose. "It doesn't seem right." He lunged for her but missed, hitting the nightstand instead, knocking the washbasin to the floor, where it shattered. Water stained the wooden floor dark as blood.

Harold stood for a moment, swaying and considering. He took a step toward Sarah Canary and his shoe came down on the broken china and the water. He slid to his knees and then collapsed in an attitude of despair, his forehead resting in a puddle on the floor. "God," he said. He covered his ears so his heartbeat wouldn't be so loud, but this only made it worse; his hands shut out all the other noises and his heartbeat echoed off their cupped walls. Jimmy had died just this way, in just this position, with his head in the mud and his hands on his ears, listening to the last sounds of his heart. Harold sat up quickly as soon as he remembered. "Don't do this to me," he said. He was begging. "Don't do this. Please." And then he softened his voice, made it as coaxing as he could. It wasn't a skill he'd practiced much. "Good girl. Be a good girl. Come over here." Sarah Canary had disappeared.

He looked for her along the wall, saw the hem of her dress. Harold grabbed for it and missed, falling painfully onto one elbow. The gun jumped out of his pocket and spun through the water and broken china, coming to rest underneath a large, curved part of the washbasin. Harold didn't go after it. There were things guns could do for you. There were things guns could not. Threatening Sarah Canary with a gun would be about as logical as telling her he loved her. And just about as effective. "I love you," said Harold. "I love you. I'm only going to love you. I'm dying. Help me. Be a good girl.''

He pushed himself to his feet, squinting into the corners of the room, looking for Sarah Canary. He thought he saw her over by the door, and there she was again, standing at the bedside, watching him, watching him. He rubbed at his eyes and tried to focus. Two figures remained, but they were close together now, more like the double image from the saloon, though never quite that close. They overlapped only at the fullest part of their black skirts, like two halves of a butterfly, like twins attached at the hip.

This was clever of Sarah Canary. Damned clever. Obviously, she was doing it with mirrors. "The Wild Woman does not recognize herself in a mirror," Harold said, laughing because he was not taken in, had never been taken in, had never believed that innocent Wild Woman act for a moment. Harold had seen a woman sawn in two once, not a woman like Sarah Canary, but a beautiful young woman with long ringlets of brown hair, and he had known immediately that it was done with mirrors. Harold was not born yesterday.

Harold had not died yesterday.

He hesitated, wondering which figure was the image and which the real woman. " 'The mirror cracked from side to side,' " he said. Both figures were silvered from the moonlight or the mirror, but the silhouette on the left was taller and shivered suddenly. " 'The curse has come upon me' "—he lunged left, gripping her shoulders— " 'Cried the Lady of Shalott.' " When he felt the solid bones beneath his hands, he knew he'd made the right choice. "Here now," he said. "Now I have you. You should be grateful, darling. There can't have been many other offers. No more tricks now," and he thought that at the same time he was talking, she was telling him to take his hands off her, but before he could be sure, something sharp and excruciatingly painful slid into his chest between two of his ribs. He stumbled, letting go of Sarah Canary in surprise. The handle of a chopstick protruded from his body. It was white and carved with those damned markings the Chinese pretended were words. You looked at Chinese writing and it looked like chicken scratchings. You heard the Chinese talking out loud and you still thought you were listening to chickens.

Harold put his hands on the chopstick and tried to pull it out, but he was too drunk and too weak. He fell forward instead, the longest fall of his life. He had plenty of time before he hit the floor to wonder that, after surviving the Battle of the Wilderness and the fire afterward and the march to Andersonville and the camp at Andersonville, which was one more thing than even Jimmy had survived, he should die like this, spitted by a Wild Woman who, as far as he knew, had never done anything before in her life. What are the odds of that? he wondered. Jimmy, he said, only no words came out. Look at me, Jimmy. Dying for love with a chopstick in the heart. What are the odds?

His head landed on a jagged piece of china. It hurt for a moment. Then it felt like a pillow beneath him.

"Come on, dear. Perhaps you'd better sleep with me tonight," he heard her say and he thought, Well, that was all I wanted, but it's a little late now, isn't it? And then he thought maybe death had said those words, that he had heard death inviting him to come to bed one more time and that he seemed to be saying yes.

V

In the November 2, 1872, issue of *Woodhull and Claflin's Weekly*, Victoria Woodhull, the Spiritualists' candidate for the presidency of the United States, accused Henry Ward Beecher of having slept with Elizabeth Tilton.

Beecher was a popular preacher who drew thousands to his church every Sunday. He had a wife, but she was not Elizabeth Tilton. Elizabeth was married to Theodore Tilton, Henry Ward Beecher's best friend. Theodore was the one who had revealed the affair to Victoria Woodhull. He had done this because he was sleeping with Woodhull.

Victoria Woodhull was continually vilified by the press for her advocacy of free love. Why should she be persecuted, she now asked, for practicing openly what the most admired men in the country did in secret? By evening, copies of the paper were selling on the streets at forty dollars apiece.

Anthony Comstock arrested Woodhull for the transmission of obscene matter through the mails and Henry Ward Beecher declared his innocence. Beecher had been the first president of the American Woman's Suffrage Association. Many of the suffragists were personal friends of his, and they were friends of the Tiltons. Elizabeth Cady Stanton, Susan B. Anthony, and his own half sister, Isabella Beecher Hooker, were all aware of the affair. They were bound to be questioned.

Unlike Victoria Woodhull, these were women known for their integrity. They could not be bought off. They could not be manipulated. They would not lie.

They had to be discredited.

Beecher began by characterizing the suffragists as "human hyenas" and "free-lovers." His half sister he accused of insanity. As for the woman who claimed he had pursued her through months of persuasion and argument, Beecher said that Elizabeth Tilton had "thrust her affections upon him unsought."

Theodore Tilton was simultaneously telling the world that he had merely feigned affection for Victoria Woodhull in the hopes of keeping her silent on the subject of his wife's affair. He had certainly never, never been in love with Woodhull.

The appearance of respectability was worth more to many men than actual respectability, Elizabeth Cady Stanton observed. Clearly it was worth more than any woman.

Theodore Tilton sued Henry Ward Beecher for the destruction of his family. Two years later, the case came to trial. Victoria Woodhull testified decorously. Beecher carried violets and was witty. The existing statutes held a wife incompetent as a witness either for or against her husband, so Elizabeth Tilton was not permitted to speak. She sat in the courtroom, listening quietly while her husband and her lover abandoned her by turns. The jury reached no verdict.

In 1873, one of Sophie Tolstoy's neighbors gave up his mistress for a younger and more beautiful woman. Anna, the discarded lover, threw herself under a moving freight train at the railroad station in Tula, and Leo Tolstoy began to write *Anna Karenina*.

In 1873, the Association for the Advancement of Women was founded.

ADELAIDE'S
THEORIES ON SEDUCTION

Whatever it is — she has tried it —
Awful Father of Love —

EMILY DICKINSON,
1871

The moment Adelaide Dixon saw the Alaskan Wild Woman in the
unsteady moonlight of the upstairs Bay View Hotel, she recognized
the infamous profile of Lydia Palmer. She had seen Lydia's picture
often in the paper; the hair so coarse, the lips so full, the nose so
very distinct. There could not, Adelaide told herself, be two such
profiles.

Lydia was wanted in San Francisco for the murder of Andrew
Hamelin, Superintendent of the Presbyterian Sunday school and a
trustee of the school district—beloved husband, lamented father,

adulterer. His body had been found about six months ago in the basement of the nest he'd procured for Lydia, three bullets all in a row across his abdomen. Lydia had removed his shoes and put them beneath his head as a pillow. One dark curl, shot with gray, was missing from his forehead; the newspapers speculated later that it had been taken for Lydia's locket. Nine blocks away, his family sat around a Sunday pot roast, waiting for him until the meat grew cold.

Lydia had attended the funeral, dressed all in black, with black net obscuring her face. She carried a black-bead bag and a small white handkerchief whose embroidered violets she watered copiously during the service. Then, through an implausible series of misunderstandings, the San Francisco police had let her simply walk away. Lydia had not been seen since.

Not until Adelaide, sitting at her desk, looking dispiritedly through her lecture notes, heard the washbasin break. Adelaide was as close to despair as she had ever allowed herself to be. The response to her evening lecture was not an unusual one here on the frontier. In Steilacoom they had crumpled their programs into balls and tossed them about the room, and drawn mustaches on her face in the promotional bills, and then Adelaide's traveling companion, Louise, had deserted her to marry the sheriff, a loathsome man. "My only regret," Louise told her, unable to meet her eyes, "is leaving you. And with so many people so anxious to hear you and so many people needing your message. Perhaps you can find another companion in Sacramento or San Francisco and finish the tour in the summer."

"Or get married," the sheriff suggested, winking. "There's no shortage of men. Catch yourself a big one. 'Better once than never, for never too late.' "

"I have my own engagements," she'd retorted. "As unbreakable as yours." And had gone on with the tour, scandalously unescorted. To Seabeck. To derision and ridicule. To frustration and despair. For what? Adelaide could not remember what she was supposed to be accomplishing, not the justifications she gave to others or the ones she gave to herself. She was too disheartened even to cry.

Then she heard the sound of smashing crockery in the next room. Suddenly she wanted to see the Wild Woman for herself. The woman raised by wolves. The woman who didn't even understand that she was a woman. Adelaide went out into the hall. She knocked on the door to the Wild Woman's room, but no one answered. "Is everything all right?" she asked, opening the door. Like all the doors in the Bay View, it was warped and neither closed nor opened smoothly.

There stood Lydia Palmer. In the upstairs of a tiny hotel in the middle of the night across a stream from nowhere. It was incredible. It was the most incredible thing that had ever happened. Not that there was time to wonder at it. Obviously, Adelaide had arrived not a moment too soon. What was it about Lydia that provoked such passions? No one could consider her a handsome woman.

But the very air tonight was a syrup of violent desire and frustrated dreams and drink. The smell of whiskey was so concentrated in Lydia's bedroom that just breathing made you dizzy. The Alaskan Wild Woman's manager, a little man with a large mustache, had obviously been breathing for quite some time. He leered incompetently. He muttered incoherently. He clutched at Adelaide until she pushed him away, then he collapsed over Lydia. He gasped, clutched his chest, and toppled to the floor, like a felled tree, into his own drunken debris. Adelaide nudged him with the toe of her shoe. He didn't move. If men could only see themselves.

"Come on, dear. Perhaps you'd better sleep with me tonight," Adelaide said, stepping over the body on the way to the door. Lydia did not follow. She knelt instead and her skirts spread across the floor like spilt wine. She put one hand underneath a large piece of pottery and flinched. She pulled her hand out. The edge of the pottery had cut her on the side of her wrist; a thin red line appeared and she brought it to her mouth, licking the blood away and looking at the wound. She was holding a gun, pointed purposelessly about the room, sometimes at the man on the floor, sometimes at Adelaide, sometimes anyplace in between, as Lydia worried over the scratch on her wrist.

"Here, give that to me," said Adelaide briskly. She moved to Lydia's side and unwrapped Lydia's fingers, one by one, until they all gave way, curling up limply into the empty palm. The gun was very cold. Lydia's hand was almost feverishly warm.

Adelaide had given a lecture to lumbermen on the finer points of female sexuality, prevented a forcible seduction, and disarmed a murderess. It was not a bad night's work, after all. "Come to bed, Lydia," she said. She took hold of Lydia's arm and steered her around the broken pottery and the puddles of water and the body, out into the open hallway.

Downstairs the men were shouting—boisterous, happy sounds. Women were rarely safe when men got drunk and happy together. "Don't stand out here," she said to Lydia, pushing her insistently forward, her hand pressing against the row of small buttons down the back of Lydia's dress. Once inside her own room, she immediately closed the door, standing on her toes, slamming the upper corner once with her fist to force it shut. She turned the key.

Adelaide folded back the bedclothes and helped Lydia lie down without undressing. She sat beside Lydia briefly, telling her to sleep now, looking without success for some sign that Lydia heard. She wanted to see if Lydia responded to the sound of her own name. "Lydia. Lydia," said Adelaide. Such a beautiful name. She called to her gently. "Lydia Palmer. You come here, Lydia." She leaned in closer to Lydia's ear. "Lydia loves Andrew." Still no response. Adelaide slipped her hand shallowly into the neck of Lydia's dress. Lydia did not even look at her. Adelaide's fingers searched over Lydia's shoulder and then she withdrew her hand in some disappointment. There was no locket. Of course, there were a thousand possible explanations, a thousand ways a woman could lose a necklace on the path between Lydia Palmer and the Alaskan Wild Woman. Not that a locket wouldn't have been a nice touch, even for the Alaskan Wild Woman. Placed around an infant neck by the loving mother. Any manager with any imagination at all would have seen the possibilities. Still. The nose was so distinct. Adelaide was almost certain.

Finally she took the top blanket off the bed for herself. The lantern continued to flicker on the little writing desk and a half-hearted fire burned in the fireplace. The inconstant light from both gave the scene a kind of uncertainty related to distance and focus, like something viewed underwater or seen through the body of a ghost.

Adelaide wrapped herself in the blanket and sat. Her quill lay on the side of the desk blotter with the gun on the other, an illustration for the old parable that the pen is mightier than the sword, only more ambiguous as to its conclusion. Adelaide looked at the gun for a long time before she picked up the pen. It was probably the very same gun that had killed Andrew Hamelin. This was more than likely. Adelaide had to force her eyes away. Above the blotter, an envelope contained her current research and her notes. She reached for fresh paper. Her topic on her next tour would be seduction, not the forcible variety commonly referred to as *female frailty*, but the variety dependent upon persuasion and deceit.

Lydia snored three times. The first snore was loud, the second quieter, the third almost inaudible. The wind blew water against the window with a sound like a handful of pebbles thrown by a secret lover. Only a little rain really, just a few drops running down the glass, spreading thinner and thinner until a dozen long trails each ended in a drop too reduced, too spent, to continue its descent. The moon came out again and the water on the window pearled against a background of black branches and black sky. Adelaide began to make black marks on the paper before her, marks that flew across the page like birds.

There was an excellent chance that Lydia's manager would want her back in the morning. Adelaide would have to think very carefully about the best way to prevent this. Something that wouldn't draw too much attention to Lydia prematurely. Some private arrangement based, perhaps, on the ugly scene of attempted female frailty Adelaide had just witnessed.

The air was cold on the back of Adelaide's neck and she stood up, releasing her hair from its pins. She readjusted the blanket, higher and tighter about her body, so that she was swaddled when she reseated herself. Only one hand remained outside the blanket, one cold hand on the pen. She heard the rain begin again, tapping on the roof, and the wind, shaking the trees. She turned to look at the bed, where Lydia lay still as stone with the light swimming over her.

Lydia might be feigning her current helplessness and confusion, of course. Insanity would be her best defense against a murder charge.

Perhaps her manager was also a party to this deception and—for what motive? for love? for money?—had agreed to conceal her. Perhaps he was blackmailing her. Except that he had chosen such a public form of concealment. Exhibiting her, again and again, in town after town when her picture had been so widely circulated and her nose was so very distinct. No. The manager was ignorant of Lydia's identity or he would never have suggested it. And Lydia herself must be truly mad or she would never have agreed.

Driven mad by disappointed affection. Destroyed by misplaced trust. It was not hard to reconstruct the events that had resulted in this; Adelaide had heard such stories many times. They rarely varied. She wrote down the outline of Lydia's affair, the way she would tell it, the way Lydia would tell it if Lydia could. Of course, he had made love to her. Of course, he had said he would leave his wife. Someday we'll be together. Not just now, though. Give me time to arrange it. Not yet, but someday. Not now. Not yet. Until the day he said he wouldn't be leaving his wife, after all. He was home for good. He loved his wife. He was a happy family man. He had children. He didn't want to lose the love of his children. If she really loved him, she wouldn't ask him to risk the love of his children. And so he wouldn't be seeing her again. Couldn't. His wife might find out.

And besides, it was wrong.

You lied to me, Lydia said, unable to believe it.

I never lied. I was very unhappy when I met you. Things changed. Things do change.

Adelaide's nose began to itch and she wiped at it with the scratchy edge of the hotel blanket. A flea appeared on the back of her hand. She set the pen down and reached over to pinch it, but it jumped away, landing in the ink pot. Adelaide watched it drown; kicking its little feet ineffectually, splashing invisible flea-sized drops of ink on the sides of the pot. She had been told not to stay in the Bay View. She had expected fleas.

And then she couldn't watch anymore. She went to rescue the flea with the tip of her pen, but the movement of her arm knocked the gun from the desk to the floor, where it spun like a bottle and came to rest, pointing back at Adelaide. Lydia jerked at the sound.

She seemed to wake up, kicking off the blankets, although the room was very cold without them. Then her breathing evened again.

Adelaide was immobilized within the cocoon she had made. She would have to unwind herself in order to retrieve the gun. Then rewind herself into the blanket. She sat still and stared instead.

I did love you, he said. I hope someday you'll believe that.

So Lydia shot him three times, because things had changed for him, but nothing would ever change for her and she needed to know that he would never change again. She needed to make him as permanent as she was. She pillowed his head, because she loved him. She cut the lock of his hair to have something she could keep.

Adelaide began to write again, punctuating one of her sentences with the body of the flea. She was not going to argue that these were the actions of a normal woman, only that they might be a little less abnormal than everyone else seemed to think. Since Lydia's disappearance, any number of experts, from alienists to phrenologists to clergymen, had been questioned and they had all agreed that suicide or prostitution were normal female responses to betrayal. Three bullets in the abdomen could not be considered part of the natural order. Lydia was either monstrously evil or she was mad.

There was little pity for her either way. Even if it was madness, the men in San Francisco were in a frenzy to find her. Even if it was madness, it could not be allowed to spread. Last year in Brooklyn, there was Fanny Hyde. And then Lydia. And only this month, again in Brooklyn, Kate Stoddart. It could not be allowed. It could not be. It could not. It could . . . not . . .

From the downstairs saloon, Adelaide heard shouts and then shots and breaking glass. She opened her eyes with a start. Her head was on her papers. Her back ached and her throat was dry. The fire was out. She had fallen asleep in her chair. She tried to stretch but was too tightly wrapped in the blanket. The rain had stopped and dawn, she guessed, was maybe an hour away. The noise downstairs grew louder, as if a door had been opened. Adelaide thought she heard footsteps on the stairs. Suddenly she was frightened. "Get up," she whispered to Lydia. She tried to stand, but the blanket prevented her. "Get up," she said, more loudly, struggling to free her arms, working herself loose. Definitely footsteps, closer now. The hissing sound of drunks trying to talk quietly. A spill of laughter. It was a party. The men had spent the night drinking and now they were coming, drunken and hilarious, for the great magnetic doctress. To show her the finer points of female sexuality.

She thrashed about in the blanket until it fell away. She should never have stayed here at the Bay View, isolated from Seabeck proper by the stream. She had been told very clearly that the United States Hotel was the place for ladies. Right in town. Clean. No saloon. No squaws. But she had been too proud to stay in the proper place for ladies. She had wanted to make a point. She always wanted to make some point.

Adelaide stepped over the blanket, scooping up the gun and running to the bed. "Lydia," she said, grabbing Lydia by the shoulder with her free hand and shaking her. "Get up. Now. We're leaving."

Lydia's dark eyes opened uncomprehendingly. "Now!" said Adelaide. She would not go without Lydia. She would never lose Lydia. She ran back to the door dragging the chair, wedging it against the knob. She grabbed her coat and the bag with her money, glanced at the pen and her lecture notes. There was no time to take anything else. She returned to the bed, where Lydia's eyes had already shut again. Adelaide took hold of her arms and pulled her upright. She kept on pulling until Lydia gave her a drowsy sort of cooperation, getting to her feet, allowing Adelaide to direct her. Adelaide unhooked the window's catch and swung it open. She dropped the gun into her pocket with her money. The window looked out on a wide, safe expanse of roof and, beyond that, the branches of a large tree. She pushed Lydia through the window ahead of her.

Lydia hovered for a moment, half in the room and half out in the bitter darkness, like a plug in a bottle's neck. "Go on," Adelaide pleaded. She heard the doorknob rattle, pulled the gun from her pocket, and fired a single shot in the direction of the door. Then she shoved Lydia from behind as hard as she could. "Ump," said Lydia. Her body tipped forward; her toes caught on the windowsill. Adelaide unhooked them, flinging Lydia's feet through the window after her. Putting the gun back in her pocket, she hoisted her own skirts and climbed out. The window swung shut again.

The roof was iced like a cake with rain. A wet wind blew over it. "Come on," said Adelaide, letting go of the window frame and edging carefully around Lydia. The branch of a tree grew alongside the eaves. She stepped onto it, holding herself steady with a parallel branch higher up. Both branches dipped under her weight and then rebounded. Her fingers tightened frantically when she felt herself dropping. It was a horrible sensation, like being bounced. Adelaide moved as quickly as she could toward the thicker, steadier wood by the tree's trunk. The wind whipped her with dead leaves. She walked hand over hand, foot over foot. When she was as close to the trunk as she could get, she began to descend. Her hair fell into her face and she stopped once to flick it back, looking back up to where, against all her expectations, Lydia was following her. "Hold tightly," Adelaide whispered. The bottoms of the branches dripped water. First Adelaide's hands and then her skirts grew damp. Once she was forced to sit astride a branch. Her skirts bunched about her and the wet cold reached into her thighs. Her fingers began to stiffen and to ache with the effort of hanging on. The branches came at safe, reasonable intervals until the very end. From the last branch to the ground was a distance of perhaps seven feet. Adelaide hung from her hands and prepared to drop.

" 'You won't find many women in Washington,' " someone to the right and below her said. "That's what they told me when I wanted to come here." Adelaide turned her head to look. A man stood and watched her, his arms across his chest. He was tall and thin, dark and bearded, warmly dressed, self-satisfied. "It was one of the things that appealed to me most. I figured it'd be so quiet. But here I stand, minding my own business, and the women are falling out of the trees." He removed the hat from his head with exaggerated courtesy. "Miss Dixon. I'm Will Purdy. Postmaster here. At your service."

Adelaide tried to pull herself back up onto the last branch. She kicked her legs and strained her arms but was not strong enough.

She tried to hold on to the branch with one hand only, fumbling inside her coat for her pocket with the other. Opening her fingers proved just as painful as keeping them clenched. "I have a gun," she said, although she couldn't produce it.

"So do I," he told her. "Fortunately, neither one of us is in any danger."

Adelaide felt her grip on the branch giving way. She reached frantically upward with her free hand. Too late. Her heels hit the ground first, her legs folding so that she sat. The man—and she recognized him, he'd been at her lecture—offered her a hand, which she refused, standing up without his help. There was a litter of glass around her. What remained of the windows in the Bay View saloon hung and dripped in their frames like icicles.

The branch over their heads shook down a shower of rain. Adelaide looked up. Lydia sat above them, swinging her legs. Her skirt was bunched beneath her, her shoes and ankles were completely exposed. "And here's the other one," Purdy said.

"My traveling companion," Adelaide said tightly.

"Absolutely enchanted."

Lydia jumped, plummeting toward them, skirts flying. Purdy moved out of her way. She landed lightly on her feet beside Adelaide, who now grasped the gun but did not display it. "If you'll just excuse us," Adelaide said.

"I'd like to. But Bill Blair is a personal friend of mine. Very popular man. Very generous with the drinks. I can't help wondering if, in your haste to leave by way of the Bay View roof, you mightn't have forgotten to pay your bill. It's so hard for Blair to make a living when guests do this."

"Mr. Blair can expect his money when he manages to guarantee the safety of his guests," Adelaide told him. There was a crash upstairs and more breaking glass. Someone shoved the chair from Adelaide's room through the window. It bounced on the roof and flew over the edge, landing on its back in the mud.

"Did you see that?" The voice from the bedroom expressed drunken exultation. "Did I tell you? It skipped. Just like a stone. I skipped it."

An empty bottle skidded across the roof and stuck in a branch of the tree. "Two skips." The second voice was higher and steadier. A man leaned out the window to look, and Adelaide stepped in nearer to the hotel, out of his sight.

"Miss Dixon!" someone called. "Miss Dixo-o-on."

The envelope with Adelaide's lecture notes fell past her face. Some of the pages spilled out and were caught and thrown again by the wind.

"Two skips."

"But that was a bottle," the first voice said. "That was a bunch of papers. I skipped a *chair*."

"Fetch me a chair!" the second voice shouted.

One of Adelaide's gloves dropped down, balled up like a fist. There was laughter. A third drenched voice. "Missed the roof entirely."

"Someone fetch me a chair!"

Adelaide stepped forward carefully, watching the upstairs window. It was empty. She ignored the single glove and reached instead for the envelope, which had landed near her. It contained her pamphlets and whichever of her notes remained: her observations on the Fanny Hyde case, her thoughts on Belle Starr, her refutation of the points made in phrenologist Orson Squire Fowler's recent treatise *Science of Life*. Fowler's enormous book had sparked yet another round of controversy about the need for antiseduction legislation. His position toward women was sympathetic and protective and pernicious. Adelaide had outlined it and it came down to three simple points:

One—the essential thing about women is that they are all seducible.

Two—it is only natural for women to respond to men with devotion, and once a woman's affections are engaged, she is bound to cling to the man with the unreasoning obstinacy of an oyster.

Three—it falls to the man, therefore, to prevent the attachment, or to honor it with matrimony. Any other course threatens not only the happiness but the sanity, sometimes the very life, of the woman. There was no creature more vile than the seducer.

Unless, perhaps, it was the man-hating woman.

Lydia started down the stony path to the footbridge. Adelaide made a grab for her skirt, but the wind took it away from her hand. "Wait for me." She followed Lydia, sticking whenever possible to the windless, dark places nearest the trees. She heard Purdy's boots on the stones behind her. "Don't try to stop us, Mr. Purdy." Adelaide turned. "I have a gun."

"I remember that. You're rather tedious on the subject."

Lydia reached the bridge and began to cross. It was a suspension affair made of ropes and wooden slats. It swung in the wind even before Lydia stepped onto it. As she crossed, it bucked and plunged beneath her. Adelaide ran to catch up. Purdy stayed with Adelaide, matching her step for step.

They paused, panting, by the stream, which was much higher and wilder than it had been the night before. "I'm escorting you!" Purdy had to shout to be heard above the water. "As a gentleman must. Ladies, even such independent ladies, cannot wander about lumber camps. Call it protection from the elements, if you like. I never saw so many peculiar things falling out of the sky as I have this morning." He stood too close to Adelaide. His breath was soaked with whiskey.

Lydia had long since made the other side of the creek and was loping away. Adelaide began to understand how Lydia had managed to elude the San Francisco police. She was so fast, moving in and out of the trees, with no hesitation.

Adelaide watched, allowing herself to imagine how, having forewarned the press, she would appear casually on the docks in San Francisco with the woman no man had been able to find. How she would speak for poor Lydia at the trial. Adelaide's eloquence and Lydia's pathos would save Lydia from the gallows. Adelaide thought for a moment of Lydia's neck, which led her to uncomfortable doubts about the missing locket. She ignored them. The whole affair would have front-page coverage from the moment they landed until Lydia's release. The press might continue to call her the great magnetic doctress, winking, as if the needs of the body were a sort of joke played upon women, but, even so, they would have to take her seriously.

"You don't like men very much, do you, Miss Dixon?" Purdy asked. His tone was accusing, but he had continued to smile. Did he really imagine that she didn't remember how he had mocked her during her lecture?

"I don't like men like you very much," Adelaide said. "Why do you suppose that is?" She didn't bother to raise her voice. She didn't care if he heard her or not. He wasn't listening anyway. Adelaide decided to make him listen. She pulled the gun from her pocket and pointed it at him. The wind blew her hair wildly about her head, stinging her cheeks. She had to force herself not to close her eyes.

"You have ink on your face." Purdy was still smiling. "Did you fall asleep over your love letters?" He put his hand out as if he intended to wipe her cheek. "You'd be prettier without it."

Adelaide stopped him by raising the gun. She resented his smile. She resented his hat. Most of all, she resented how safe he felt with her. She had a gun and she was still the one who was afraid. She had a gun and they were bouncing chairs out of second-story windows and she was still the one who was afraid. Men were dangerous and women were not, and when men loved women, women were still not dangerous to them, and when women loved men, then men were the most dangerous of all.

She had no more time to waste getting rid of him. She was so cold. She was losing Lydia. She needed to find a way out of Seabeck for the two of them, and the sooner, the safer. "Take out your gun," she said. Her voice was too quiet. He didn't respond. "Take out your gun," she shouted. "Carefully. Now throw it in the creek."

"No."

"Yes." She aimed at his face. "Skip it if you can."

He stared at her for a moment, stepping back, the smile finally gone. Then he took out his gun and tossed it away, side-arm. She didn't look to follow its movement, but she heard it hit the water. Once. "Now give me your knife. I know you must have a knife. Take it out carefully and throw it on the ground there. I *will* shoot if you do anything else. There is no one here to see.

"Now!" she shouted.

He removed a small pearled knife, something for cutting his nails, from his breast pocket. "I'm sure you can do better than that," Adelaide told him, sighting down the gun. He reached into his boot and pulled out a second knife, which had a long blade and no mother-of-pearl. He lobbed it to her. It landed in a puddle. "You just hold still, Mr. Purdy." She stooped to pick up the knife, keeping the gun level and steady the whole time. Then, with the gun in one hand and the knife in the other, she began to back carefully over the footbridge. She could never hit him if he moved now; the bridge swung with every step and she swung, too, hardly able to stay upright with both her hands full. He shifted his weight. "No!" she said quickly.

They stood watching each other, and the bridge swung less and less until it only trembled beneath her. She began to back up again. She was over half the creek. She was almost over the creek. She could see the white water in the spaces between the slats. The closer she came to the other side and the closer she was to making her escape, the more her nervousness grew. By the time she could see the other bank out of the corner of her eye, her tension was almost unbearable.

Then she bumped into someone stepping onto the bridge from the other side. Adelaide screamed. Her heart exploded in her breast. The gun went off. Purdy dove for the ground. She had been holding the envelope with her papers between her left arm and her body. Now it lay just past the bridge in the mud. Two more sheets of paper fell out, blew down the bank and into the creek.

Adelaide turned around. She had backed into a Chinese man, very short, no taller than she was herself, his hair tumbling out of his queue. "I'm sorry," he said. "I thought you were somebody else. Please don't shoot me." He had a blanket roll tied to his back and he held his two empty hands in the air.

Behind him, back by the trees, was a second man, much taller, with pale skin and pale hair. "Has Sarah Canary stopped shooting?" His voice squeaked with the effort to be heard over the noise of the creek. "Why is she shooting, Chin?" He crossed the patch of bare ground that separated them, looking eagerly and then less eagerly at her face. "She is *not* Sarah Canary," he told the Chinese man in a tone that suggested he had been contending this all along. The Chinese man remained frozen and frightened. "Who is she? Is she the Alaskan Wild Woman?" When the Chinese man did not answer, the pale man shouted at Adelaide directly. "Are you the Alaskan Wild Woman? I hope not. Chin and I spent the whole day and the whole night on the *Biddy* coming in from Port Gamble, because we didn't think the Alaskan Wild Woman would be you."

A pamphlet had slipped out of the envelope at her feet, and muddy water was working its way through the cover to the pages inside. The pale man bent and picked it up for her, wiping it on the front of his coat. It was the popular tract entitled *The Victim of Seduction: An Affecting Narrative of the Tragical Death of Miss Fanny Salisbury, A Native of New Jersey, Who, Having Been Enticed From Her Widowed Parents and Basely Seduced By a Young Man of the City of New York, After Enduring Incredible Hardships in That City, Terminated Her Own Existence By Hanging Herself In a Forest Near Newark, on the 23rd of January Last.* He shook his head. "This is so sad, Chin," he said, putting the pamphlet back into the envelope and handing them both to her. "What are 'widowed parents'?"

"Who is the Biddy?" Adelaide asked. Her heart had still not settled back into its usual rhythm. Perhaps it never would. Two more men who wanted Lydia. For what purpose? What was she to do?

"The *Biddy*. She's a sloop."

"A what?" Adelaide was having trouble hearing him. She thought he had said something rude.

"A sloop. The *Biddy!*" he shouted. "You have ink on your cheek. Did you know that? It's a word." He moved closer and bent over the gun as if he didn't even see it, to get closer to her face. "It's a word, but it's in code."

On the other side of the creek, Purdy got to his feet, wiping off his knees. Adelaide pushed the pale man away, swinging around again so that the gun was leveled at Mr. Purdy.

"Don't you move!" she screamed over the water to him. "Don't you dare."

"Are you talking about the *Biddy?*" he called back. "The *Biddy's* the mail sloop. In and out of Port Gamble. I was just on my way to her."

"When does she leave?" Adelaide asked the pale man.

He was still squinting at her face. "It's the word *someday*. You have the word *someday* written backward on your cheek."

"When does she leave?" Adelaide shouted to Purdy.

"She leaves when I get there."

"Oh," said Adelaide. She took a deep breath to clear her head and calm her heart. "All right." She moved the barrel of the gun in a repeated semicircular gesture between the pale man and Will Purdy. She was telling the pale man to cross the bridge.

He was too busy reading her face to notice. "Someday what?" he asked. "What does it mean?"

"The Alaskan Wild Woman is in that hotel," Adelaide shouted. "Over there. I want the two of you to cross now. Go stand next to Mr. Purdy. Do it as quickly as you can." She made the gesture with her gun again, a smaller, more hurried semicircle.

"It's a message for you," the pale man told her insistently. "It's on *your* cheek. And it's backwards. You're supposed to read it in a mirror." The Chinese man sidled past with his pinched unhappy face, dragging the pale man along by his sleeve. "Don't you wonder what it means?" the pale man asked. "Yes, Chin. I'm coming. Don't you wonder what it means, Chin?" Every time the pale man took a step, the bridge threw the smaller Chinese man a few inches into the air. He clung to the ropes at the side, dancing desperately to keep his balance. When they were both across, Adelaide began using Purdy's knife to saw through the ropes that held the bridge.

"Wait a second!" the pale man called back in surprise. "We may want to get back." The Chinese man spoke to him, said something Adelaide couldn't hear. "But, Chin, she may not even be the right Alaskan Wild Woman. Then we'll want to get back for sure."

"You're making a big mistake here!" Purdy shouted. "The sloop won't leave without me. When I do get to the shipyard, you'll still be sitting there, waiting, and sorry to see me again. Trust me for it."

"*You* may want to get back," the pale man pointed out. "You

136

may have left something in the hotel that you need. Did you ever think of that?''

Adelaide cut the last strands of the knots. Her end of the bridge fell away, landing in the water, dipping underneath, and then rising to the top, riding out its length, but held back finally by the ropes, which still anchored it on the other side.

The sky was beginning to lighten in the east. Adelaide put her weapons into her coat pockets and ran in the opposite direction, through the trees and toward the bay. Occasionally she saw part of a footprint, the cast of Lydia's heel in the wet ground. To the best of her recollection, the shipyard was about three quarters of a mile away. Lydia seemed to be heading straight for it.

Adelaide caught up with Lydia in front of the Washington Mill Company lumberyard. A white seagull flapped through the air above her. Lydia was gazing up at it, her naked neck stretched and exposed. She seemed to be speaking. Adelaide could not hear it, but she saw the movement along Lydia's throat. The rain had melted but not obliterated the lines of a baseball diamond.

The sun came up. Adelaide was filled with joy. She stood over the bare patch of ground that marked home plate, her hair wild about her face, her nose and fingers stinging with cold, and imagined she had hit a ball straight out at Lydia, straight out toward third. It touched down in left field, just where Lydia was, just barely fair, before it rolled underneath the pile of logs in the lumberyard and was lost.

C H A P T E R
T E N

MORNING AT
THE BAY VIEW HOTEL

Remorse — is Memory — awake —
Her Parties all astir —
A Presence of Departed Acts —
At window — and at Door —

EMILY DICKINSON,
1863

"Would you like some chewing gum?" Mr. Purdy asked.

Chin turned to look at him. Purdy had taken a handkerchief out of his pocket and was unfolding it awkwardly with his gloved hands. The gum was inside. He held it out to B.J. "Thank you," said B.J., taking a piece and passing it to Chin. Purdy was already refolding his handkerchief. He opened it again and gave B.J. a second piece. Chin sniffed at the gum, which smelled of pine trees. He bit off a piece. Saliva filled his mouth, but the gum grew harder and harder. Chin chewed it into a small pebble, which he swallowed. The texture was somewhat medicinal and he hoped it might ease the stabbing pain he had in his shoulder from sleeping awkwardly on the sloop and carrying the bedroll. He took another bite, swallowed it, and shifted the bedroll from one side of his back to the other.

The three men walked together up the path to the Bay View Hotel, Purdy a few steps ahead, Chin just a few steps to the rear. B.J. twisted his head around to talk to Chin as he walked. "Oh, well," B.J. said around the gum. He was chewing with his mouth open so that Chin could see his teeth. B.J.'s teeth were always a surprise to Chin, white and healthy against his sallow skin. B.J.'s toe hit a fist-sized stone and he stumbled without facing forward again or appearing to notice his own clumsiness in any way. "We can worry about getting back later. Someday. At least we're where we want to be now." He was about to walk into a tree. Chin grabbed his arm and pulled him sharply to the left.

"Later," Purdy called back to B.J., "the creek will drop on its own. It's tide-fed. When the tide is out, there's still a creek, but not much of one. We'll be able to cross without the bridge in a couple of hours. 'Course the *Biddy*'ll be an hour up the canal by then."

"I thought you said it wouldn't go without you," B.J. reminded him.

"I lied. Sloops haven't been used for the mail run for two, three years. The steamer picks up the mail. If Miss Dixon wants to rent the *Biddy*, she can go to Port Gamble or anywhere else on the canal, unless the captain figures the wind is too high."

Purdy slowed their pace as they neared the Bay View, stopping at a bifurcation in the walk. Half of the stones led on to the main door. Half turned right and began a circle around the hotel.

"What's that?" said B.J., pointing out a small wooden cross hammered into the mud under one of the trees.

Purdy moved his gum into one cheek to answer; Chin could see the lump that it made. "That marks the spot where William Gassey died." He touched his forehead, his chest, and then each of his shoulders with one hand. "William was a ticket-of-leave man from Australia, worked at the mill, used to come here drinking when the

Cliff House went dry. Nasty creature, really. Shouldn't speak ill of the dead, of course, but there it is. One stormy summer night he's put away more than a few; he's one of those men who gets drunk by design instead of by accident. The creek is roaring up over the bank and we've all agreed to sit the storm out in the Bay View. No one can get home in that kind of weather. But suddenly William's all afire, like he's had a vision. 'By God, Blair,' he says to the innkeeper. 'I must be the luckiest man alive,' he says. And then he weaves out the door without saying good-bye to anyone and he's struck by lightning, right there by the tree, right there where the cross is. There are designs *and* designs in this world," Purdy said, which is what Chin had always thought himself.

"We bowl sometimes when it's dry in that flat stretch of dirt past the cross." Purdy indicated the area with his hand, loudly sucking in the saliva that had collected around his gum. "I'm going to build an alley out by the mill this summer. Hire an Indian to stick up tenpins. Do you bowl?"

"I play the violin," B.J. answered. "Is that story true? The one about William Gassey?"

"May lightning strike me if what I've given you is not a true and faithful account of the events of the evening of July 3, 1870. I don't blame you for doubting me, though. Not a bit. No offense intended, I'm sure, and none taken. If you're staying in Seabeck and the rain lets up, I could teach you tenpins. Anyone who plays the violin would have the wrist for it."

"Thank you," said B.J. His gum chewing grew noisier. He was evidently pleased.

Purdy turned back to face the hotel, shaking his head. "Would you look at the poor old Bay View?" Chin did so. He saw that the hotel had three chimneys, although smoke rose only from one of them. Chin was very cold. He stared at the smoke longingly.

"It's not enough that her bridge is out. She's not got a window left in her frame." Purdy seemed to take a certain pride in the fact. He pointed with his finger to each glassless hole, one by one, until despite his words he came to the shut eye of a single intact window whose drapes were drawn. Purdy's finger stopped at the undamaged glass. "Oh, well, there's your Alaskan Wild Woman," he said. "Still sleeping the sleep of the innocent."

Chin heard a man's voice above them, somewhere on the second story. "Ho-o-w do!" it said, thick with phlegm and elated. Chin had seldom heard a more unpleasant sound. The gum was heavy in his stomach. Chinese men were rarely safe when white men got drunk and happy together. Even without liquor, groups of the white demons were always much more dangerous than solitary white men. Chin wondered at this. Demons like B.J., who were essentially harmless unless you made them otherwise, had no friends. You found them alone; you dealt with them alone. But the dangerous and cruel demons were always together. The white culture rewarded cruelty with honor and friendship.

Chin gave up his thoughts of a warm seat by a fire. He knew better than to enter a building where white men were shouting "Ho-o-w do!" He would send B.J. to talk to the owner, just to the owner, nothing too tricky, and he himself would squat and wait for B.J. on the porch in the cold like a Chinaman.

The main door to the Bay View opened and the bits of frosted glass that remained in its small ornamental pane fluttered and clinked like wind chimes. An Indian girl came out. She stood beside the doorjamb, brushing her hair. She might have been twelve years old or thirteen or fourteen; she was wearing a shift and had no breasts and her skin was as fresh as peeled fruit. She looked to the east and the sunrise. Chin wondered if there were more Indians about than just this girl. Drunken white men, drunken Indians, a solitary Chinese man, the creek up and the bridge out. Through the open doorway, Chin could just see the bodies of men lying on the stairs.

"The bridge has been cut loose," Purdy told the girl.

She had not seen them yet; she stiffened slightly in surprise, and the expression she had turned to the sun was not the expression she had for Purdy or B.J. or Chin. She smiled at them, but this was a calculated smile, like light stretching over a pool and making it shine so you could no longer see through to the rocks and the weeds and the fish. Not really a happy expression, merely an unrevealing one.

"That suffragist cut the ropes on the other side," Purdy said.

"That magnetic doctress. Blair will be so pleased, won't he? With all his windows gone and the hotel full of drunken lumbermen? Would you like to tell him or should I? It might come sweeter from you." The girl turned and reentered the Bay View, walking stiffly, awkward because they were watching her.

"Was that the Alaskan Wild Woman?" B.J. asked.

"That was Jenny," Purdy said. "Do you think she went to tell Blair? I think I'd better go tell Blair myself. He's going to want to know exactly what happened. And the *implications*."

The edge of the sun had appeared over the mountains, but the moon refused to abdicate. It made Chin think of the Dowager Empress and the end of the Regency. Had it happened? Had the grasping big-footed Manchu woman really relinquished the throne? If so, his uncle would be pouring back the tiger whiskey in celebration. How long since Chin had read a Chinese newspaper?

The Chinese character for *bright* was a picture just like this of the sun and moon together in the sky. Chin wished he had told Tom this when they spoke about the moon. Perhaps Tom would have been satisfied to hear something he had never heard rather than see something he had never seen. But surely not in the words of men. "The earth talks to us," Tom had said, and he had understood the owl. But if the world was a dream, then the words of men were only the memories of a dream. The moon grew paler. The wind stirred the dead leaves on the ground and the dying leaves on the trees.

He followed Purdy to the porch. Beer had been drunk and beer had been spilled; Chin could smell beer even outside the door. Someone was snoring. Someone was dreaming. Chin spoke to B.J. softly so that Purdy wouldn't hear him telling B.J. what to do. "Go and talk to the proprietor," he said. "This Blair. Ask if the Wild Woman's manager is named Harold. Describe Harold to him." B.J. started to follow Purdy through the open door, but Chin caught him by the sleeve, holding him back.

"Describe Harold to me first," he suggested.

B.J. blinked several times and chewed. "A little man with a large mustache."

"Tell him what kind of mustache," said Chin. "Show him

the . . . the wings." Chin was not sure of the word and drew the shape of Harold's mustache with his fingers beside his own lips. "And say that he's dark. Dark hair, light eyes. And if he asks why you are interested, just tell him you want to see the Alaskan Wild Woman. Nothing more."

"Maybe you'd better do it yourself," B.J. said.

"Just ask if his name is Harold," said Chin. "And then come back out here. *Don't* go up to see Harold yourself. If Harold should appear and you see him before you can talk to Blair, come back out here quickly and tell me. Don't let Harold see you."

"I'm not going in." B.J. folded his arms decisively. "Not all alone. It's too hard."

"Not hard," Chin said. "Forget everything else. Just follow Mr. Purdy to Blair and ask if the Alaskan Wild Woman's manager's name is Harold. That's all. Not hard."

B.J. dropped his arms to his side. He chewed on his gum. Then he stepped resolutely into the Bay View. He pivoted immediately and stepped back out, pulling the door shut behind him. The door did not shut easily. He had to tug at it. The shattered glass jingled and a triangle broke loose, falling from the door to the porch. "There are bodies all over the stairs. It's a message not to go inside."

"Those men are sleeping," Chin said, "because they are drunk. They are so drunk they wouldn't wake up if you stepped on them. And you won't step on them, because you won't be going upstairs at all. You're just going to find Blair's office."

B.J. sat down on the porch. "You go."

"Who-o-o-ee!" the voice upstairs shouted. "Whoo! Whoo!"

"Please, B.J.," said Chin.

"You go."

Chin squatted down on the porch beside B.J. He had done astounding things for Sarah Canary. He had taken her to Steila-coom. He had kidnapped her from the hospital. He had gotten on a boat to follow the Alaskan Wild Woman to Seabeck without even being absolutely certain she was Sarah Canary, and he had told himself more than once after his long, bitter, and involuntary voyage from Hong Kong on the *Ville de St. Louis* that he would never board

143

a boat again, never, never, never, unless he was returning to China, a rich man.

Chin had stopped asking himself why he did all this. The doing had become its own reason. And anyway, so much time had passed now, it would be difficult to go back to his uncle. His uncle must believe he was dead. His uncle had probably written his mother to tell her so. Great rejoicing when he reappeared, of course. Great, great rejoicing. And yet a lot of awkward questions. He had not been gone long enough to have been enchanted. He had made no money and had squandered much of what he had brought with him. His uncle would know just exactly how much. Squandered it pursuing a strange and ugly white woman while his own treasured mother sat neglected and mourning him. And after the great rejoicing, which would be brief, and the awkward questions, which would be long, would come the railroad work, which would be forever.

"You are a free man," the Company had said when his contract was fulfilled and they returned it and he tore it in pieces and threw the pieces into the sky, where they danced like little kites, like snow, until they blew away. And so he was, as free as any man who had to eat and keep warm and send money to his parents. Could a man appear to disappear, the same way snow melts into the wind? Could he vanish into the forest around Fort Lewis and, dead to his obligations and responsibilities, walk out somewhere else? Someone else? It seemed to Chin that he could, and this was a tantalizing freedom that frightened even as it dazzled. Chin remembered how he'd stood with Tom, only a few moments before putting the rope around Tom's neck, and looked out onto the peaks of Mount Rainier. He remembered feeling that a man could lose his soul to those peaks, so dangerous, so beautiful were they. That a man might even want to.

"A ghost took my soul," Chin would tell his uncle if he ever saw him again, which might even be true. The ghost was Tom or it was Sarah Canary, seducing him with freedom, which was a thing so much closer to death than Chin had ever realized.

But however close it was, it was not death, and Chin had not lost sight of this. He would not enter into a hotel full of drunken white demons while the bridge was out. "I can't blame you, B.J.," he said cunningly. "An old, dirty place like this. Probably filled with fleas."

B.J. closed his eyes so as not to hear.

A man's face appeared in the hole behind the broken door pane above Chin, looking to the right and to the left, unable to locate Chin and B.J. where they sat. "Gentlemen?" the man asked. The door handle turned and the door opened. A light-eyed Indian stepped onto the porch, extending a hand to B.J., who still hadn't opened his eyes and therefore did not take it. "Please come in," the man said. "Please. I'm Bill Blair, the owner of the Bay View. Will Purdy has been telling me about your ordeal at the bridge. You're lucky to be alive. You're a lucky man. Come inside and have a drink. The saloon is rather cold, but I can offer you a fire and a comfortable chair in the kitchen. Perhaps a bit of breakfast. Eggs," he promised. "And bread."

B.J. opened his eyes. "That would be nice," he said, and Chin, too, thought how nice that would be. An egg, fried and then chopped into little pieces with perhaps some bits of mushroom. A little garlic for flavor and for health. Bread to fill the stomach. He had gotten quite used to bread. Blair led them past the stairs and into the kitchen. It was a small room. A rough wooden table and six chairs filled it. Purdy sat in one of the chairs.

Blair fetched whiskey and poured each man a small glass. Chin drank his immediately and felt a warmth surrounding his heart.

Blair cooked the eggs himself while the other men sat. Chin took an inconspicuous chair slightly behind B.J., with Purdy to his right. Purdy leaned across him. "I recollect being afraid that the Bay View might prove too rough for Miss Adelaide Dixon," he told B.J. "Will you believe me? Remember, Blair? Remember me saying that the Bay View was not the place for ladies?"

"I will believe you," B.J. promised. "I don't know what Chin will believe."

"I let her stay because another woman had taken rooms as well," Blair said. "Otherwise I wouldn't have. Not unescorted, the way she was."

"Her and her companion," said Purdy.

"No companion," said Blair. "I never had an unescorted woman stay here before. I never will again."

"She left with a companion."

"No companion."

"I saw a companion."

"I believe you," said B.J.

Purdy's voice was increasingly excited. "By God," he said. "I *thought* her companion was a little wild-eyed. Now I recollect that she growled at me like a dog. She swung out of the trees like an African ape. She ran to the river like a deer. So Miss Adelaide Dixon escaped through the window with the Alaskan Wild Woman, did she? But why would she do that?"

It was all too plausible to Chin. Why did anyone run off with Sarah Canary? It was a question beyond why. Blair set a plate of eggs in front of B.J. He reached past to give Purdy the second plate. Both men put their hands in their mouths and pulled out their gum. B.J. set his out on the plate rim. He looked at it. He shaped it into a little mountain peak. He smashed it down with his thumb. Chin turned to Purdy to see if this was simply what one did with gum, but Purdy was already eating his eggs and his gum lay relatively untouched on the table, like a bird dropping. Chin felt slightly embarrassed for having swallowed his.

"What a *lot* of eggs," said B.J.

"Did you see two women?" Blair asked him.

"No," said B.J. "But the woman I saw looked a lot like the woman I didn't see. I thought I was seeing the woman I didn't see, at first. So did Chin. Didn't you, Chin?"

"I don't understand," said Blair.

"It was confusing," B.J. agreed. "That's all I'm saying. I was confused." Blair returned to the stove and scraped another plateful of eggs out of the pan. He held the plate out to Chin along with a metal spoon. Bits of uncooked white dotted the eggs. Chin's mouth filled with water and he ate quickly without chewing. Purdy cut the bread into thick slices and passed it.

B.J. rubbed his bread in circles over his plate to clean it. Chin imitated him. He drew rings in his cooked eggs and then erased the rings.

B.J. put his bread into his mouth. "Is the Alaskan Wild Woman's manager's name Harold?" he asked. "I don't want to see him or anything. I just want to know. He's a short man with a big mustache."

"Yes," said Blair. "That's him."

Chin's thoughts straightened into lines. Sarah Canary would take the *Biddy* to Port Gamble. And from there, who could guess? Perhaps with Miss Adelaide Dixon, wherever her business might take her. Perhaps with any other man or woman who happened along. They had missed her again.

"Dark hair." B.J. was being very thorough. "With light eyes."

"Right upstairs," said Blair. "Unless he climbed out the window with the ladies."

"Which he wouldn't have," Purdy added. "She wouldn't have taken a man. She doesn't like them."

"Are you a friend of Harold's?" asked Blair. "Or a creditor? Would you like to go up and see him?"

"No," said B.J. "We just wanted to see the Alaskan Wild Woman. Nothing more."

Chin cleared his throat inadvertently. B.J. misunderstood. "Oh," B.J. said awkwardly. "I guess I *do* want to go up and see Harold."

Chin coughed in alarm.

B.J. stared at him. "But not now?"

"Why not?" said Blair. "It's just up the stairs. First door on your right."

"Why not?" said B.J. in some confusion. He looked at Chin. "You come with me, Chin," said B.J., and Chin, who knew that Sarah Canary was gone but that some white demon was hidden upstairs instead, shouting "Ho-o-w do" and "Who-o-o-ee" at irregular intervals, was still afraid to risk anything so un-Chinamanlike as refusing. Besides, B.J., left to himself, was likely to go to the first door on the right.

Purdy followed them all the way to the foot of the stairs. The light was very dim and the smell of beer made Chin want to cough, which he couldn't do, not without waking someone. His eyes watered instead and he could hardly see to pick his way among the legs and arms and heads of the men on the stairs. Toward the landing he reached a spot where there was no gap left for his foot. His boot hovered over the face of a man, then over his palm, then over his white beard.

"Are we going up the stairs now?" B.J. whispered behind him.

"Yes," said Chin.

"I thought it had gotten steep," B.J. said. Chin straightened his knee, stretched his leg to the stair above, set his toe down in the middle of a plate of bread. It took both his hands on the rail to pull himself forward. The plate cracked as his weight shifted onto it. He took a final, long step and stood at the top of the stairs, looking back to see if Purdy was still watching. It was too dark to see past the landing where the staircase turned. He heard a second crack as B.J. stepped on the plate behind him.

Chin passed up the first door on the right. He paused at the second, put his ear against it. He was mentally matching it to the hotel exterior, to the draped and intact window outside. Sarah Canary's room would be right next to Harold's, of course. Locked, he imagined, although he did not try the knob. Harold would have locked her in at night and kept the key with him as he slept, underestimating her cunning. She'd escaped him through the window.

"Whee-yoo-oo!" the white demon called out suddenly from behind a door across the hall. The doorknob rattled as it turned. The third room on the right was open and Chin, in a panic, grabbed B.J.'s sleeve, pulling him inside. He could not shut the door behind them. It was split and appeared to have been forced.

"Chin?" said B.J. Chin hushed him. They stood for a moment, still as stones, and listened. No more sounds came from across the hall. A noise behind them turned out to be the wind, coming through the window frame unchecked, rustling papers that earlier had blown off the desk and into corners where they beat against the walls in the wind like trapped moths.

Chin shivered, from nervousness or from cold. The room was

extremely cold, colder than the porch had been. The open window channeled the wind right toward them over the bed, which was unmade and unoccupied, but B.J. stared down at it in a way that made Chin go and look, too. On top of the rumpled blanket, someone had set out the articles of a white woman's dress in the shape of the woman. Perhaps it was a joke, because the undergarments were laid on the top. Most of them were unknown to Chin, although he recognized the function of the stockings and the shoes, which had not been quite properly placed, so that one leg appeared longer than the other. One shoe had fallen over onto its side, so Chin could see the whole length, how very big the shoe was. One shoe pointed merrily up to the ceiling.

It was very easy to imagine the woman inside the clothes. The wind disturbed the hem of the skirt so that it beckoned with a disembodied, unearthly sexuality. Chin was aroused even as he recoiled. Noises through the doorway, a gasp and a groan and a series of secretive footsteps, quickly took his attention instead. He could not tell where the footsteps were headed. He could not take a chance on being found in some white woman's room. Not with the bed unmade and her clothes so intimately displayed. Chin hurried past the bed and climbed out the empty window to the roof.

B.J. followed him through the window. "Chin?" he said.

Chin hushed him again. He crossed the roof to the one room he knew was empty, the one with a window and the drapes drawn. He pushed at the glass, levered it open enough to reach through with a finger and flick loose the catch. There was something wrong with this, but he couldn't, for a moment, think what. He was already scrambling inside when he remembered. This particular window shouldn't have been locked.

CHAPTER ELEVEN

THE STORY
OF CARMILLA

But never met this Fellow
Attended, or alone
Without a tighter breathing
And Zero at the Bone —
EMILY DICKINSON,
1865

Harold was sitting on the floor, leaning against the bed frame. His face was drained of color and his eyes were those of a madman. He was looking right at Chin. "Demon from hell," he said. His voice croaked like a cricket's. "Chinese devil." He spat. In one hand he held something; now his fingers uncurled so that it fell to the floor. "Pick it up," he told Chin. "Read it to me."

Chin had heard of snakes in India that hypnotized their prey so they walk right into the snakes' open mouths. He took three steps into the room, moving like a little mouse, like a dreaming rabbit, carried forward by his own sense of inevitability. Beside the bed, he squatted slowly, until his eyes were just opposite Harold's. He picked up the item, which he didn't look at, but that his fingers recognized as a chopstick. He rolled it to the flat side, felt for the characters like a blind man. He couldn't take his eyes off Harold's eyes. "It says good health," said Chin. "Good fortune. Long life." What did chopsticks say?

Harold laughed and it was a horrible whistling laugh, like a breath over the top of an empty bottle. "Long life. I just bet it does," he said. "John Chinaman."

"Chin," B.J. said from the window. Chin didn't know if B.J. was speaking to him or correcting Harold. Neither responded. They continued to look at each other, Harold attacking with his insane stare, Chin defending, until his strength gave out. His soul began to leak from his eyes and he was forced to close them quickly.

Harold made a sound, breath and demon music. The air from his mouth was very foul. "Am I a dead man?"

"No." Chin looked at the chopstick in his hand and saw that it was his own chopstick, his own good fortune, his own long life. "Did Sarah Canary give you this?" he asked.

"That's what she did," said Harold. He coughed, holding both his hands over his stomach, and the cough was unproductive and apparently painful, but Harold repeated it anyway. He brought one hand up, wiping away the spit at the corners of his mouth. Chin saw that his nails were stained the color of bean sauce and there was a matching stain on his shirt where his hand had been. "I found it in my heart. Is it wooden?"

"Yes."

"Of course, it would be. She used to come at me in my dreams, standing over me in the moonlight and gloating and her dress all made of blood. I'd wake up in a sweat and have to drink to steady myself so that I could sleep again. I don't have a gift for sleep. Too much like death, I suppose. And now, of course, we've gone beyond dreams. Now she's tried to kill me. She doesn't understand that I can't be killed. You tell them, Jimmy. You know that I can't be killed."

151

"B.J.," said Chin. "Go downstairs and get Mr. Blair. Harold needs medicine. A doctor, too, if Blair can find one."

"I can't be killed," said Harold with more emphasis, as if Chin were missing the point. "But I think she can be."

B.J. had not moved. "B.J.," Chin said authoritatively, and B.J. began picking his way through the puddles of water and islands of crockery on the wooden floor. He opened the door and disappeared into the hall.

"Where is she?" Harold asked.

"Gone," said Chin.

"No." Sweat coated Harold's forehead. "How long? Gone where?" Chin was afraid to touch him. He squatted on the heels of his boots and tried to see how badly hurt Harold was. He tried to see this from a distance, but Harold's hands were in the way.

"I don't know. She was gone when I got here."

"I want to ask you a question, Chinaman." Harold's hands were shaking. He paused a few moments to breathe. Chin could see nothing that looked like fresh blood, not on Harold's hands, not on his shirt. The color was coming back to Harold's face in two small circles that burned in his cheeks. "Since you found Sarah Canary in the forest, how many people have died?"

"None," said Chin. He thought of Tom, of course, but what did Tom's death have to do with Sarah Canary?

"Think harder."

"None," Chin repeated. "Not one." He had troubled himself from time to time, wondering how Sarah Canary had gotten the warden's keys to the asylum gate, but there was no reason to think anyone had died over them.

"Except for Bergevain." B.J. was standing in the doorway to the room.

"Who?" said Chin. "I thought you were getting Mr. Blair."

"Louis Bergevain. The wardens beat him to death in December. I tried to tell you before, Chin. And I can't get Mr. Blair, because there's another dead man on the stairs."

"Step over him," said Chin. "Those men are just drunk."

"I don't think so." B.J.'s voice was apologetic. "Please come, Chin."

Chin rose and followed B.J. The light was much better in the hall now. There was only one small glassless window, but it was on the east side of the hotel and the sun had risen enough to come through it direct. Naked and dirty patches in the flocked paper on the walls were visible now. Chin stood at the top of the stairs and looked down at the man whose blood-caked, matted white beard contrasted with his nice clothes. Blood ran from the man's throat onto the step beneath him and off that step, in defiance of gravity, up the sleeve of another man below.

A kitchen knife lay beside the man's hand. Behind a pair of small spectacles, the man's eyes were open, flat and dead, and larger than they should have been.

"What did I tell you?" said Harold. "What did I dream? So Sarah Canary killed him, too. *La belle dame sans merci.*" Chin turned in surprise. He wouldn't have believed Harold could get to his feet, but Harold stood unsupported and quite steady in the hall behind them, and the look on his face was one of satisfaction. "*La dame sans merci,*" he said, giving it more thought. He uncapped his silver flask and took a drink. "I met him last night," Harold told B.J. "We had a drink together. Jim Allen. A nice man."

"Sarah Canary didn't kill him," Chin said. "She's gone. I told you. She's been gone since sunrise. Since before we got here. And this man wasn't dead when B.J. and I came up the stairs."

"I could hardly see," said B.J. "How could you see, Chin?"

"I couldn't. But I stepped there." Chin pointed to the lower stair. "Where the blood is. And then I stepped on the plate of bread. So did you. If he'd been dead then, there would be blood in the bread."

"I heard someone on the stairs when we were in that other bedroom," said B.J.

" '. . . often from a reverie I have started, fancying I heard the light step of Carmilla at the drawing-room door.' " Harold's voice was pitched poetically high. He took another drink. He grew steadier and steadier. "Have you read Sheridan Le Fanu? The story of Carmilla?"

"No," said B.J.

"No. I wouldn't have expected you to," Harold said. "Nor seen *The Vampyre* performed either, I suppose. So you won't understand even though the evidence is all there. Her unnatural teeth. How she can't see herself in mirrors. The wooden stake through the heart. Blood. Horrible lusts. It takes an immortal to recognize the undead," said Harold. "Mind you, she had me fooled, too, at first, with that innocent Wild Woman act. Just like she fooled Burke. Just like she's fooled both of you. She does it well." Harold shook his head. "She does it well. I didn't really suspect the truth until this morning. In spite of the dreams."

Chin looked away from Harold, back at the dead man. There lay the dead man's hand, right on the stair where it had blocked his footstep, turned up and cupped as though waiting for someone to drop something into it. The little finger wore a thick gold band; the index finger was curled and yet still almost touched the knife. If the man had killed himself, could his hand have fallen back into that same position?

" 'Find a crime, hang a Chinaman,' " said Harold. "Perhaps you're more familiar with that quotation. How about 'a Chinaman's chance'?"

"I know these sayings," Chin said slowly. "I have no reason to hurt anyone. I didn't know this man. And I've been with B.J. Or with you. I haven't been alone."

"You're ignoring the evidence again. We have one man who's been stabbed on the stairs with a knife. And an unknown Chinaman who was the last man up those stairs. We have a second man who was stabbed. With a *chopstick*. And a lot of men who won't feel well when they wake up and won't remember very much. They'd lynch you even without my testimony. But I'll say it was you, Chin."

"That's a lie," said B.J. "*I* was the last man up the stairs. I'll tell them Chin didn't stab you."

"Very convincingly, too," said Harold. "I'm sure."

"They'll believe me," B.J. told him calmly. "It's not like it was Chin's own chopstick."

"What do you want from me?" Chin's voice was as flat as a white man's.

"I want to know where Sarah Canary is. I'm going to stop her. She has to be stopped. Don't try to stop me. Stop protecting her." Harold licked his fingers and used them to smooth his mustache.

"This is code," B.J. told Chin in a whisper. "This is the way they talk on the telegraph."

"You worship her," Harold said penetratingly.

"Stop," B.J. suggested.

"Stop," said Harold. "Tell me where she is or I'll shout for Blair." He opened his mouth.

"Stop," said B.J.

"She left with another woman," Chin told Harold. It was a betrayal, but what could he do? If this was another test, designed by the immortals, then it was a test too hard for him. His situation was exactly as Harold described it. What point was there in hanging Tom if he himself was only to hang later? "Miss Dixon. Miss Dixon was asking about the sloop B.J. and I came in on. It's called the *Biddy*. I think she's gone to Port Gamble on it. I suppose Sarah Canary is with her. I don't know where they'll go next. Really, I don't." He kept his eyes down. He was hiding nothing, but the truth is no servant to man. You can't make someone believe you just by telling the truth any more than you can make the truth false just by not believing it. "Really, I don't," Chin said again. He remembered suddenly that white demons showed their truthfulness by looking at each other's eyes. He forced himself to look at Harold's face. He focused on the tip of Harold's nose, looked up at Harold's eyes once, quickly, but couldn't sustain it and dropped his gaze to the wide wings of Harold's mustache. Harold had obviously gone mad. Chin's hands were shaking and he hid them in his coat sleeves.

"Well, that makes sense," said Harold thoughtfully. "That she would leave with another woman. That's straight from Car-

milla. I suppose they struck up a rather passionate friendship?''
Harold closed his eyes, tipped his flask to vertical, and emptied it
into his mouth. "She made me hit her," he said. "Did I tell you
that?"

Of course, Chin had hit her, too. That was why he was so eager
to prevent anyone else from hitting her. Why he had removed her
from the asylum when he had seen another woman hit. And then
Harold had taken her and struck her anyway. Chin surrendered himself to shame.

"She aroused unnatural feelings in me," Harold said. "She
wouldn't stop." He capped the flask, pocketed it. "I just hope I'm
not too late."

One of the men further down the stairs stirred suddenly. He sat
up. "Good God, Blair," he said. "You've forgotten to fill my glass."
He closed his eyes and slumped sideways again.

Harold turned to him and then turned back to Chin. "Give me
the chopstick." He took it, smiling, sheathed it in the pocket of his
coat. "Good fortune," he said, like a blessing. "Long life," he said,
like a curse. He moved the plate of bread out of his way and put his
foot in its place on the stair. His second foot hovered over the bloody
pool; he could stretch it no farther and finally withdrew it again to
the top step. "Well," he said. He put his first leg over the railing,
swinging around so that he faced Chin and the upstairs hall, seated as
if on a horse. Then he slid down, his face receding from them. The
railing turned at the landing and they saw his profile slipping away.

"He's getting smaller," B.J. remarked. "Do you see that?"

Harold disappeared from view. They heard a thump at the bottom of the stairs. "Would you like some breakfast?" Blair's voice
floated upward.

Harold answered, words Chin could not make out.

"Have you heard that your Alaskan Wild Woman is gone?" Blair
asked. "I'm dreadfully sorry. It seems Miss Adelaide Dixon is to
blame."

Another unintelligible response.

"But you don't have your bag," Blair pointed out.

"The window," Chin told B.J. as he pushed back past him. He hurried through Sarah Canary's room and out onto the roof. A tree grew at the roof's edge. It would have been easy to climb down if Chin's boots had not been so large. His foot slipped out entirely once, leaving the boot wedged by the toes in the joint between a branch and the trunk. Chin had to sit on the branch to pull the boot free. He put it back on his foot, and it fell off again when he hung from the last branch by his hands, dropping like a ripe apple when Chin swung out and down.

Will Purdy was standing before him on the walk. He held out one hand, palm up as though he were checking for rain. "You'd think the Bay View didn't have stairs," he said. Chin said nothing. What could he say? He stood on his one booted foot and thought that at least there was no sign of Harold. B.J. landed beside him.

"I don't suppose you paid Blair for breakfast?" Purdy suggested.

There was no way Chin could go back inside. There was no time to let B.J. handle this. "We could pay *you*," he said, trying to keep the desperation from his voice. "You could give the money to Blair."

Purdy regarded him for a moment and then spoke to B.J. "It was a big breakfast," he said. "Won't be cheap."

"A lot of eggs," B.J. agreed cheerfully.

Simply getting away from the Bay View would not be enough. Chin needed to get out of Seabeck and he had only a few coins left. He was forced to bargain. He spoke to B.J. in a low tone, but calculated for Purdy to hear. "We can't spend a lot on breakfast. We won't have the money for more boat trips."

"How much money do you have?" Purdy asked B.J., who looked to Chin.

"Enough for boat tickets and a small breakfast," said Chin. "Nothing more."

Purdy thought for a moment. "I'll tell you what. I figure the creek might have dropped now, enough for us to cross. You pay me for the breakfast, the big breakfast, and I'll help you hire a *hyas canim*. An Indian canoe. That would be cheaper than the steamer and you might just catch the *Biddy*. Assuming that's what you want to do." His hand was out.

Chin dropped his money into it and went to retrieve his boot.

The creek had fallen dramatically but still came to Chin's knees in the middle, and then, just when he expected it to drop again, he stepped into a hole that, even walking on his toes as he was, sent the water alarmingly high up his legs. It reached his thighs but, much to his relief, went no higher. Purdy splashed straight across, leaning to the right against the current and passing Chin, who, being smaller and lighter, found it hard to keep his feet. Chin held on to B.J.'s arm and the two of them made a crooked crossing, scrambling up the bank slightly downstream. Water ran from Chin's pants and spilled out of the tops of his boots. His feet were soaked. Chin's teeth began to click together.

He followed Purdy through a stand of trees, up a hill, down a hill, up a hill, grateful for the constant motion. At last they passed the Washington Mill Company lumberyard. The bay glittered behind it, crystalline, like the scenes that grew inside certain kinds of egg-shaped stones.

Purdy stopped at a shanty, a building made of scrap lumber from the mill that slanted so far to one side, it might have just been something the tides left, except that it was placed too high. A small stretch of grass separated the shanty from the beach, and there was dirt, too, where someone had just turned the grass, preparatory to putting in a spring garden. Purdy chose a spot for the three of them, in the sun and out of the wind. Chin stood behind B.J. and tried not to draw attention to himself by shaking with cold. His pants had dried and they chafed him with salt when he walked or shivered, stiff as the sails of a boat. Inside his boots, his feet were as wet as ever.

"Sam!" Purdy called out. "Sam Clams?"

The door to the shanty was a hanging blanket, which whipped about the empty space in the wind. An Indian came out from behind it, holding it to one side in his hand. *"Klaxta o'coke?"* he asked. He was missing one of his wolf teeth and his legs were bowed.

158

"We want a *hyas canim*," Purdy told him. "We want to catch the *Biddy*. You come and paddle. *Delate hi-hu chickerman.*"

"No," said the Indian. "You take the canoe. Buy the canoe. Pay me chickerman. But I'm not going. Too much wind."

"*Mika wake tickery momak?*"

"*Delate halo*. Boston man wants *cultus coolley* in my *canim*. Boston man *delate hyas pilton*. Boston man can paddle his own canoe."

"He'll sell us the canoe," Purdy translated for B.J. "But he won't rent it and he won't paddle it. He's being very insulting. He called me a *hyas pilton*. A big fool." He shrugged. "Indians. Nothing you can do. You just have to live with them."

"Do you?" asked B.J., suddenly interested.

"Do I what?"

"Do you live with Indians?"

"Not right with them," said Purdy.

"Oh," said B.J., turning back to Sam. The interest had faded from his voice. "I thought you said you had to."

"When did the *Biddy* go out?" Purdy asked Sam.

"Fifteen minutes ago. No more. Take the little canoe." Sam pointed down to the beach, where a small canoe was lodged on its bottom in the sand between two larger canoes, right at the water-line. As he gestured, he lost his grip on the blanket. It whipped about the doorway. B.J. gasped. Sam grabbed for it again, securing it in his fist.

"He says we can have the little canoe," Purdy translated. "He says the *Biddy* went out fifteen minutes ago." He turned back to Sam. "Isn't this canoe kind of small for the canal? I want the *Chinook canim*. The wind is too high for us to take the little one."

"Are you coming with us?" Chin asked Purdy. He tried to decide if this would be good news or bad. In the distance, seagulls called to each other over the water.

"Well," Purdy said. "Now the steamer has the boiler. I could sit there and get warm. That's pretty tempting. But I'd like to see Miss Dixon again. She owes me a gun."

159

"Boston man *hyas pilton.*" Sam stared unconcernedly off in the direction of the beach.

"I know," said B.J.

"Take the little canoe," said Sam. "I have crossed the canal in it many times."

"What do you think?" asked Purdy.

"I think it's semaphore," B.J. said. "I'm getting most of it."

Chin ignored him. "The wind is so strong," he said carefully. "It is dangerous to be on the water when the wind is strong." Tigers controlled the wind. Dragons controlled the water. A wise man did not get caught between the two. A wise man did not get caught between the white men and the Indians either.

Purdy nodded. "I want the Chinook canoe," he told Sam again. "The *hyas canim.*"

"It's not for sale. Just the little one."

Purdy was getting angry. "I don't want to buy it. I just want to rent it. I've rented it before. *Mika wake tickery momak?* We have offered you much *chickerman.* Why are you wasting our time?"

"Belle Starr lives with Indians," B.J. said. "I don't know if she has to. She's married to one of them."

Sam spat from between the gap in his teeth. He had to smile to do this. The wind carried the spit away. Then the wind dropped suddenly. The blanket barely shivered in Sam's hand. It made a noise like a small clap. The wind came back.

"Is this a good thing?" B.J. asked. "Would Indians want this?"

Sam stopped smiling. "Is that man with you?" Chin turned to look where Sam was looking, down to the beach. Harold was there, standing in the space between the two larger canoes. He glanced up at them briefly. Then, as they watched, he began to push the little canoe out into the water, splashing along behind it.

"Why is that man stealing my canoe?" Sam asked, while Chin shouted at Harold to stop, but the words came out in Cantonese and Harold couldn't have heard them anyway. Harold was knee-deep in the bay now, tipping the canoe almost horizontal in order to climb inside. Once he was settled, sitting toward the back, he pulled a paddle from the bottom. The wind was behind him and blew his hair into his face. It pushed the little boat quickly forward across the lines of the waves to the choppy circles of deep water.

VI

In 1854, the new governor of the Washington Territory, Major Isaac I. Stevens, stopped in Seattle village to address the Indian population. Good times were coming for them, he said. All the blessings of civilization plus free vegetable seeds from the Department of Agriculture. He invited Chief Seattle to respond.

The chief, who was more than a foot taller than Stevens, made a very long speech, resting his hand the whole time on the governor's head. According to eyewitness accounts, Stevens looked pained. The Battle of Seattle took place two years later.

The original name of Seattle village was Duwamps. The early white settlers felt that this sounded too much like someone being sick to his stomach and did not want it on their letters and packages. They changed the name to Seattle in honor of the chief. It was a gesture that upset him enormously.

Among Seattle's early landmarks was the Mad House, a house of prostitution run by John Pennell. Although there were a few white women, most of Pennell's prostitutes were Indians from the Dwamish tribe. Pennell had purchased the women from their chiefs with Hudson Bay blankets. The Hudson Bay Company wanted money and sometimes land for their blankets, so Pennell's offer was a real bargain. The blankets were of the first quality, but Pennell did not even demand the most beautiful of the Indian women in exchange, although all the Dwamish had lush and glossy hair, an effect they enhanced, according to tribal custom, with frequent urine rinses and fish oil rubs, until they came to the Mad House and such treatments were forbidden. Pennell's clientele was so squeamish.

By 1873, the Mad House had closed and the Chinese occupied that section of Seattle. Most of the Puget Sound Indians wore white men's clothing, lived in houses, and found employment in white men's homes and mills and on white men's boats. They had adopted

163

white methods of fishing; they retained their own canoes but outfitted them with sails and oars; they played games of skill with bows and arrows, but baseball was a more popular pastime. Their condition was characterized by their white contemporaries as a state of half-civilization.

In this same year, on the California–Oregon border, the Modoc War ended with the trial of Captain Jack and five other Modoc leaders. For six months, fifty Modoc warriors had engaged a thousand U.S. soldiers in a conflict whose every twist was thoroughly covered for the Eastern newspapers by correspondents on the scene. These reports were a continual source of humiliation for the Army. On June 1, 1873, Captain Jack allowed himself to be captured, explaining that his legs had given out. He and the five codefendants were charged with the murders of two peace commissioners: General Canby, the only General to be killed in an Indian war, and the Reverend Mr. Thomas. The trial was conducted without defense council and in a language none of the defendants really spoke. The sentence was death.

Public opinion favored clemency toward Barncho and Slolux, the youngest of the captured Modocs. President Grant commuted their sentences to life imprisonment, stipulating that they not be told of this until the hangings one month later. Six men rode to the gallows seated on four coffins. Barncho and Slolux spent five years on Alcatraz Island and then were released. Captain Jack, Schonchin John, Black Jim, and Boston Charley were executed. Their Modoc names, the names they had in their own language, are not remembered.

William Cody won his new name while working as a buffalo hunter for the Kansas Pacific Railroad. For eighteen months he supplied buffalo meat to the railroad hands. They called him Buffalo Bill, a title, he said in his autobiography, of which he was never ashamed. He had killed 4,280 buffaloes.

In 1871, a small technological breakthrough in the process of tanning buffalo hides resulted in the final massacre of the prairie buffalo. By 1873, a traveler to Fort Dodge described the north bank of the Arkansas River as "a continual line of putrescent carcasses" so that the very "air was rendered pestilential." Buffalo hunter Frank

Nixon boasted of having killed one hundred and twenty buffalo in forty minutes, an average of one every twenty seconds, and to kill one hundred from a single stand was not uncommon.

The buffalo were not reproducing at the rate of one every twenty seconds. It was soon necessary to follow them into the Comanche lands of the Panhandle, a place where white men were forbidden to go. In 1873, the 7th Regiment, disassembled over the last two years and sent to protect the South against the Ku Klux Klan, was reunited to serve again on the plains under the leadership of George Armstrong Custer.

Chief Seattle's address to the territorial governor of Washington is supposed to have ended with these words: ". . . At night when the streets of your cities and villages are silent and you think them deserted, they will throng with the hosts that once filled and still love this beautiful land. The white man will never be alone. Let him be just and deal kindly with my people, for the dead are not powerless. Dead, did I say? There is no death, only a change of worlds."

CHAPTER TWELVE

A RAINY DAY
ON HOOD CANAL

Too distant to arrest the feet
That walk this plank of balm —
Before them lies escapeless sea —
The way is closed they came.

EMILY DICKINSON,
1873

The blanket in the doorway to Sam Clams's house was made of cotton from fireweed, duck feathers, and the hair of a white dog. A Salish woman's wealth had once been counted in these dogs, but the breed was extinct now and the blankets were rare. B.J. knew a lot about Indians, because the Indian agent had been interned periodically at Steilacoom. He had told B.J. that Indians were less sensitive to physical pain than white men; he had described religious ceremonies, ceremonies of *black tamahnous*, in which they cut and bit themselves, and he said that they could endure easily numbers of fleas that would drive a white man out of his mind.

Their susceptibility to other kinds of pain was a subject on which the agent was less sure. They were seldom insane; Dr. Carr had told B.J. that. There were exceptions, of course: a Clallam Indian who was struck in his youth by a falling tree so that some of his brains spilled out; a Twana who had a long series of troubles with different wives and developed a quiet, self-deprecating insanity, eventually running away and hiding in the forest.

There were occasional suicides, always women. The Indians described sorrow as the sensation of being stuck with a needle in the heart. The white men named villages and rivers after men, because it did not hurt white men to hear the names of the dead. The Indian heart was made of mud, the Indians had told the agent. The white man's heart was made of stone.

B.J. noted two iron spearheads leaning against the doorway and decided that Sam Clams was probably a seal hunter and might be a wealthy man if he didn't hold to the old potlatch way of thinking that giving things away made men important, if he understood that money was now wealth. "Pay me *chickerman*," Sam had said, so he probably did understand, and, anyway, the days when Indians could be paid with a cotton handkerchief for a day's work were over. Seal hunting was becoming a profitable business and the white men kept as much of it to themselves as they could.

Look at me, the blanket in the doorway told B.J. insistently. I am trying to tell you something.

Before things changed, the blanket said, twisting about in Sam's fist, animals were much more like people than they are now. In this time, Coyote had a daughter who was known for her speed. She wished to marry Raven, a man from another village, and he wished to marry her, but Coyote opposed the union, saying that Raven was not her equal. He was not as fast as Coyote. He was not as skilled with *syuid*, the language of power. Why should she marry someone less than her father?

I've heard this story, B.J. told the blanket in his mind. Only instead of Coyote, it was a king, and instead of being known for her speed, she was known for her goodness, and instead of wishing to marry a Raven, she wished to marry a woodcutter. Except for that, it was the same story.

B.J. wondered for a moment if the blanket itself was talking or if Sam was secretly directing the blanket in coded patterns for B.J. The Indians on the plains communicated with blankets and smoke. Why not blankets and wind? B.J. looked more closely at Sam's hand. A tattoo of three semicircles decorated his wrist. His hand did not appear to move.

Suddenly the blanket escaped from Sam's fingers and flew at B.J.'s face, making him gasp. Pay attention now, it said sharply. Stop thinking and listen to me. Just listen.

Coyote wished to marry his daughter himself, the blanket said. He would tell his daughter she must marry a certain man from the Yakima tribe and then he would disguise himself as this man. B.J. could scarcely imagine such perfidy, but he had the impression that the blanket rather admired it.

Sam caught the blanket again. The story became quieter. Coyote's daughter ignored his wishes and married Raven. And then Coyote took some pine and made a box big enough for two people. He put his daughter and his son-in-law in the box and he nailed it shut. He towed the box out into the ocean behind his canoe and cut it loose.

He thought the box would sink. But it did not. Coyote tried to push the box under the water. It rose again to the top. Coyote stepped out of the canoe and danced on the box. When he danced on one end, that end dipped under the water. When he danced on the other end, *that* end dipped. But the box would not sink. Coyote jumped up and down on the box. He jumped high into the air and a great wave moved the box from beneath him. Coyote fell into the water. His canoe had already floated away.

The Changer came by in another canoe. "Where is your daughter, Coyote?" he asked. "What are you doing?"

"*Syuid*," Coyote answered. "I am making fog." And he made a great fog to hide himself from the Changer and he made this fog by correctly naming the part of his body through which he urinated.

His male member? B.J. asked in silent surprise.

That is not the correct name, said the blanket. The blanket was laughing at him.

"I know," said B.J.

"You can't hide from me, Coyote," said the Changer, and he woke the Thunderbird, who flapped his wings and spit lightning and blew Coyote's great fog away. Then, without the fog, the Changer saw Coyote and the Thunderbird saw the box. The Thunderbird thought the box was a whale. The Thunderbird ate whales and so he sent a lightning bolt from his mouth to kill the whale, but the lightning went wide into the water. The Thunderbird circled lower to try again, but there was no whale, only a box, and the Thunderbird was now close enough to see this. The Thunderbird took the box in his talons and carried it into the sky. The sky was much closer to the earth than it is now. It was not so high. The Thunderbird left the box on the ground of the skyworld.

Day came by and found the box. He opened it and saw the man and the woman. He took the man out. He didn't want the woman, so he left her inside and nailed the box shut again. Day had five beautiful daughters, and he told Raven they would all be his wives if Raven came home with him. Day left to chase an elk and told Raven to wait for him to come back. Raven sat on the box and waited until it grew dark. Then Night came to Raven. "I have five beautiful daughters," Night told him. "Come with me and they will all be your wives." So Raven followed Night home on the bright paths that Night used. Being so dark himself, he couldn't see to find his way on dark paths.

Four of Night's daughters were waiting for him at Night's house. They were very beautiful, and on their foreheads each had painted one aspect of the moon. The youngest girl wore the full moon, the next youngest wore the waxing moon, the next the waning moon, and the oldest wore only a tiny crescent. The girls bathed Raven and rubbed his body with the oil of the dead so that he became as black as Night. They offered him food, but it was the food of the dead, and Raven did not eat it. He ate roots instead. He went to bed with the four daughters of the Night. In the morning, the girls got dressed to go hunting. "Why are there only four of you?" Raven asked them. "Night told me he had five daughters."

The girls pointed to a box at one end of the room. "There is our eldest sister," they said. "She is the dark moon that no man can see. She is your wife, too, and she slept with us last night, but she never comes out of her box in the daytime. She is very beautiful in the dark, but the brightness of day would kill her. You must believe us and not try to see her for yourself." The four daughters of the Night left Raven alone with the box. Raven opened it at once.

"I know this story," said B.J. Only instead of Raven, it was Pandora, and instead of the daughter of the Night, it was all the troubles of the world. Plus hope. Except for that, it was the same story.

Stop thinking, said the blanket. Just listen. When Night had found Raven, he had seen Coyote's box. Inside, he thought, there must be a woman as beautiful as my eldest daughter. And he had gone back later to fetch it. This was the box that Raven opened, so the woman inside was not Night's daughter, but Coyote's.

"You stink of death," she told Raven. "You have eaten the food of the dead."

Raven denied it. "I ate only roots," he said. But she would not listen. She left the house of the Night and went on the dark paths and Raven followed her, knowing as long as he stayed in the dark, Night could not see him. "Roots!" he called to the daughter of Coyote. "Roots!"

The daughter of Coyote walked many miles in the skyworld looking for Spider. She wanted to talk him into lowering her back to earth. She could not find him, but she found his cord. She threw it out of the skyworld and began to descend it. Raven flew behind her. "Roots!" he called. "Roots!" The cord did not reach to earth. The sky was much higher than the daughter of Coyote expected. She fell the rest of the way and it was a long fall.

On earth, everything had been changed. Everything was the way things are now. The Changer had changed everyone except for Coyote's daughter, because she had been hidden in her box in the house of the Night and the Changer had not seen her. And so Coyote's daughter is more like a coyote than most women and more like a woman than most coyotes.

"What do you think?" Purdy asked.

"I think it's semaphore," B.J. said. "I'm getting most of it." He expected Chin to be pleased with this, but Chin wore his usual unhappy, eyes-closed-to-slits expression and didn't respond to B.J. Chin spoke to Purdy instead, which was rude of Chin, but B.J. understood. In Chin's defense, B.J. had noticed that Chin suffered from some sort of phobia about boats and another about Indians, and right now Chin was trying to rent the one from the other. Of course, he was unhappy.

Boats had maimed and killed many more people in the Puget Sound area than Indians had, even counting the war in 1855–56, and yet a certain uncomfortableness around Indians was considered only natural and this same uncomfortableness around boats was a sign of insanity. B.J. didn't understand. One of the men in the Steilacoom asylum had been bruised and scalded on the *Fairy* when her boiler exploded just out of the Steilacoom dock. He had been thrown into the air like a Fourth of July rocket and he'd lost the hearing in his left ear. He still had a red mark on his chest, shaped like the pad of a bear's paw and just about the size of a watch, B.J. thought, but he couldn't be sure about the size and it might have been smaller.

Dr. Carr specialized in boat phobias and would have found Chin an interesting study. He had told B.J. once that a sudden irrational fear of boats was common in women about to give birth. And then B.J. knew, the whole nation knew, about Abraham Lincoln's recurring black boat dreams. Although Chin might not know. B.J. made a mental note to tell Chin about this sometime when he had nothing else to say.

In fact, and less in Chin's defense, Chin often didn't respond to B.J., not just when they were around boats and Indians. B.J. minded this, because it made him wonder sometimes if he had spoken at all, which made him wonder if he was really there. He could always ask

Chin, though, and when he did, Chin always told him he was, so it was better than before he had met Chin.

Chin often didn't respond to other people either, making B.J. answer for him. B.J. minded this, too, because he was afraid to be wrong, but he was becoming less afraid. Chin was smart and often he told B.J. how to respond to people so that B.J. looked like the smart one. It wasn't as hard to look smart as B.J. had always thought. He could do it himself sometimes, even without Chin. He said something to Purdy now about Belle Starr, something Chin probably wouldn't have known any more than he'd know about Abraham Lincoln, although Chin could surprise you sometimes and he knew about Patrick Henry and he could recite the first two lines of "Paul Revere's Ride" just like everyone else could.

B.J. looked back at the blanket. It was trembling in anticipation. But the Changer knows that he missed her, the blanket said with a sharp flap and two small flutters. He looks for the daughter of Coyote. He looks for a woman who is followed by a black bird. When he finds her, when he changes her, the Change will be complete. Then time will stop. Then everything will stay, always, the way it is now. Then there will be no more changes.

"Is this a good thing?" B.J. asked the blanket. "Would Indians want this?"

"Is that man with you?" Sam was looking away from them, down toward the beach. B.J. turned to see Harold pushing the smallest of the canoes into the water. The smallest canoe was a fishing canoe, made of a single piece of fir, meant for rivers and lakes. It was too little for the canal, unless Harold stayed close to the shoreline.

"Why is that man stealing my canoe?" Sam asked.

Harold gripped the dugout by the gunwale and tilted it. Water poured off the legs of his pants as he climbed inside. B.J. watched Harold and let Chin answer Sam. Chin's answer was a shout in a code B.J. couldn't translate, but this didn't mean Sam might not understand. Except that Sam repeated his question. "That man has stolen my canoe. Why?"

Purdy cleared his throat. "That man is the manager of the Alaskan Wild Woman. She left Seabeck this morning on the *Biddy* with someone else. Probably he wants to get her back. We were hoping to catch up to her ourselves."

"Is there some way we could get to her first?" Chin asked in a funny voice, as if he might have hurt his throat with his shouting, as if his throat was full of fog. He looked at B.J. Help, his expression said. It was an expression B.J. had become familiar with. Chin was telling B.J. to say something, but he was not telling B.J. what to say.

"Harold wants her to stop," B.J. told Purdy. "He's not fooled by her innocent Wild Woman act any longer." He looked at Chin for guidance, for approval or disapproval.

Chin offered neither. He was staring instead out over the water, where Harold and the little canoe grew even littler. "He does not have her interests in his heart," Chin added in his low unhappy voice as if he wished he were not speaking at all.

"No," said B.J. "Nor her chopstick. Not anymore."

"Three dollars to rent the *hyas canim*," said Sam.

"Fine," said Purdy.

"I will take you to the *Biddy*. On the way you will help me recover my stolen canoe." Sam looked out over the canal, where Harold could no longer be seen. "Three dollars and my wife will come and paddle, too," Sam said.

The sky behind the shanty darkened, the wind died, and somewhere in the distance, somewhere in the mountains, there was thunder. Everyone stopped for a moment and looked toward it. Even the seagulls were silent.

"The dwarves are playing tenpins," said Purdy lightheartedly.

"The Thunderbird is flapping his wings," said Sam Clams, and his tone was one of ominous import.

"The Thunder God is punishing lazy dragons," said Chin, whose boat phobia was showing again in the trembling of his voice.

The blanket was still.

. . .

The canoe had a flat stern for rough waters and a bow carved with the face of a frog. It tilted wildly until Sam slapped the blade of his paddle against the surface of the water, holding it there a moment to keep them from capsizing. Sam was steering from the backmost position. B.J. heard the sound of the paddle striking the water. He turned from his place just behind Purdy in the bow in time to see Chin dropping his paddle onto the floor of the canoe and grabbing with both hands at the gunwale. B.J. thought that Chin was probably as white as he was ever going to get.

Sam had given Chin a woman's paddle, which was an insult if Chin had only understood it as one. Instead Chin had simply accepted the paddle he was offered. Now he retrieved it, dipping into the water with the shallow, splashing stroke of a woman, only more awkward. B.J. had seen mother ducks feign injury and flap above the water as if they had only one good wing in order to draw a hunter away from the nest. This charade was what Chin's paddling reminded him of.

Behind Chin sat Sam's wife, a short woman with long hair. No one had actually told B.J. her name, but Purdy had called her Old Patsy when they first took their seats in the dugout. Really she wasn't that old. She had waited behind while the men climbed aboard, pushing the men and the canoe into the water over a track of sticks and then wading after it to scramble in. "Come on, Old Patsy," Purdy had said from his seat in the bow. Old Patsy spoke only to Sam and not in a language B.J. could decipher or in one Purdy seemed to know. She had a paddle like Chin's and a quick, graceful stroke. Sam steered. His paddle was made of yew, five feet long, a fine expensive *Makah* paddle that he drove deep into the canal. They all sat to one side and leaned against the wind, which came from behind and across them. The paddling was almost unnecessary to their forward motion; the wind moved them northward, but without their own efforts and without Sam's steering, it would have also blown them back to shore.

Sam and Purdy had begun the trip with an argument about the advisability of using a sail. Sam had two sails stowed in the bottom of the canoe. They had been pieced together out of old flour sacks, but Sam said the wind was too strong to risk them. "One sail only," Purdy suggested, but Sam still refused, hinting that the crew was unreliable.

A wave splashed up and over the gunwale. B.J. was already tired. His hands were wet and cold where the water ran down the paddle every time he lifted it for another stroke. He was beginning to feel the strain in one spot beneath his shoulder blade, the same spot that had always hurt him at the asylum when he had wood-chopping duties. He rested a moment, rubbing his back, and watching the shoreline. The dugout moved quickly. The scenery was continually changing as if a long painting were being rolled by them: sometimes beaches, sometimes forest, once a group of Indian shanties thrown up together along the stony coast and all tipped in the same direction as the wind. Small, muddy children came out as they passed, singing and whistling and pounding on a drum to give them good weather. B.J. waved, turning when they were behind him, until the shore curved out and he couldn't see them anymore. Sometimes B.J. saw logs that had been lost on their way to the lumber mills and were now beached or wedged against rockier parts of the coast. An occasional seagull flew overhead. Once, they passed a tree that bent double in the wind right before their eyes and cracked across its trunk. It fell over into the canal several yards behind them with an enormous splash, sending them skidding forward. The incident made B.J. remember Dr. Carr's suspicions concerning the magnetized trees left behind for the French Revolution. It was a dangerous world, no doubt about it, and there was really no way to anticipate its many dangers. Not when trees were willing to sacrifice themselves for malice.

They rounded a small point, struggling with all their weight and muscle against the wind, the big canoe blown almost sideways. Then their direction changed and the wind was entirely favorable now, throwing them forward at great speed. They all pulled their paddles in, setting them on the thwarts to rest. They flew past the entrance to a small bay with a stony beach. A large rock jutted out into the water, the waves battering themselves white against it.

Behind the big rock was another stand of trees, whose tops were bent and tossed in the wind. Halfway past, B.J. saw a canoe lodged between two of the trees, the bow and the stern set within the two forks of four branches. The branches beneath it bent. Those above blew about. The canoe seemed to shake precariously in midair. B.J. turned, pointing to make sure that Chin saw it as well. "Rock-a-bye baby in the treetop," B.J. said.

"How did a canoe get into a tree?" Chin asked. B.J. wondered if Chin thought the canoe might have simply blown there on an earlier occasion when someone had been foolish enough to try to take it out onto the canal in bad weather. He looked that frightened.

"The Indians bury their dead in canoes," B.J. told him, "since they don't bury them. They put the canoes in trees or sometimes they build scaffolds if there are no good trees." When the wind blows, the cradle will rock.

"And sometimes when white men want a *canim* but do not want to give their *chickerman* to an Indian, they come and dump the dead man out," Sam said. The wind blew Sam's voice up to the bow of the canoe. Sam spoke very little and always with an expressionlessness that suggested what he was saying was unimportant, but there was something important in what he was not saying. B.J. couldn't imagine what this might be, but surely Chin knew. B.J. didn't let it trouble him. When the bough breaks, the cradle will fall.

"Bad white men!" Purdy added in a shout over one shoulder. He swiveled around to address them head-on. "So now bad Indians stab holes in the burial canoes and cover the holes with mud and sticks. A man takes the canoe out on the canal and doesn't know about the holes until it's too late and the mud has washed off."

"The dead man's canoe," Sam repeated. He said something else, something to Old Patsy, something simple and short that B.J. couldn't understand. Something the wind blew away.

CHAPTER THIRTEEN

THE STORY
OF THE DRAGON'S GATE

The Clouds their Backs together laid
The North begun to push
The Forests galloped till they fell
The Lightning played like mice

EMILY DICKINSON,
1870

The trees stretched endlessly to the right and ahead. All their branches were empty now. It was early afternoon, although the sky was dark with clouds and the water was dark and clouded, too, having no sunlight to reflect. Small, child-sized pops of distant thunder came rolling across the choppy water from the mountains. B.J. was cold. He paddled hard to warm himself.

"We've had a good wind," said Purdy. "We must be close to halfway there."

"Shouldn't we be catching Harold soon?" Chin asked anxiously. He had taken up his paddle again himself. Old Patsy paddled on the right. The men were arranged in the left side of the dugout. The canoe flew forward like a large bird with many wings, like a water bug with an asymmetrical number of legs. They reached another small point where the direction of the coastline changed. Now the wind drove the canoe out toward the deeper water. Sam worked with a pole against the bottom to prevent this.

"We would be going faster if we left the coast a bit," Purdy suggested over his shoulder. "More in a straight line."

Sam used his pole to push them in closer to the beach. "Too dangerous," he answered.

"That's probably what Harold's done," Purdy called back. "And then, he had a bit of a headstart." Purdy paddled vigorously, then twisted around again. "We may have already passed him. He might not have been able to hold a course, one man by himself. It took all of us to keep from being blown into shore back there."

They worked in silence. B.J.'s hands were so cold they wouldn't tighten on the paddle, but his left hand, the one on the paddle's throat, slipped up and down along the wood with every rhythmic stroke. His arms ached. Soon he would have blisters, a reddening just under the heart line on his palm. Suddenly his paddle grew enormous in his hands. He could still pull it through the water, but at the end of each pull, he could scarcely lift it to finish the circle. He let it drag a few feet, resting his arms and rubbing the painful spot beneath his shoulder blade. The paddle bounced over the waves, splashing him with water until he pulled it back into the canoe. He looked for something to wrap his hands with. Old Patsy had packed them a lunch in a basket. B.J. removed the lid. There was bread and cold potatoes and crackers wrapped in a blue checkered handkerchief. B.J. unwrapped them, sampled a cracker, and bound up his hand.

The canoe tipped, throwing him sideways and forward against the thwart, scattering the crackers into the bottom of the dugout, and sending Purdy sprawling onto his knees in the bow before him. They were about thirty yards out now, too deep for poling. He heard the sound of Sam's paddle hitting the water. B.J. forced himself to lean back, to counter the tipping dugout. He thrust his body far out over the gunwale into the spray of the waves. The water beneath him was murky. Somewhere below B.J., below the waterline, was a darkness shaped vaguely like their canoe. B.J. might have been imagining it. It seemed to slide along beside them, pacing them, like the boat's own shadow, only unattached. There was a second slap as Sam struck the water. Their shadow disappeared.

"I think we're going to get some rain!" Purdy called down to the stern. Even as he spoke, the first few large drops hit the inch or so of water at the bottom of the canoe. The drops punched holes into the water and then filled the holes with themselves. The rain stopped.

When it started again, it came in a downpour, slanting in slightly from behind them. Purdy set his paddle aside. The wind was more moderate now that it was raining. Purdy unrolled one of the mats that had been stowed next to the lunch basket. He unrolled a second mat, held the first over his head to cover himself, and gestured for B.J. to join him. "Take a break," he suggested. "Come in out of the rain."

B.J. slid forward in the dugout and slipped under the second mat. The two of them were faced backward now; the rain drummed steadily above their heads. B.J. sank down so that the sides of the canoe provided some shelter from the wind. The crackers he had spilled floated at his feet like tiny rafts.

The two Indians wore coats woven of cattail rushes and fastened at the sides. These coats seemed to shed the rain so that only the Indians' heads were unprotected. Chin's clothing was quickly soaked. His queue drew whatever rain fell on his hair, gathering it into one stream of water that ran down from his shoulder.

"Bad luck," said Purdy. "Cursed luck. Of course, bad luck for Harold, too, wherever he is." He lowered his arms so the mat rested directly on his hair. His curly beard was spangled with drops of water. Drops dangled from the hairs above his mouth. "That he would threaten a defenseless woman. It's unthinkable." Holding the mat on his head with one hand, he wiped his beard dry and then reached for one of the cold potatoes. He chewed on it reflectively. "I tried to tell that to Miss Adelaide Dixon," he said. "She was in no danger last night. Not that I would have had a lady stay at the Bay View, if the choice had been mine. Certainly, a great deal of drink was consumed, and certainly, the fun was a bit on the rough side. A sort of chivaree almost, only without the bridegroom, and, of course, that's always been Miss Dixon's choice."

He took another bite of potato. "I'm not trying to excuse anything, but we've had a spot of trouble at the Washington Mill Company recently and a great deal of stress for the men. Still, the fun was of a rough sort and nothing a lady needed to witness. It was my intention to escort her out of there myself. But she was in no actual danger. Out here in the west, women are like precious jewels. Out here in the west, a woman, any woman, is a queen." He called against the wind, down to the stern of the canoe. "Sam, Old Patsy is going to have to start bailing soon."

B.J. fetched a potato for himself. He chose a large one for Chin since it was past lunchtime. He put his mat down and slid forward without lifting his feet while the crackers danced about his toes. B.J. walked like a duck with his knees bent, one hand on the gunwale for balance, the potatoes cupped against his chest, back to where Chin was paddling steadily if futilely. He tried not to make the canoe rock. Raindrops pounded on Purdy's mat behind B.J. They dripped down to the canoe floor below. Rain fell into B.J.'s face and onto the potatoes. Chin put his paddle down to eat. He took big bites. He looked unhappy, but when didn't Chin look unhappy? The moment he stopped paddling, Chin began to shiver. B.J. went back to the bow and picked up his mat. Chin finished the potato and picked up his paddle.

The water around their feet was rising. B.J. leaned out over the gunwale again, holding his mat carefully above his head. He got wetter anyway. The spray around their boat was only half made up of water falling down from the sky. The other half was water tossed back up by the wind and the paddles. B.J. couldn't really see into the water with all the disturbances on the surface, but he thought that their shadow was back. Chin's paddle appeared to be chasing it, hovering in the air just above it, but always cutting into the water a foot or so behind.

In China, dragons control the water and the rain, Chin had told B.J. on their long trip into Seabeck when the wind was against them. The *shen lung* rule the sky and the sea and the marshes. In China, Chin said, there is a certain waterfall in a certain western mountain stream, which is named the Dragon's Gate. If a carp is able, as few are, to jump from the lower pools beneath the falls to the higher pools above it, then the carp has passed through the Dragon's Gate and is rewarded for its strength and its bravery. It is transformed into a spirit dragon.

B.J. liked this story particularly because of its democratic message. Any ordinary carp has the chance to become *shen lung*. Chin agreed, and told him about another category of dragon, the *lan lung*, the lazy dragon. Lazy dragons hid when it was time to make rain, sometimes in people's clothing. When a man was hit with lightning, the way William Gassey, Purdy's ticket-of-leave man had been, it was usually because the Thunder God had hurled it at the lazy dragon sleeping in his sleeve. Chin's mother had called him *lan lung* sometimes and so had his uncle, Chin told B.J. And Chin said sadly that this was partly an evaluation of what they thought he could do, and partly a statement about what they thought he would do. The Dragon's Gate, said Chin, was sometimes used as a metaphor for the Imperial Examinations. Chin had studied for the Imperial Examinations; his mother, like all mothers with clever sons, had hoped he would become a mandarin. But Chin had ended up in Golden Mountain instead.

B.J. raised his mat to look back at Chin, who was paddling hard, breathing through his mouth sort of like a fish. B.J. didn't have a mother or an uncle himself, but Chin's story had reminded him of another story he heard once, so he had told his to Chin in his turn, only instead of a carp, B.J.'s story had been about an ordinary mortal, and instead of jumping a waterfall, the mortal had to be kind to an annoying old woman who was really a beautiful fairy in disguise, and instead of becoming a dragon, the mortal had been granted three wishes. He thought that Chin had liked B.J.'s story as much as B.J. had liked Chin's. Chin had said that he, too, knew stories where ordinary mortals were rewarded for their kindness to annoying old women. Chin had appeared quite cheered up by the exchange, wearing a completely different expression for a while, until B.J. had made the mistake of telling him that here in Washington the Indians said that the Thunderbird controlled the rain, which gave Chin back his thinking-of-Indians face.

"Have you ever seen a dragon?" B.J. had asked Chin, who said no, but he knew a man who knew a man who'd seen a dead one once, washed up on the beach in his village. It was fifteen feet long, blue in color, with eyes like a cow and four legs and scales all over its body.

B.J. searched for the shadow. He tried to gauge its size, but the water was an unsteady lens and B.J. was not good at sizes. It might have been fifteen feet. It might have been smaller. It might have been blue.

It might not have been there at all. B.J. didn't really believe that a Chinese dragon would be out here on Hood Canal. He wasn't *that* crazy. He wouldn't have believed in Chinese dragons at all if Chin hadn't known a man who knew a man who'd seen a dead one. Chin hadn't lied to him yet, not as far as he knew.

"Mind you, some women take advantage of their position," Purdy said. "I've seen women smoking cigarillos. Out in public. I've heard language you wouldn't expect from a miner. If I told you some of the things Miss Adelaide Dixon said in her lecture, you would refuse to believe me. I've seen women ride with the horses right between their legs."

B.J. sat back in the canoe. "Like Belle Starr," he agreed. "But you mustn't make too much of the horses. Not when the women have access to pens and knives as well. Although I've done this myself," he added generously. "Until Dr. Carr explained things. Anyone could."

"I don't know much about Belle Starr," Purdy answered. "But

Miss Adelaide Dixon certainly has access to both. Adelaide Dixon has *my* knife, if we want to get technical about it. And I miss it sometimes.''

Old Patsy squatted, rocking from side to side, the bottom of her coat just touching the floor of the canoe. She had a bailer with a handle about six inches long and a cup about five inches deep. Old Patsy worked to scoop water out, tossing it cupful by cupful into the ocean. Without the rocking, she could have been digging in her spring garden. The motion was very much the same. The water in the canoe didn't diminish, but it stopped rising. She harvested the sodden crackers that had floated into her reach and bailed them out with the rainwater. B.J. watched them dotting the waves behind the canoe like a trail of bread crumbs. He felt anxious suddenly. He wouldn't have believed in mermaids either until he had seen a dead one himself. What if, in spite of what Burke had said, they existed in places other than Australia? What was to prevent it? The ocean was the same, wasn't it?

What if—B.J.'s heart was sitting in his throat now—what if the Australian mermaid was a dwarfed variety and larger specimens frequented colder coasts? He had a sudden vivid vision of Sam, standing up in the stern and thrusting his spear over the gunwale and into the water. The head on a seal spear was made to detach from the handle but was wound with fishing line. In B.J.'s vision, Sam played the creature with the line, slowly and patiently, playing her like a big fish but always bringing her up closer to the surface and that inevitable moment when she broke through, the spear head deep in her womanlike neck, her tail thrashing, and her face the same eternity of agony he'd seen in Burke's cabin. Only very much larger.

Sam would not do this if he knew what he was going to catch. The Indians did not like to see anything odd—a white squirrel, for instance, or a frog with its head cut off. They thought such oddities were messages, were omens of evil. When an Indian saw something he had never seen before, it might mean a bad storm was coming or a bad illness or it might mean a death, which could always turn out to be your own. And the Indians put a great deal of faith in dreams, sleeping dreams and waking visions like the one B.J. had just had.

"Ladies should be ladies," said Purdy. "That's all I'm saying. Miss Adelaide Dixon wants to be treated like a lady, but she doesn't want to behave like one. You know the type?"

"Yes," said B.J., who hadn't been listening at all but was still able to reconstruct the words after he realized a question had been asked and felt, in any case, that *yes* was generally the safest answer to anything. Behind them one cracker crested a wave and then disappeared suddenly, too suddenly, not as if the wave had simply curled over it, but as if something had come up from beneath and swallowed it. A moment later a second cracker vanished. B.J. could see none of the crackers now.

"I was hoping to have a chance to talk to you alone," Purdy said. "After we'd left Seabeck safely behind." His voice was low beneath the sound of the rain on the mats. With a great effort, B.J. put mermaids out of his mind. He stopped watching for crackers. He moved closer to Purdy in the bow. He wished he could talk to Chin instead. Chin would know if there was a mermaid following them or not and why. Shouldn't the mermaid be following Harold? Harold was the one who'd purchased her. Harold was the one who planned to exhibit her, breasts and all. What had B.J. done? He hadn't known it was her blanket he was taking. He'd put it right back.

"We left a bit of nastiness back in the Bay View Hotel this morning," Purdy told B.J.

"*We* left a dead man," B.J. remembered suddenly. "On the stairs What did you leave?" Ordinarily he would have said less and allowed Purdy to say more. He was upset. This made him thoughtless and reckless, and he recognized it, but too late.

"You saw him?" Purdy crossed himself with the remains of his potato and then popped it in his mouth. "Yes. Jim Allen."

"Stabbed."

"Yes."

"Dead."

"Yes."

"The knife was the same knife Blair had in the kitchen," B.J. said. "I recognized it. Unless it was bigger." Probably the knife had told someone to kill Jim Allen. Knives were nasty things and full of

185

their own suggestions. That didn't mean you had to listen. What if everyone went around doing whatever knives told them to do?

"I see where your thinking is leading you," Purdy said. "But you mustn't blame Blair. He's half white, you know. And he's got his little girl, Jenny, to think of. He would never risk going to jail and leaving her unprotected. It would be different if she was married, of course. She *should* be married. Most Indian girls are married at twelve, and Jenny's fifteen. Treating her like a white woman won't make her one, will it, B.J.? More likely to make her dissatisfied and sulky. I've said as much to Blair myself. She's got considerably less white blood than he does."

B.J. began to chew on one end of the checkered handkerchief with which he'd bound his left hand. He hoped Purdy wasn't hinting what he thought Purdy might be hinting. That was all B.J. needed. A wife. He undid the knot with his teeth, wiped his face with the handkerchief, and watched the trees sliding past on the shore. The canoe was farther out now and the shoreline was blurred through the curtain of rain, but he could see the tossing of the treetops. He looked over the murky water between him and the trees. He never looked down at all.

"I don't imagine the man who killed Jim Allen intended to implicate Blair," Purdy said. "I imagine he just didn't have his own knife for some reason or other." Purdy looked straight at B.J. "I want to say something in defense of the men of Seabeck," he said.

He was quiet then, long enough for B.J. to conclude that while Purdy *wanted* to say something in defense of the men of Seabeck, he couldn't, in fact, think of anything to say.

B.J. tried to help. "They seem to be very good shots," he suggested. "They got almost every window." Or maybe he didn't say it, because Purdy cleared his throat and went on as if B.J. hadn't spoken.

"When the Indian Department issued their order for all the squaws to be taken from the white men and put onto the Indian reservations, *except* in those cases where the white men married them, I don't know of a single man who put his faithful squaw away,"

Purdy said. "You hear these stories from other towns. Tragic stories. Tragic for the squaws. But not in Seabeck."

B.J. watched Chin paddle so as not to look back at Purdy. He was more and more certain what Purdy wanted. He could only pretend he wasn't. He waved the handkerchief at Chin. There was no response. Chin was soaked with rain and shivering violently. His paddling was frenzied, completely unproductive. His mouth was still open as if he were out of breath. "Many half-breeds resulting from these unions, like Blair, have risen to positions of responsibility in the community and in the Company," Purdy said, dropping all pretense of subtlety. "But I cannot say that I have seen any full-blooded Indians rise in similar ways, and I think we must credit the success of the half-breed to the blood of the father rather than that of the mother."

That was all B.J. needed. Children. He tried to say something that would make his feelings about marriage clear. "Women are crazy."

Purdy pointed back down the canoe past Chin to where Old Patsy squatted in the rain working steadily with the bailer. "Take Old Patsy. Refuses to learn English. Refuses even to learn Chinook." He shook his head sadly and lay back against the bow, closing his eyes.

B.J. had suddenly lost the thread of the conversation. Why were they talking about Old Patsy? She was already married. He didn't know how to respond, so he repeated himself. "Women are crazy," he said again, but he put more stress on the last word so that maybe Purdy would think he'd said something new.

"The Indians have a legend," Purdy told him, "about an earlier time when the white men and the Indians and the animals were all the same. Then Do-ki-batl, the Changer, came. And he changed flies into flies and minks into minks and blue jays into blue jays and he made Indians dark-skinned and ignorant, but he gave white men books and learning and a light skin, and that's just the way things are."

"I know this story," said B.J.

"There's a lot of truth to these fanciful old legends," Purdy said. "Not on the surface maybe, but underneath."

B.J. looked over the surface of the water, avoiding any possible truths underneath. He wondered why Chin had not waved back at him. Had he done something to annoy Chin? B.J. walked without straightening his legs, down the belly of the boat to Chin, taking his mat along like an umbrella and holding the handkerchief balled up in his other hand. This prevented him from gripping the gunwale, and made him proceed sideways, cautiously balanced on the balls of his feet. "Chin," he whispered. "Chin. Are you mad at me?"

"No," said Chin. "What's that?" Chin sprang to his feet so as to see over B.J. and his mat. The canoe rocked violently. B.J. dropped the mat and grabbed Chin's sleeve to keep him from pitching over the side. Chin swung in a half-circle at the end of B.J.'s grip, shading his eyes from the rain with one hand.

"Sit down," said Sam sharply, but Chin didn't appear to notice.

For a moment he had stopped shivering. B.J. looked where Chin was looking. A distant, dark shape rolled in the waves before the bow. "Is it Harold?" Chin asked. "Paddle out that way."

"You don't stand up in a canoe," Purdy said, turning to look ahead.

Sam shifted course.

"It's just a log," Purdy told them. "It's floating deep, like a log."

B.J. hoped it was a log. There was nothing upsetting about a log on the canal. There were lots of logs. No one could think a log was an evil omen.

Chin began to shake again, uncontrollably. The movement of the canoe pitched him from side to side. "He's about to fall in and take all of us with him," Purdy said. "Over a log."

"*Make* him sit down," Sam told B.J. in a hard, important voice. B.J. pulled on Chin's wet sleeve until Chin sank to his knees. Not once did Chin look away from the object as the canoe approached it.

"It's a log," Purdy called back. B.J. took three deep breaths to celebrate his relief. He gave the checkered handkerchief to Chin, who used it to wipe rainwater from his face. Then Chin tied it low around his forehead, just above his eyes. His teeth were clicking together. He picked up his paddle.

B.J. rejoined Purdy in the bow. "Excuse me," he said.

"Not at all," said Purdy. "I was wandering anyway. I didn't mean to go on and on about Jenny. I didn't think you knew about Jim. I just wanted to make sure you understood that you can't go back to Seabeck. Not with your Chinaman."

So he didn't want B.J. to marry Jenny. B.J. had misunderstood. He was relieved but not surprised. B.J. misunderstood things too often to be surprised. "What's Chin done?" B.J. asked.

"Nothing. As far as I know. It's unfortunate that Chin's sudden flight looks so suspicious. But if he'd stayed, they would still have lynched him."

"He didn't stab Harold. It wasn't even his chopstick," B.J. said. "And he didn't kill Jim Allen. There would have been blood in the bread."

"Look," said Purdy. "When a murder takes place in a small community, everyone is happier to think that the murderer is someone from the outside. Could have been Harold. That would have been fine. But your Chinaman is even more outside. Your Chinaman is perfect."

"I don't think that Harold killed Jim Allen either," said B.J. He might have, though, B.J. supposed. He might have snuck out into the hallway while Chin and B.J. were trying not to look at the woman's clothes. All those undergarments laid out on the bed. B.J. had *heard* someone in the hall when he was trying not to look. So then Harold could have stabbed Jim Allen and hurried back into Sarah Canary's room and slumped against the bed so as to be there when Chin and B.J. came through the window. Except that the knife had been in the kitchen with Purdy. So Harold could have snuck out into the hallway and gone down the stairs and past Purdy and snuck into and out of the kitchen and past Purdy and climbed back up the stairs and stabbed Jim Allen and hurried back into Sarah Canary's room and slumped against the bed so as to be there when Chin and B.J. came through the window. It could have happened that way.

The canoe tipped sideways. This time no one was moving around. It didn't feel like the wind or like a wave. It felt like a hand had come up underneath the canoe and was steadily pushing it over. B.J.'s heart squeezed into a little ball between his lungs. Sam hit the water with his paddle. The hand released them. B.J.'s heart pumped slowly back to normal size.

"He had money," Purdy said. "Suddenly. Jim Allen. He had lots of money." B.J. looked over the side of the canoe. No shadow. He leaned forward, around Purdy, and looked over the other side. No shadow. He sat back against the bow again, under the drumming of the rain on the mats.

"I shouldn't tell you this," Purdy said, which, of all the ways to begin a sentence, was B.J.'s absolute favorite, "but last year in San Francisco the Hood Canal lumbering interests entered into an agreement to keep up the price of lumber." Purdy was biting with his top teeth beneath his bottom lip into the sparse hairs that began his beard. He counted on his fingers. "Port Gamble," he said. "Port Ludlow, Port Discovery, Tacoma." He came to his thumb. "And the Washington Mill Company, too, of course. Seabeck. Only"—Purdy closed his fingers into a fist with the thumb on the outside—"the Washington Mill Company has been discounting its bills. The books look regular, the initial price charged is according to agreement, but then adjustments are made. Very profitable for Seabeck, of course. Disastrous, though, if it should become known throughout the rest of the Concern." Purdy opened his fist and reached into Old Patsy's basket for another potato. "Jim Allen sold the Company out," he said. "Everyone thought so. Straws were drawn to see who would kill him. You couldn't shirk the short straw, now could you? Even if you'd known him a long time? It's a Company town and we all live there together."

Purdy skinned the potato with his teeth, bit into the white flesh. "I don't suppose the original agreement was strictly legal. Still, it was nasty to break it. And nasty to tell for money."

"And nasty to kill the man who told," suggested B.J. "And nasty to blame Chin."

"This way, nobody else gets hurt. As long as you keep your Chinaman away from Seabeck, nobody else gets hurt."

"What's that?" Chin shouted.

"Nobody else gets hurt!" B.J. called back, but Chin was pointing again with his paddle out over the canal. B.J. turned. A dark, loglike shape rolled in the wind and waves and the rain far ahead of them. "There!" said Chin. "Take the canoe that way."

"It's a log," said Purdy, not looking, not taking his eyes off B.J. He lowered his voice. "Now. We never had this conversation."

B.J. was alarmed to hear it. Who *had* had this conversation and what had he been doing while they had it?

Sam turned the canoe away from shore. "More," said Chin, taking four long, deep strokes himself. "Turn us more." They paddled farther and farther out. The trees shrank in the distance behind them. The loglike object grew.

"It's a canoe," said Purdy. "By God. It's Harold's canoe. He's capsized." Purdy crossed himself. "Can he swim? Can he swim in rough waters? How close to the shoreline do you suppose he was? Look for a body," Purdy said quietly.

"Look there," said Chin. A small object glittered suddenly in the sunless water by their dugout, but it wasn't nearly large enough to be a body. B.J. was sure. The rain struck the object, making it bob first this way and then that. Chin reached for it with his paddle, trapping the object underneath the blade, pushing it down into the water, and then losing it. It popped back to the surface, where it began to float past Chin. He reached again. He cut into the water with the paddle blade about a half-foot behind the object and batted it clumsily closer. It was Harold's whiskey flask. Still capped, and filled with air, it bounced just out of arm's reach. Chin leaned. The dugout leaned with him.

"Don't," said Sam loudly, pounding with his paddle. The side of the canoe continued to drop until B.J. lay stretched out over the waterline. He still held the mat on his head, but what was up and what was down had shifted faster than B.J. could shift his thinking to compensate. The rain fell on him sideways. Sometimes the waterline was beneath him and he was in the air. Sometimes the waterline rose up to meet him. Purdy landed on him from behind.

"Lean!" Sam shouted. "Lean against it." But B.J. was pinned beneath Purdy and couldn't.

B.J.'s face was on a plane with Chin's face, which was on a plane with Chin's fingers as they opened and closed over the air, under the water, around Harold's flask. He saw Chin's hand. He saw the reflection of Chin's hand in the dark water. Five fingers reached down to the surface; five fingers reached up. In another moment they would have met, joining Chin to his other self, like Siamese twins, but the water rose instead, eating Chin's hand away to the first knuckles. The water dropped. Chin's fingers were whole again.

B.J. looked down to find his own reflection. The proof of him. Sometimes bigger than he was, but sometimes smaller. Reaching for him when he reached. Leaving when he left. But never leaving him first. Never.

The water was too agitated to hold an image. The sky was too dark for reflections. Puzzled, B.J. looked back toward Chin's hand. Nature was fond of pairs and partial to symmetry, Burke had told him that night in the little cabin, but the Wild Woman did not see herself in mirrors. What a sad way for Sarah Canary to live. All by herself.

Purdy struggled to right himself. He pushed B.J.'s shoulder. He kicked B.J.'s knee. His elbow went between B.J.'s ribs, removing all the air from B.J.'s lungs. As B.J. drowned there just above the waterline, his eyes dark with breathlessness, he thought he saw the hand beneath the water break through. It groped for Chin's hand and missed, grabbing the gunwale instead. The canoe went over completely.

B.J. fell deep into the canal. It was shockingly cold, but windless beneath the surface. It was quiet. There were other legs and arms about him, kicking gracefully in the black water. He saw a curtain of dark hair, which made him think frantically of the mermaid, although it was only Purdy's beard, floating in all directions, his cheeks above it puffed with air. B.J. felt something scrape by his back as he fell. He twisted around. There was nothing, only Chin, blurred in the distance and too far away to touch him. B.J. squinted. Chin's braid stretched up in the water behind his head, above the checkered scarf, like a snake rising from a basket. Old Patsy shed her cattail coat like last year's skin and swam away from it. B.J. saw the overturned canoe receding from him in the ceiling of water with the blades of the paddles floating around it. He saw the bottoms of Sam's two boots, together beside the canoe in the water above him. B.J.'s empty lungs burned in his chest. They tried to make him open his mouth.

B.J. was kicking back up to the dugout when a cooked potato fell past him like a thrown stone. He was rebounding to the surface himself at such a speed that the potato shot by. B.J. was going too fast. Rebounding into the air, he struck his head on the carved, upside-down nose of the frog on the canoe's bow. He heard the sounds of the wind and the rain come back, but only for a second. He took one breath before he sank again, his ears filling with water.

Then he was being pulled like taffy in two directions. Something had a grip on his ankles. Something else had him by the wrist. He was stretched out between the two, one grip drowning him, one grip rescuing him, but he was too disoriented to know which grip was which.

He began to be dizzy, almost giddy. He began to blame his reflection, or Chin's. Perhaps these other selves were not so benign. Perhaps they had tired of swimming along underneath the dugout. Perhaps they had overturned it so that they could ride inside for a while. Or perhaps his reflection had leapt up into the air as he had fallen and taken his place. How would anyone know the difference? Would B.J. even be missed? If B.J. drowned, wouldn't his reflection wander about in his world in much the same artless, untethered, unconnected way Sarah Canary did?

Why couldn't the Wild Woman see her own reflection?

B.J. kicked frantically. The grip on his legs came loose, but he was still attached at the wrist to a second figure, which floated out from him, above him, like an angel in a mirror, kicking the same way he was kicking, looking back at him the whole time he looked. The second figure pulled him closer. B.J. resisted. The grip tightened.

Closer. It was Chin or Chin's reflection. How was B.J. to know one from the other, under water in the dark? B.J. saw Chin's face just for a moment, then it passed through the waterline and disappeared, pulling B.J. with it to the surface and air and rain.

B.J. lay on his back in Chin's arms, breathing. A salty wave broke over his mouth. B.J. coughed. Out of the corner of one eye he could see Purdy, Old Patsy, and Sam clinging to the sides of the large, upside-down canoe. Chin dragged B.J. by the armpits through the water to join them. He clutched along the wood for a handhold. B.J. did the same.

"We could probably make it to shore!" Purdy shouted. The trees were distant ghosts, gauzed behind the rain.

"Probably," said Sam.

"The longer we wait, the farther out we drift," Purdy said.

B.J. had no intention of going back into the canal. He tried instead to pull his legs completely out of the water. He couldn't. He was too tired. The canoe rode too low. "Chin," he said. He coughed. "Chin?"

"Yes?"

"Why can't the Wild Woman see herself in the mirror?"

"Can we all swim?" Purdy asked.

"I don't know," said Chin.

Their paddles, Sam's pole, Sam's spear, the basket, the mats, and Chin's boots bobbed about them, dispersing in a wider and wider circle. The bedroll sank. Something thin and white floated by. Chin picked it out of the water. It was a chopstick. Chin put it in his pocket.

"We'll freeze if we stay like this," said Purdy.

Chin's teeth were clicking like the telegraph. B.J. shook with cold. He continued to cough, but in between he tried to listen. Chin's teeth said that the Puyallup Indians could sleep in the woods at night without a blanket or shelter. Stop.

"Some of us faster than others," said Sam.

An enormous wave covered and uncovered the entire canoe. Sam put his hand on Old Patsy's shoulder and spoke to her. The two Indians slipped into the water, first Old Patsy and then Sam.

They swam off in the direction of the tiny ghostly trees. On the way, Sam retrieved his seal spear.

Purdy took a deep breath, removed his shoes and dove, kicking against the canoe. His head resurfaced immediately. His beard floated out beneath his chin, his hands paddled furiously. "Come on," he said to B.J. "Come on! We'll build a fire. We'll get dry. We'll find something to eat. Oysters! Clams!" He offered another inducement, which the water swallowed. A wave moved him farther from the canoe. "Come on!" he called insistently. B.J. didn't hear him again. B.J. watched Sam and Old Patsy and Purdy's progress for as long as he could. When he thought that they had probably made it to shore, he told Chin so.

"You don't have to stay here just for me," B.J. told Chin. "I'm probably going to be swimming in to shore myself soon."

"I know," said Chin. "I will, too."

"I'm just waiting for the trees to get a little bigger." B.J. tried to guess how far out the canoe was. Three hundred feet? "I'm just going to give Purdy and Sam time to get the fire started." He searched the water for signs of shadows and reflections. He searched the clouded sky for smoke. Nothing. "How long does it take clams to cook?" he asked.

"Not long," said Chin.

"Of course, Old Patsy'll have to dig them first," B.J. said. Raindrops puddled in the spaces between his knuckles and ran down his arms. They hung from the tip of his nose. "I'll let you know before I go," B.J. promised Chin.

"Thank you," said Chin.

vii

The routes of several steamboats known collectively as the Mosquito Fleet lay across the waters of Hood Canal and Puget Sound. The *Phantom* ran to Seabeck; the *Zephyr* between Tacoma and Olympia; the *Eliza Anderson*, whose deck was mounted with her own calliope and whose coming could therefore be heard for miles, ran the international mail route; and the *Enterprise* carried passengers between Victoria and New Westminster. The routes and functions of these boats changed periodically, but the boats themselves worked until they sank, and then afterward many of them were raised to work again.

The perils for the boats were frequent and varied. The *Fairy* was the first of many to sink when her boiler exploded. The *Sea Bird* was destroyed by fire. The *Peacock* ran onto the sands of Cape Disappointment. The *Zephyr* went under while in dock when a Swedish logger, recently hired as a fireman, left the hoses running to her water tanks and sank her with the weight of the extra water.

The *Capital* was returning to Olympia from the oyster beds when her chief engineer, Indian Vic, realized the injector was no longer operating. *Halo chuck skookum kettle! Alki hiyu pooh! Nika klatawa!* he told the captain. "There is no water in the boiler. Soon there will be a big explosion. I am leaving." He dove over the side, followed by the rest of the crew, but the explosion did not come. The unpiloted ship continued on, eventually running herself into the mud flats at low tide, very close to her home dock.

The *Eliza Anderson* floundered at Deception Pass. Her captain, Captain Fitch, ordered eight head of cattle thrown overboard and then dumped seven pianos until the steamer righted herself and limped into Seattle with all the passengers and a shipload of whiskey intact. The company agent questioned the decision to dump the pianos and save the whiskey. "Can you drink pianos?" Captain Fitch asked incredulously.

The passengers retired to the nearest saloon to celebrate their survival. They drank a toast to the pianos and the music they made, hitting the water. "Like a host of angels was playing the keys," one of the passengers said, his glass raised. "And the wind blowing and the cattle all bellowing. By God, it was glorious."

CHAPTER
FOURTEEN

EMMALINE
RECITES LEAR

The Leaves like Women interchange
Exclusive Confidence

EMILY DICKINSON,
1865

The steamboat captains were the heroes this hazardous life required. They dressed the part: uniforms with epaulets, caps with gold braid, loud, loud voices, full beards or broad handlebar mustaches. Captain Wescott had all of the above and the command of the eccentric, tubby little steamer that ran between Seattle and Tacoma as well. The steamer was named the *Lotta White*, but she was known to the locals, affectionately, as the *Pumpkin*, because of her size and her speed.

Those boats whose routes confined them to the sheltered waters of the Sound tended to be flat-bottomed stern-wheelers, but the *Pumpkin* had side wheels and a walking-beam engine. Her colors were white and black and brass. When she ran, she poured black smoke and white steam into the air above her. Her paddle buckets roared, churning the black water to a white wake that followed her like a bright shadow as she pulled out of Port Gamble and throbbed her way toward the Pacific. *Adelaide Dixon* was written on the *Pumpkin*'s register in a slanting hand. Followed by an oddly shaped blot. A smear. *And nurse.* It was the best Adelaide could come up with. If Lydia was recognized as Lydia, of course, the game was up. If she was recognized as the Alaskan Wild Woman or if Adelaide was recognized, then considerable confusion would result, but some fanciful story could perhaps be concocted and then Adelaide's own name, right there on the register, might ultimately satisfy everyone. And if neither was recognized, then Lydia could pass as Adelaide and Adelaide could be the nurse. This was what Adelaide anticipated. She had no illusions of influence or renown in this territorial mudhole.

Adelaide sat with Lydia in the captain's own cabin. The communal passenger cabin was, of course, out of the question for Lydia. Adelaide had demanded a private space, which was provided for them out of deference to Lydia's obvious frailty and, perhaps, an unspoken concern that whatever made her so odd might be contagious. Adelaide sat in their tiny quarters and sang to Lydia to keep her calm. Lydia did not seem to notice or, in fact, to be particularly upset. She'd drawn a great deal of attention to herself during the hours they spent in Port Gamble waiting for the steamer, and especially as they were crossing the gangplank onto the *Pumpkin*. She picked and fretted at the dark net Adelaide had made her wear over her face until her hands had to be held, all the while making throaty noises of displeasure and resistance. "Is she ill?" asked a tall young woman on the deck, validating the ruse Adelaide had chosen to adopt. The woman stood under a black umbrella with a carved ivory handle. A pretty little blond girl, ten years old perhaps, or eleven, and obviously her daughter, held her mother's skirt with one hand and felt outside the shelter of the umbrella for rain with the other. The raindrops sounded on the umbrella like the ticking of a clock.

"She's making funny noises," the little girl pointed out, staring at Lydia's veiled face.

"Emmaline!" Her mother rebuked her quietly.

"She *is*," Emmaline insisted.

"It's not something a nice little girl would notice." The woman contrived to frown at her daughter and smile at Adelaide simultaneously.

"Yes," said Adelaide shortly, hurrying Lydia past them. "She is very ill." Lydia made a sound like a seal. "And developing a nasty cough. I'm taking her to a specialist in San Francisco. I only hope we get there in time. Come here, dear." Adelaide addressed Lydia in a careful public voice. "We must get you out of the damp."

"Aakk," said Lydia. "Awk. Kk-kk-kk."

Adelaide would have liked to stand out on deck after signing the register, watch the rest of the passengers board, and assure herself that there had been no pursuit out of Seabeck. But she was afraid either to leave Lydia alone or to take Lydia with her. Lydia sat on the bed and faced the wall while the boat shuddered out of its dock. Adelaide tried to relax. Her emotions were particularly unsteady; bouts of the joy she had felt upon leaving Seabeck alternated with doubts and anxieties. She had just begun her monthly bleeding, which was especially difficult to deal with while traveling. Her luggage was back in Seabeck. She had no change of clothing, no place to clean up, no bucket for her used menstrual rags, and no menstrual rags except for those she had just made, tearing up the bottom of her petticoat. She felt heavier than usual; the heaviness concentrated itself into something in her abdomen that was not really a pain but nagged at her unpleasantly. Adelaide wished there were room to lie down. She let herself think about San Francisco. Baths. Dressmakers. Hot and cold running water. In the tiny cabin, she was acutely conscious of the smell of her bleeding, a mineral sort of smell, an animal sort of smell. Not a smell she had ever liked.

Adelaide sang to the back of Lydia's neck, which was not really very clean, to her short, rumpled hair, to the buttons down the back of her dress. She noticed suddenly that the buttons seemed to be ornamental only, and puzzled over this as she sang. The dress was tight around Lydia's neck. How did Lydia get in and out of it? " 'Twas there as the blackbird was cheerfully singing, I first met that dear one, the love of my heart.' " The silent space between *my* and *heart* was filled unexpectedly with the sound of a fist thumping on the door. Adelaide's voice dropped and then stopped. Knock, knock, knock went her heart. Why would anyone need to see her now? They were less than fifteen minutes out of dock.

Adelaide took the two steps between herself and the door but did not open it. "Who's there?" she asked.

"Captain's compliments," a man outside answered. "And could he speak with you below, please? We've picked up a bit of a problem and the captain is hoping you might help."

Adelaide stood at the closed door. She believed there were going to be more arguments about the cabin. A request to share perhaps with the angelically golden-haired Emmaline. Adelaide had thought that the other travelers in the passenger cabin would only last a little while with Emmaline before the idea of closeting her with someone who might possibly be contagious occurred to them. Well, Adelaide had stormed the captain's cabin herself and she would hold it. No one could get in if the door never opened. "What sort of problem?"

"I think Captain Wescott would prefer to explain himself. If you don't mind. He could attend you here if necessary."

"That would be preferable," said Adelaide. "I don't wish to leave my invalided companion alone." No further sounds came from beyond the door. Adelaide went back to the bed. This problem, she told herself, had to do with the cabin and not with Lydia. No one could have possibly recognized Lydia. No one had seen her face. Adelaide sang now to calm herself. " 'Twas there as the blackbird was cheerfully singing . . .' " She couldn't remember what came next. She tried again. " 'Twas there . . .' "

"Captain Wescott," a loud masculine voice through the door informed her. "Begging your pardon. Begging your indulgence."

"My companion is quite ill," Adelaide said. "Is it really necessary to disrupt her rest in this way?"

"Quite necessary. Quite unexpected. I am sorry. But it's you I need to talk to. With your permission. If you'll just step out, perhaps we can manage to speak without disturbing her." Adelaide considered and then decided there was no help for it. She opened the door as minimally as was possible to pass through, closing it immediately behind her. She felt at a great disadvantage—untidy, unbathed, and smelling unpleasantly female.

Captain Wescott wore a uniform of white and gold. His beard was brushed, his mustache was waxed. "Captain Wescott," he said again, bending over her hand, which was quite gloveless. "Miss . . . ?"

"Bird," said Adelaide, raising her chin. No, that was silly. She revised it quickly. "Byrd. Mrs. Byrd."

"I trust you're finding the cabin comfortable, Mrs. Byrd," Captain Wescott said. "I always did."

Adelaide looked at him sharply but could not read his face. "I'm grateful to you for giving it up."

"It's my pleasure." He released her hand. "I'm delighted to have you making this voyage with us. The pleasure would be even greater if you joined me for dinner later. Please say yes."

"I'm afraid I must dine with Miss Dixon in our room." There was no temptation to do otherwise. "But how kind of you to ask me."

"This is a great disappointment, of course. But I do understand. I only wish there was something more I could do to increase your comfort. You and your companion." The captain's words were gracious, even unctuous, but his manner seemed to Adelaide a bit stiff. She guessed that gallantry toward the female passengers was something Captain Wescott saw as part of his job, but that it was not the part he enjoyed or even the part he thought he was good at. She guessed that it had rarely entailed giving up his quarters and that he was only pretending not to sulk about this. Adelaide began to like him a little for the stiffness.

"I would send a doctor to attend Miss Dixon if we carried a doctor as part of our crew, but the run to Tacoma is simply not long enough to warrant one." He held his hands out, palms up. Empty. Nothing to hide. "Which brings me, Mrs. Byrd, to the reason I have disturbed you. We've just picked up two men from a capsized canoe.

Both have spent quite some time in the water. Both are chilled to the bone. I want to know how serious their condition is. Must we turn back to Port Gamble and the closest doctor? I would welcome the opinion of someone such as yourself who has had experience with the ill and the invalid."

The great magnetic doctress was being asked to confer. It was a good joke. It was a good thing. Adelaide had no intention of returning to Port Gamble and giving Lydia's pursuers a second chance of catching them. "Poor, unfortunate men," she said. "But how lucky for them that you happened by. Of course I'll see them. Where have they been taken?"

"To the boiler room. Warmest place on the boat. I'm much in your debt," the captain said, waiting while she locked Lydia into the cabin.

Adelaide followed him down a deck. Several crew members stood by the rail in the rain, leaning over the side, hauling on ropes and arguing, their faces and hands red with exertion. "We're trying to save the canoe," Captain Wescott told her. "It seems to be quite a large and valuable one. Between you and me, only a madman would be out on the canal in a canoe in this wind." He slid the barnlike door to the cargo hold aside. The *Pumpkin* was carrying several bales of hay, seven sheep with black faces, three large wardrobes, and a grandfather clock. Captain Wescott allowed her to precede him through the door, then jostled by her to regain the lead, taking her past the crew's quarters to the boiler room. "One of the men we rescued is a Celestial," he warned her just before she stepped into the room and saw for herself.

The Chinese man lay on the floor with his back to her. Had Adelaide not been told otherwise, she would have assumed, from this angle, that he was an Indian. His hair was still braided even after everything he'd been through. Above the braid was the knot of a blue kerchief.

The white man was thin and pale and recognized her as quickly as she recognized him. "Look, Chin," he said over the sounds of hissing steam and the scraping of the fireman's shovel in the coal.

The pale man reached across and poked at the Chinese man, who did not respond. "It's that woman who took Sarah Canary. What was her name?"

"B.J., this is Mrs. Byrd," Captain Wescott said.

"No," B.J. told him. "No, I don't think so. Chin will remember." Chin said nothing. Neither man was dressed. They stretched across the floor in the heat of the boiler, wrapped in blankets. A partially filled whiskey bottle, obviously medicinal in intent, stood between them. Their flesh, what Adelaide could see of it, was fish-colored with cold. What dreadful luck, Adelaide thought to herself, but not resignedly. What awful luck, but she would not be thwarted by two such men, one of whom was Chinese, after all, and one of whom had to be a madman to have taken a canoe out on the canal in this weather. No one would listen to them. She focused on B.J. "What luck," he told her, with quite a different emphasis than she had been giving the words. "We came to rescue you and here you are. It's so perfect." He smiled at her brilliantly. In the dim light provided by the glow of the coal fire, Adelaide saw the pale man's irrational smile. "You do remember us, don't you?" he asked. His smile faded and brightened again. "You had a gun. You pointed it at us. That was us! You cut the bridge while we were on the other side. At the Bay View in Seabeck. You had *someday* written on your cheek. I kept trying to tell you." He squinted at her. "It's gone now. Did you ever figure out what it meant?"

Adelaide glanced nervously aside at Captain Wescott. "Delirium," she said. "Delirium and shock. Just as I would have expected."

"The Celestial is in even worse shape," Captain Wescott answered. "You'll see when you attend him."

"Someday," said B.J. encouragingly. "*Someday* you'll figure out what it means." He giggled, covering his teeth with one hand.

Adelaide knelt by B.J. first. He shivered and smiled. She put her hand on his face. His skin was wet, but Adelaide couldn't tell if this was seawater or rain or sweat. Their clothes lay in a heap beside the boiler; Adelaide was glad that the task of stripping him had not been left to her. The clothes would never dry, all bunched up like they

205

were. Really they should be rinsed of salt water and then spread flat. Adelaide wondered if this suggestion would pass for medical expertise.

"Have another drink," she told B.J. "Best thing to ward off chill." If she could get him drunk enough, he could say anything and no one would listen. Adelaide reached for the bottle herself. She helped raise his head, tipping some whiskey into him. "This man will be fine," she told Captain Wescott. "Bit more whiskey to warm him up. Some rest here by the boiler. And just wait for the delirium to run its course. Which may not happen before we reach Tacoma. I really wouldn't expect it to. But I don't see that a doctor is necessary."

She turned to look at the Chinese man, whose condition was obviously more serious. His breathing was slow. His skin was quite cold when she touched him. His eyes were glazed but open, the pupils tinier than she would have expected even in this dim light. She thought that he saw her but wasn't sure.

Adelaide did not have a very high opinion of the Chinese. She had heard a story about the Chinese mining camps around the Comstock Lode and a slave girl named Spring Moon. Finding her life unendurable, finding one moment in this life when she was untied and unwatched, Spring Moon escaped from her owner into the hills. The Chinese miners organized to go after her, to bring her back. When she was found, her feet had frozen and had to be amputated.

Of course, the Chinese liked their women even better without feet. *Fairy feet*, P. T. Barnum called the painful, crippled stumps the Chinese created from the ends of their little girls' legs. Barnum had a fairy-footed Chinese woman in one of his exhibits. Adelaide had seen her, seated on a pedestal, right next to the Mechanical Arab, a machine that played chess. Really, what the Arabs did to their women wasn't much better. Harems that were little more than prisons. Adelaide had read that middle-class women might be kept secluded in rooms with courtyards and gardens, but that the daughters of a wealthy man would live in rooms with windows so small and so high they would never see the outside. These were the women men really desired: imprisoned, untouched, and half-alive. Adelaide leaned toward the Chinese man, lowering her voice so that no one but him would hear her over the sounds of the boiler. "Very bad," she said. She lifted the blanket and looked at the bottoms of his heels, the cold purple color of his toes. The muscles of his legs looked stiff; his feet seemed somewhat swollen. She leaned back to his face, dropping the edge of the blanket. "We may have to cut them off," she whispered. "We may not be able to save them." His eyes focused on her eyes in confused alarm, then glazed again. "Your feet," she told him.

"Tom," he said. "Tom?" Followed by words she didn't understand. *Bright*, maybe. And *moon*, definitely. And something that sounded like *striped horses* but was probably Chinese instead. He spoke slowly, like a man who has been dosed with laudanum.

Adelaide really wasn't interested. She raised her voice. "I don't see that a doctor could do anything here either. I don't see any reason not to press on to Tacoma. I'm not saying his condition isn't bad. He's in the hands of God now. We can keep him warm. Watch him for convulsions or signs of fever. God's will be done." She looked back down at the Chinese man's face. Beneath his eyelids, his eyes darted about nightmarishly. Adelaide softened. "I am concerned about his hands and his feet. Can we adjust him so that his feet are closer to the fire?" Pity was a trap. Adelaide knew this and she cursed herself for continuing to fall into it. She stood up, finished with the man.

"Of course," said Captain Wescott. "One of the prettiest steamers I ever served on was made in China. The *Diana*. She murdered her engineer and her fireman in San Francisco with an exploding boiler, but she was always a perfect lady to me." He adjusted the Chinese man's body by pulling on the blanket until the Chinese man started to unwrap. Then the captain grasped him by the shoulders. B.J. slithered out of their way, tightly sheathed in his own blanket.

"He will be all right?" B.J. asked Adelaide. "I mean, of course he will be. Won't he?"

"Yes, of course," said Adelaide. B.J. had high cheekbones and hair like hay. Scandinavian heritage, she guessed. Vikings. Pillagers. Rapists.

Two crewmen appeared in the doorway to the boiler room. "Captain," the taller of the two said with obsequious urgency. "You're needed on deck."

"Excuse me," Captain Wescott told Adelaide. She watched the back of his white and gold suit as he left her. Something else white and gold approached, something smaller, which stopped opposite Captain Wescott and then continued toward Adelaide. The approaching white and gold turned into the child, Emmaline. Emmaline's hair had been gathered together into an enormous blue bow, but still reached halfway down her back. Adelaide imagined the battles there must be, brushing out that hair. Rapunzel, Rapunzel, sit still or I'll smack your hand with the hairbrush. Emmaline's mother entered the boiler room behind her, tall but still girlish, a brown-haired version of Emmaline, only with her hair twisted up in a respectable Psyche knot.

"May we join you?" Emmaline's mother asked. "Poor Emmaline was cold."

"I wanted to see the shipwrecked men," Emmaline said. "Is this them?"

"Yes," said Adelaide, thinking that she really must get back to Lydia soon and that this was lucky, that perhaps Emmaline's mother could be persuaded to watch the men until Captain Wescott returned. "Were they worth the trip?"

Emmaline looked at both men. "Oh, yes," she said. Her voice was delighted, clear as a chime. "One of them is Chinese! The sailors were just raising their canoe as we came down the stairs. It had a big face carved on it like a mask. And Mr. Wellman, up in the passenger cabin, he said you'd have to be some sort of *lunatic* to go out in a canoe in this kind of storm. He said he wouldn't have even stopped to rescue such a lunatic. He said it would be no great loss."

"Of course, he didn't mean that, Emmaline," Emmaline's mother added quickly, glancing at B.J. "I told you so."

"It's just like Mr. Lear's poem. Remember, Marmy?" said Emmaline. "The Jumblies went to sea in a storm and a sieve? Only their heads were blue and their hands were green. And they wrapped their feet in a pinky paper fastened with a pin."

208

"Emmaline has a wonderfully retentive memory," Emmaline's mother told them.

"I can see that," B.J. answered. He seemed to admire it.

"I suppose you've lost everything you own now," Emmaline suggested to B.J. "All your worldly possessions lying on the ocean floor. I suppose you are as poor as a church mouse."

"She's such a comfort to me." Emmaline's mother's smile hardened and broke. She sniffled twice. Her face turned red in the dim, red firelight, blotched over suddenly like a case of hives. She began to cry.

This made it awkward to ask her to sit with B.J. and the Chinese man. Adelaide would have to wait until Emmaline's mother had pulled herself together. Adelaide felt in the bosom of her dress for her handkerchief, which was warm from her skin, limp and perfumed. She offered it to Emmaline's mother. "I'm Mrs. Byrd. Sea voyages can be so unsettling," she said, rather lamely. "I myself cry frequently when I'm at sea."

"How very peculiar," Emmaline said, staring at her. The wings of her blue bow poked up from behind the curve of her head like a cat's ears.

· · ·
viii

In 1873, Anna H. Leonowens, tutor to the king of Siam's sixty-seven children, published her second book. This was a work of nonfiction based on her own observations of the lives of King Mongut's nine thousand wives and concubines. *Around the World in Eighty Days*, with its nod toward the problem of sati, was the current best-seller, but *The Romance of the Harem* had its own fascinated audience. Its publication coincided nicely with the escape from Utah of Ann Eliza Young, the seventeeth or nineteenth or twenty-seventh wife, depending on how many of the others you counted, of Brigham Young.

In 1859, in a political climate of virulent anti-Mormonism, Horace Greeley had traveled to Salt Lake City to study the religion and to look at some of those households wealthy enough to be polygamous. He reported that, while the husbands were, without exception, fanatic in their support of the system of polygamy, the wives "seemed lifeless, inert, inactive." He concluded that the system was a degradation of women. A year later, Captain Richard Burton, the English explorer and adventurer, made his own visit and gave a more favorable report. He granted that polygamy had removed much of the romance between men and women but felt this might be an improvement. As opposed to the Eastern states where womanhood was petted and spoiled, the Mormon system had "rather placed her below par, where," Burton said, "I believe her to be happier than when set upon an uncomfortable and unnatural eminence."

"The more the merrier," was Burton's final word on the subject of multiple wives. He returned to England to deliver a lecture to the London Anthropological Society on the Native American custom of taking scalps.

Ann Eliza Young began lecturing to Gentiles on the subject of Brigham Young's love life. The career choice was suggested to her by P. T. Barnum, who, three years earlier, had offered to exhibit

Brigham Young himself for $100,000 a year. Ann Eliza took Barnum's advice but refused his management. She was in the process of suing Brigham Young for divorce. He had filed a countersuit charging adultery. The audience for her lectures was enormous and avid.

Ann Eliza's main difficulties arose from the ambiguity the Gentiles felt toward Mormon women. If the Mormon women were victims of polygamy, then the Gentiles were sympathetic. If they were participants, however, then the Mormon women were whores. Ann Eliza was a key activist in the campaign to force the federal government to outlaw polygamy. Her political effectiveness and her own personal success on the lecture circuit would be compromised if anyone believed she was a whore. Her attire and her manner were accordingly genteel and chaste. Her topics were sexual, but the context was religious. She told the Gentiles what they had long suspected, that Mormon men were stealing Gentile wives. She was a great success.

In 1874, the *Chicago Times* accused her of sleeping with Major James Pond, her business manager. A Salt Lake City paper repeated the charges under a headline that said Ann Eliza was "reveling in a 'Pond' of illicit love." The scandal was immediately confirmed by Victoria Woodhull, who told the press that she had seen the amorous couple in Illinois, although it turned out later that Woodhull herself had actually been in Nebraska at the time of the alleged sighting. Women should sleep with whomever they pleased, Woodhull said. She always did.

Further investigations and her own demure bearing worked to clear Ann Eliza's name. Later in 1874, she spoke for two hours to Congress, detailing the miseries endured by plural wives. The next night, she gave a public lecture entitled "My Life in Mormon Bondage," to an audience consisting largely of congressmen and their families. President and Julia Grant attended her second lecture, "Polygamy as It Is," and congratulated her personally afterward. Within a few weeks, Congressman Poland's bill against polygamy had been passed and signed into law.

In 1883, Ann Eliza married a Gentile banker who had hastily

divorced his first wife just after their silver wedding anniversary to make this possible.

In 1890, the adulterous Grover Cleveland offered the Mormons amnesty for polygamists, legitimization of the children born of polygamous households, and statehood for Utah in return for their submission to the laws opposing polygamy. The Mormon elders finally agreed.

By 1891, Ann Eliza had grown tired of finding her husband in the beds of their maids and servants. Her husband said that she had driven him to this. He said that she was frigid. She said that his inhuman sexual needs had damaged her health. He said that she was a whore. He began to openly patronize prostitutes. Ann Eliza divorced him in 1893. She never married again.

THE CAPTURE
OF LYDIA PALMER

Only lest she be lonely
In thy beautiful House
Give her for her Transgression
License to think of us —

EMILY DICKINSON,

1871

Emmaline's mother wiped her face with Adelaide's handkerchief and blew her nose delicately. "Thank you," she said. "You're very kind. I'm Mrs. Maynard. No matter what anyone else may tell you." Tears spilled out of her eyes again, running down the length of her nose. She held the handkerchief over her face and took several quick, audible breaths through her mouth.

"We came all the way from Boston," Emmaline told Adelaide with maximum drama, "to be with Papa again. He said he would send for us, but Marmy wanted to surprise him." Mrs. Maynard's sobbing grew in volume. "All the way from Boston on trains and in nasty, bumpy little carriages with fleas and on boats. And then when we got here, Papa had another wife."

"That woman is not his wife," Mrs. Maynard said sternly. She sniffled and blew her nose. "There is a word for what she is, but it's not a word I would permit myself to use."

"Trollop," Emmaline told them.

"Emmaline!"

The *Pumpkin*'s whistle sounded three sharp blasts. The fireman looked up for a moment, then set his shovel aside and left the boiler room. "Well, that's the word you used before," Emmaline said.

"The Territorial Legislature gave him a divorce," Mrs. Maynard told Adelaide. "No one bothered to inform me. And I said it didn't matter anyway. It wasn't legal. God knew who his wife was. Do you know what the Methodist minister said to me then? The minister? He said that nothing in the *Bible* forbids a man to have more than one wife." Mrs. Maynard took a sodden look at her daughter and covered her eyes again. "My poor Emmaline. My poor little girl."

"He doesn't have another daughter," Emmaline said. She located the blue satin tail of her bow and stuck it in her mouth. "And I wouldn't care if he did."

"The other women said it was my own fault for leaving him alone too long. What could I expect, they said. I would have come the moment he sent for me. I came *before* he sent for me."

Adelaide shook her head. "Someday," she said, "someday we will learn that when one woman is wronged, we are all wronged."

"Someday," said B.J. pointedly and then didn't finish the sentence, flinching away from the look Adelaide sent him. There he lay, she thought, with his mouth open, naked and snug as an oyster inside his blanket. Lying there just expecting to be nursed. "How many wives do you have?" she asked him, her voice edged like broken glass.

His pallid complexion paled even more. "None," he said, losing his pitch so that the word slid out of control from a lower register into a higher. He reached over and shook the Chinese man's shoulder. "Chin," he whispered. "Chin," he pleaded. The Chinese man was a dark hill in his blanket, its contours outlined from behind in red by the light of the coal fire. The Chinese man sighed and muttered something in a language Adelaide supposed was his own but might almost have been German. What was passing for art in Germany now was really the most virulently misogynist poison Adelaide had ever seen. Still-lifes of dead women. Garroted women with stab wounds and fruit. B.J. turned back to Adelaide, looked at her face, licked his lips nervously with the tip of his tongue. "Not even one. But I can't marry her. All my worldly possessions are lying on the ocean floor."

"*I am already married,*" Mrs. Maynard sobbed.

"See? There's another reason," said B.J.

Adelaide looked at him in disbelief. "And if she were not, do you imagine for one moment that this poor woman would want you? Or any other man? After what she's been through? We assume that the men who come out here, left alone too long, will seek female companions. But what about the women abandoned in Boston? Are they marrying multiple husbands? Do you ever wonder why not?" She had been using her hands, her angry public voice. She had been making a speech. She tried to stop, turning back to Mrs. Maynard, cutting off B.J.'s answer, because she really couldn't have been less interested in anything he had to say. Mrs. Maynard held the handkerchief over her face while her shoulders shook with sobs. "And just when do you suppose he was planning to tell you about the other woman?" Adelaide asked.

"Why didn't you tell us about the other man, B.J.?" Captain Wescott reappeared suddenly. His voice was just as angry as Adelaide's and even louder. The *Pumpkin*'s fireman followed Captain Wescott into the boiler room, returning to his station, checking the fire. He loaded in another shovel of coal. The fire spit and reddened.

"Chin!" said B.J. He shook the Chinese man desperately. "Wake up, Chin. Please wake up." No response. B.J. withdrew his hand and glanced unhappily around the room from face to face. His eyes stopped on Mrs. Maynard, who was crying quietly. "I didn't know it was important," he offered. She sobbed. He looked at Adelaide. "I didn't think you'd be interested?" He slumped closer to the floor and turned his face to Captain Wescott. "I thought Chin had already told you?" He pulled the blanket up about his neck. "What other man?" he asked Emmaline piteously. He pulled the blanket over his face. "I'm not feeling very well right now." His voice was muffled. "Could we discuss this later?"

"What other man?" Emmaline asked the captain. Her mother reached over and removed the end of her ribbon from her mouth.

"When we succeeded in raising the canoe, there was a third man clinging to the gunwales underneath. He escaped from the crew, who were only trying to help him, and ran like a madman into the ship. The Lotta White is not a big boat and we have not searched her thoroughly, but we have not yet been able to locate him. He is a passenger now, B.J. I would like to know who he is."

"He's a stowaway!" said Emmaline. "He's a shipwreck and a stowaway."

Adelaide felt that Captain Wescott's approach was too threatening. She knelt beside B.J., making herself smaller, although B.J. wouldn't see this unless he came out from beneath his blanket. "Who else was on the canoe with you, B.J.?" she asked gently. Emmaline came to stand beside her, her white dress flickering red, reflecting the coal fire.

"Two Indians and a postman."

"A postman?"

"From Seabeck." The blanket moved. "Will Purdy. You remember. You held a gun on him, too. They all swam into shore, though. They were going to make a fire and eat clams and oysters."

"Like Mr. Carroll's poem," said Emmaline. " 'The Walrus and the Carpenter.' Remember how the Walrus held 'his pocket handkerchief before his streaming eyes'? Like Marmy." She was sucking on her ribbon again, covertly using the side of her mouth farthest from her mother. Mrs. Maynard sniffled.

"I know Purdy," said Captain Wescott. "This man was not Will Purdy. Who else?"

"No one."

"Who else?" Captain Wescott demanded. "A very short man with a large mustache."

B.J. lowered the blanket to just below his eyes. "Dark hair?" he asked.

"Yes."

"Light eyes?"

"I think so."

"Oh," said B.J. "Oh. Well, that must have been Harold. His canoe tipped over, too."

"Tom," said Chin. He tossed restlessly about in his blanket, exposing his naked chest.

"Or Tom," said B.J. "Might be Tom." He moved himself and his blanket closer to the Chinese man, covered him up again. More coal went into the fire. The red light flickered across the gold of Emmaline's hair like some unnatural dawn.

As soon as Adelaide understood who Harold was, she returned to the captain's cabin. To her relief, the door remained locked. Inside, Lydia lay on the bed sleeping, curled up like a cat, her knees at her chest, her full skirts mounded over her legs. Adelaide's coat lay kicked to the side, by Lydia's feet. Adelaide remembered suddenly that she had left the gun and the knife in the coat's pocket. She sat on the foot of the bed to retrieve them. Careless, careless. The cabin felt especially chilly after the warmth of the boiler room. She covered Lydia with the coat.

She was as stealthy as she could be, but still she woke Lydia. One of Lydia's cheeks was creased from the folds in the bedding. Her eyelids were heavy and hung at half-mast. She appeared to recognize Adelaide, although Adelaide couldn't have said exactly what about her face or eyes communicated this recognition. But she wasn't mistaken, because Lydia hummed at her, eight notes in sequence from the song Adelaide had been singing earlier. *Twas there a-as the-e blackbird.* The last note went sharp, but Adelaide was touched. This was the most responsive Lydia had ever been to her. "I won't let you hang, Lydia," she promised, slipping the weapons into her dress pocket. "Lydia Palmer. I wouldn't take you back if that were going to happen to you." No woman had been hanged yet in California, although Laura D. Fair had come pretty close. There simply weren't enough women on the West Coast to be wasting them in this way.

Adelaide thought she had dealt fairly deftly with B.J. and his Chinese companion. She was no longer concerned that they could stop her. And there was no reason to worry that Harold would be any more of a problem. It was just that he was the third obstacle to appear unexpectedly on board the *Pumpkin*. Adelaide had a sort of fairy-tale foreboding about the number three. Three wishes. Three dragons. Three tasks. One, spin a handful of straw into gold. Two, spin two handfuls of straw into gold. Three, spin a roomful of straw into gold. Do it by morning and the king will marry you. Fail and the king will have you killed. And then, the creators of that particular fairy tale would have you believe, the girl had a happy marriage and a reasonable sex life with that murderous, avaricious bully until some dwarf stole her son. If this was the best love could do in the fairy tales, it was no wonder love in the real world was a bit of a disappointment.

The *Pumpkin*'s whistle sounded three blasts. Adelaide found that her hands were shaking.

She tried to calm herself by making plans. Adelaide had always been a forward-looking person. So, when the trial was over, she would take Lydia with her on the lecture circuit. People would come to see Lydia and stay to hear Adelaide. Adelaide would dress Lydia just as she was dressed now: modest, nothing tasteless or exploitative. A locket, perhaps. Adelaide heard someone running in the corridor past her door. Followed by someone else.

Of course, Lydia would not be expected to perform in any way. Or even to appear if this were difficult for her. Absolutely no more Wild Woman shows. But she probably wouldn't mind merely sitting to the side of the stage with a nurse to care for her. A nurse could be paid for out of the proceeds of the lectures. No expense would be spared in Adelaide's efforts to restore Lydia to sanity or to keep her safe and comfortable. Shouts at the end of the corridor. *Here! Where? There! Stop! Stop!*

Adelaide stood up and turned her back on Lydia, pulling up her dress to substitute a clean menstrual rag. She tried to find a way to dispose discreetly of the used one. The little cabin did not have many hiding holes, but a recent newspaper lay folded on a board that had been hammered into the cabin wall as a desktop. Adelaide tore away a section on the Modoc Indian's murder of General Canby and dropped the little packet beside the bed, telling herself she would deal with it better later. She wiped her hands on her inside hem and sat beside Lydia again, cross-legged in the space between Lydia's feet and underneath her own coat. Once she was seated, she became very tired. Body tired only. Her mind still hopped from thing to thing to thing. Modocs, her mind said briefly. Seabeck. Her mind created a funny picture of B.J. and Purdy at the bridge with their hair blown all about by the wind and their mouths open. Someday, her mind said, with no explanation. San Francisco. Menstrual rags (a thought directed at her body with some contempt). Harold. Harold. Footsteps raced back through the corridor.

Just let me lie down, her body asked nicely. Two minutes. Give me two minutes. It's been a long day. It had been a long night. Sleeping in chairs. Climbing in trees. Sailing in sloops. Sky, land, water. The full ticket. Just let me sleep a little. Adelaide yawned. Her mind and body were always wanting different things. It was pretty much a permanent condition. Probably this wasn't true only of her. Probably everyone felt this way.

One blast from the *Pumpkin*'s whistle. Was this an all clear? Had Harold finally been brought to bay? "Harold is here," she told Lydia, who yawned back. "Now, why do you suppose he's come?" And why hadn't Harold declared himself as the manager of the Alaskan Wild Woman? Why had he tried to hide? Just how much did he really know about Lydia?

Rain coated the porthole. Adelaide listened to the sound of the engine, paddle buckets, whistles, and steam. Everything working to its own rhythm. *Pumpkin, Pumpkin, Pumpkin,* the engine said. The steamer rocked. The door was safely locked. *Peter, Peter, pumpkin eater,* Adelaide thought sleepily. *Had a wife and couldn't keep her. Locked her in a pumpkin shell. And there he kept her very well.* An insidious, ugly little rhyme that made her mind skip like a stone over water, back to harems and across to keyholes. The captain's cabin was as small as a cell. There was only the one tiny window. She reminded herself that she was protecting Lydia, not imprisoning her. She was rescuing Lydia. What would have happened to Lydia if Adelaide had not come along? She only wanted to help. Adelaide leaned against the wall of the cabin, closing her eyes.

Someone knocked on the door. "Mrs. Byrd?" Captain Wescott stood outside. Adelaide looked at her watch. Seven o'clock. Time for dinner and then the dock at Tacoma. Soon she and Lydia would be sailing to San Francisco, or they would not be. "Mrs. Byrd," said Captain Wescott, "I'm afraid I must trouble you again."

"What is it?" asked Adelaide, ready to be alarmed, but not alarmed yet, still sleepy, quite hungry. Perhaps the Chinese man's condition had taken a turn for the worse.

"This is rather difficult. Please open the door so that we can talk."

"What about?" Adelaide didn't like the tone of his voice. Behind the forced gallantry, a new awkwardness. An embarrassment.

"Please open the door."

Harold must have revealed himself and demanded Lydia. Adelaide tried to think what to do. She sat up, patting her hair into place. "Has that madman been captured?" she asked, stressing the *mad* before the *man* in hopes of discrediting any claims Harold might make.

"No. Not yet. Soon." But there were whispers outside. Captain Wescott was not alone. Adelaide rose and went to the door. She knelt beside it, putting her ear to the keyhole, trying to hear.

Captain Wescott spoke. "We are conducting a thorough search. We would like all the passengers to gather together in the passenger cabin until we are finished. For their own safety."

"We're safer here," said Adelaide. "But thank you."

More whispers. Adelaide heard her name. Her real name, the name she had signed onto the steamer's register for Lydia. She slid one hand down the bubbled white paint of the cabin door. She tried to look through the keyhole. A round blue eye looked back. It blinked. Adelaide jumped to her feet. "She's in there!" Emmaline said excitedly. "I can see her."

"Mrs. Byrd, you must open the door. We must search my cabin. Indeed, we've looked everywhere else."

"Really," said Adelaide in amazement. What was she being accused of now? "There is no one here but me and my companion. Who is very ill. I do assure you. Your quarters are too small for me to be mistaken."

"I was suspicious the moment she demanded a private cabin." Adelaide identified Mrs. Maynard's voice, whispering, but loudly enough to be heard over the engine, loudly enough to slip through the brass keyhole.

"Mrs. Byrd, you must open the door," the captain said.

Adelaide looked at the porthole. Far too small for her hips. Far too small for Lydia. And anyway, where would she go next? She retrieved the veil and pinned it into Lydia's hair. Lydia's nose made a large bump in the middle of the veil. The black net clung to her face and dipped into her nostrils when she inhaled. It waved like a flag when she exhaled. "Please," Adelaide said to Lydia. "Just for a few minutes." Lydia removed the veil at once, pulling at the pins so she lost some of her hair. Adelaide replaced the veil. Lydia removed it. Adelaide replaced it, catching Lydia's hands and lacing the fingers together. Lydia struggled away from her, freeing her hands, batting the veil onto the floor.

"Mrs. Byrd, you must open the door." Adelaide pulled her coat tighter around Lydia's chin. She pushed Lydia until Lydia rolled onto her side with her back to the door. "Mrs. Byrd." Adelaide glanced back at Lydia, whose face, at least temporarily, could not be seen. She fitted the key to the keyhole and turned it. The doorknob rotated. Captain Wescott opened the door. His splendid uniform was untarnished, but his face was slightly red. He stood there holding his hat. Emmaline's hands were clasped together under her chin in excitement. She had evidently been pressed against the keyhole. There was a keyhole shape on her cheek and she stumbled forward into the room when the door swung open. Mrs. Maynard hovered in the corridor behind.

Adelaide heard Lydia's body shifting on the bed. Emmaline's eyes widened. Adelaide blocked her at the doorway. "Perhaps now you can explain this intrusion, Captain Wescott?" she said icily. "Although I doubt very much that your explanation will satisfy me."

"I do apologize." Captain Wescott would not look at her. "Mrs. Maynard believes you have a man inside the cabin. Of course, she is mistaken. If we may just see your companion?"

"I recognized you." Mrs. Maynard's voice was shrill and certain. "And I went straight to the captain. Who showed me the ship's register. You're not Mrs. Byrd. You're not even married. You're Miss Adelaide Dixon. The suffragist. I heard you speak once in Boston on a topic I will not even allow to pass my lips."

"Trollops," said Emmaline. The ears of her bow had started to droop and the ends of her hair had started to snarl. A bit of blue stain marked the corner of her mouth. Adelaide thought she looked better this way.

Captain Wescott's face betrayed shock. He leaned down to correct Emmaline. "The fair but frail," he suggested stiffly.

"Exactly," said Mrs. Maynard. Her brown hair was coming loose and strayed about her temples. The corner of Adelaide's own handkerchief showed in the bosom of her dress. "Miss Dixon. A trollop by any other name. And since you *are* Adelaide Dixon, your companion cannot possibly be. I was suspicious the moment I saw your companion. No woman walks like that. Not a womanly walk. Not a womanly voice. I know a man when I see one, even if he's wearing pannier and a veil. You have concealed your identity in order to frolic with a man right under our noses in the captain's own cabin. Don't try to deny it, Miss Dixon."

"I don't understand," Adelaide said and she really didn't. "I am being accused of smuggling on board in Port Gamble a man who was later pulled onto the *Pumpkin* clinging to a canoe?"

"The *Lotta White*." Captain Wescott corrected her. "You're not being accused of anything, Mrs. Byrd. I am merely asking you for access to my own cabin." He brushed the top of his hat with the side of one hand and adjusted an epaulet, apparently still unable to look at her. "Possibly you've never heard of Jimmy Jones, skipper on the *Jenny Jones*?" He paused to let Adelaide agree that she did not know of this man. Adelaide refused to give him the satisfaction.

After an awkward moment, the captain continued anyway. "Well, I wouldn't expect a lady from the East to know of him, but he's rather famous in these parts. Jimmy was thrown into prison in Victoria for debt and his schooner was seized. She was a flea-ridden vessel, but all he had. He caught up with his creditors and the *Jenny Jones* in dock at Steilacoom. He'd escaped from prison by dressing as a woman. All the riggings—bustles, bonnets, and veils. I'm sure he looked a picture. But he stole back his own ship while the crew was ashore and made it all the way to Mexico. You tell a steamship captain in these parts there's a man dressed as a woman on board his ship and he's just as likely to believe you."

"Are you quite finished?" Adelaide asked. "Because the point I was making is that the man arrived *after* my companion and I were already settled into the cabin. Your story is as preposterous as it is irrelevant."

"It's not preposterous. It's absolutely true," said the captain. "Jimmy's a lecturer now, like you. I've heard him myself. Or at least he was a lecturer until he spoke at Seabeck. Just before his speech, one of the local wags gave him a drink. Jimmy was never known to turn down a free drink. Only this one was doctored with ipecac and cascara. The mill towns take their entertainment rough, as I'm sure you don't need me to tell you, Mrs. Byrd, if you are, in fact, Miss Dixon."

"The point I am making . . ." Adelaide began again, speaking slowly since no one here with the possible exception of Emmaline appeared acute enough to follow her otherwise. But she was not able to finish. Mrs. Maynard snapped her sentence in two.

"Oh, you're very cunning," Mrs. Maynard conceded. Fury had blotched her cheeks and made her voice shake. "I noticed that at your lecture. Always an answer for everything. I told Captain Wescott not to underestimate your cunning. But the truth is, if you've got nothing to hide, you've no reason not to let the captain search his own cabin. Do you?"

"This is a matter of principle. You wouldn't understand." Adelaide regretted every moment of pity she had felt for young Mrs. Maynard. Certainly she had faced charges such as these before. She expected the approbation of her own sex no more than she wanted the approval of men. Which was lucky since she never got either. But it was galling to remember that she had been comforting this woman only a short while ago. She heard herself adopting her public voice again. "I will set principle and dignity aside, Captain Wescott." She reached past the captain, brushing over Emmaline's head, flattening one of her cat's ear bows, to retrieve her handkerchief from Mrs. Maynard's bosom. She pulled it free with a snap. Mrs. Maynard recoiled from her hand as if she expected Adelaide to strike her. Adelaide had not stopped speaking. "I see you are determined to look and that no appeal to courtesy or decency will dissuade you. When you have satisfied yourselves as to the injustice you do me, I will accept no apology. And I will entertain no further intrusions." She backed into the cabin, sweeping her skirts aside with one hand.

Lydia had rolled around, facing Captain Wescott, following him with her large dark eyes as he came into the room. She shifted onto her back, showing them all her famous profile. Adelaide could hardly breathe. "Has everyone seen enough?" she asked.

Mrs. Maynard crowded into the cabin behind the captain, who was behind Emmaline. One more person could not have fit into the tiny room. "It is a man," she insisted, but somewhat uncertainly.

"I don't think so." Captain Wescott also did not sound sure. He took a step forward to the bed, treading on Adelaide's used menstrual rag. He bent over to look at it curiously, unwrapped it with the toe of his shoe. Adelaide was hot with embarrassment. The captain reddened like a boiled lobster. The *Pumpkin*'s whistle sounded on deck, a continuous blast like a teakettle. "Madam, I am deeply sorry." He straightened up and addressed Lydia. "The way we have disturbed you. In your condition. There is no excuse for it. I can only assure you I was concerned for the safety of my ship. And her passengers. And that I deeply regret this whole episode."

"She is a man," Mrs. Maynard insisted, whispering through her teeth. "Look at her." But even as Mrs. Maynard spoke, Captain Wescott took her arm and piloted her firmly through the door backward. She continued to accuse Adelaide as she retreated. "Doesn't the Redpath agency handle your engagements? And isn't Redpath's business manager missing? Vanished with a great deal of money. I read it in the papers."

"I'm not with Redpath," Adelaide said. Of course, she was much too scandalous for the Redpath agency. "I handle my own career."

Captain Wescott pushed Mrs. Maynard farther out into the corridor. "Emmaline!" Mrs. Maynard called back. "Come away from there." Emmaline remained in the cabin, staring at Lydia. At the sound of her mother's voice, she turned and smiled inexplicably at Adelaide. An unforced little girl's smile. Perhaps slightly conspiritorial, but perhaps purer than that. Adelaide had always told herself that she didn't want children. Such a bother. Such a responsibility. Far too bestial. She reached over and straightened Emmaline's ribbons. The truth was that the prospect of child-bearing had always filled Adelaide with terror. It was painful to admit that she lacked the ordinary courage of her sex. But it would be even more cowardly not to face the truth of the matter.

"Good-bye," said Emmaline. She ran away from Adelaide, her shoes tapping lightly and then more lightly down the corridor in the direction of the passenger cabin and her mother.

A crew member arrived just outside the cabin door. "There's food missing from the galley," he reported to Captain Wescott. "Cheese and bread. And whiskey."

A second crewman ran up from the other direction, shouting. "We spotted him up by the bridge!" He reached the captain, paused to catch his breath. "He swung down the companionway and headed toward the stern. One of the passengers says he went back over the side. We can't see anything in the wake."

"Search the stern," Captain Wescott said, sending the crewmen back off on a run. To Adelaide's surprise, he did not follow. He stood there a moment, rotating his hat nervously in his hands. "The *Columbia* lost an Indian deckhand off the stern once," Captain Wescott offered. Adelaide was not interested and would not pretend that she was. "Nobody missed him. He was dragged in the wake for three days but was recovered when she docked in Olympia. Hungry, but otherwise fine." The more Adelaide refused to answer, the more embarrassed the captain seemed to become. Adelaide was still embarrassed herself, so this seemed only just. "Well," said Captain Wescott. "I had better go see to this." He put his hat on his head. "I am sorry, Mrs. Byrd. I hope someday you'll believe that." Adelaide closed the door.

Lydia rose and stood at the porthole. Nothing could be seen but water and the horizon. Adelaide had already looked. Adelaide picked up the newspaper. She tore a long strip to rewrap her rag in, then noticed the words *a Palm* at the top. She placed the strip back on the little desk, matching the torn edges. Now it read *a Palmer*. Adelaide had to retrieve the bloody section on the floor to piece together the entire article. Lydia Palmer had been captured six days ago while attending a performance of *Love's Hidden Heart* in Sacramento.

Adelaide was surprised at how little surprise she felt. What were the odds, really, that she, Adelaide Dixon, would be so lucky as to find the fugitive no one else had been able to find? A woman who couldn't hold an audience, was afraid to have children, was afraid to fall in love. A woman who didn't even sleep with men often, although once was more than enough as far as most people were concerned. Still Adelaide had magnified it. She had found that people would come to be scandalized when they wouldn't come to be instructed. So she had made a lie of her sexual past in the service of great truths, and the truths were still true and the truth was still great, but Adelaide herself was only one small lie.

Adelaide looked at her fingertips, smeared with blood and newspaper ink. Adelaide might tell a lie, but she was a great believer in seeing the truth. And the truth was that she hadn't done this only for her work. The truth was that Adelaide was afraid, and perhaps she was the only woman in the world who felt this particular fear. She had never heard another woman say it. Adelaide was afraid that if she ever once allowed herself to feel the full range of her sexual desires, that this would be a need too great for any man. That these desires, once allowed to come to life, would never be silenced or satisfied again. Adelaide had read Darwin's *The Descent of Man and Selection in Relation to Sex* to find the answer to one question. Why were men's sexual needs so easily accommodated, when women's were so difficult? She knew what a minister would tell her, if she asked him. She had hoped for something new from Mr. Darwin. But Darwin didn't talk about women's needs at all.

Some tiny hold on reality had prevented Adelaide from telegraphing her triumph ahead to San Francisco, as would have been a more sensible course of action if she had really captured Lydia Palmer. So Adelaide wasn't surprised and she wasn't disappointed and she wasn't angry. She was just tired. She had been emptied out like a bottle.

The Alaskan Wild Woman had the hiccoughs. They were a noisy and arrhythmic variety. Who in the world was she? Poor crazy woman. What was Adelaide to do with her? She couldn't return her to Harold, who had been clearly terrifying and mistreating her. Perhaps B.J. knew where she belonged. Hadn't he been looking for her, too?

Adelaide locked the door behind her and went back to the boiler room. Past the sheep with their black, heart-shaped faces, past the wardrobes, past the grandfather clock whose pendulum was wrapped in an Irish blue quilt and whose hands were frozen, one on top of the other, at midnight.

The boiler room glowed. She knelt beside B.J. "Look," he said. He held his fist out to her, then withdrew it. "Well, I can't show you. If I open my hand, it will get away. But my blanket has fleas. I've caught one."

"Where did you find the woman?" Adelaide asked. "Who is she?"

"Chin found her. In the forest. Her name is Sarah Canary. Have you ever seen a flea dressed up like a bride or a groom?"

"No," said Adelaide. "Can you take her home?"

"If you tell me where. Chin and I would do it."

"I would do it, too," said Adelaide. Of course she would. "I was hoping *you* would tell *me* where."

"Ask Chin," B.J. suggested. "And keep her away from Harold. Harold is looking for her. Have they found Harold?"

"I don't know," said Adelaide. "Not the last that I heard." She wanted sympathy suddenly. She had been alone such a long time. Or perhaps she was frightened by her own emptiness and wanted a

229

respite from it. A friend, however temporary. To be taken medicinally. "The last I heard, they were accusing *me* of dressing Harold like a woman and hiding him in my cabin," she told B.J., thinking how very brave it was of him to come in a canoe through a storm only a lunatic would face to rescue an ugly woman who couldn't even thank him. It was almost romantic.

"Dressing him like a woman?" B.J. repeated. "All in black? And then putting him with other women in black like yourself and Sarah Canary? So no one would notice him? I heard a story like that once. Only instead of women dressed in black, it was purloined letters. Except for that, it was the same story. Have you ever seen trained fleas? A flea circus? Like they have in England?"

"I saw some fleas once who were dressed as little soldiers. They shot off a little cannon and raised a little Union flag," said Adelaide. "In a carnival. Of course, the fleas aren't really trained. No one could train a flea. They're just hopping about. They're just trying desperately to escape. I thought it was too much like the real war to be entertaining. I thought it was too much like life." Something in her answer distressed B.J. Adelaide could see it in his face. She wanted to reassure him, but she didn't know what she had said.

"There she is, Tom," said the Chinese man. Adelaide turned. His breathing had normalized, his color improved. He looked less stiff. He was warmer; Adelaide felt his forehead.

"Oh, he's much better," said Adelaide, hoping to please B.J. with this news. But the look the Chinese man gave her was startling, a look perhaps of defenseless joy. A look as if, of all the faces in the world, hers was the one he had most wanted to open his eyes and see. Adelaide smiled at him involuntarily. "Mr. Chin," she asked gently. "Who do you think I am?"

"An enchantress," Chin answered. His voice was weak from fever and rough as a frog's.

"Delirium and shock," Captain Wescott opined sadly. Adelaide did not know when he had entered the boiler room. He was standing behind her, looking down on the Chinese man, shaking his head. "Absolutely starkers."

Adelaide removed her hand from Chin's head. "Have you found Harold?" she asked tartly.

"Not yet," said the captain. "He's been seen up by the pilot-house, but we haven't actually caught up with him yet."

"B.J. says he's looking for my companion," Adelaide told him. She turned to B.J. for confirmation. B.J.'s face was shadowed, but his hands were open and empty. Apparently he had allowed his captive to slip away.

iX

Below Nob Hill lay Tangrenbu, San Francisco's Chinatown, an area comprising about ten city blocks and housing an expanding population. In 1871, the Sandlot Orator, Denis Kearney, told the city of San Francisco that the contest against the Chinese would not end until there was enough blood in Chinatown to float their bodies to the bay. He spoke, he said, for the working man. He represented the Workingmen's Party.

H.J. West printed and disseminated an influential pamphlet entitled "The Chinese Invasion: They are Coming, 900,000 More. The Twenty-three Years' Invasion of the Chinese In California And The Establishment of a Heathen Despotism in San Francisco. Nations of the Earth Take Warning!"

In 1869, one month before the completion of the transcontinental railroad, a Central Pacific crew of 848 Chinese had set the world track-laying record, ten miles of track laid in twelve hours. In 1871, the San Francisco medical community explained that the nerve endings in a typical Chinese man's body were farther from the surface of the skin than those of the typical Caucasian. This made the Chinese inferior to the Caucasians since they were able to work longer hours and were less sensitive to pain. These findings were published in the California 1871 Biennial State Board of Health Report.

In his inaugural address, Newton Booth, the governor of California, opposed the law that prevented the Chinese and Indians from giving testimony in court and succeeded in overturning it by statute in 1872. In 1872, a group of boys selected a Chinese man at random and stoned him to death in broad daylight while a large crowd of San Franciscans watched.

In 1873, the San Francisco Board of Supervisors passed the Queue Ordinance, which required all prisoners in the city jails to have haircuts, established a special tax on laundries, and began to apply the Cubic Air Ordinance (which penalized crowded living conditions) to the Chinese only. The Cubic Air Ordinance was overturned on the grounds that it was beyond the jurisdiction of the Board, and the mayor, William Alvord, vetoed the Queue Ordinance and the tax. His action was applauded by the majority of newspapers, countrywide. Prejudice must not be allowed to become persecution, the New York *Herald* said. And from the Chicago *Inter-Ocean*, "They have a brave man for Mayor of San Francisco."

CHAPTER SIXTEEN

THE STORY
OF CASPAR HAUSER

Stands the Sun so close and mighty
That our Minds are hot.

EMILY DICKINSON,
1872

Chin had only been in San Francisco once before. Unlike most of his compatriots, his original point of debarkation was New Orleans. An American clipper-ship company had advertised the *Ville de St. Louis* with the following handbill:

ALL CHINAMEN MAKE MUCH MONEY IN NEW ORLEANS, IF THEY WORK. CHINAMEN HAVE BECOME RICHER THAN MANDARINS THERE. PAY, FIRST YEAR, $300, BUT AFTERWARDS MAKE MORE THAN DOUBLE. ONE CAN DO AS LIKES IN THAT COUNTRY. NO-

BODY BETTER NOR GET MORE PAY THAN DOES HE. NICE RICE, VEGETABLES, AND WHEAT, ALL VERY CHEAP. THREE YEARS THERE WILL MAKE POOR WORKMAN VERY RICH, AND HE CAN COME HOME ANY TIME. ON THE SHIPS THAT GO THERE PASSENGERS WILL FIND NICE ROOMS AND VERY FINE FOOD. THEY CAN PLAY ALL SORTS OF GAMES AND HAVE NO WORK. EVERYTHING NICE TO MAKE MAN HAPPY. IT IS NICE COUNTRY. BETTER THAN THIS. NO SICKNESS THERE AND NO DANGER OF DEATH. COME! GO AT ONCE. YOU CANNOT AFFORD TO WAIT. DON'T HEED WIFE'S COUNSEL OR THE THREAT OF ENEMIES. BE CHINAMEN, BUT GO.

Chin was carried aboard with a bag over his head. He had been out running an errand for his mother.

Several of the Chinese men on board the *Ville de St. Louis* jumped into the bay in Canton. Some of them drowned. More died during the long trip. It was a part of his life Chin tried never to think of, but these memories surfaced like bodies whenever he was forced to travel over water. He had been on boats for five days now. He was a haunted man.

Three years ago, Chin had landed in New Orleans, seriously mal-nourished, desperately homesick, and covered with fleas. He escaped immediately and made his way across the country to San Francisco, where his uncle was working. His English was good when he started his journey. It was excellent by the time he arrived. And he had learned many other things: mysterious beliefs, strange customs, odd sayings. *I am all ears*, the white demons said, with typical Caucasian overstatement. *I am all thumbs. You are all heart. You are all wet.* But he had not really understood until Adelaide Dixon explained it to him that the issues of the Civil War had been largely sexual.

In the slave system, she said, one group of men (white) had ab-solute power over one group of women (black). With nothing but their own sense of decency as a restraint, the white plantation own-ers had been, essentially, unrestrained. At a recent exhibition in Chicago, a statue entitled "The Slave" was unveiled. This was a figure of a beautiful white woman in chains and despair. The re-sponse had been sensational. But no one, Miss Dixon said, wanted

236

to examine too closely all the things the statue might mean. The sculptor seemed to be making a point about the condition of white women; the audience understood this simple statement. Only Miss Dixon wondered if something even more radical was being said. *Don't trust your eyes,* the statue had told her. *Now what do you see?* In San Francisco, Miss Dixon said, she had seen many black people with so much white blood that they could pass either way.

"And was it an accident that, just as women in the East were demanding equality and the vote, men in the South were employing the method of rape to create a new race of subjugated women?" Miss Dixon asked, standing next to Sarah Canary, leaning against the rail on the deck of the large steamship she had bought them all tickets on in Tacoma. Miss Dixon knew of a women's rescue mission on Kearny in San Francisco that might take Sarah Canary until her family could be found.

"No," said B.J. "It was not." He stood on Miss Dixon's other side, next to Chin, leaning his back against the rail in a glorious flood of sunlight. Chin had been sun-starved. He closed his eyes and let the sun bleach away the dark times in his memory.

They passed another steamer headed north. B.J. turned to look. Whistles sounded on both boats; passengers shouted greetings from the decks. The man standing on Sarah Canary's right cupped his hands and hallooed through them. Sarah Canary howled, only once, but the passengers standing around her fell immediately silent and edged away.

Chin watched, waiting for the moment when the waves from the wake of the second boat would collide with their own wake. The surface was a chaos of glittering and shaded mountains, which rose and fell in an instant beside other mountains. A diorama of the history of the world. A statement made in the full light of day. If mountains were brief, then what were men?

". . . corruption," said Miss Dixon. "If slavery had been allowed to continue another three generations, the slaves would have become visually indistinguishable from the masters. The physical evidence of the white man's corruption would no longer be possible to ignore." A flock of gray and white sea gulls whirled above them, screaming to be fed. Two small boys in sailor suits threw handfuls of bread and crackers into the air. Sarah Canary watched, opening and closing her mouth soundlessly. "How much white blood would it have taken until the white women in the South were forced to recognize the slave women in the South as their sisters?" asked Miss Dixon. "Literally, their sisters."

"How much," B.J. echoed, shaking his head in an ambiguous gesture of agreement or disagreement, depending on which was appropriate. Chin had frequently seen him employ this strategy when he had been asked a question and didn't have a clue as to the answer.

"Now the only slaves in this country are Chinese women," Miss Dixon said pointedly. She didn't look at Chin, but he suspected she wanted him to do something about this. What did she think he could do? Miss Dixon was probably unaware of it, but once every seven years on the Festival of the Good Lady, Chinese women were permitted to walk the streets freely, just as if they were men. Chin made a decision not to tell her.

Miss Dixon already recognized the Negro women as sisters and the Chinese women and the Indian women as well. Miss Dixon didn't have a racist bone in her body, she told Chin quite frequently, and she proved it by bringing Sarah Canary all the way down to steerage every day to see him.

So Chin thought she might notice that she did all the talking when they were together. She was the first white woman he had ever talked to. So much yang to her yin. She had something to say about everything. This was not an attractive female quality, probably not even in the white culture. In fact, there was something sexless in the unrestrained way she confided in him, not that he wanted it any other way. Speaking with white women was always a dangerous activity for Chinese men, but the danger did not go both ways, so perhaps it was unfair to expect Miss Dixon to see this.

Still he felt that Miss Dixon did like him, although he didn't know why. It was a whimsical approval at best and he knew better than to count on it. B.J. said that Miss Dixon had nursed him very tenderly on board the *Pumpkin*, and that Chin had been near death. Chin thought he must be right, because Chin remembered spending the time with Tom, remembered that he and Tom had finally settled some things between them, and death was certainly where Tom would be. Chin didn't remember Miss Dixon at all until the time Sarah Canary was brought in to the boiler room to see him just before their arrival in Tacoma. Sarah Canary had recognized him. Not that there was any show of happiness. Sarah Canary had simply held out her hand, palm up, until Chin fished through his clothes for one of his chopsticks. He was resigned. Nature was partial to pairs, B.J. kept reminding him, but Chin seemed doomed to own a single chopstick. He hadn't really wanted to eat with something that had been in Harold's heart, anyway. Sarah Canary had immediately put the round end into her mouth.

"Don't let her swallow it," B.J. said anxiously, but she had already withdrawn it and stuck it into her nose. "Just like Dr. Carr said," B.J. told Chin, shaking his head. " 'Every orifice,' he said. 'Women are so prone to this,' he said." B.J. whispered so that Miss Dixon, who had accompanied Sarah Canary, wouldn't hear. She heard anyway.

"And just who is this Dr. Carr?" she asked nastily, making Sarah Canary take the chopstick out of her nose. "When he is at home?"

"The doctor at the Steilacoom asylum." B.J.'s tone was careful. "I didn't say it."

"I should think not."

"I did say that maybe women who liked to ride horses wanted"— he stopped suddenly, blushing. "wanted to be men. The kind of woman who won't ride sidesaddle. You know."

Miss Dixon shook her head. "I'm not sure I do. A sidesaddle is a lot harder to stay on. Have you ever ridden with one?"

"I didn't mean that." B.J. tried again. "I just thought maybe these women wanted to have what men have. So they ride horses. Without the sidesaddle."

Miss Dixon looked bewildered. She turned to Chin for an explanation. Chin didn't know what B.J. was talking about.

"It doesn't matter," said B.J. nervously. "Forget it. Dr. Carr set me straight."

Miss Dixon stared at B.J. "Oh," she said. "No. You can *go* somewhere on a horse." She laughed suddenly. "Calamity Jane likes to ride her horse standing on her head," she said.

Bringing Sarah Canary out of her cabin and down a deck had been Captain Wescott's idea, a daring stratagem to entice Harold out in the open. It hadn't worked. Harold continued to haunt the *Pumpkin* like a ghost: the child Emmaline saw him everywhere—in the porthole, on the poop deck—but the sightings grew more and more outlandish. Chin thought Harold must have gone back over the side. In a just world, he would be washed up on the beach near Steilacoom and interned under Dr. Carr and Houston's anxious care. Presumably security had been tightened since Chin, Sarah Canary, and B.J. had made their escape. Harold could just stay there eating boxty until he got better.

The flags snapped on their poles above first class, barely audible over the sounds of the engine. Crewmen swarmed about the decks, working the pumps, washing the vessel down with water and rags before they docked in San Francisco. All the passengers had dressed up, with the exception of their own party, who had no other clothes to change into. Yet even Miss Dixon had fastened a paper rose to her breast, and put another in Sarah Canary's hair. The petals rustled slightly, rubbing against one another in the wind. Shh, they said. Shh. Of course, Chin was only imagining this. Such a small sound could not be heard against the backdrop of boat, passengers, water, and wind. The flowers were a gift, B.J. told Chin, from a man in first class who had been markedly attentive. Chin wondered if this man always traveled with flowers for women. Chin didn't ask for details.

The coastline changed in an unchanging way, rocks and cliffs and trees. Never the same ones, but always more of the same. Somewhere north and inland, the Modoc War had begun and Chin would never have known, if Miss Dixon had not told him, that the Modocs had never made beads or baskets, but traditionally bartered their women to other tribes in exchange for necessities. "Flesh peddlers," was how Miss Dixon characterized the Modocs, and after that, there didn't seem to be much else to say.

Chin leaned out over the rail, his long braid spilling forward.

Schools of fish were eating the bread that the sea gulls missed. Round rings of mouths showed themselves like a pox at the waterline. Occasionally there was the flash of a silver tail. A seal surfaced among the fish, scattering them, its face wet and shiny, its neck encircled with a collar of water. This was the third seal he'd seen.

Chin counted the seals to ward off his unpleasant boat memories. First, the omen seal he had seen while the earth trembled at Steilacoom Lake. Chin remembered how he had thought the first seal was a woman, just for a moment, before he saw it clearly. The same way he had mistaken the mermaid for a dead child. Second, the seal that had followed Sam's canoe like a pet dog all the way up the canal from Seabeck to disaster. Chin had almost touched it once or twice with his paddle. And now a third one. They were strange creatures, boneless and wormish, not quite fish and not quite beasts. The third seal called to the steamer with its unlovely voice.

Miss Dixon unpinned the rose from her dress and threw it out, overarm. It hit the water, floated away from the boat. The seal swam up beneath it, tossing it aside. "I'll take you to see the sea lions at the Cliff House," she offered, and Chin didn't know which of them she was speaking to, but he doubted it was him. "When we're settled." She replaced the empty pin into the black pleats of cloth at her bosom, brushed the back of Sarah Canary's hair with her fingers.

"I've been thinking some more about Sarah Canary," she added. She folded her arms on the deck rail, gazing out into the waves. The sun made a bright circle like a mirror on the back of her hair, turning it just in that spot from black to gold. "One of the pieces of the puzzle is Harold," she said. "And I don't know that we've paid enough attention to him. If Sarah Canary is just what she seems, harmless, vague . . ." Chin thought that Sarah Canary had never seemed harmless or vague to him. Mysterious, rather. Possibly powerful. Certainly purposeful. He said nothing. ". . . then why is she being trailed by an assassin? Why would anyone want to kill a harmless, vague woman?" Miss Dixon looked straight into Chin's face, her eyes large and intense, awaiting his answer. Chin was afraid to look at her eyes.

"Harold is crazy," Chin told her, looking past her to the curving horizon of water. He had no doubts about this. He remembered Harold's face, like a gargoyle, Harold's voice, like water on coals, when Chin had first come upon him again sprawled on the floor in the Bay View Hotel with a bloody chopstick in his hand.

"Maybe not," said Miss Dixon. "Why does one person want to kill another person?" She began to count on her fingers. "Revenge. The person has done something." She held up a second finger. "Avarice. The person owns something." Three fingers. "Fear. The person knows something." She dropped her hand back to the rail.

Chin noticed a few omissions. "Hate. The person is something," he added. Chinese, for instance. A gull had landed on the deck railing near Sarah Canary. It tipped its head, stretched its neck, ruffled its feathers. It watched Chin from the absolute center of one red-rimmed eye.

"I was just about to say that. Have you ever heard of Caspar Hauser?" Miss Dixon asked.

"No."

"This is a very mysterious story. Caspar Hauser appeared out of nowhere in Nuremberg about fifty years ago. He looked to be sixteen or seventeen years old. He didn't speak. He walked only with difficulty. The sun seemed to hurt his eyes. There was a note pinned on to him that said he wanted to join the army. No one knew where he had come from." Miss Dixon looked down and the circle of sunlight on her hair became a crown.

"Later, as he learned to talk, things became even more mysterious. He said he'd been raised entirely secluded inside a closet. The whole time he was growing up, he had no contact with anything or anyone except that three times a day a man's hand would place his meals into his room. He could remember nothing else, no other life but this. Until the day he left the closet, he never saw any more of the man than his hand. Sometimes the food was drugged, and when he came to, he would be clean, his hair and fingernails cut. Maybe he had some toy horses to play with. I don't quite remember," Miss Dixon said.

"I heard a story like this once." B.J.'s voice was unhappy. "Only instead of a closet, he lived in a tower, and instead of toy horses, he had books and lots and lots of wonderful toys and a magic rug, and instead of having trouble walking, he was completely lame, and instead of being alone, he had a godmother who loved him." B.J. had complained to Chin that Miss Dixon said a lot of very ugly things. What he really didn't like about it, B.J. said, was how you couldn't ever say she wasn't right. Listening to Miss Dixon was like seeing the mermaid's face. There it was, but why did you have to look at it? B.J. had resumed his position, back against the deck rail, face tilted sunward, shading his eyes with two hands like the see-no-evil monkey. Chin couldn't tell what his expression was. "This is a nicer story," B.J. suggested gently.

"Yes, it is," Miss Dixon agreed. "But yours is a fairy tale and mine is true. Caspar lived only a few more years. Because someone kept trying to kill him, someone he identified as the man from the closet. Finally, one day while Caspar was walking in the Hofgarten at Anspach, the man succeeded. They found a lady's handbag in the snow where Caspar was murdered." The wind lifted the hair off Miss Dixon's cheeks. "With a note inside. You'll like this, B.J. The note was written backwards. You had to read it in a mirror. And even then it didn't make any sense. But now it seems that Caspar was an heir to the Royal House of Baden. Which is why he was hidden and why he was killed."

"Same story," B.J. insisted. "Except that the king died of natural causes and the prince didn't die at all. He became the new king. There was a coronation. Everyone was happy about it."

Another steamer passed them, whistling, pouring out its clouds of white and black smoke. "We must be very close," said Miss Dixon. They could hear how close they were in the voices of the other passengers. The noise level rose slowly but steadily. The dirt of factories began to color the sky in the distance. The smell of the ocean intensified and turned slightly rotten, became a shore smell. Dead fish and garbage. The ocean cleansed itself by sending its refuse all the way to the shore.

"This story makes you think of Sarah Canary," Chin said. It made Chin think of *ren*. *Ren* was the tolerance or benevolence a man felt toward others. There was no good translation. But *ren* was a product of community, of relationships, manifested only in inter-action. A man raised in isolation would show no *ren*. Caspar Hauser would show no *ren*. And Miss Dixon was quite right. Sarah Canary also showed no *ren*. In the Confucian system, *ren* was the most fundamentally human quality. The ideogram was the same as the ideogram for *man*.

"Yes. I'm reminded of Sarah Canary by Feuerbach's description of Caspar. When he was first found, Feuerbach said he seemed to hear without understanding and to see without perceiving. So it made me wonder if Sarah Canary might also be someone special. Something like a princess." Miss Dixon looked a bit embarrassed. "Fairy tales," she said. "I know. But she does sort of resemble portraits of some of the Stuarts. Have you ever seen a painting of James II? He has a kind of dark misshapen look. I think his eyes don't quite match."

Chin knew nothing about English kings and queens except that they had wanted the Chinese to continue to consume opium badly enough to go to war with the Manchu dynasty over it. It had something to do with the revered position merchants held in British society. It had something to do with a mystic principle of cosmic harmony the British called the Invisible Hand. Inverted, this was an image right out of Miss Dixon's story. For sixteen years, Caspar Hauser's entire visible universe was nothing more than a single hand. Which made Chin think of the Christian god, which made him think of the Taipings and Hung Hsiu-ch'üan, which made him think of failed Imperial Examinations, and he did not really have these thoughts one at a time: rather they all existed about him, ringing him like a landscape, though he could only bring one into focus at a time.

Meanwhile, the landscape of the bay grew rapidly larger and more detailed. On the right was the fortification that protected the entrance. Straight ahead, the little island of Alcatraz. The steamship rounded the point. Another boat passed them, a boat headed for China. Chin knew what it carried. Flour and bones. The polished bones of dead Chinese. Some twelve hundred men had been killed on the railroads the year before Chin came to Golden Mountain.

Two thousand pounds of bones arrived in a single shipment to Canton just as he was leaving. Chin was stabbed with the sharp edges of homesickness. Treasured Mother. Home.

"I always thought Sarah Canary's clothes were expensive," B.J. said. "They mend themselves. How much do you think a dress that does that would cost?"

Chin extricated himself from his thoughts and returned to the conversation. What was B.J. saying? He looked at Sarah Canary. Her dress had held up very well considering how long she had been wearing it and everything it had been through. It was probably cleaner than you would expect. But mended itself? It had never been torn. Had it? Chin wasn't sure.

Miss Dixon ignored B.J. "Well, anyway, it's a possibility," she said. "An upbringing like Caspar's would explain the way she behaves. And it would explain Harold." A host of small boats was moving out to meet them, carrying agents who shouted advertisements for various hotels and restaurants. Chin watched as they came up beside and below; the agents swung on board, distributing their cards among the passengers.

"Dinners, seventy-five cents." An agent spoke to B.J. He tipped his hat to Sarah Canary. "Breakfasts, half a dollar. Lunch, twenty-five cents. All meals include potatoes, bread, butter, and coffee." He held out a flier. "Homelike surroundings."

"We will stay at the Occidental Hotel," Miss Dixon told B.J. before he could be tempted in some other direction. "I always stay there."

B.J. refused the flier. He was looking particularly docile, practically insensible. He was paler than his usual pallor. "I've never seen this many people," he whispered to Chin. "I mean, maybe if you counted them *all*, everybody I ever saw, I have, but not in a group like this. Not all in the same place at the same time." He clung to the rail while their steamer nosed its way through a maze of boats and wooden docks. The sounds of voices on shore were so loud now that no single one could be distinguished from any other. B.J. put his hands over his ears. Miss Dixon was obviously too purposeful to mind and Sarah Canary seemed unfazed. The steamship scraped into its dock. The gangplank opened outward and down while the passengers cheered.

Miss Dixon held tightly to Sarah Canary's arm as they debarked so that they merged into a single body. This slowed their progress considerably; such a large space had to be emptied around them. B.J. and Chin followed, one after the other, B.J. first and then Chin. The people were so close on all sides that Chin hardly had room to notice what walking on solid ground felt like again. He enjoyed the unyielding dirt, although his body still remembered the boat and tipped him slightly from side to side as he stepped. If he stopped walking to savor it, the other passengers leaving the ship carried him forward anyway.

"The Master of Pain," a tall, beautifully dressed man with a gold watch around his neck told B.J., stepping along beside him. He had a deep, trained voice. "You need do nothing. Don't say a word. I can diagnose your disease merely by looking at you. And I can cure it. I can provide testimonials from patients as far away as New York. I have worked with the crowned heads of Europe. I am as close to a miracle as you will ever come." B.J.'s mouth was open. Miss Dixon reached behind her with her free left arm and seized B.J.'s hand.

"Fairy tales. Come along," she said, pulling.

"Oysters!" a woman with a tray shouted after them.

Miss Dixon guided them to a row of coaches, choosing one that looked particularly clean. It was hitched to a brown mare in blinkers whose tail whipped about restlessly while she stamped her back feet. The horse froze a moment, releasing a stream of urine into the street, then resumed her stamping. "The Occidental Hotel. Montgomery Street," Miss Dixon told the hack-driver. She looked at him sternly. "No whip." He shook his head, held out his hand to help Sarah Canary. But Sarah Canary did not want to get into the coach. She had to be coaxed. She had to be wheedled. B.J. got on and off again twice to show her how easy it was. During this process a young, sandy-haired man hurried up from the dock behind them. He was carrying two carpet bags and panting.

"Miss Dixon," he said breathlessly. "I would have been gratified if you had allowed me to find you a carriage." Was he the man who had given Miss Dixon the flower on the boat? Or were there others? How many others? Why did Miss Dixon attract so much male attention? Chin had no reason to dislike this man. He tried to find one.

Miss Dixon swept her skirts into the coach. "I'm sorry," she said pleasantly, "if my ability to find my own transportation has caused you unhappiness. I'm afraid I was thinking only of myself." Her answer pleased Chin; he didn't ask himself why. The sandy-haired man retreated, choosing a buggy for himself, setting his bags into it, climbing aboard. His buggy left in a clatter, heading around Tangrenbu, where the Chinese all lived one on top of another, up the hill to the big houses where, the Chinese house servants said, a man might have a dozen rooms, one room to cook in and another whole room for eating, one room for reading and another for sleeping, and none of these rooms shared with even one other person.

Miss Dixon reached down for Sarah Canary's wrists, dragging Sarah Canary up to the seat beside her. Sarah Canary resisted at first, then shot through the coach and out the door on the other side. Chin ran around the rear to catch her, but before he could do so, his head was jerked painfully back. He slid to a stop. His head was jerked again. He tried to turn. Out of the corner of his eye he could see a little boy behind him, dirty and in short pants, holding the end of Chin's queue.

"Stop that!" Miss Dixon said, looking out from her seat in the coach. The little boy released Chin and ran away back toward the docks, into the crowd. Chin looked around again, conscious of a new stiffness in his neck. Sarah Canary was running away from him, across the street and down along the bay.

She was not so far ahead. Chin began to run after her. "I will get her, Miss Dixon!" he shouted.

He heard a horse whinny behind him and the clatter of hooves. B.J. called out, something Chin could not understand. The distance between Chin and Sarah Canary had shrunk. He did not dare take the time to turn and look back. He did not dare take his eyes from

247

Sarah Canary's fluttering black skirt. He reached out a hand as he ran.

"Chin!" B.J. shouted. "Please, Chin."

Chin approached a vegetable vendor, Chinese, wearing a bamboo hat, baskets of fruit and greens on either end of his pole. Sarah Canary ducked under one basket. Chin ran around. "What are you doing?" the vendor asked in incredulous high-pitched Cantonese, turning so that his baskets swung like a scale, up and down on his shoulders. "Why are you chasing the white demoness? Are you crazy? Now the demon is chasing you."

A large, red-faced man blocked his path. Chin bumped into the man before he could stop. B.J. ran into Chin from behind.

"What are you doing to the lady?" the white man asked, pushing Chin away, which pushed B.J. back as well. His tone did not suggest that this was really a question. His hands were curled up threateningly. He seized Chin's shirt in one fist, raising Chin onto his toes until they were face to face. Chin could smell peppermint and brandy on his breath. "Let her alone."

Behind them, Chin heard the sharp, sudden clap of a gunshot. For one moment, all other noises stopped. The white man dropped him. "Chin," said B.J., panting. "Will you listen? It's Miss Dixon." Chin looked behind him back to the coach where they had left her. It was moving at great speed up the street in the general direction of the Tangrenbu Gate and the Lane of the Golden Chrysanthemum. The neck of the brown horse arched with the effort she was making. And instead of the driver, Harold sat in the driver's seat. He was using the whip, but not on the horse. Miss Dixon leaned from the coach with a gun. She was trying to hold it steady, trying to sight along it. It was her right hand and the left-side window, so her angle was very awkward. She leaned farther out, almost to her waist. As Chin watched, Harold brought the whip down again and again on Miss Dixon's hand. The gun flew up into the air, spinning like a firecracker.

Sarah Canary pushed back past the angry white man. Her mouth was open and she was panting slightly from her recent run, her rib cage growing and contracting against her dress with each breath.

She came to stand docilely between Chin and B.J. as they watched the carriage turn uphill, the horse straining in her long strides, her blinkered muzzle rising and dipping, and Miss Dixon calling from the window, calling, surprisingly, for Chin. The angry white man ran after them, although he was obviously far too late. Chin would have gone himself, of course he would have, if it hadn't been obviously far too late.

C H A P T E R
S E V E N T E E N

AFTERNOON IN
WOODWARD'S GARDENS

No Notice Gave She, but a Change —
No Message, but a Sigh —
For Whom, the Time did not suffice
That She should specify.

EMILY DICKINSON,
1863

"What do we do now?" B.J. asked frantically. He had taken Sarah
Canary by the hand. "This is all your fault," he told her, and Chin
thought how true that was. All of it. All of it from the very beginning. Sarah Canary stood and panted. Her brief run along the bay
seemed to have worn her out. Chin thought she did not look well.
Her eyes had an opaque, inward turn to them. A feverish cast. Even
her dress drooped like a wilted flower. If Chin had not been so
worried about Miss Dixon, it might have concerned him.

"I don't know," Chin answered. His thoughts flew like agitated birds from one roost to the next. Miss Dixon. Harold. Sarah Canary. Miss Dixon. He forced himself to think the situation through in one straight line. Perhaps things were not so bad. "Harold must believe he has Sarah Canary. Soon he will discover his mistake. He doesn't want Miss Dixon. He will release her and she will go, as she planned, to the Occidental Hotel. She never talked about anyplace else. Except for the women's rescue mission."

"Except for the Cliff House," said B.J. "She did say she'd take us to the Cliff House."

"Why would she go there?" Chin asked.

Chin and B.J. could go to the police, of course. But Chin had never enjoyed his encounters with police. Never found the police to be helpful. His relationship with Sarah Canary was so hard to explain. And then he and B.J. had left the Steilacoom asylum under conditions that were probably illegal and certainly not ideal. It would be so much better if someone else informed the police. Miss Dixon had been kidnapped with gunfire in front of a dock full of witnesses, after all. A hack and a horse had been stolen. The police were bound to notice.

Chin led Sarah Canary and B.J. over the blocks to Montgomery Street. A carriage would have been nice, or a streetcar, and then Sarah Canary might have rested inside it instead of stumbling up and down the hills at the end of B.J.'s hand like an opium addict. One of San Francisco's balloon cars rolled by, a globe on wheels, a pumpkin drawn by a single horse.

The balloon cars each ran a regular route. A wooden disk had been set into the street where the routes ended, a disk large enough for both horse and car. When a car finished its run, it would park on the disk, which was manually rotated until horse and car faced the opposite direction, ready to reverse the route. B.J. pointed to the car in amazement. But Sarah Canary had made her feelings about carriages all too clear. It was better to save the money, anyway. Chin had very little money left. Montgomery Street was not so far from the docks.

They turned toward Market Street. The pavement was crowded with pedestrians and lined with shops, all sporting the same green blinds. The windows displayed tortoiseshell earrings, little hats with veils of different colors, dresses, men's neckties. In the bank windows, the currency from many countries was arranged in fans. A beggar woman, wearing a shawl and an apron whose pockets were all filled with flowers, tried to hand a bouquet to B.J. He reacted in alarm, backing almost into a small fountain, trying to escape. Three times Chin saw a small woman in black approaching them and his heart skipped and fluttered anxiously, but it was never anyone he knew. He made B.J. ask a banker how much farther the Occidental Hotel was.

But when they actually arrived he was a little sorry. The Occidental Hotel had been such a clear goal. On-the-way-to-the-Occidental-Hotel had been an unimpeachable condition. They were doing something. Having reached the hotel, they were no longer doing something. They entered, instead, the condition of wondering what to do next. This was a much harder place to be.

Chin went into the lobby quietly. The hotel was more elegant than he had expected. He began to think, uncomfortably, of Miss Dixon as a wealthy woman. She had provided steamship tickets as well as pocket money for Chin and B.J. in Tacoma. He had been under the impression that the money came from a group of Caucasian monks who specialized in aid to the shipwrecked. Now he was forced to wonder.

The hotel was a gaslit world. Voices were hushed. Soft footsteps descended the mahogany staircase. Each stair was carpeted and edged in brass. Chin, B.J., and Sarah Canary would have been out of place here even if they'd been clean.

"May I help you?" a large, clean white woman in a long black apron asked B.J. She wore her hair piled in curls on top of her head.

"May she?" B.J. asked Chin.

"Tell her you are here to meet someone," Chin suggested awkwardly. "Someone who may not be here yet but will be coming soon. A Miss Adelaide Dixon. Tell her you wish to wait."

"Not here," the woman said to B.J. firmly. She guided them instead into a private sitting room, small but very elegant. Sarah Canary sat astride the arm of a stuffed chair, her skirts pulled up rakishly beneath her. She rolled forward and back pleasurably. B.J. watched her but said nothing. His expression was so pronounced, Chin tried to read his face. If it wasn't disapproval, then it was triumph. It was definitely one of the two.

B.J. took the chair beside her. Chin remained standing. "Would you like something from the kitchen?" the woman asked B.J.

They had eaten lunch on the steamer not so long ago. Chin felt through his pocket for his money. "Tell her you would like some coffee," he said to B.J. "Bread and butter. Tell her to please notify you immediately when Miss Dixon comes in."

B.J. opened his mouth. "Certainly," the woman said.

A flea appeared on B.J.'s forehead. Chin reached for it hastily, hoping to catch it before it was seen, but it must have leapt from his fingers. He scratched B.J. without meaning to.

"What are you doing, Chin?" B.J. asked in an interested, unoffended tone.

Chin did not answer.

"I'll just get the food then," the woman said. She looked at him with suspicion, sweeping her skirts aside as she turned away, and Chin was certain that whatever she'd thought he was doing was something much more contemptible than flea catching. Some exotic, heathen Chinese custom that only Caucasians knew about. He tried to imagine what it could be.

On her way to the door, the woman stopped to speak to Sarah Canary. "Perhaps you'd like to tidy yourself, dear?" she offered. Sarah Canary put her hands together on the chair arm and raised herself slightly by straightening her elbows. She dropped herself back. The chair teetered.

"Maybe later," said Chin to B.J.

"Maybe later," said B.J. to the woman. She nodded suspiciously and left the room.

A Negro waiter brought the coffee and bread. He returned to clear the dishes. Chin chose a chair. When he closed his eyes, the floor rolled beneath him as if he were still on the ship. His blood rocked inside his body. Sarah Canary nodded and hummed with her eyes closed. B.J. dozed fitfully in his chair, waking every five or six minutes to ask Chin what was happening. He had one bad dream, started awake with a very white face.

"What is it?" Chin asked him, but he wouldn't answer. He shook his head, breathing heavily. "Women," he said. He went to the bathroom once. When he came back, he asked if anything had happened while he was gone.

"No," said Chin. He was wondering if they oughtn't be doing something else besides wait. He was wondering how long they would be allowed to go on waiting. If Miss Dixon did not come by nightfall, they would surely be asked to leave. Then what? He tried to remember the name of the women's rescue mission. Kearny. He remembered it was on Kearny. Even if he could find the mission, Chin could not imagine sitting and discussing Sarah Canary or Miss Dixon with a group of white demonesses. He had been counting on Miss Dixon to do the talking. She was such a vocal person. He could not imagine sitting to one side and quietly prompting and wondering what B.J. would say next while a whole group of white demonesses stared at him. It was unthinkable.

Chin could go to Tangrenbu and buy information. The Chinese were not likely to know anything about an affair involving only white people. But it was always possible that Miss Dixon had been taken to a house that had a Chinese servant. Information was expensive in Tangrenbu. Even if no one had any, it would cost Chin to find this out.

The waiter came in with a note. "It's for you," he said, handing the paper to Chin. The note was folded four times over into a triangular shape like a flag. A single word was printed on the outside. *Trade*.

"Who brought it?" Chin asked.

The waiter shrugged. "A boy."

"Did he stay?"

"No."

Chin unfolded the paper. *Woodward's Gardens. The large animal cages. Twenty minutes. If you're late, you're too late.*

"Where are Woodward's Gardens?" Chin asked the waiter.

"Mission Street between Thirteenth and Fifteenth. Fourteenth runs down the middle of the park."

"Can we get there in twenty minutes?"

"Possible. Let me get you a carriage."

B.J. opened his eyes. "Has something happened?" he said.

"We have to go to Woodward's Gardens," Chin told him. "And trade Sarah Canary for Miss Dixon at the large animal cages."

"Then we'll have Miss Dixon," B.J. pointed out. "But we won't have Sarah Canary."

"I know," said Chin. "We'll have to think of something while we go."

He was already thinking. He continued to think all the way to the gardens, bouncing up and down on the cushions as the wheels spun into potholes and out again. He thought that there would probably be other people at the large animal cages. This should make it difficult for Harold to carry out a second kidnapping. As the carriage arrived at the Mission Street entrance, Chin thought they had, at most, five minutes to spare.

The gate to the garden grounds was adorned with sculptures of seals balancing stone balls on their snouts and monkeys holding real flags in their stone paws, flags that snapped in the wind. Chin ran inside, but Sarah Canary moved only at a stumble. Chin tried not to feel impatient with her. He had anticipated great difficulties and much lost time getting Sarah Canary into the carriage, but she had chosen to cooperate. She was quiet and ladylike. She went anywhere she was pushed. She just could not be pushed anywhere fast.

A large two-story building stood opposite the gate. MUSEUM, it said in large block letters just under the roof. And next to the museum was a building that was all windows, the conservatory, a collection of hothouses for orange trees, tropical plants, and animals. Rockeries of exotic ferns flourished just inside the doorway. The greenery could be seen through the glass. The air in the gardens was scented by flowers and trees.

In front of the museum, a bulletin board listed the times of animal feedings and suggested other exhibits of great interest. A young father, carrying one child and holding another by the hand, stood reading it. B.J. joined him.

"They have a five-legged buffalo," B.J. told Chin. "Wouldn't you love to see that?" The baby in the father's arms reached out and patted B.J.'s hair. It made B.J. jump. He looked at the baby. Then, cautiously, he gave the baby his thumb to hold.

"Where are the large animal cages?" Chin asked. The gardens were a great deal larger than he'd expected. He could not see to the back fence. They didn't have time for any wrong turns.

"There's no map," B.J. said.

"Ask the man," said Chin.

B.J. stood provokingly still, reading the board. "This is lucky," he said. "We should be just in time to see the tiger fed." The man left the bulletin board, ignoring them, dragging B.J. along by his thumb, but apparently unaware of this. The baby's face reddened as if it were about to cry. B.J.'s thumb popped loose. He inspected it briefly. "Isn't the five-legged buffalo a large animal? Won't everyone want to see it? We can just follow everyone else," B.J. suggested.

"Ask the man," said Chin, "please." But the man was already gone, taking his children down the path between the museum and the conservatory. Chin hurried after him, one hand on Sarah Canary's arm. They passed a set of swings and rings. Before them was the rotary boat. It sat in the center of an artificial lake only slightly larger than the boat itself.

B.J. paused to stare at it longingly. It was propelled in its endless circle by sails and oars. Some twenty or so people were seated on it; it could easily have held a hundred. Small boys splashed with the oars and shouted. "Like the balloon cars," B.J. said. "San Francisco has a lot of ways to travel in a circle."

"Come on!" Chin's tone turned nasty. He couldn't help it. He was losing patience with both Sarah Canary and B.J. They were so slow. Recreational boats were certainly no temptation to Chin. On their right, deer stood and watched them from a grassy hill. Among the deer, inexplicably, one large Australian emu went about its business.

Behind the boat and on Chin's left, a brook ran down from the lake through the middle of the gardens. It shot into the air in a white fountain opposite the skating rink. Beside the fountain stood a woman made of marble, sheltering herself from the spray with her arms. PANDORA, her pedestal read. Soft music came from the rink, spread as thinly through the air as the fountain water.

"I know how to skate," B.J. told Chin, running to catch up to him. "I learned at the asylum. I could teach you. I don't know about Sarah Canary. Houston could probably teach Sarah Canary to skate. Houston could teach anybody to skate. But I wouldn't do that. Not unless it was really important that Sarah Canary learn to skate. Not unless she might die otherwise."

Chin didn't respond. Where were the cages? He turned and hurried along a shady path at the back of the gardens. Almost hidden among the shrubbery, he saw the small entrance to a man-made cave. Live oaks had been planted in columns beside the path. What were five minutes in the long, slow lives of trees? How many minutes had ticked away since Chin had entered the gardens? Minutes that would never be retrieved, never come back to be done differently. Chin heard time passing in every sound. In the music from the skating rink. In the barking of seals at the distant whale pond. In the clicking sails of the rotary boat. He grew more desperate with every click. "Where are the large animal cages?" he asked, seizing the arm of a white man.

The man shook loose of his hand. "Here now," he said sternly. He brushed his coat sleeve and cleared his throat. "There." He pointed along the back of the gardens. "Through the tunnel under Fourteenth Street. Then turn left."

Chin held Sarah Canary's hand and ran against her resistance. White people stared at them as they passed. They ran down into the dark tunnel under the street. Just as they came up into sunshine again, Chin heard a child scream.

The large animal cages stood in a line along the fence to Fourteenth Street. A crowd of people gathered in front of one of the cages. The crowd was growing. Harold detached himself from it and walked out to meet Chin.

The exaggerated expressions, the disarrangements of hair and clothing that Chin remembered from their last meeting were gone. Harold appeared relaxed and sane, a man in full possession of himself, a visitor like any other visitor to the gardens. Just a man who enjoyed a large animal now and then. This frightened Chin more than any visible manifestation of lunacy could have.

"You're a bit late," Harold said.

"Where is Miss Dixon?" Chin gripped Sarah Canary's hand tightly. He was not giving her up.

Harold smiled, pointed back behind himself in the direction of the crowd. The child screamed again. Chin pulled Sarah Canary along, pushing through the people until he could see what everyone else saw. Miss Dixon stood inside Cage 6, backed against the bars on the left. A large Bengal tiger sniffed at her feet. She had a knife in one hand, but she was not using it. She was not moving at all. "Please don't scream," she told the crowd. Her voice was stretched thin with fear. "You're agitating him." There was a click as the cage door swung slightly. It had been pulled closed but was not latched.

"Miss Dixon," said Chin, and at the sound of his voice, she began to tremble. Chin pushed his way to the opposite side of the cage. "Come here, tiger," he pleaded.

The tiger rotated its ears in his direction but did not take its eyes from Miss Dixon. It raised one paw, patted her dress. One large claw caught in the cloth. The tiger worked it free with its teeth. "Mr. Chin," said Miss Dixon. "Please do something."

The tiger's tail whipped from side to side like a pendulum, striking the bars at the front of the cage with so much force that they rang. "Tiger," said Chin helplessly. The tiger growled without turning, licking its paw.

"Has someone gone for its keeper?" Chin asked. "Will someone go?" He didn't turn to see if anyone responded. Instead he searched the ground for something to throw. Nothing. This was a garden, not a forest; an exhibit, a model of what the world should be, but not the world. Nothing so untidy as rocks. Chin edged along the front of the cage. The tiger growled again and rotated a single ear to show that it knew where Chin was. Chin dropped to his knees. "Tiger," he said.

The tail lashed back and forth. The bars rang rhythmically as it hit. Time was passing. It was time for Chin to do something. The tiger reached with one paw toward Miss Dixon's face. Chin reached through the bars.

"Now!" he called to Miss Dixon, grabbing the tiger's tail. He pulled the end out of the cage, held it tightly with both hands. The tiger turned and lunged at him, hurling itself into the bars, its tail slipping easily through Chin's palms. The tiger hissed and spat; its tail snaked about the cage. Chin had made one final grab as the tail slid back through the bars, but he was much too late. The tiger caught him by the sleeve of his coat instead. The fabric shredded. Shallow red tracks appeared down his arm. The tiger's claws hooked in the material at his wrist.

The tiger began to reel him in. Its face came very close. Chin could smell dreams of blood on its breath. He saw the rings of its eyes, the lines of its narrow pupils. Somewhere inside those dark lines a tiny Chin stared out in horror.

But it was all right, everything was all right, because Miss Dixon was there, on the outside of the bars, stabbing into the cage with her knife. She circled the paw, slid the blade into Chin's sleeve, and cut the cloth loose. Chin pulled his arm back, sitting and cradling it.

"Are you all right?" he asked Miss Dixon, just as she was saying the very same words to him. Some people in the crowd behind them clapped their hands. "Are you all right?" a man asked Miss Dixon. "Are you all right?" a woman said, and then she said it to Chin, too. "Are you all right?" She laughed as she said it, because everyone was all right and everyone knew it, even the tiger, even the tiger's keeper, who had arrived at last with slabs of ripe meat and was latching the cage, demanding explanations, tossing in bits of dead animal as a special treat through the bars.

"There, there, love," he said. "Here's a lovely steak for you." He whirled about to confront Miss Dixon. "Don't get into a cage with a Bengal tiger," he told her angrily. "Such a stunt. I know you. You're one of those suffragists." But Miss Dixon hardly noticed him.

She was staring at Chin, her eyes so huge and bright he couldn't look back at them.

"Where is Sarah Canary?" Miss Dixon asked.

Chin felt his stomach twist as suddenly as if he'd been punched. He scanned the crowd, but of course he didn't recognize a single face. No Sarah Canary. No Harold. No B.J. "He must be taking her out of the gardens," Chin said.

"I'm not through talking to you," the keeper told Miss Dixon. "Don't you try to leave now." But she was already running with Chin back along the cages, back through the tunnel, turning to the right now, back along the opposite side of Fourteenth Street, past the polytechnic hall and the aquarium, past the whale pond, where the sea lions called out anxiously, past the glass walls of the conservatory. The gate was empty. Chin looked outside, down Mission Street in both directions. He could not see Harold.

A row of carriages lined the street at the entrance. Miss Dixon asked the nearest driver if he had seen a short man and a woman dressed in black leaving the gardens. "Just in the last ten minutes or so," she said. "They would have only just left."

He shook his head.

"Would you have seen them?" she asked.

"Coming out the gate? Oh, yes. No one's come through the gate, madam, but you."

Miss Dixon and Chin returned to the gardens. They walked slowly back along the path. Behind the conservatory, they peered through the glass into the tropical animal house. Copper pheasants from China ran about the ground, first this way, then that, pecking at nothing. In the shaded corners, blood-sucking vampire bats hung by their hooked toes, their wings wrapped about their bodies. Parrots called from the trees. There was no public door into the tropical animal house. This was a sealed world. There was no sign of Sarah Canary here.

They crossed a bridge over the brook behind the rotary boat. Couples with children and couples with skates draped over their shoulders walked by them. A little girl called for her mother to come quick and see the emu. "He's being so funny," she said.

B.J. shouted for Chin.

He stood at the end of the path just about where Chin had last seen him, in front of the columns of oaks. "Chin! Chin!" Chin and Miss Dixon ran past the fountain and the frightened statue of Pandora with her arms over her head. B.J. was gesturing wildly, pointing into the opening of the artificial cave. Nothing he said was intelligible.

The entrance was perfectly rounded, not the door to a real cave, but the door to someone's dream of a cave. Chin saw something dark moving about inside. He entered. Miss Dixon came with him and she still had her knife. The cave was just deep enough to be dim. Chin could see to the back where Harold knelt on the cave floor. Beneath him lay a still, black form. Blood danced from Chin's head to his feet and back again. He was dizzy and his eyes went even dimmer. The air became thin.

Harold had a knife, too. Chin could see its dull metallic glow in the gloom, an ugly, underground sunless shining. "What have you done?" he asked Harold from some other part of himself, some part that could still think and talk. He walked slowly over the distance between them, dropped to his knees beside Harold. Sarah Canary's dress lay on the ground, split open from collar to hem. It was empty.

"She metamorphosed," Harold said in an airless whisper that was almost nothing more than breathing. The marked madness of Seabeck was back upon his face. "This was just her larval stage. She shed her cocoon."

"Where is she?" Chin asked.

"Gone," said Harold. "She overpowered me with her inhuman strength. She threatened me with her chopstick. This is all that's left." He lifted the dress with the tip of his knife. "First, a mermaid. Half woman, half fish. Then, a wild woman. Half woman, half beast. Is there a pattern here, Chinaman? What comes next? Half woman, half—" He stopped suddenly, cunningly. "Now, that would be telling," he said. "I will find her again. I will never stop looking. It is my destiny. I am not afraid."

"You're crazy," Chin said. "I will find her, too. I will find her first."

Harold laughed, a sound like air leaving a bellows. "You don't even know what she looks like. You wouldn't know her if you saw her now."

"B.J. was here," said Chin.

"Her dress came off," B.J. reminded him, "in the struggle. I tried to help, but I certainly didn't *look*."

"You helped," Harold agreed. "You helped, all right." Harold folded the dress over one arm. He held his knife in the other. "Have you ever seen a butterfly that someone has helped out of the chrysalis?" He edged toward the light of the cave entrance, growing brighter as he went. "One good wing," he said. "To show what was supposed to be. And one wing that is twisted and folded and useless. I'm stronger than she is now. And do you know why? It's because you helped." He feinted once at Miss Dixon, laughing again as she ducked. "You remember that," he said. "The next time you're tempted to help someone."

He ran away between the lines of live oaks and vanished into the skating rink.

Chin went to the cave opening. He could hear people on the rink shouting at Harold. "Get out of the way!" "No one allowed without skates, sir." "Are you crazy?" "Get out!" "Look out!" "Now look what you've done." The shouts faded to nothing beneath the hushing sounds of the fountain.

Miss Dixon came to stand beside Chin. "Madness and moonshine," she said. "You go and look through the gardens for Sarah Canary again. I will go to the museum and demand the police. We'll meet back there."

Chin started his search on the other side of Fourteenth Street. B.J. was with him but disappeared somewhere among the Large Animals. Chin refused to go back and look for him, as well. He saw no evidence of Sarah Canary. He returned to the museum to report his failure to Miss Dixon. His new boots, purchased in Tacoma and therefore a gift from someone, he did not like to ask himself who, clicked across the stone floor of the museum. Glass cases of stuffed animals lined the walls of the entry room. Like all museums, it had the feel of trapped ghosts.

The policeman arrived about the same time as Chin. He wrote down the details of Miss Dixon's report in a floppy brown notebook. Miss Dixon began with her own kidnapping this afternoon on the docks. Then she mentioned the second missing woman.

"Yes?" The policeman was alert. "Description?"

"Short. Dark eyes. Dark hair. Big teeth. Prominent nose. About thirty-five years old," Miss Dixon said.

"Name?"

"I'm afraid I don't know."

"Dressed how?"

"Undressed." Her voice dropped.

"I see." The policeman snapped his notebook shut. "We're certainly going to give this our full attention," he said. "You're one of those suffragists, aren't you?" He pulled on the brim of his hat, ducking his head politely as he left.

"We'll never hear from him again," Miss Dixon told Chin, glaring after the policeman. A second man, weasel-thin, waited to see her, loitering by the case containing the Diurnal Birds of Prey, pretending to examine the stuffed King Vulture. "Yes?" she asked him sharply.

"Reporter," he said. "From the *El Camino Real*. I'm interested in your adventure with the tiger. Which seems to be only one of many adventures you've had today. Forgive me. I only heard the bits I couldn't help overhearing. Would you mind going through it all again, Miss Dixon? For the record? For our readers? The *El Camino Real* reader loves a good adventure and is interested in social issues. Forward-thinking people."

"Oh," said Miss Dixon. She was obviously pleased. "Well." She brushed at her hair with one hand, tidying herself, using the glass of Case 1 as a mirror. She stared straight into the artificial eyes of a wedge-tailed eagle as she primped. Then she turned to the reporter. "We arrived in San Francisco early this afternoon," she said. "On the steamer from Tacoma. Apparently our assailant followed us all the way here from Washington. We were unaware of that. There'd been no glimpse of him since we left the *Lotta White* in dock at Tacoma, and we assumed we'd left him there or someplace even

263

farther north. His motives remain a mystery. I can only say that he is relentless and cunning."

"All the way here," the reporter repeated, writing it down. "No glimpse of. *Lotta White.* Cunning."

Miss Dixon recounted the incidents at the docks, her kidnapping, Harold's use of the whip upon her in the carriage. "A case of mistaken identity," she said. "The woman Harold really wanted is still missing. In fact, she was the whole reason for our trip. We hoped to find a haven here in San Francisco for her. She's just that bit dim, that bit helpless. We had hoped eventually to find her family. Perhaps your readers could assist us." Miss Dixon described Sarah Canary as gallantly as she could for the forward-looking *El Camino Real* readership. She made no reference to clothing at all. The reporter took it all down.

"How was she dressed?" he asked.

Miss Dixon paused. "I'm afraid I can't be too specific as to her dress."

"We were told that she changed," B.J. said helpfully. He had only just arrived in the museum, coming to stand beside Chin.

"Changed into what?"

"We weren't told. And we didn't look."

"I see," said the reporter, who clearly didn't.

"No," said B.J. "No gentleman would."

Miss Dixon moved resolutely on to the Bengal tiger. She gave Chin full credit for her escape from the tiger's cage. She was smiling. Had Chin ever seen her smile before? It dazzled. "A crowd of stricken witnesses was too horrified to move," she told the reporter, "but Mr. Chin seized the tiger by the tail and would not let go, dragging it from one side of the cage to the other, even as its claws raked through the sleeve of his coat, leaving bloody marks on the skin of his arm."

"Not at all," said Chin, happy and uncomfortable.

"Show him your arm," Miss Dixon ordered.

Chin held it out, folding back the jagged edge of fabric. Well. Now he had made himself very visible indeed. Appearing in Caucasian newspapers couldn't be a good idea, no matter how flattering the portrait. And yet Miss Dixon's gratitude pleased him very much. He couldn't refuse it. Perhaps he had not been so heroic, but he had been useful, no doubt about it. The reporter took his full name, checking the spelling of *Ah Kin* twice, although without Chinese characters it only approximated his real name, so who cared how you spelled it? How could you say one spelling was correct but not another if the whole ideographic system was flawed? Chin had a sudden, uncalled for stab of loneliness. China. Home. People who knew his real name. What if he died here, where nobody knew his real name? What would it be like to be Tom, dying in *your own home*, with the wrong name?

"I rode in the rotary boat," B.J. told him, and it took Chin a moment to remove the sudden omen of the words and remember it was just B.J. What kind of a name was B.J.? "No Sarah Canary there. I went round and round."

B.J. had spent another quarter hour looking for her at the five-legged buffalo's cage. "The fifth leg is just as big as the first four," B.J. told Chin, "but it hangs down from the buffalo's shoulder. The buffalo is a hermaphrodite. It said so outside the pen. What does that mean? Does it just mean five-legged?"

"I don't know this word," Chin said. He turned to Miss Dixon, but she was studying Case 3 as if she had never seen a Goshawk before. The *El Camino Real* reporter shuffled from foot to foot. "I better get back with the story," he said. "If I hurry, you can look for it tomorrow. Thank you, Miss Dixon."

B.J. wandered back through the museum, leaving Chin trapped with the ghosts, and returning in a great rush to tell them that Case 105 held a Union flag made entirely from the feathers of California birds. In their natural colors. He recommended that they see it at once.

Chin and Miss Dixon moved irresolutely in that direction, searching the museum again and then the hothouses and then the skating rink. A naked woman should not have been able to leave the grounds unobserved, but apparently Sarah Canary had managed it. Finally, late in the evening, the gardens closed. Miss Dixon took B.J. with her to the Occidental Hotel. Chin went to Tangrenbu.

The smells and sounds—roast duck and wind chimes, ginger, garlic, and loud, loud Cantonese—intensified his homesickness. The slave girls called to him from their cribs, high voices like breath through wooden flutes, promising him a half-dollar's worth of ecstasies, telling him he could do anything he wanted for a dollar, making him think uncomfortably of Miss Dixon, so that he noticed what he might not otherwise have noticed, that the cribs were not so large as the animal cages he had just left at Woodward's Gardens. Chin remembered B.J.'s complaint about Miss Dixon, that she was always making you see something ugly. She didn't create it or imagine it or misperceive it. It was there, all right. But you might not have seen it for yourself if she hadn't made you.

"Chin Ah Kin! We thought you were dead!" Wong Woon ran from one of the street kitchens and threw his arms about Chin. "Your uncle is here. Have you seen him? We must go. We must eat. We must drink!" Chin found himself dragged joyously through the streets. There was no time to resist.

But Chin's uncle rejoiced at his reappearance. He asked fewer awkward questions than Chin had anticipated. He had too many things of his own he wished to tell Chin. His mole quivered as he talked. He bought Chin dinner and they shared a bottle of tiger whiskey. The Washington Territory had become unsafe for the Chinese, Chin's uncle told him, his face beginning to flush from the heat of the liquor. Chin was right to get out of it. Steilacoom did not get the railroad terminus, after all. It went to Tacoma. Hadn't Chin's uncle said that it would?

"San Francisco has become unsafe for the Chinese, too," Wong Woon said, setting down his rice bowl, picking up a square of boned fish with his chopsticks. "You cannot leave Tangrenbu at night. You must stay away from the parks even in the daytime. Small boys will throw stones at you. Or worse."

Chin's uncle thumped the bottle of whiskey on the table. "Yes," he said. "This is true. You have lived among the white demons and you have come back from the dead. Do not tempt fate twice. Now you must stay within the gates of Tangrenbu."

How good it felt to be safe, to speak freely, to speak loudly. How wonderful rice tasted. Chin could not eat enough. He shouted at Tom's moon, floating above him, fat and ghostly. "I see you!" Chin called. "There you are. Hello from someone." The sky above Tangrenbu was full of stars. If Chin squinted, he could imagine the stars were falling toward him, bright and soft and no larger than snowflakes. How many dangers had Chin faced? He began to count them. His life since the sudden appearance of Sarah Canary receded from him, became unlikely, became dreamlike. As white men counted their sheep to fall asleep, Chin counted dangers to wake up. Boats and Indians. Hangings and Hank Webber. Harold and Seabeck. Tigers and Miss Dixon. Chin was a man waking up from an enchantment.

Chin was a man waking up from a great deal of drink. The next day was wrapped in fog. There was an odd, unfamiliar pulse drumming behind his eyelids. His mouth had been wiped dry. It was noon before he was able to see a copy of the *El Camino Real*. "San Francisco's Own Tiger Lady," the headline read. Chin needn't have worried. He was not mentioned at all.

CHAPTER EIGHTEEN

THE STORY OF T'UNG HSIEN NU

Now I knew I lost her —
Not that she was gone —
But Remoteness travelled
On her Face and Tongue.

Alien, though adjoining
As a Foreign Race —
Traversed she though pausing
Latitudeless Place.

EMILY DICKINSON,
1872

Miss Dixon had hired a Pinkerton detective to search for Sarah Canary. Chin was surprised, hurt, and then resigned to this. It was, Chin was forced to concede, a good idea. Certainly the detective was more efficient, more clever than Chin could ever be. Certainly the readers of the *El Camino Real*, who continued to see vague, lost women wherever they went, would be more comfortable sharing their sightings with a Caucasian detective. For four weeks now, Chin had looked and found nothing. "I only wish you'd called me in earlier," the detective said, sitting with them in the little room at the Occidental Hotel. "While the trail was still fresh."

Miss Dixon had given him every letter she had received from the *El Camino Real* readership. He spread them in his lap like a fan. He aligned them like a deck of cards. He selected the most promising. "You've given me so little to go on. And"—the detective glanced briefly at Chin with his round blue eyes—"muddling amateurs may have destroyed whatever leads existed initially. I will have to undo the damage before I can even begin the search."

There had been just enough that was odd about Miss Dixon's story, however she tried to slide quickly over it, to attract a second set of responses. The detective left these letters behind. Chin picked them up off the little marble end table and began to read them.

A Mrs. Bastion forwarded a small newspaper clipping from Tenino, Washington, where a train had struck a creature, first assumed to be an Indian, knocking it senseless. The engineer had stopped the train and found the body of an extremely large, extremely hairy manlike beast, still alive but damaged about the skull. *Jacko*, they were calling him. Jacko had recovered consciousness and was being shipped to Chicago for further examinations and possible exhibition.

A Mrs. Farrell wrote that, in 1869 during the last solar eclipse, she and her husband had seen a small but exceedingly bright point near the limits of the corona, just below the circle of the moon and in the general area of the anvil-shaped protuberance. They had assumed it was a star, but no star in that position can be seen by the naked eye. She now believed it was a ship from another world. She had just finished reading *20,000 Leagues Under the Sea*, and she begged Miss Dixon to remember that the world was full of possibilities.

An unsigned letter told Miss Dixon that a funeral home in Seattle had opened its doors one morning to find that a coffin had been left on the porch. They tried to bring it inside, but it was unusually heavy. Upon prying it open, they found the statue of a woman inside, or perhaps a real woman's body that had been turned into stone. The woman, the letter said, was smiling.

Chin thought that Miss Dixon's interest in Sarah Canary had

waned and he surprised himself by taking this a little personally. Miss Dixon spent her days now at the Lydia Palmer trial and came home from each session in a fine rage. Chin couldn't figure out if this was because of the way the trial was going or because the suffragists had found Miss Dixon too scandalous to sit with them.

"You'd think he was a saint," Miss Dixon said. "The way people talk about him. We love dead people. As soon as they die, we start loving them."

"Not all of them," said B.J.

Miss Dixon looked at him. "Oh, well," she agreed. "Some people are never dead enough." Miss Palmer had proved to be an excellent witness, remembering nothing about the murder and fainting four times under cross-examination. But public opinion was against her. Her fate was far from assured.

Chin was spending his days delivering laundered clothes to white demons on Nob Hill. Usually he let B.J. come with him, not up to the doors, which would have required too much explanation, but along on the deliveries. B.J. spent his nights at the Occidental, where Miss Dixon was paying for his room. Miss Dixon certainly did not need Chin. B.J. was fine. Chin told himself, self-pityingly, that he was clearly no help to Sarah Canary either. He was a free man again. He should go somewhere. No one would miss him.

Chin told himself that Sarah Canary was gone for good. Gone for good. It was a peculiar phrase full of Caucasian optimism. Chin had done his best for Sarah Canary, but his best had included striking her, losing her repeatedly, and, at the very end, choosing Miss Dixon instead. Wherever Sarah Canary was, surely she had found someone more worthy.

It was time for Chin to move forward along the straight line of his life. It was time for him to marry. It was time for him to return home and prove to his mother that he had not died in Golden Mountain, no matter how many times she had heard otherwise. He put aside the notes from the readers of the *El Camino Real* and explained this to Miss Dixon. She was sitting in the stuffed chair, one white hand spread out on the chair arm where Sarah Canary had

270

sat. She wore a dress the color of plums. Chin would not look at her face. He stared at her hand, which whitened as she gripped the chair arm. Chin told her that he would not go, of course, until he could find a happy situation for B.J. He would not go if the Pinkerton detective returned any word, any word at all, about Sarah Canary. The room was filled with the smell of gardenias sent to Miss Dixon by some admirer.

"I am Chinese," Chin pointed out. Could Miss Dixon deny it? The Chinese did not let go of their dead the way Indians did. In fact, Confucianism subordinated the living to the dead as surely as it subordinated the individual to the group and the wife to the husband. The Chinese spoke the names of their ancestors forever.

They did not let go of their living families either, not like the Caucasians, making permanent moves to new homes on the other side of oceans. Chin believed that white people loved their parents, but he wasn't sure they loved them as much as Chinese people did. Chin said none of this. "I cannot stop being Chinese. When I am home, I may even take the Imperial Examinations."

Miss Dixon said she understood. Miss Dixon understood nothing. What did she know of the sacrifices a family made so that a son could study for the examinations? How could she know of the success that family had every right to expect in return?

Miss Dixon said there would be a verdict in the Lydia Palmer case in a day or two. She, in fact, was just about to purchase a train ticket to New York. She was, she reminded Chin, a forward-looking person. The episode with the tiger had brought her some small attention. It would not last forever. The condition of women had not improved while she sat idly in the Occidental Hotel. The time had come to start her new lecture series.

Chin was surprised. "I thought you were staying. I thought you were giving lectures here."

"No, not on the West Coast," said Miss Dixon. "The West Coast has not really worked out for me."

Her face was rather drawn. B.J. watched her anxiously. "I will marry you, Miss Dixon," he offered, and she said how very kind of him, but it really wasn't necessary. She excused herself to go to her room and lie down. The exertions of the prosecuting attorneys! Just watching them had made Miss Dixon quite tired.

"I will be coming back, of course," Chin said. He was knotted with unexpected unhappiness. "I am only going for a visit to China. I will come and see you when I get back."

"Won't that be nice?" said Miss Dixon. "Of course, if you pass the examinations, you will be too important to leave, won't you? I wish there were a country I could go to and be important. I wish it were that simple for me." She left the room quickly, turning once at the door, but careful to keep her face shadowed. "Good-bye, Mr. Chin. I wish you the best of luck."

"Did I tell you about the exhibit called the Happy Family?" B.J. asked Chin when the door had closed. "At Woodward's Gardens?"

"No," said Chin.

"It was a bunch of different kinds of animals all in one cage together. Monkeys, two bear cubs, dogs, pigs, peccaries. The bulletin board said the bear cubs were orphans who'd been suckled by a pointer bitch and that they still lived with their foster mother."

"It sounds like something you would like," Chin said, surprising himself by letting a white man know how well Chin understood him.

"I didn't, though," said B.J. "The bears cuffed the dogs around. Even their *mother*. The monkeys fought with the pigs and with the dogs and with the other monkeys. I wished they all had their own cages."

His adventures were over. Chin rejoiced in the straight, simple line his life had become. How glad he was to be free of complications and responsibilities. How could he ever miss Sarah Canary, who hadn't spoken a word to him, or done him one kindness, but had involved him, again and again, in messiness, and even peril? Did you miss spending nights in jail and being forced to hang men in the morning? Did you miss red-faced white men shouting "Whoo-oo-ee?" from hidden rooms? Did you miss Indians who overturned your canoe and swam away and left you to drown? Were you crazy?

Chin returned to his narrow bed in Tangrenbu. He lay upon it, listening to the gossip and complaints of the men all about him. There was an argument over the debaucheries of the Manchu Emperor. There was an argument over the possible medicinal uses of tiger claws. There was an emptiness inside Chin that he tried to fill with sleep.

He tried not to hear the calls of slave girls. In the safety of Tangrenbu, his prolonged celibacy became physically painful. His dreams were erotic and unsatisfying. He needed desperately to be touched. It was harder and harder to think about anything else. Late at night he was awakened by Wong Woon. Wong Woon had just shaved his forehead. It glimmered in the darkness like a new moon. Chin remembered vividly how Miss Dixon had looked at him when he had his own forehead shaved. "You look so Chinese," she had said in a tone that sounded startled and unhappy.

"A white demon has come," Wong Woon told him. "He is looking for you."

Chin rose, cleaning his eyelids with his fingers. B.J. stood, shivering, coatless at the door. His light hair blew about his ears.

"It's Miss Dixon, Chin," he said. He was breathless, as if he'd been running.

"Is it Harold?"

"No, it's Miss Dixon." B.J. paused. "I didn't see Harold. I guess he could have been there," he admitted. B.J. took two noisy breaths. "The verdict on Lydia Palmer came in this afternoon while we were at the hotel. It was for acquittal."

"Yes?" said Chin. "Isn't that what Miss Dixon wanted?"

"Miss Palmer was released. She came to see Miss Dixon at the Occidental. They were both happy."

"What is it, B.J.?" Chin asked. "Why are you here?"

"Lots of men were unhappy," B.J. said. "They're outside the hotel. Some of them say they are going inside. Chin, there are lots of them. Maybe fifty."

"You stay here." Chin's uncle had risen and stood at his shoulder slightly behind him. He spoke in Cantonese. "What is this to you? What can you do?"

"Where are the police?" Chin asked B.J. B.J. was always getting sizes wrong. Probably there weren't fifty men. Probably there were ten. Probably there were two.

"Miss Dixon sent me for the police. They said they won't come. They said it looks too dangerous."

Chin reached for his coat. "They will kill you," Chin's uncle told him. "If the police will not come to save a white demoness, who do you think will come to save you?" Chin joined B.J. in the street. They began to walk. The bodies of plucked chickens hung by their legs in a store window. Twisted, candied roots gleamed on the shelves beneath.

They hurried past the opening to the Devil's Kitchen. An addict watched them incuriously through the opium ghosts in his eyes. "What can you do?" his uncle shouted after him, switching to English in his last appeal.

"What will we do, Chin?" B.J. asked.

What would they do? "We will be there," said Chin.

"I was doing *that*," B.J. told him. "It wasn't helping."

Chin began to walk faster. Hurrying after B.J. over streets or through forests, with no particular plan, to help imperiled white women had become the pattern of his life. He felt a curious sort of joy. He was concerned about Miss Dixon, of course. But the emptiness inside him was gone. He had been useful to Miss Dixon before. Perhaps it would be his fate to be useful again.

They left Tangrenbu. The stars dimmed. The streetlights brightened. They walked from one circle of light through darkness to the next. The streetlights reflected from the shop windows, double images of astounding brightness. The closer they got to Montgomery Street, the more men they saw, all going in the same direction they were. Chin and B.J. turned a corner. B.J. had indeed been mistaken about the size of the crowd. There weren't fifty men. There were hundreds. They loitered at the edges of the block, talking in small groups, sitting, smoking and drinking, on the fountains and the pavement.

"If she was a man, she would have been hanged," one of them was saying, a tall, gaunt man. His voice was not strident, but reasonable, heartfelt, and persuasive. He paused to blow clouds of cigar smoke from his mouth above the heads of his companions. "That's all I'm saying. A woman out here can get away with murder. And now they all know it. What's to stop the next one?"

A second man spoke. Chin couldn't see him. "Open season on men. That's what the courts said today. Any one of us can be shot with absolute impunity."

"All the same, you wouldn't have wanted to see a woman hang," a third man answered. "What else could the jury do? It's too horrible to think of."

"I'm thinking of it," the first man said. "It's not so horrible. They hang women in their shifts."

A man down the block laughed suddenly and just as suddenly stopped. Someone broke a bottle against a lamppost. Chin heard the glass shatter.

Chin and B.J. walked more slowly. The closer to the hotel entrance they came, and quieter it got. The men here were the participants. They had not come to watch. They were not sitting or climbing the fountains or discussing the case. They stood outside the hotel in a single unit, like a leaderless army, like an ocean, swelling and spilling over at the sides. Chin could smell liquor and gunpowder and anger. He kept his eyes on the backs of B.J.'s shoes, following B.J. closely. He looked at no one's face.

A small group began to smash the glass door to the hotel. Chin looked up at the sound. The group was thorough, methodical, and rhythmical. Glass fell to the pavement in sheets and broke again there. No one came to stop these men. The hotel lobby was empty. None of the hotel staff could be seen.

Chin was cold with fear. His sense of contentment had vanished. He had iced over gradually as he walked, his face, his hands, his feet, until he was so stiff that the walking became difficult. Why had he come? What could he do? He was a frozen man, a man who might break. He stayed very close to B.J. He was the invisible frozen Chinese servant.

The mob surged toward the hotel. "There she is!" someone called. "There she is!" The mob stopped moving. Above them, on the second story, a woman had appeared. She opened the window to her room, leaned out. She was veiled, but Chin knew her. Adelaide Dixon started to speak. "Listen to me," she said. The men stepped back and looked up. "Are you all listening to me?"

She was so brave, clearly illumined in the window, masquerading as Lydia Palmer. This was just what Chin would expect of Miss Dixon. Chin thought he had never seen anyone so brave. Or so beautiful. "I have a gun," she said, although her hands were on the window frame and held nothing.

"You always do!" one man shouted. "How many of us do you think you can get when it takes you three bullets to kill a man?"

"It was your law," she said. "It was your judge and your jury. God knows, it's never been ours."

Inside the hotel, through the empty hole of a doorway, Chin could see a second veiled woman creeping down the mahogany stairs. He held his breath and hoped no one else was looking. The woman stopped in the shadows of the landing. "There she is!" a man behind Chin shouted.

"What is the value of a woman's heart?" Miss Dixon called desperately from her window. The woman on the stairs was still. But the man behind Chin was pointing at neither of them. "Back here!" he called excitedly. "She's back here!" Chin stretched to see over the white men's heads. He was too short. He jumped once and still saw nothing but the backs and necks of white men.

"Chin," said B.J., seizing his shoulder. "It's Sarah Canary."

"Are you sure?" Chin asked B.J.

"She's bigger," said B.J. "Chin, she's so big."

The men were surging again, away from the hotel now, carrying Chin with them. "It's not the right woman," Chin told the man on his left. The man turned to look at him. "It's not Miss Palmer. Leave her alone."

The white men would not let him stop moving. B.J.'s hand tightened on his shoulder, trying to stay with him. "B.J.!" Chin called. It was an appeal for help. He twisted around.

There was a horrible look on B.J.'s face. Chin recognized the look, although it took him a moment. It made him think of the mermaid back in Burke's cabin, but it was not the mermaid's look. It was the look B.J. had worn when B.J. had seen the mermaid. Chin turned back, wondering why B.J. wore this face now, when he had just seen Sarah Canary. "He has a gun," B.J. said.

Chin saw it, too. A man near them was pointing a gun at the window of the Occidental Hotel. Chin followed the line of the barrel. He tried to reach for the gun but couldn't. He could not get to the man.

"Adelaide!" Chin shouted her name so that everyone turned to him. He became visible all at once. "Adelaide! Get down!" he cried. There was one shot, a sound like a branch snapping in two. Adelaide disappeared into her room. Chin looked back to the gun. The men around him moved away. The barrel was pointing at him. Chin could see straight into its empty mouth.

B.J.'s hand pulled him back as B.J. pushed past. "Don't listen to it, Chin," said B.J., stepping in front of him. "Guns always say that." And Chin would swear, Chin would always remember it this way, that he heard the second gunshot only after B.J. fell.

B.J. lay in a heap at Chin's feet. Chin knelt beside him, pulled B.J. into his lap. Blood fell out of B.J.'s chest. Chin pressed his hand over the hole. "Don't die for me, B.J.," he said, but when had B.J. ever done what he was told?

"It was an accident," he heard a man say. "I only meant to frighten the woman. I only meant to hit the Chinaman." The man's voice was thick and liquored. Chin's hand rose and fell with B.J.'s chest. His palm was filled with warm blood. Blood seeped out around Chin's hand. He couldn't stop it. He couldn't hold B.J. together. B.J. stared at him.

"The police are coming," someone told Chin. Chin did not look up to see who. The pant legs of white men were all about him, like a forest of trees. Chin wanted to ask B.J. if he could remember now the carp who became a dragon by leaping the Dragon's Gate. Chin wanted to tell B.J. that this was what B.J. was doing. But he wasn't sure it was true and he wouldn't say good-bye to B.J. with a lie. Chin was crying too hard to speak anyway.

"Chin," said B.J. He sounded surprised. "You're getting so little, Chin." He stopped breathing. In the silence Chin could hear horses' hooves on the pavement. The police had decided to come at last.

Two policemen lifted B.J. by the shoulders and the feet. Chin stood and followed as they carried him out of the crowd. Chin kept his head down; his eyes streamed with tears. He searched through the forest of pant legs for one black skirt. Was Harold right that Sarah Canary was a killer? Had Sarah Canary killed B.J.? Or had she saved Chin? Or had she never been there at all?

There was no sign of her. There was no one else to rescue. The police told Chin that the hotel room was empty. Apparently, while B.J. died, Adelaide and Lydia Palmer had escaped.

Chin stood at the police station and tried to answer their questions. "What is your name?" they asked Chin. "What was his name?" Hard questions. Chin found it hard to listen. So many ghosts he had to take care of now. The ones he could name and the ones he could not. But Chin knew what B.J.'s ghost would like.

Chin stood by B.J.'s body and told his ghost a story. "One day an old woman had a dream," Chin said. "She dreamt that she took a pear and cut it in half. She and her husband shared it. She told her dream to Chou Kung. He was the most powerful fortune-teller in all China. 'What does it mean?' she asked him. 'It means that your son will die,' Chou Kung said.

"The woman ran home, weeping. Her weeping was so loud, it was heard by T'ung Hsien Nu, the Holy Maiden who walks with immortals. 'Chou Kung can foretell the future,' she said to herself. 'But I can change it.' She took a rooster, called it by the old woman's son's name, and killed it quickly.

"The old woman's son was on his way home when he was caught in a rainstorm. He saw an old brick kiln and decided to shelter there until the storm passed. But when the wind was at its very strongest, he heard his mother's voice in it. 'Come to me, my son,' his mother called. He ran out of the kiln to find her, and just as he left it, the kiln collapsed. He would have died if he had been inside. He returned home and told this story to his mother.

"She went back to Chou Kung. 'My son is alive,' she said. 'You

278

made a mistake.' But Chou Kung knew that the Holy Maiden had meddled with fate again. He shook his head. He said nothing.''

Chin told this story to B.J. in Cantonese while the San Francisco police watched. He began to cry again. "Poor little rooster," he said to B.J.

He sat on the steps of the police station, bent over, and cried until he heard footsteps. Over the obstruction of his tears, from the space between his knees, he saw the black skirt. "Did you kill him?" Chin asked, but when he raised his eyes, the face was Harold's.

"No," said Harold. "I didn't. I'm not the man I was." Harold was standing in front of the San Francisco police department and he was wearing Sarah Canary's old dress. The dress was slit up the center and Harold wore it over his other clothes, fastened at the neck like a cape. "I'm not the same man who left you in a cave in Woodward's Gardens," Harold told him.

Chin got to his feet immediately and started for Tangrenbu. Harold followed along. Chin walked faster. So did Harold. They covered several blocks without a word.

"Go away," said Chin. He had never been so tired.

"I'm sorry," said Harold. "Another one dead. I am sorry. Who was it?"

Chin walked on. Harold was so very eye-catching. Did this mean Chin was invisible beside him? Or would he be part of the attention Harold was certain to attract? Would people say, "Look! A man in a dress"? Or would they say, "Look! A man in a dress following a Chinaman"? And wouldn't it make B.J.'s death absolutely useless if Chin allowed himself to get killed outside the gates of Tangrenbu by Harold or any other white demon on the very same night?

"Was it B.J.? I never had anything against B.J." Harold's shoes snapped on the empty streets behind Chin. "I know what it's like to lose someone."

"Did you find Sarah Canary?" Chin asked.

"No," said Harold. "Did you?"

"No." Chin had a sudden suspicion. He voiced it without stopping, without looking back. "B.J. saw you outside the Occidental Hotel tonight."

"Did he? I wasn't there," said Harold. "I've been up in Chico. There were sightings, but I was too late. I wonder who B.J. saw."

"Not Sarah Canary," Chin said hastily. "We never saw Sarah Canary again." It might even be true. It was not given to him to know. A man says something. Sometimes it turns out to be the truth, but this has nothing to do with the man who says it. What we say occupies a very thin surface, like the skin over a body of water. Beneath this, through the water itself, is what we see, sometimes clearly if the water is calm, sometimes vaguely if the water is troubled, and we imagine this vision to be the truth, clear or vague. But beneath this is yet another level. This is the level of what *is* and this level has nothing to do with what we say or what we see.

Harold caught up with Chin, stepping in front of him. He appeared a bit embarrassed. "If B.J. had been wearing this dress, he'd still be alive today," Harold said. "I shouldn't have taken it. I don't need it. Since I'm immortal already. It was selfish of me."

Chin began to walk again.

"The dress sheds bullets," Harold told him. "And fire. You can't be drowned in it. It makes you immortal. Overkill in my case. To coin a phrase."

"Go away." Chin stopped at the gates of Tangrenbu.

"I don't blame you for not liking me," Harold said. "Immortality was a burden. I wore it gracelessly. I'm learning to handle it better. Take the dress."

Chin stared at him. "No."

"Please. You earned it. Wear it and no one will ever hurt you again."

"No," said Chin. He did not believe Harold. He did not disbelieve. It did seem possible, finally, that this dress was Sarah Canary's gift to him, her reward for all his patience and peril. He could just picture himself, a Chinese man dressed as a white woman. He could just picture no one hurting him. "I'm not brave enough for immortality." Hadn't he once said this very thing to B.J.?

"I know I've made mistakes," said Harold. "Things I wish I

280

could undo. I must have been crazy. She made me so crazy. You remember?" There was a wistfulness in his voice.

"I didn't notice."

"I don't mind telling you, I see things quite differently now. I see things quite differently since I've been wearing this dress."

Harold stood behind Chin and did not follow him through the gates of Tangrenbu. Chin turned around once. Harold was still standing there, staring after him. Chin had a moment of inspiration. "Half woman, half man," he said. And Harold answered:

" 'All look and likeness caught from earth
   All accident of kin and birth,
   Had passed away.'

"That's poetry, Mr. Chin. That's Coleridge." Harold unhooked the dress from his neck and slid it from his shoulders. He held it out to Chin.

" 'She, she herself, and only she,
   Shone through her body visibly.' "

The street lamp behind Harold flickered so that the shadows, the dark shapes stretching over the street, vanished for a moment and then reappeared as if Chin had blinked. "I have to go now," said Chin. "I have to go home."

X

The Taiping Rebellion ended with the death of the Heavenly King in 1864. The Heavenly King's other name was Hung Hsiu-ch'üan. He was a failed candidate for the civil service examinations and a Hakka convert to Christianity.

The foreign, Christian elements of the rebellion may have cost Hung Hsiu-ch'üan the local support he needed. Ironically, it may also have cost him the support of the foreign communities in China. The missionaries certainly found him difficult. He had read the Bible, which was to his credit, but then he had visions and this could not be encouraged. He claimed to be a prophet, to have direct inspiration from God. He purchased a fire engine and baptized his troops with it. The imperialist powers joined forces with the imperial powers to crush the movement. The victorious commander of the Imperial Army reported that, at the end, Hung betrayed his religion and killed himself. Much later, new evidence surfaced that proved he died instead, conveniently, just before the collapse of his rebellion, of natural causes, at the hand of his God.

In all important respects, the dynasty was defeated as well. The foreign powers imposed conditions that made China helpless. In 1873, the Ministers of the United States, Britain, France, Russia, and the Netherlands stopped performing the *ta-li* or *kowtow* at the foot of the Dragon Throne. The Manchus became a puppet regime, unable to inconvenience the imperialists, but permitted to continue to wreak havoc on their own people.

The unpopular regency of the Dowager Empress, Tz'u-hsi, ended in 1873. It was hoped that the young Emperor, although currently debauched by the palace eunuchs, would in time develop into a forward-thinking leader. Time was not given him. The reign of the new Emperor lasted only two years and ended with his death from smallpox. His Empress, much disliked by her mother-in-law, died soon after, murdered by persons unknown.

Tz'u-hsi chose as new Emperor an infant named Kuang-hsü. With this choice, Tz'u-hsi prolonged her regency by another twenty years. It was a brazen violation of the laws of succession. One official felt compelled to commit suicide over it.

CHIN'S THEORIES
ON FATE AND CHANCE

It will not harm her magic pace
That we so far behind —
Her Distances propitiate
As Forests touch the Wind

EMILY DICKINSON,

1872

In 1875, Chin was given a quotation from the story of Chou Kung, from the very story he had last told B.J., as part of the civil service examinations. Chin had fresh paper before him and a beautiful brush that was a gift from his mother. He was thinking of Adelaide. She had ceased to be a regret to him and became instead a sort of perfume that hung about his years in Golden Mountain, sweetening every other memory. He thought of her often, daily, almost ritually. He remembered that she talked too much, that she always knew every-thing, that she had often been tactless and disapproving. He woke up every morning and remembered that, whatever else the day brought, it would not bring Adelaide.

He would marry a woman his mother chose. Because of Adelaide, he would treasure his wife and he would treasure his big-footed daughters as they came. He hoped that his memory was also sweet to her, but this was unlikely, leaving as he had, without a word. He wondered if Adelaide was the sort of person who could let her whole life be poisoned by regret. He was afraid that she was.

He tried to tell himself that he had left her out of kindness rather than cowardice. He wasn't sure this was true. Certainly, he had wanted to see her again. He had wanted to tell her how brave she was. "Are you all right?" he had wanted to ask her. He had wanted to tell her lies beginning with the word *someday*. He couldn't let himself do this. In the end, he had decided to let Adelaide stay forever in the happy world where B.J. was still alive, although this meant, of course, that Chin could never see her again.

Chin began to write down the side of the page. "This reminds me of another story I heard once," he wrote. "In this story, instead of a kiln, there is a cage, and instead of a son, there is a woman, and instead of a storm, there is a tiger."

Chin had felt so completely Chinese in Golden Mountain. But back in China, every word he spoke seemed odd and Western. Half Chinese. "You are too flexible," his uncle had always told him. "Make a place to fit yourself." Perhaps he would pass the examinations and become important. Perhaps the time in China was just right for him. A new approach to the Western imperialists was being cautiously suggested. In this approach, Chinese learning and culture remained as the theoretical base, or *ti*, but Western learning was recognized for its many practical applications, or *yung*. Chin had a vision of steamships on the Yangtze.

Chin wrote:

> There are many stories of the conflict between Chou Kung and the Maiden, which is the conflict between fate and chance.
>
> We imagine ourselves as creatures of destiny. We listen

to stories and forget that the listening also tells the story. The story we hear is ourselves. We are the only ones who can hear it.

Without our listening, all the stories are the same story. They all tell us that nothing is meant to be.

That nothing is meant.

That nothing is.

They tell us nothing. We dream our little dreams, dream that we are dreamers—

Chin dipped his brush in the ink again.

—while all about us the great dream goes on. Sometimes one of the great dreamers passes among us. She is like a sleepwalker, passing through without purpose, without malice or mercy. Beautiful and terrible things happen around her. We discern symmetries, repetitions, and think we are seeing the pattern of our lives. But the pattern is in the seeing, not in the dream.

We dare not waken the dreamer. We, ourselves, are only her dreams.

He had blotted the paper with a long, mounded worm of ink. Neatness counted. Chin would have to start over. He folded the ruined paper once down the middle, running the fold between his thumb and forefinger. He opened it up to look at it. The wet ink had spread under the pressure of his fingertips into a curved shape on both sides of the fold. With no intent of any kind, except to discard the paper, Chin had drawn the Caucasian ideogram for the heart, which, when broken like this, into two parts, is also the butterfly.

XI

Nineteen eighty-seven was the Year of the Rabbit. Religious leader Jim Bakker lost his pulpit in a sexual scandal involving a twenty-one-year-old church secretary; the police in Utah exchanged gunfire with polygamists; animal-rights activists burned a partially constructed laboratory in Davis, California, while in Berkeley, university officials were accused of enforcing an unspoken quota system that limited the number of Asian Americans accepted as students. Ronald Reagan, the American president, made a speech about the American Indians.

The Australian *People* magazine took considerable heat over a projected charity program whose schedule included a dwarf-throwing and bowling contest. During this event, dwarves were to be strapped onto skateboards and rolled at the pins. The editor of the magazine defended the program by saying that only stunt-dwarves were to be used. These men are professional projectiles, the editor said. These men like being thrown.

In 1988, a genetically engineered mouse with an enhanced susceptibility to cancer became the first animal to be patented. The Pullyap tribe was given $162 million in land, cash, and jobs in exchange for their claim to some of the most valuable land in Tacoma. Religious leader Jimmy Swaggart was involved in a scandal of sex and prostitution.

In 1989, herpetologists at Seattle's Woodland Park had a hatch of hundreds of Solomon Island leaf frogs. These frogs had never before been successfully bred in captivity. Suddenly the herpetologists were drowning in them.

In 1989, the Chinese government killed an estimated four hundred to eight hundred civilians as a response to the demonstrations in Tiananmen Square.

According to eyewitness accounts, President Reagan's speech went something like this: "They from the beginning announced that they wanted to maintain their way of life . . . And we set up these reservations so they could, and have the Bureau of Indian Affairs take care of them . . .

"Maybe we made a mistake. Maybe we should not have humored them in that wanting to stay in that kind of primitive lifestyle. Maybe we should have said, 'No, come join us. Be American citizens along with the rest of us,' and many do."

The President went on to say that some Indians had become very wealthy from oil on their reservations, "and so I don't know what their complaint might be."

In 1990, the *Wall Street Journal* and the *New York Times* reported new evidence, in the form of hairs, of the existence of a Chinese wild man, a creature weighing five hundred to six hundred pounds, standing six to seven feet tall, and having humanlike features.

The following headline appeared in the *Weekly World News*: "Wounded Civil War Soldier Found in Georgia. 'This man is not from our century,' experts tell police."

And in the *Worldwide Gazette*: "Flea Circus Horror! Trainer Attacked by Ravenous Fleas!"

ACKNOWLEDGMENTS

I offer my thanks to Donald Kochis, Nina Vasiliev, Sara Streich, Alan Elms, Ann Kenny, Barbara Lorenzi, and Debbie Smith for help with the first draft.

For editing and support in the later stages, I owe a great deal to Damon Knight, Kate Wilhelm, my wonderful editor, Marian Wood, and my wonderful agent, Wendy Weil.